"I'm here to talk to you."

"To talk to me?" Her voice rose with incredulity. "About what? The weather? No, wait. Maybe we can talk about local bars. Bars where badass vampires go to pick up prosecutors. Seems to me that would make one hell of a conversation opener." She snapped off her words, as if embarrassed that she'd shown her hand.

"No," he said, determined that she know the truth. "There was no ulterior motive between us. I saw you in the bar. You pleased me, and I wanted you. Hungered for you even as I do now. I took only what you were willing to give."

Guilt washed over him, because though his intentions that night had been innocent, now they were anything but.

"Don't," she said, shaking her head, her eyes sad. "Don't come here with sweet words and try to twist me up in knots. It won't work."

"Do you want me to go?" The words were out before he had considered them, and he stood frozen, waiting for and fearing her answer.

BOOKS BY J. K. BECK

When Blood Calls
When Pleasure Rules
When Wicked Craves

WHEN BLOOD CALLS

J. K. Beck

BANTAM BOOKS
NEW YORK

When Blood Calls is a work of fiction. Names, characters, places,
and incidents are the products of the author's imagination or are
used fictitiously. Any resemblance to actual events, locales, or
persons, living or dead, is entirely coincidental.

2010 Bantam Books Mass Market Original

Published in the United States by Bantam Books, an imprint of
The Random House Publishing Group,
a division of Random House, Inc., New York.

BANTAM BOOKS is a registered trademark of Random House, Inc.,
and the colophon is a trademark of Random House, Inc.

ISBN 978-0-440-24577-3

Cover design: Scott Biel
Cover art: Cliff Nielsen

Printed in the United States of America

www.bantamdell.com

2 4 6 8 9 7 5 3 1

Book design by Diane Hobbing

To my mom

ACKNOWLEDGMENTS

I want to express my thanks to so many people who helped bring this book to life. My friends, plot helpers, and general whine buddies: Kathleen O'Reilly, Dee Davis, Jessica Scott, and Aaron de Orive. My family: Don, Catherine, Isabella, and my mom, Anna, along with Nana, of course. The LAPD folks for answering questions about concealed carry permits and the criminal justice center. And, most especially, my agent, Kimberly Whalen, and the fabulous folks at Random House, especially Nita Taublib and my wonderful editor, Shauna Summers.

PROLOGUE

The judge's body lay sprawled on the ground, eyes still open in surprise and terror. He'd known what was to befall him in his last seconds. Known that his betrayals had finally been avenged, his crimes soundly punished.

Without thinking, Lucius licked his lips, tasting the bitter flavor of Braddock's fear. Fear, but no remorse. Of all the monsters that moved in the night, Marcus Braddock had been among the most vile.

He was dead now. Justice delivered. Fate sealed.

It was over.

Lucius took one last look at the Los Angeles officer, standing stiff in his uniform and talking rapidly into the radio on his shoulder as the lights from his patrol car painted the drizzled night in red and blue. Nearby, a female sobbed, the foolish jogger who'd discovered the body and called 911, setting the wheels in motion.

Soon more officers would descend. And then the others would come. The ones who would understand what had truly happened here tonight.

The ones who would search for Braddock's killer.

He needed to be gone before they arrived.

And with that thought, Lucius Dragos melted back into the night where he belonged.

CHAPTER 1

"Rain," Tucker said. "You wanna tell me why we're always getting called out in the goddamn rain?"

"Clean living," Ryan Doyle answered, eyeing his partner with amusement as he slid his '63 Pontiac Catalina in beside an LAPD black-and-white. The flashing lights cast eerie shadows over the thickly wooded park, illuminating an ambulance and two unmarked piece-o'-shit vehicles that had homicide written all over them.

"And that," Tucker said, pointing to the nearest patrol car as he continued his diatribe of bad fortune. "We got cops coming out our a-holes. Now we gotta deal with the whole f-ing system."

Doyle slammed the gearshift into park. "I'm gonna assume you didn't get laid last night, and temporary celibacy has soured your mood. 'Cause if this is going to be your attitude for this entire investigation, I'm putting in for a new partner."

Beside him, Tucker spread his arms wide, then flashed the smile that had made him a celebrity among all the Division 6 females. "I'm good, man. Don't get your panties in a wad."

Doyle grabbed his umbrella off the floorboards and shoved open the Pontiac's door. "Let's do this thing."

Tucker fell in step beside him, and they slogged toward

an officer in a rain-soaked slicker who was currently roping off the area with crime scene tape. The officer stiffened as they approached, his eyes widening like a deer caught in the headlights. *Rookie,* Doyle thought, as the officer held up a hand. As if that could keep them out.

"You might want to step aside, junior," Doyle said, flashing his badge out of politeness, but not bothering to slow as he lifted the tape and started to slide under.

"I'm sorry," the officer said. "No one passes."

"We got authority here," Tucker said, staring hard at the guy. "So come on, rookie. Get off our backs and let us through."

The officer's face went through the usual jumble of confusion before smoothing out. He smiled, all polite cooperation. "Absolutely, sir. Detective Sanchez is right over there." He pointed to a woman with a heart-shaped ass. "She's in charge."

"Not anymore," Tucker said.

Doyle followed his partner inside the crime scene tape, unable to stifle his grin. "One of these days, you gotta teach me how you do that."

"It's a gift," Tucker said. "Comes in handy with the ladies, too."

"I bet it does. Doubt you could get the ladies any other way."

"You wound me, man," Tucker said, pressing his palms over his heart. "I'm seriously wounded."

Doyle shook his head at his partner's antics, but didn't bother to respond. Sanchez had already spotted them and was on her way over, her Noxzema-fresh face pinched.

"Hold up, hold up," she said. "You want to tell me who you boys are and what you're doing at my crime scene?"

"That's just it," Doyle said, pulling his shield from the pocket of his raincoat. "I'm not so sure it's still your crime scene. I'm Agent Ryan Doyle." He nodded at Tucker. "My partner, Agent Severin Tucker."

She peered at his shield and ID, then met his eyes, her own filled with confusion. "Homeland Security?"

Doyle nodded. Technically, it was true. With the passage of the Patriot Act, his employer—the American arm of the Preternatural Enforcement Coalition—had been formally set up as a division of Homeland Security. A secret division, but there nonetheless. And considering the type of terror the PEC chased, there was a certain circular beauty to the ancient organization's new cover story.

She stared him down. "Are you shitting me?"

"No, ma'am," Tucker said. "We at Homeland Security do not have a sense of humor of which we're aware."

She tilted her head and sent Tucker a scathing glance, because despite the soft shape, she was clearly a hardass. "Since when did killers mimicking some creature out of a bad B-movie cross the line into a federal crime?"

"Sorry, Detective," Doyle said. "That's classified."

"Suffice it to say there's been chatter," Tucker added.

She looked from one to the other, obviously not buying their bullshit. Doyle watched Tucker's face, saw that he was getting the look, and stepped in front of his partner. Tucker's trick came in handy, but he couldn't pull his sort of heeby-jeeby on the whole crew. And while

Sanchez might be the only one making noise, there were at least seven officers hanging back, circling the body with intent to claim grazing rights.

"We got jurisdiction here, Sanchez. You need confirmation, you call this number and ask for Nikko Leviathin." Doyle handed her a card. "Otherwise, we're gonna go check out our crime scene."

The gal stepped up, getting right in his face. He clenched his hands into fists, fighting a temper that rose like molten lava, ready to explode at any moment. He sucked in air, stifling the urge to lash out and show her right then exactly who was in charge there.

"You wanna play who's got the bigger dick?" she said, unaware of the increasing danger. "You go right ahead. But this is my crime scene until my lieutenant or the district attorney tells me otherwise."

"Those'll work, too," Tucker said, his hand firm on Doyle's shoulder, the pressure just enough to keep Doyle grounded, to bring him back from the rising red danger. "In the meantime—" He cut himself off, then shot Doyle a warning look before turning and heading toward the body.

Doyle drew in a breath, then another, forcing the final remnants of the dark back down before he followed in Tucker's wake. Sanchez looked ready to spit nails, but she hung back, her cell phone now plastered to her ear.

"So what've we got?" he asked, peering down at the ghostly pale form of retired judge Marcus Braddock. By all accounts, the man had been a shape-shifting son of a bitch, but that didn't mean Doyle would wish murder on him. And this particular cause of death was the worst kind of murder. The draining of a human or a para-human was a Class Five homicide in violation of the Fifth International Covenant, and punishable by public execution. Bad shit all the way around.

Tucker was already squatting near the body, his hand reaching for Braddock's collar.

"Do you mind?" a rat-faced little man said, firmly shoving Tucker's hand out of the way.

"Careful," Tucker said mildly. "Do that again, and you'll lose a few brain cells."

The rat hesitated, confused. Then Sanchez stepped up, her expression pure business. "Let him see," she said. "They've inherited this mess. Guess that means they've got access to whatever they want." She faced Doyle head-on. "Including my resources, I'm told. At least until your own team arrives."

"And we appreciate the cooperation."

Sanchez's smile was like ice. "I'm sure you do." She nodded toward the uniformed officer. "You're relieved," she said, then smiled at Doyle. "*Limited* resources." She signaled to the rat with a jerk of her chin. "Go ahead. Show the Feds what they want to see."

Ratboy slid his hand into a latex glove, then tugged the collar down, revealing the ripped flesh and brutalized muscle.

Bloody vampires. Despite the Covenant and the strict laws against contact feeding, it seemed like every time Doyle turned around one of the fuckmongers had sucked somebody dry.

He clenched his fists at his sides, hating their weakness. Disgusted by their lack of restraint. And, yeah, he'd seen all the damn statistics that showed that the vast majority of vampires could control the daemon within. That they didn't feed on humans. That they didn't kill. That they obeyed the law.

That they weren't the walking, talking incarnation of pure, fucking evil that Doyle knew they were.

Statistics be damned. As far as Doyle was concerned, the only good vamp was a dead one.

Marcus Braddock may have been a prick—on and off the bench—but Doyle was going to make sure that the rogue vampire who sucked the life from him went down—with either a stake through the heart or an ax to the head.

"I would have said serial killer until you boys showed up," Sanchez said, her comments pulling Doyle back to the moment.

"No, ma'am," he said. "This is much worse."

The rat and Sanchez exchanged a glance, and when she nodded, Ratboy cleared his throat. "We found this under the body," he said, holding up a clear evidence bag.

Doyle took it, his eyes not needing the illumination from the flashlight that Sanchez politely held up. A silver signet ring, caked in mud. Even half hidden by the earth, the intricate craftsmanship stood out. A delicately carved dragon with a ruby eye, the body forming a circle as the beast consumed its own tail.

Tucker leaned in for a closer look. "Isn't that—"

"The Dragos crest," Doyle said, his smile cold and hard. Lucius Dragos, the last Dragos standing. Finally, after all these years, he had his old friend's balls in a vise.

"Holy fuck," Tucker said. "Talk about a gold-star evening. All this time without one piece of solid evidence, and now Dragos goes and makes a mistake like this? It's too fucking good to be true."

"That's what worries me." Doyle squatted beside the body, then tilted his head to look at his partner. "I need to see if there's more."

Tucker shook his head, then looked meaningfully at Sanchez and Ratboy. "You really want to deal with the paperwork?"

Doyle thought of the stack of reprimands and warnings that already peppered his file. Any more, and he was deep in some serious shit. "I'll only get dinged if Division finds out."

"Is there a problem?" Sanchez asked.

"Not yet," Doyle said. To Tucker, he added, "You know I have to do it."

"Aw, hell," Tucker said, then rolled his shoulders in defeat. "Fine. Go for it. What's a little official reprimand between friends, right?"

As Tucker looked deep into the eyes of Detective Sanchez, Doyle pressed his palm over Braddock's forehead. Ratboy's feathers ruffled almost immediately. "Are you insane? You're not even wearing gloves. How can you—"

"I can explain," Tucker said, crouching down next to the man as Detective Sanchez wandered away, suddenly remembering that she had an elsewhere to be. While Doyle concentrated on finding Braddock's last thoughts, Tucker put some mumbo in Ratboy's jumbo and sent the little worm on his way as well.

"I couldn't go deep," Tucker said. "Too risky. So you better find it fast."

Doyle nodded, but didn't speak. He was getting close.

Darkness. Surprise. Pleasure, even. At least until it turned. Shifted.

Then the fear came.

A mishmash. Horror. Pleasure. Pain.

None of it coming together, none of it coalescing into an image.

Just confusion. A jumble of confused emotions and reactions. Nothing to grab.

Nothing to hold on to.

"Come on, come on," Tucker said, as Doyle closed his other hand over the body's heart, trying to get purchase on the fading aura.

Dizzy. Gone.

Remorse.

And death, so cold and familiar.

And then, finally, a face.

The last image of death. The last conscious thought.

Doyle looked. And in his mind saw Lucius Dragos, fangs bared, as he bent close to suck the last vestiges of life from Judge Marcus Braddock.

Doyle's teeth chattered and his body shook as he pulled free of Braddock's mind. But he had Dragos now, had him dead to rights.

Exhausted, he tilted his head up to face Tucker. "We finally got him, partner. And we are going to nail his ass to the wall."

faces were hidden behind masks designed to withstand both human-style weapons and dark tricks, the camouflage material of their body-hugging uniforms accomplishing the same purpose.

To a civilian on the street, the team appeared to be an elite SWAT team. But they were so much more. And so much more dangerous. And there was Doyle at the head of it all, arms moving with purpose as he issued orders, dotting all the i's and crossing all the t's.

He turned then, his face tilted toward the camera, almost as if he wanted Luke to see his resolve. But Luke saw more than that; he saw Doyle's wariness, too.

Luke grinned. If a beast like Doyle felt even a hint of unease around him, then Luke must be doing something right.

Of course, word on the street was that Doyle had reined in his famous temper, this time perhaps for good. That he'd reformed, and now he got his rocks off bringing the bad guys to justice.

Luke cringed at the word. *Justice.* As if the bastards outside his home even knew what the word meant.

His cell phone rang, and he grabbed it off the console with a low, irritated growl, half expecting it would be Doyle, asking him to come quietly. Not damn likely.

He glanced at the caller ID, saw the familiar number. Immediately, his aggravation faded, and he flipped open the phone. "Are you all right?"

" 'They say the neon lights are bright on Broadway,' " Tasha sang. "But there's no magic, Lucius. I wanted there to be magic."

He drew in a breath, forced himself to use a quiet voice. His ward had always been wired differently. Even

CHAPTER 2

They were coming.

Even through the thick stone walls of his Beverly Hills home he could smell them, their determination so strong it almost masked the scent of their trepidation. Almost.

They knew him, these hunters. These men who would shackle him and interrogate him and try their best to render justice upon him.

They knew him, and they feared him.

As they should.

Within the dark confines of his interior office, he tilted his head, his nostrils flaring as he breathed more deeply. They were two. One, a gifted human. A man whose scent Lucius didn't recognize. The other, a para-daemon he'd once called friend. A beast who masked his native fury inside a knot of clean living and playing the system.

Ryan Doyle.

With an efficient movement, Luke flipped on the bank of monitors, each of the fifteen screens displaying scenes from the cameras scattered around his house. He found Doyle right away, near the main gate, talking to the human, their faces tight with purpose.

Behind them, in the shadows, lurked the RAC officers—Recon and Capture. As per procedure, their before she'd been brought over, her mind hadn't worked like other girls'. Now, at almost three centuries, she still saw the world in the most simplistic of patterns.

"You arrived safely?"

"Where were you?" she said, not answering the question. "During the night. Where did you go?"

He glanced at the monitor, at the RAC team checking weapons and conferring on details. "You know perfectly well," he said.

Her delighted giggle rose up. "Not last night. That was for me, for me, because you love me. The night before. Where did you go? I wanted you at home, but you weren't there."

His body tightened with the memory of the night, of the woman.

"Who were you with, Lucius?"

A warning bell clanged in his head. "Were you spying on me?" He forced his voice to stay flat, with no hard edges.

"Sometimes I watch and don't see. Sometimes I don't watch and see more than I want to."

"That's not an answer, Tasha."

"You promised me I would never have to leave you. You promised me you'd take care of me."

"I did promise," he said. "But to take care of you, I must see you away, and safe. You are safe now, aren't you? Safe with Sergius?"

"I'm here," she said. "But why didn't you come, too?"

"I had to stay," he said slowly. "We talked about this, remember? There are things I have to take care of in Los Angeles."

"But what if they come for you?"

He looked at the monitors, clenched his fists at his sides. "They won't."

"Then why did I have to leave?"

He almost laughed. Sometimes he really didn't give Tasha enough credit. "Just in case," he said. "Don't worry. Everything's going to be fine. Is Serge there?"

A rustle as she handed the phone over, then Serge's rough voice came over the line. "What kinda shit you got yourself into this time?"

"Nothing I can't get out of," he said, with another quick glance at the monitors. "Although to make sure that happens, I probably should hang up now."

"You will tell me," Serge said.

"I will," Luke agreed before hanging up. Someday, when the truth wasn't so dangerous, he would share everything with his friend. In the meantime, he needed to make this look good.

And yeah, it was gonna look beautiful.

Everything was in place. The system's inherent corruption working for him, rather than against him. Plans within plans within plans.

He focused again on the monitors, because although Luke had anticipated Doyle's participation, the paradaemon was a wild card. A pawn of the PEC with a hard-on for Luke, and enough power that he just might manage to bring Luke's carefully constructed house of cards crashing down.

"Fuck him," Luke growled. The plan would work. It had to. Because if this didn't go down exactly the way he'd laid it out, he'd soon feel the sting of the executioner's stake slamming home.

No.

His time upon this earth was not yet over. He had to stay; had to ensure that Tasha was never without protection.

More than that, though, he had no desire to die. Even after all his centuries, there was too much yet to live for. The pattern of stars that played across the night sky. The steady pulse of the surf outside his Malibu condo. The sweet nectar of a woman's lips beneath his own.

Oh, yes, he would miss the women.

Over the past two decades, he hadn't sipped from that cup nearly often enough, so he supposed he owed a silent thank-you to the raven-haired beauty in whose arms he'd lost himself only one night before. As the saying went, at least he would go out with a bang.

Lord knew, she qualified.

Sara. Her name alone triggered lust in his veins, and he reveled in the memory.

When he'd picked her up in the bar Wednesday night, he hadn't planned to sleep with her. He'd been perched on a stool, his sights on Braddock, his daemon screaming for release. But then Braddock had looked straight toward him, and Luke had done the first thing he'd thought of to shield himself from recognition—he'd pulled the woman sitting beside him close and pressed his lips to hers, never expecting the maddening heat that burst through him when she gasped, then relaxed and opened her mouth under his.

She'd been soft and pliant in his arms, yet utterly *there,* as if she controlled the moment as much as he. And then she'd deepened their kiss, and the daemon within had purred and backed off, abandoning the anticipation of a kill for the pure pleasure of the woman.

His head had spun from the desire rolling off her, wanting to soak it in, to explore its depths, but hesitating because he knew her reactions were fueled in part by alcohol. His cock suffered from no such moral quandary, its hard length demanding only satisfaction.

He'd had no doubt that she would provide exactly that. He could smell it on her—the arousal, the need. *The victory.* She'd come into the bar to celebrate. And Luke was the spoils of her war.

With fresh triumph pumping through her veins, she'd deepened their kiss, and he'd drunk his fill of gin and olives and the merest hint of vermouth that sweetened her mouth. The keen edge of his lust had been like nothing he'd experienced for centuries, and it had taken all his restraint not to take her right then, right there, and damn the consequences.

When she broke away to look at his face, her eyes soft with drink and her smile quivering with lust, he was certain she felt the same way.

He scanned the bar, saw Braddock leave with two other suits. Tonight, at least, the man would live.

He'd slid off the bar stool, held his hand out for the woman. The scent of hesitation faded beneath the heady fragrance of her desire, and she touched her fingers to his.

"Come with me," he said.

She quirked a brow, then looked him up and down, a sultry smile blooming on those deep, red lips. "Yeah," she said. "That's kind of my plan."

Luke stiffened, remembering how well they'd executed that plan. Remembering the way her naked body had felt beneath his. The way she'd traced soft fingers over his rough skin. The way her hips had bucked when he'd lost himself deep inside her.

The way reason and sanity had disintegrated in the fiery passion of lust and physical need.

Oh, yeah. She'd come with him, all right. And him, with her.

Even now, his cock stiffened, and if he concentrated, he could still detect her scent lingering on his skin. Even now, he wanted to claim her once again, this woman who had managed to both rile him and soothe him in ways he had never imagined.

Stop.

He clenched his fists, forcing himself to scan the monitors, to calm down and see how much further his ultimate doom had progressed.

Not much. Doyle really was playing it safe. The RAC team still circled the property, but had moved in no closer. Luke glanced at the clock and realized why—dawn was approaching. And what better way to keep him contained during the takedown than to make sure he couldn't race outside the walls of his mansion.

Of course, Luke had expected just such a plan. Still, it amused him to watch Ryan Doyle run around with his head up his ass, thinking that he was running the show.

In the meantime, the earth continued to rotate, and dawn would come, with Doyle and his team moving in on the heels of the sunlight.

He pushed back from the monitors and stood, raw energy flooding his veins.

When it was all over, he would be a fugitive.

He could live with that. If it kept Tasha safe, he could live with that for eternity.

◆

"He's not stupid," Tucker said. "He might not know you popped a vision, but the guy's gotta know he lost the ring. Not like he's going to hang around the house watching *Oprah* while we pull our party together and storm the place."

"I think Lucius is more a *Cops* kinda guy," Doyle said as he stepped into the RAC jumpsuit. Not standard procedure—broke about a dozen regulations, actually—but no way was he hanging back and letting the strike team go in first. With Dragos, Doyle intended to be front and center. And close enough to see the hate in the smug SOB's eyes when Doyle snapped the binders around his wrists.

But Tucker was right. Lucius Dragos wasn't stupid. Far from it, in fact. If Doyle didn't hate the bloodsucker so much, he'd actually respect the hell out of him.

So Doyle had to assume that Dragos knew he'd lost the ring. And if he knew that, he also knew they were coming.

And if he knew *that* . . . well, he was either long gone, or the wily bastard had one hell of a contingency plan.

The only question was what?

Beside him, Tucker started climbing into a RAC suit as well.

"What the hell do you think you're doing?"

"Going with my partner."

"You think that's a good idea? Your brand of mojo ain't gonna work on a guy like Lucius. And as fucked up as it might be, I've gotten used to having your scrawny human ass at my side. I'd rather not see it get ripped to shreds."

"You go, I go." He smiled broadly, then slipped on the face cover. "Besides, I got my magic duds."

Doyle bit back a curse. "I'm not watching your ass."

Tucker returned an evil grin. "But I got such a cute one." His eyes narrowed, the levity fading as he squinted at Doyle. "Seriously, man, you up for this?"

Doyle knew what Tucker was driving at. The visions drained him, and until he recharged, he wasn't operating at full strength. Any other perp, and he'd hang back, head over to Orlando's for a little pick-me-up. With Dragos, though, Doyle could be weak as a kitten, and he'd still go in for the takedown. "Wouldn't miss it for the world," he said, then turned to Tariq, the RAC team leader, before Tucker had the chance to slide another protest into the mix.

"We ready?"

Tariq's yellow eyes flashed in the glow of the rising sun. "Let's do this thing." The muscular jinn lifted an arm, signaling to the team, and then Tariq rushed forward, his magic disintegrating the lock on the mansion's front door.

"Clear."

"Clear!"

"Over here, too. All clear."

Within moments, the team's calls echoed through the marble entrance hall as the men split up and searched the premises. Eight thousand square feet, and not a soul, dead or alive.

"He's here," Doyle said, cutting off comment before Tucker or Tariq could raise a counterpoint. "The bastard is here someplace."

"Crypt?"

"None in the plans," Tariq said, paging through his handheld. "But the property survey shows it backs up to Silver Dreams Cemetery."

"Fuck," Doyle said. The cemetery dated from the late 1800s as the resting place of the local rich and powerful. During the silent film heyday, it had become the burial place for many a silver screen celebrity. A tourist destination, the place was modeled after European cemeteries, with crypts and mausoleums instead of the traditional stone lawn markers. It was, Doyle thought, the perfect place for a vampire to hide.

"That's his escape route," Doyle said. "He's got his little rat tunnel from here to there."

"Hang on..." Tariq tapped the screen, navigating through electronic pages. "Just give me some time."

Doyle waited, impatient. "Where's Murray?"

"In the vehicle, running ops."

"Why the hell isn't he in here?"

Tariq stared him down. "Because he's damn good at coordinating, and when I put together a team, I make it solid."

Doyle nodded, thinking. Wasn't one thing suspicious about Tariq's answer, and yet his bullshit meter was tingling. "You know the suspect?"

"Who doesn't?" Tariq answered, which was a fair

enough response. But Doyle knew that Tariq and Dragos had gone head to head a half dozen centuries before. And they were both still standing. On most days, the question of why would be an academic one to discuss over a pint. Today, Doyle's gut was telling him that the question was key.

Not that he needed the answer; he simply needed to address the problem.

"Switch," he said, looking Tariq full in the eyes and watching as his diamond-shaped pupils shrank to nothingness.

"Come again?"

"Murray in here. You in the van."

"You wanna tell me why?"

"Not really," Doyle said, stepping closer. "Why don't you tell me why?"

"I don't know what the fuck you're talking about," Tariq said, rage boiling behind his usually calm features.

"And you don't need to," Doyle said. "So long as you go out, and Murray comes in."

Tariq looked from Doyle to Tucker and then back again. "Fuck it," he finally said. "You want to play hot cop in charge, you go for it."

He shot a withering look back toward Doyle, then stormed out of the room.

Tucker looked at Doyle. "What was that about?"

"Ancient history," Doyle said.

Tucker pondered that, nodded. "And who the fuck's Murray?"

"Werewolf. And I want his nose on the job."

Five minutes later, J. Frank Murray stopped in front of an oak bookcase. "In there," he said, his nose twitching.

Doyle gave the order. "Open it or go through it, but get us inside now."

"Damn shame we gotta ruin a nice piece of furniture like that," Tucker said.

"Don't fuck with me," Doyle replied. "Just get me inside."

Murray cocked his head, and two RAC techs rushed forward. Within seconds, they'd bypassed the hidden mechanism. A sharp *click* rang out through the room. And then the entire shelf rotated slowly inward. "Told ya it was a nice piece of furniture."

They found themselves in Dragos's security room, the banks of monitors still showing footage from around the house, each now set in playback mode so that Doyle and crew were watching themselves suit up outside.

"Son of a bitch."

"Least we know he was here," Tucker said.

Doyle pointed to Murray. "Find the exit."

But Murray was already on it, nostrils flaring and muscles twitching as he walked the entire perimeter. Nothing.

The men in the room looked at one another.

"Maybe he backtracked out," Tucker suggested.

"And maybe he's making fools of us all," Doyle countered. He turned in a circle, taking in the walls, the ceiling, the floor.

The floor.

He pointed to the marble floor, the seams between the tiles appearing perfectly sealed.

They weren't. Only moments after Murray confirmed that Dragos had slipped through the floor, the team's techs had pried up the marble, exposing the tunnel below.

"In," Doyle said, and followed Murray into the black.

Two hundred yards later, they reached a set of stone stairs. The beam of Murray's flashlight followed the stairs to an ornate iron door and the blackness behind it.

Doyle cocked his head, drawing in the scent. His prey was in there, playing dead.

"Blow it," he said.

Within seconds, the door exploded, dust and bits of iron scattering as the team rushed in, stakes at the ready. They fanned out, backs to the stone walls for safety, as they quickly laid a hematite perimeter, the mineral barrier that would prevent Dragos from transforming into animal or mist. Someone lit a flare and tossed it on the ground, and the cramped tomb filled with an eerie reddish glow.

And there he was.

Lucius stood not seven yards away, clad in black jeans, a black T-shirt, and a long black duster, which undoubtedly hid a variety of weapons in its folds. His arms were crossed over his chest, his hands hidden.

His quarry wore wraparound sunglasses, the lenses so opaque that Doyle couldn't even glimpse his eyes. But Doyle didn't need to see the bastard's eyes to know that Lucius was looking straight at him.

And then he turned, his gaze sweeping over the group, examining each face.

"Tariq's not here," Doyle said. Then he smiled. "Psych."

Lucius's face remained hard as stone, his jaw firm. But

the angry scar that cut across his right cheek twitched. Fear? Doyle couldn't imagine Lucius Dragos being afraid of anything, no matter how much he should be.

No, Dragos wasn't afraid. The sorry bastard was plotting.

Not that it would do him any good.

"Hands where I can see them," Doyle said. *"Now."*

One second of insolent hesitation, then Lucius slowly pulled out his hands. He held them up, showing the backs and then the palms as the team rushed in. Five men surrounded the perp, crossbows at the ready.

Another five fanned out, inspecting the crypt.

"Over here," one cried, shoving the stone lid off a sarcophagus. "Tunnel."

"Place is wired," someone else chimed in, bending down to inspect the floor. "Not explosives, though." He followed a lead wire around the room. "Aw, shit. Nerve gas. Gonna put us all to sleep."

"And without any vamps on the strike force, you'd be the only one not affected. Then you slip into your tunnel and go your merry way?"

"Seemed like a good idea at the time," Lucius drawled. "Right now, I'm thinking a few more hours at the drawing board would have served me well."

"Glad you're so amused," Doyle said, "considering we have you dead to rights on a solid murder charge."

"I seem to recall something about a trial," Lucius said. "This isn't over, Ryan."

"Oh, it is. You're done, Dragos. Finished. There's nowhere left to run."

"There's always somewhere."

Doyle's hand fisted at his side. He wanted to smash Lucius in the face. Wanted to wipe away that smug grin.

Oh, yeah. Doyle wanted to see the bloodsucker burn.

Lucius turned his head, then the beast reached slowly up and pulled off his sunglasses. The familiar amber eyes stared straight at Doyle. Calm eyes. And too damn arrogant.

"You're going down," Doyle said, stepping forward to slap the binders on his wrists.

"Right now, perhaps," Lucius said. "But there's always a plan B."

CHAPTER 3

There was a balance to Manhattan, Sergius thought. Wants warred with disappointments. Pain complemented pleasure. And in this empire that never slept, the darkness was beaten back by nothing less than the sheer force of will.

He belonged here, both his homes fulfilling his ever-dueling needs. The deep, windowless den he'd acquired beneath abandoned train tracks, far away from prying eyes. And this penthouse of marble and glass in which he now stood, peering down at the city below.

The glass had been manufactured to his own specifications. Glass that blocked the rays of the afternoon sun, casting the city below in eternal night.

It pleased him to stand there now, looking down at the humans scurrying like ants forty-seven stories below. Did they have any idea of the horror he could wreak upon them should he choose? Did they know the effort it cost him to stay here, behind glass, fighting the urge to take and to kill? To rend and become?

Every day, the battle within him grew more fierce, and every night he fought to remain inside, to keep himself far from the scent of blood.

He had told no one of his growing hunger, not even Lucius, his closest friend. His *kyne*.

Soon, though, he would have to reveal his secrets. Either that, or he would have to kill.

And then, of course, he would have to run.

"How long must we stay here?"

He looked up, startled by the female voice that echoed his thoughts. Then he saw her reflection in the window and relaxed. *Tasha*. Luke's ward.

"I don't know." He spoke without turning, transfixed by the image of her as it approached him, gliding across the polished wood floor. Her auburn hair hung in loose curls to her waist. She moved in front of his floor lamp, and for a moment, she was illuminated from behind, a halo of red and gold dancing around her, her hair crackling with unknown power. A vision. *A goddess*. Something untouched and pure, her face carved by the gods themselves, her fiery red lips seeming to call to him. To lure him in. Begging him to discover if the purity was only an illusion.

She wore a gown of white silk with nothing under it, and he clenched his hands tight at his sides, fighting his body's reaction to her soft curves and moon-white skin. A seventeen-year-old's body, yet it had walked this earth for centuries. A saint with a seductress's form.

He bit back a curse. She was Luke's, and she was innocent, and he would not be the man who took that from her.

"Serge?" she said, the press of her hand turning his blood to molten lava. "Will he be okay?" Her lips curved into a little pout, and tears filled her eyes. He turned and pulled her close, pressing her head to his shoulder and forcing himself to steady. To keep his hands where they belonged, and to offer only the proper sort of encouragement.

"He'll be fine. He's been in tighter scrapes."

She pulled back and blinked blue eyes so pale they had almost no color at all. "It's because of me," she said, in that singsong voice. "Me, me, me. Shouldn't have told him. Naughty girl, telling secrets." She pulled away from him and moved to a black leather armchair, curling herself up so small she looked like a child.

Her suffering moved him. *Beauty. Innocence.*

She was everything he was not. Everything Luke was not. And yet the horrors of their world had spilled over on her.

Not for the first time, he felt a pang of regret that Luke had turned her at all. Serge had been there, of course, on that snowy night in France. He had witnessed what Lucius had done to her father, to her household. Hell, he'd participated.

And, yes, he understood why Luke brought the girl over. His friend had looked upon Tasha and seen his beloved Livia. He'd seen the dying girl and believed he could quell his nightmares by snatching her from the arms of death.

From that night on, she'd become Luke's responsibility. His talisman, even. But Serge couldn't help but wonder if Luke truly saw redemption when he looked upon her sweet face. Or did he instead see guilt.

Perhaps, Serge thought, his friend saw both.

"Watching me," she sang. "Pretty, pretty me, and you're a naughty boy for looking."

He released a breath that was almost a laugh. There were many times he looked at her with naughty thoughts. Now was not one of them. "I was thinking of Luke."

At the mention of his name, she frowned. "His eyes don't touch me like that." She stood, arms out, naked beneath the soft film of her gown. "He does not let me see the way his pulse burns for me, even as yours now does. It's a secret," she said. "A naughty little secret."

She stepped toward him, her head tilted to the side as if he were a mystery to her. "It does burn, yes?" Her whispered words tickled his ear, the lavender scent of her hair wreaking havoc with his self-control. "Does your blood throb with desire? Do you want what you cannot have?" Her eyes dipped down, and he was certain she could tell that his cock had sprung to attention and was now straining against the tight confines of his jeans. "Naughty boys," she murmured, her voice low and singsong. "Naughty boys want their toys, and pretty girls have them."

"Tasha." His voice was hoarse, but firm. "Sit down." He wouldn't do this. Not to her. She didn't understand. Didn't have a clue, really, what she was playing at. Her mind was a child's. Innocent.

And above all else, she was under Luke's protection.

Serge had done a lot of regrettable things in his long life, and he was certain that he would rack up more in the future, but never would he stoop so low as to count fucking his best friend's addle-brained ward among them.

"Don't want to sit. Want to play." She slid her hand down over her belly, over the mound between her thighs, and the only thought in his head at the moment was that Luke had damn well, *damn well,* better value their friendship, because keeping his hands firmly in his pockets was costing Serge all his willpower. Every last drop. "Don't you want to play with me, Sergius?"

"You don't know what you're asking," he said, his body so tight and hot he could barely force the words out. "I need to get some work done." He made to move past her, felt her fingers close over his arm. "Let go, Tasha. I need to get out of here." *Talk about an understatement.*

"But I do know," she said, sidling closer, her gown brushing against him, her soft thighs pushing close. "He showed me," she added, easing around in front of him, then cupping her palm over his frustrated, desperate cock. "He showed me how to play."

Warning bells sounded like Klaxons in his head, and he stepped back, gripping her shoulders and looking firmly into her face. "Who?" he demanded. "Who showed you?"

"Judge not," she giggled. "Lest ye be judged."

"Judge not?" he repeated, not understanding. But as he looked at her and saw that glint of sexuality spark in her eyes, he knew. He knew what had happened to her.

More than that, he knew what Luke had done. And why.

"Braddock," he said, the name like a curse on his lips. The judge had always been oily, and for decades there had been rumors of bribery and blackmail. If Serge was understanding Tasha right, Braddock had gotten his hands on her—and had gotten himself killed for his trouble. Luke might have been unwilling to give Serge details during their last phone conversation, but that didn't mean Serge didn't have sources of his own within the PEC. He'd found out easily enough that Luke had been taken into custody for Braddock's murder. Now he knew why.

The only surprise was that those incompetent RAC fools had been able to take down Lucius Dragos. Even now, Serge thought, they were probably lifting a pint and reliving their glorious victory.

It wasn't over, though. Whatever Luke's endgame, Serge was confident they hadn't reached it.

Still, Braddock was dead. And that was a damn good start.

He looked down at Tasha, unable to conceal his fury. "What did the bastard do to you?"

"Do you want me to show you?" she asked, pressing herself up close, her body swaying dreamily from side to side. "I promise to only share the part that felt nice. So nice. All soft and sweet." She scowled and shook her head, her brow creasing. "But not the part that hurt. That's the secret part. Not for sharing. And I don't like it. I don't like it when it burns. *No pain,*" she added, the vixen shriveling to reveal a terrified child. "Please, no pain. Not again."

She fisted her hands in his shirt and looked up at him with wild, terrified eyes. As she whimpered in his arms, he understood what Luke had done. Oh, yes. He understood.

He only regretted that he hadn't been there to help.

"Tasha," he said, wishing he could extinguish the fear in her eyes. "You're safe. He can't hurt you anymore."

"No more pain..."

"No."

"Only pleasure..."

"That's right."

"I can make it stop," she whispered, her dreamlike voice working on him like a trance. She lifted herself onto her toes, her hands still lost in his shirt. Her lips brushed lightly over his. "I know things. I know things about making the hurt go away. About turning pain into pretty, pretty pleasure." She tilted her head back, and he saw the raw need in her eyes. "Do you want me to show you?"

"*Tasha.*" He ground out her name, his hands closing over hers, pushing her away. "Don't."

"Don't what?" She moved closer, the gossamer gown caressing curves that he wanted to touch.

A lump formed in Serge's throat and he tried to swallow. He would *not* bed his friend's ward. He wouldn't. He couldn't.

And yet as she moved ever closer—as his body tightened with need and the daemon raged in his blood—he feared that no matter how hard he fought, in the end, he would betray his friend.

CHAPTER 4

"Sara!" Emily Tsung's heels clattered on the smooth marble floor. "Hold up a second."

Sara Constantine paused outside of Department 103 of the Los Angeles County Criminal Justice Center, moving aside to avoid the flood of humanity spilling from the courtroom. After all, in only twenty-seven minutes, Judge Kelly would reconvene the hearing on the defendant's Motion to Suppress. And folks had to hurry if they wanted to beat the lines at the coffee stand in the lobby.

Not Sara. She was off to the library. The stale coffee she'd downed before the hearing would have to suffice.

"Come on," she said as Emily drew closer. "I've got three cases to pull and Shepardize. You want to talk, you have to help."

"Don't bother." That from Dan Cummings, the defendant's attorney who had waylaid her not moments before by arguing New York case law not cited in his brief. Hardly binding authority, but definitely persuasive to a court that had yet to rule on a similar issue.

"Nice try, Dan," she said. "But I have this burning desire to fully understand the law cited in my cases."

"Not what I meant." His blue eyes twinkled. If the man hadn't been an attorney, he could have easily worked in Hollywood. Or radio. He had a voice that would make most girls melt.

He opened his briefcase and removed three anorexic printouts, then handed them to her. "I like to win on the merits, not because your eyes fell out reading three dozen New York cases that cite my authority without adding a damn thing to the jurisprudential landscape. It's a policy argument, Sara. And may the best man win."

She flipped through the pages and saw that he was true to his word. Dan or his paralegal had Shepardized all the cases, meaning they'd pulled the list of every other written opinion out there in legal-land that cited Dan's authority. And according to the report, none of those cases relied on Dan's New York case law for anything remotely pertaining to this motion.

"Thanks," she said. "This is decent of you."

"I'm a decent guy," he said with a grin. "Remember that the next time I ask you out for coffee."

"I'll keep it in mind," she said, wryly. "Now excuse me while I go figure out how to beat the pants off you when we reconvene."

"Put that way, I'm not sure I'd mind that much."

She grinned. "Keep wishing."

"By the way," he said. "Congratulations. The Stemmons conviction was a hell of a thing. Didn't think anyone could manage to put that son of a bitch away."

"Why Dan," she said. "Your inner prosecutor is showing."

He chuckled. "Don't tell anyone." He pressed a hand gently to her shoulder. "Seriously. Congrats."

"Thanks. That means a lot to me." She opened her

mouth to say more, then stopped herself, not inclined to reveal tidbits of her personal history to opposing counsel, no matter how nice a guy he might be. But the truth was, in putting away Xavier Stemmons, she'd scored one more victory in the name of her father.

The man who had murdered her dad may have walked free on a technicality, but because of Sara, one more murderer was behind bars. And at the end of the day, wasn't that why she'd become a prosecutor? To balance the scales? To put away the monsters?

To find, at the heart of it all, some semblance of justice?

She told none of that to Dan, but something in his face made her think that he understood. "The DA is lucky to have you," he said. "Truly."

Sara managed a thank-you as he moved on, and when she met Emily's eyes, her friend was smiling. "What?"

"Not only is he right—that you're kick-ass, I mean—but you have got yourself one very hot man there if you want him."

Sara shifted the strap of her briefcase on her shoulder and headed down the hall, with Emily falling in step beside her. "I don't think Dan is exactly my type." An image of dark hair, a surprisingly sexy scar, and intense amber eyes flashed in her head. No, Dan really wasn't her type at all...

"No, I guess he's not."

Something in Emily's voice made Sara stop and stare at her friend. "Spill," she said, shifting into cross-examination mode. "What do you think you know?"

"Think? Honey, I have eyewitnesses."

"Is that a fact?"

"From what I hear, your type is tall. At least six foot four. Deeply sexy. And looks beyond hot in jeans and a starched white shirt."

Sara licked her lips. *Hot* really didn't do the man justice.

"Score one for me," Emily said, not missing a trick. "So come on. I got that far on my own. Tell me the rest."

"Nothing more to tell," Sara said, putting on what her mother used to call her innocent angel face.

"That is such bullshit. My secretary saw you walking down Broadway with him. Actually, hanging all over him, I believe was the way she phrased it to me. And, gee, isn't your condo on Broadway?"

"Objection, Your Honor. Circumstantial evidence."

"I'm your best friend," Emily protested. "And I haven't gotten laid in over four months. Toss me a bone here and share the dirty details."

Sara laughed. "Get me drunk one day, and maybe. But my mother taught me that a lady doesn't kiss and tell."

"So there was kissing. Anything else?"

Sara waved the papers. "You gonna help me or not?"

"Can't. I have a hearing in Van Nuys. So I get to brave the traffic on the 101. Color me totally joyful." Emily pointed at the papers. "I don't care if Dan is cute. You kick his butt, you hear?"

"Absolutely."

"And you're not off the hook about the mystery man."

"I pretty much figured that out all on my own."

Sara watched Emily disappear down the hallway,

then settled on a bench and pulled out Dan's cases. She had just under twenty minutes to study the law, find an opposing argument, and figure out the best way to articulate it. Plenty of time. She was good at thinking on her feet. Always had been. And the law came easy to her, both the advocacy and analytical arms of the beast. She'd spent law school buried in books, arguing the impact of obscure passages with her professors. Hours would pass when she thought of nothing other than Blackacre or Whiteacre or the fruit of the poisonous tree.

So why was it that now, when she needed to be back in court in mere minutes, she couldn't even focus on three simple cases?

Luke.

Well, there was a big, fat duh. Of course he was the reason she couldn't focus. He was the reason she'd spent all of yesterday glowing, though everyone around the office assumed her sparkle and pop came from Wednesday's victory in the Stemmons matter. Only Sara had known the truth—that her mind had been more on sex than on the fact that a serial killer was finally behind bars. A sweet victory, yes. But not as sweet as Luke's lips on her breasts.

One day of mooning around was enough, though, and she'd spent the entire morning methodically forcing the man out of her mind so she could concentrate on this hearing. But obviously she still had some serious mind-over-matter issues, because one word from Emily, and every sweet, sexy, erotic moment came rushing back, like an IMAX movie in her mind.

She shivered, the typed words on the page swimming

in front of her as she remembered the way he'd pulled her to him in the bar. One moment he was beside her, casually nursing a Scotch. The next moment, she was tasting the Glenfiddich that still clung to his lips.

For an instant, she'd been shocked, her mind screaming at her to pull back and let the bastard feel the sting of her palm against his cheek. But the next moment, all thoughts of retribution faded against the desperate, fervent urge building within her. *She wanted him.* She'd never met him. Didn't know him. But damned if she didn't have to have him. Right there. Right then.

The power of her need had confused her as much as it had excited her. She wrote it off to alcohol and victory, a potent combination. She'd nailed her first high-profile felony, after all. For months, she'd lived and breathed the law and the evidence, burying herself in blood and horror and the fucked-up brain of a psychopath. A devil. Exactly the kind of criminal who had drawn her to the law in the first place. The kind of man who, since she'd been eight years old, she'd wanted to put behind bars. No, not wanted. *Needed.*

Was it any wonder that once it was over she wanted to revel in her victory? Wanted to ease the tension that had built up during the long nights lost in the law and the horrible, gut-wrenching evidence?

Wanted to lose herself in passion and pleasure?

And she had. So help her, she really had.

They'd left the bar before they caused a scene, stumbling arm in arm onto the sidewalk. She'd taken him back to her condo then, not only because it was close, but because she had a doorman. Security cameras. She was in lust, yes, but she wasn't stupid. She wanted him to see that people knew her. That they'd remember him.

More than that, she'd wanted some tiny illusion of control. Because the real truth was that every ounce of control had drained away at the moment his lips first touched hers, her body responding in a way it never had before.

She was no stranger to sex, but so often lately it had been more of an aerobic workout than a mind-numbing, body-tingling experience. Not so with Luke. Her body had practically glowed under his touch, and she'd wanted more. So much more.

And he'd delivered.

They'd stumbled to her condo together, groping, touching, kissing. The heat between them so intense Sara feared she'd melt, and the fact that they arrived at her building without her slamming him against a parked car and demanding he take her right then was a supreme testament to her self-control.

In the elevator, though, all bets were off.

He pulled her close, his erection pressing against her thigh and leaving no doubt that he wanted her as much as she wanted him. His growl of frustration shot straight through her, making her sex tingle. She was wet, so wet, and security cameras be damned, she couldn't wait any longer to feel his hands on her.

She'd taken his hand, slid it along her thigh, hiking her skirt up as they went, then pressed his palm over the soft satin of her panties.

He'd made a low noise in his throat, his hand cupping to stroke her, his clever fingers pulling aside the band of her panties, finding her slick and wet. He'd thrust inside her, and she'd come in his hand, her quivering body drawing him in as the orgasm ripped through her, shattering her so that she had no choice but to cling to him or else burst into a thousand pieces.

It had been one hell of a start to a long, sweet night. A night she desperately wanted to repeat. A night that, surprisingly, hadn't been solely about sex. They'd lain together, calm and quiet, and she'd told him about the Stemmons conviction. More than that, she'd told him about the case itself. How it had become personal, almost as if it had been her and Stemmons in the ring, each blow designed to do maximum damage.

The words had spilled out, and had she stopped to think about it, she would have been mortified that she was revealing so much to a stranger. Except he hadn't seemed like a stranger. Not then. He'd seemed like Luke, and though she knew it was silly, she felt as though she'd known him forever.

That, of course, was an illusion, and she wasn't foolish enough to share the fantasy with the man in her bed. She'd made no noises about future dates, suggested no plans for dinner or coffee. If she didn't ask, he couldn't make false promises.

He knew where she lived. Where to find her.

And when he'd left before dawn the next morning, she'd sent him off into the world with a kiss, but with no request for promises of a future, no matter how much her body still craved him.

She'd shut and locked the door, then succumbed to the girlish angst that inevitably followed a night of passionate sex with a perfect stranger. By the time she'd showered and dressed for work, she'd convinced herself that theirs had been a singular encounter. The kind of night she would remember and hold up to judge other men by. The kind of memories that would keep her warm at night.

But she didn't expect to see the man again.

Then she grabbed her briefcase and opened her door. There, lying on her mat, was a bundle of perfect tulips, their stems tied in a blood-red bow. She'd never been given flowers before, hadn't even realized there was a hole in her heart until his gift had filled it.

There was no note, but it didn't matter. Somehow, she knew. They'd marked each other. Gotten in each other's heads.

And, yes, she would see him again.

The thought had been enough to keep the glow all day yesterday. Even now, she could feel the tingle of pleasure running through her. And, yes, she'd been sappy and girlish enough to tuck the red ribbon that had bound the flower stems into the pocket of her suit jacket.

She slipped her hand in now, twisted the satin ribbon around her fingers, and lost herself to a wave of sweet anticipation and contentment.

He'd moved her. And damned if she hadn't wanted to be moved.

"Sara?"

With a start, she jerked her head up and found herself looking into Sergeant Pearson's worried eyes. "You okay?" the bailiff asked.

"Yes. Fine. Just tired." She gathered her papers, hoping she wasn't blushing, and hurried to stand.

"Judge wants you inside. He's ready to start back with the arguments."

She nodded, trying her best to appear confident despite having blown off her case review in favor of an X-rated rerun of her night with Luke.

A pleasant diversion, but somehow she doubted that her ruminations on sex with Luke would prove useful in arguing her case.

In other words, time to march into court, face the judge, and wing it.

CHAPTER 5

"Thank you, Counselors. I've heard enough." Judge Kelly rapped the gavel on the polished oak bench. "You'll have my ruling in the morning."

Sara rose along with everyone else in the courtroom as the judge stepped down and disappeared through the door to his chambers. As soon as he'd cleared the room, she exhaled, then dropped into the chair.

It had been brutal, but at least she hadn't made a complete fool of herself.

"Good job, Counselor," Dan said. "For a moment, I didn't think you were going to raise the jurisdictional question, but then you snuck it in at the last minute. Really caught Kelly's attention. And pretty much blew my argument out of the water."

"For a guy on the opposing side, you're far too nice to me."

He grinned. "You caught me. Let me make it up to you with a coffee. Hell, let me make it up to you with dinner."

She shook her head, unable to fight her smile. "You never stop."

"That's why they pay me the big bucks." He nodded toward the door. "Seriously, a coffee? I promise I'll keep my hands to myself and my conversation on the law. My thoughts, however, might drift."

"I've got work," she said. "But thanks."

He nodded. "Another time maybe."

"Sure," she said, but they both knew she didn't mean it.

He left ahead of her, and as he stepped out past the heavy oak door, Martin Drummond, the senior assistant district attorney, stepped in. "I caught part of your argument," he said, his voice level.

"Oh." She swallowed, noting how quickly the glow faded. True, she hadn't been at her best, but she hadn't sucked. Even Dan had paid her a compliment, though he'd also admitted to ulterior motives. Even so, surely Marty wasn't about to call her to the carpet for not being better prepared.

Was he?

"I'm pulling you off the case."

Apparently, he was.

Her entire body went cold, most likely the result of all the blood draining out of her. "What? But—"

"You're being reassigned."

"No! I mean—" She felt the hot sting of tears and hated herself for it. She would *not* cry. She'd argue her case. To the district attorney himself if she had to. One time—one lousy time—she wasn't completely on her game, and she was being punished this severely for it? It wasn't right. It wasn't fair. It wasn't—

"Hell of a promotion, actually," he said, smiling now. "Looks like you've been plucked from the obscure ranks of the ADAs."

She stepped back, her body backtracking as much as her mind. "Wait. A promotion?"

Marty chuckled. "You're doing a great job, kid. Guess it got you noticed by the right folks. You've heard of Division 6?"

"Sure. I don't know a lot about it. Their offices are upstairs, right?" She hoped that made her sound at least somewhat on the ball. The truth was, she didn't have a clue about Division 6. On occasion, late at night, she'd run into someone with a Division 6 badge in the lobby. She knew the group was under the jurisdiction of Homeland Security. And considering the shady edge to the few employees she'd bumped into, she tended to think the division specialized in undercover antiterrorist ops. But other than that, she knew next to nothing.

"No one knows much," Marty said. "But I guess you're about to." He took a few steps and then stopped, turning back to her. "Only the best get the opportunity to work for Division 6," he said. "Great for Division 6, not so great for the District Attorney's Office. You decide the job's not for you, and you can have your old position back. Any day. Anytime. No questions asked."

"Thank you," she said. "I appreciate that." All the more so since Marty wasn't the type who bothered with niceties or compliments. He'd bothered today, though, and that made her even more curious about this mysterious position for which she'd been chosen.

He was walking again, and she followed him through the halls to the elevator. He slipped a key into a slot, then pressed the button for the twentieth floor. Authorized Access Only. Sara had to smile. Apparently she was now authorized.

The doors opened on a reception area with a lanky

receptionist sporting spiked orange hair. Not the generally proper demeanor most courthouses tried to convey. The Division 6 crew, it seemed, was a little wilder.

"I've got Sara Constantine for a meeting with Nostramo Bosch and Alexander Porter," Marty said. He turned to Sara. "Here's where I leave you. I don't have authorization beyond the reception area. Good luck."

And then he was gone, and she was all alone, staring at the unremarkable reception area and the completely remarkable receptionist.

"Water?" the girl asked.

Sara shook her head, wondering if she ought to sit down. But there wasn't time. A pair of frosted glass doors opened, and District Attorney Alexander Porter stepped inside, his hand out in greeting. "Sara," he said. "Good to see you again. You've been doing excellent work. Coming up fast through the ranks."

"Thank you." Technically, Porter had been her boss for the three years she'd been working at the District Attorney's Office. But the job was a huge one, and Porter knew how to delegate. Which meant that Sara's day-to-day contact had always been Marty. And now he'd gone and abandoned her, leaving her to the mercy of the big man himself. "Um, Marty didn't know a whole lot about what I'm going to be doing."

"No, he wouldn't. Walk with me." He headed back through the doors, and she followed him. "The truth is, I don't know a lot about it myself, though I am the liaison between Division 6 and the District Attorney's Office.

"Homeland Security," Sara said. "Terrorists."

"Something like that," Porter said, but Sara had the feeling he was smiling at her, though she wasn't at all sure what was funny.

He stopped inside the doors, bringing Sara up short. "I actually owe you an apology. On any other day, you'd be sitting in the conference room with an orientation packet and a rep from Employee Relations giving you an overview of how things work here. The PowerPoint presentation is actually quite interesting. I'll make sure you get a copy."

"But today?"

"Charges were filed this morning in a new matter, and Bosch thinks you'll get more out of sitting in on the initial interview with the defendant." The corner of his mouth lifted. "To be honest, I think Bosch wants to gauge your reaction. Throw you into the deep end of the pool and watch you swim."

"I can understand that," she said, determined not to drown. After all, she was a trained prosecutor. It's not as if there was much that could surprise her. "And Mr. Bosch is . . ."

"He's the subdirector of the Violent Crimes Division. He'll be your immediate supervisor."

"Got it. Thanks." She cleared her throat, not inclined to rush her boss, but still anxious to know the details of the kind of matters she'd be handling. "So, what's the nature of this new case?"

Instead of answering, he started walking again, and Sara noticed that the hall didn't actually go anywhere. It was simply a hall, and it ended at an elevator.

"Mr. Porter?"

"The truth is, I don't know. But I can tell you generally about the type of work you'll be doing for the Division."

She nodded, hoping she didn't look too eager.

"Again, bear in mind that under normal circumstances, you'd have the benefit of an orientation day."

"No problem. I'm sure that moving straight into a case will give me a much more solid understanding of the job than any orientation video ever could."

"Probably true." He punched the down button and turned to face her. "But I think the point is to ease new prosecutors in. To reduce the shock."

"Shock?"

The elevator arrived and she followed Porter on, noting that there were no buttons for floors nineteen to one, or for the basement and courthouse parking levels. Simply labels. But there were seven sublevels she'd never seen before, as well as P-Sub-10, which was apparently a parking level below the final sublevel. All in all, very mysterious, and Sara had the sense she was about to get sucked into the world of international espionage where she'd find James Bond's full-out tech center accessed through the back of a broom closet.

Porter pushed the button for Sub-7. "Get ready, Sara. You're about to go down the rabbit hole."

She cocked her head, considered her response, and decided on complete honesty. "I'm sorry, sir. I don't know what you're talking about."

"No. You wouldn't. Not without seeing it." He grinned. "Or seeing the PowerPoint." He paused. "The truth is there's an entire world out there that most of us never see."

"You're talking about the criminal underground?"

"I'm talking about the stuff of human nightmares."

She nodded, hoping she looked as if she was following. "Right. Like . . . ?"

"Like vampires. Demons. Werewolves. All those beings you thought were only myths. That you thought were the stuff of nightmares or stories told to scare children or populate horror movies. All those things are real. They're real, and they're out there, and some of them are just as evil as Hollywood has portrayed them."

"Some of them?" she asked, because it was the only question she felt competent at the moment to form. Was this a big joke? Some sort of test of how well she handled the absurd?

He nodded. "The breakdown percentages are quite similar to our world. Most of the Shadow creatures are law abiding. It's the ones who break the law that Division is concerned with."

"You're serious," she said, trying to imagine Count Dracula on the stand. *But he can't be serious.*

The elevator lurched to a stop, and the door slid open. Sara stared out into the cavernous room and took an involuntary step backward, not able to believe what she saw, but also unable to deny her own eyes.

Outside the elevator lay a whole new world. A world where wolves slunk across a reception area. A hulk of a man with pale orange skin and cloven feet stood at a granite counter calmly filling out a form. And the woman behind the counter seemed to have some sort of mist swirling around her.

There were humans, too. At least they looked like

humans. But they really weren't the ones drawing her attention.

"A little overwhelming the first time, isn't it?"

Hell yes. Her heart was pounding so loud she could barely hear herself think, and her palms had started to sweat.

The rabbit hole, he'd said? Try a wormhole to hell.

She looked at Porter, calling on every ounce of self-control to keep her voice from shaking. To keep from revealing how much her world had just tilted. "This is for real?"

"You okay?"

She smiled, bright and perky. "Absolutely." And then, just to prove the point, she stepped out of the elevator and took a deep breath. Since nobody with fangs rushed to assault her, she took another tentative step, then boldly looked around.

And the truth was, that despite the rather bizarre appearance of some of the beings occupying the space, the room had a familiar feel. The hustle and bustle of the judicial system at work. "This is a reception area?" she asked.

"You got it, but there's no public access. That's on sublevel four, which can be accessed from the main reception area we came through, or the secondary reception on the Division's primary parking level." He shot her a wry smile. "As you might imagine, a number of the creatures who work here or are brought in for questioning or detention would cause a bit of a stir if they marched through the building's main lobby."

"Yeah. I guess they would."

"Bottom line is that no one comes past reception

without an escort." He pointed to a long, dark hall. "Investigation to the right. Prosecution to the left. Detention and Security section are accessed through Sub-9."

"I didn't see a Sub-9," she said.

"You wouldn't have. Highest security—some of these creatures are quite the escape artists. Sub-9 is accessed only through an elevator across from Leviathin's office."

"Who?"

"Nikko Leviathin. My counterpart down here." He looked at her. "You ready to keep going, or do you need to take a minute?"

She scanned the room, her mind processing. As unbelievable as this was, Marty had been right—this was one hell of a promotion. More than that, it promised to never be dull.

She looked at Porter. "I'm ready," she said. "Lead the way."

His quick smile included a heavy dose of pride, and she was glad she hadn't hesitated. For the first time, she realized how much was riding on her successful insertion into this world. Clearly, Porter had recommended her. If she froze up, her failure would reflect badly on her former boss, as well as on the entire District Attorney's Office. *Political games.*

They moved swiftly through the lobby and underneath a stone archway into which two words had been carefully carved: *Judicare Maleficum.* "To judge the evildoer," if her Latin was correct. "We'll introduce you around later," Porter said. "Right now, Bosch is waiting."

Sara followed, a million questions still swirling through her mind.

Always go back to the basics. "So what am I going to be doing?"

"Exactly what you're trained for." He flashed a badge at a security desk. A set of steel doors swung open, revealing a hall that could have been in any law office. Doors on one side, cubicles for support staff on the other.

She tried to peek inside one of the cubicles and caught a glimpse of blue skin. Definitely not in Kansas anymore.

"And here we are." They'd reached a corner office. Porter knocked, and Sara held her breath, wondering what they would find behind that door.

"Enter." The voice was low, clipped, but sounded entirely human.

When Porter pushed open the door and they stepped inside, Sara saw that the man looked as human as his voice sounded. About sixty years old, with salt-and-pepper hair, Nostramo Bosch exuded the air of a distinguished elder statesman.

He stood, and when he came around the desk to shake her hand, she caught the subtle scent of cinnamon.

"Sara Constantine. I'm Nostramo Bosch."

"Nice to meet you."

"We're very excited to have you on board. I've been monitoring your career for quite a while. I hope you decide to accept the position."

She had absolutely no intention of walking away. But she couldn't help but wonder what would happen if she did.

Bosch chuckled, as if he could read her thoughts.

Then again, Sara supposed that maybe he could. "Don't worry. You have a perfect right to say no. And if you do, you'll simply go back upstairs and slip back into your old job."

"No way," she said, then realized she'd blurted the response out far too quickly for propriety. She turned to Porter. "I didn't mean—"

"I understand," he said, amusement in his voice.

"But I'm curious," she admitted. "I could just go back? After having seen all of this?"

Bosch waved his hand, as if dismissing that complication. "We have creatures on staff more than capable of adjusting your memory. At most, it would seem like a very vivid dream."

She was digesting that tidbit of information when Bosch's phone buzzed. "Mr. Porter's needed back on the main floors," a melodic voice announced. "And the suspect is settled in Interview A."

"Thank you, Martella."

"I'll take my leave, then," Porter said. He turned to Sara, then took her hand in his, giving it a friendly pat. "I'm the only one in my office who knows the true nature of Division 6. You're welcome to speak with your friends, of course, but don't forget the cover story. A division of Homeland Security, and you're not at liberty to share any more information."

"Right. Thank you." She smiled politely, surprised to find she wasn't nervous about him leaving her alone down here. Just the opposite, actually. She was eager to get on with it. To find out the details of this strange new world.

Bosch was watching her face, his expression approving. "We'll walk out with you," he said to Porter.

He slipped into his suit coat and they followed Porter out into the hall. But when he turned back toward the reception area, Bosch led Sara further into the bowels of the building, moving through doors, striding down crowded hallways, and finally stopping outside a room labeled Interview A. "Porter didn't have the chance to explain my job in much detail," she said.

"Your job's exactly the same," Bosch said. "It's only the rules that have changed."

"The rules?"

He opened the door and they stepped into an anteroom, completely empty. The walls were concrete, painted a dull gray, with one exception—the far wall featured a window of opaque black glass beside a heavy steel door. A control panel was mounted between the door and the glass.

"Normally, I'd give you a little more time to take it in. To get your bearings. But I want you in at the ground floor of this case."

"That's what Mr. Porter said." She looked toward the closed door, imagining the defendant waiting beyond it.

"Right now, the shorthand version. Division 6 is the cover story for one arm of an ancient organization we now call the Preternatural Enforcement Coalition. The PEC's been functional in some form or other almost since the dawn of civilization, though I'll admit it's become more bureaucratic of late. We have one purpose: to bring those of our kind who would do evil to justice."

"But?"

"You could say that we are a self-regulatory agency.

We do not operate under the laws of humans. We operate under the Covenant, a series of laws created and modified over millennia."

"And these laws have jurisdiction over whom? Werewolves? Vampires? All the spooky things Porter mentioned when we were in the elevator?"

"The Shadow creatures. Exactly."

"Okay." She licked her lips, forcing herself to look at this like any job, any problem. "But I'm human. Doesn't that matter?"

"No, though humans are rare among our ranks. We only offer positions to the best and the brightest. Humans we have determined to be psychologically capable of moving into this world."

"Oh." She looked at him. "Are you human?"

"No."

She nodded, desperately wanting to ask what he was, but fearing that would cross some sort of prosecutor-boss etiquette line.

"You said it's a new case?"

"New, and high profile. The enforcement wing apprehended the defendant this morning. He's finished processing and is waiting for us. I don't expect you to participate today, but I do want you here for the preliminary interview."

"What's the charge?"

"Murder. He killed a retired judge. One of our judges."

"What was the murder weapon?"

"The defendant was the weapon," Bosch said as he pushed one of the buttons on the control panel. "He can't see us," Bosch said. "One-way glass."

As he spoke, the glass shifted from opaque black to transparent, revealing the interior of the interrogation room. Sara stifled a gasp, carefully schooling her face into absolutely no reaction at all.

Not that Bosch was watching her. He was staring at the defendant. *He was staring at Luke.* At the man whose hands had brought her skin to life. The man whose tongue had laved her. Whose cock had filled her. Whose urgent thrusts had left her moaning and begging for more.

The man who'd shared her disgust when she'd outlined Stemmons's crimes, and who'd helped celebrate her victory when she'd shared the jury's verdict.

The man who'd left a bundle of tulips on her doorstep. Who'd filled her thoughts and eased her dreams.

The man now sitting there accused of murder.

"Sara? You okay? I know it's a lot to take in."

She cleared her throat, remembering the gentle way his fingers had caressed her neck. "You said the defendant was the weapon? What exactly did you mean by that?"

"Pretty standard stuff in this division," Bosch said. "Lucius Dragos is a vampire."

CHAPTER 6

She had no time to process, no time to realign her reality with this new perception of the world. *Luke was a vampire. Luke was a murderer.*

A vicious, cold-blooded killer. The very epitome of the evil she'd dedicated her life to putting behind bars.

There had to be some sort of mistake.

And he wasn't simply a murderer. No, he was also an in-your-face, straight-out-of-your-nightmares vampire. It was outrageous. Unbelievable.

Mortifying.

He'd had his hands on her. He'd touched her—he'd *claimed* her—and surely, *surely* she would have known if she'd been sleeping with a killer.

She remembered, though, the strength in those powerful hands and the determination in his amber eyes. She'd seen control there along with an undercurrent of violence that had both scared and excited her. He'd practically thrummed with a potency and raw carnality that had wreaked havoc on her. She'd wanted him, yes, but he'd wanted her, too, and he was a man who took what he wanted.

He'd taken her, leading her to where he wanted her to go and then watching with unabashed rapture as she'd shattered under his touch. He was dangerous, all right.

She'd seen it, and she'd simply ignored it. In his arms,

she'd felt no risk. The opposite, actually, because he'd made her feel more secure than she ever had in her life.

Clearly, she'd been a fool.

"Constantine? Do you need a minute?"

She tilted her face up, caught her own reflection in the glass as she did. She'd gone slightly pale, but there was nothing in her face that gave away her secret. Nothing that would reveal that she'd been thrown.

It was the face of a trial attorney, and a damn good one. A prosecutor who could get the shit kicked out of her by a witness in front of twelve citizens good and true and make it look like the witness said the exact right thing to put the final nail in the defendant's coffin. It was, she realized, the face that had gotten her this job.

"I'm fine," she said, meeting Bosch's eyes. "Let's go hear what Mr. Dragos has to say for himself."

If Bosch could see her surprise, he didn't show it. Under the circumstances, she supposed he would assume she was tossed a bit off balance by the fact that she was about to come face-to-face with a vampire. Bosch, of course, had no way of knowing that she'd been significantly closer to Dragos than arm's length. And, yes, she needed to tell him about that little conflict of interest. For that matter, she considered stopping him as his fingers tapped out a code on the control panel. She shouldn't be working this case. Not with the baggage she was going to be lugging into that room.

Except she said nothing, determined instead to walk into the interview room and face a defendant she'd slept with not forty-eight hours before. Not because it was allowed, and not because justice demanded it. But because she needed to see firsthand the kind of monster who had taken her body and toyed with her heart. The killer who'd gotten under her skin.

An electronic beep signaled that Bosch had entered the correct code, and a green light flared above the door. Sara took a step forward, anticipating, but Bosch didn't open the door. Instead, he pulled a sheaf of paper from a folder and handed it to her. "Initial report. I'll be handling this round of questioning, but don't feel you're locked in the role of observer. You want information, you ask."

"Thank you," she said, though she didn't intend to accept the invitation. This round, she would be content to watch and learn.

She flipped through the pages, her gaze skimming over Luke's picture along with his vital statistics. Height, six foot five. Weight, 220. Both stats that jibed with what she knew of the man. The next statistic, however, had her mouth going suddenly dry: born in Italy in the year 122. Apparently she'd been a few years off when she'd guessed that the man she'd taken back to her apartment was five years her senior.

The report indicated no prior arrests, but the lead dectective, Ryan Doyle, had methodically itemized the homicides worldwide in which Luke's name had been thrown in as a suspect. The list was enough to make her stomach turn despite the fact that each of the investigations had been marked as closed, and Luke had ultimately not been implicated.

The slight queasiness shifted to downright dread as she turned to Doyle's summary of the crime scene. The killer had violently punctured the victim's throat in two places, leaving his exsanguinated body to molder in

MacArthur Park. She swallowed, trying to hold her own memories at bay. *His throat. His dead eyes. Her terrified scream.*

And the coppery scent of his blood smearing her hands as she'd held him close and begged her daddy to please, please, please wake up.

Dear God. Dear God, no.

She drew in a shaky breath, her hands tightening on the pages as she tried to shut off the flood of images. Her knees weakened, and since she feared that she would fall, she gripped the pages tighter still, forcing herself to focus on Braddock and Luke and the evidence in *this* murder, not a chillingly similar one that she had witnessed more than twenty years ago.

"Turn the page, Constantine," Bosch said. His voice was firm, businesslike, but she thought she detected a hint of compassion under the professional veneer. He would know, of course. The county ran extensive background checks on all prosecutors. Her father's murder was part of her file. And if the county knew, then surely Division 6 did as well.

Rather than comfort her, though, his compassion shamed her. *It shouldn't show.* Her emotions shouldn't spill out into work like this, and her past should never interfere.

"Sir, I'm fine."

"Turn the page."

She did, her mouth going dry as she turned to an eight-by-ten glossy photograph. "Meet Marcus Braddock," Bosch said. "Our victim."

The photographer had used a flash, making the colors pop, primarily red and white. The pale white of the victim's bloodless skin contrasted sharply with the fiery red bloom where the neck had been brutally punctured.

"Anyone familiar with a vampire's bite would recognize this murder for what it is," Bosch said kindly. As he spoke, the chill of cold certainty ripped through her. She'd suspected it when she'd skimmed the text of the file, but she hadn't given voice to it until the vivid colors of reality had reached out and grabbed her—*her father had been murdered by a vampire.*

She swallowed, working to hold it together despite the one-two punch to her gut that was Luke and then her father.

Suck it up, Constantine.

Aware that Bosch had to be watching her, judging her, she focused on the photograph, examining it not as a daughter mourning a lost father, but as a prosecutor seeking justice for a murdered victim.

As murders went, it was brutal, but not more brutal than some Sara had seen. Stemmons, the serial killer she had so recently put away, had been particularly fond of cutting thin slices into his adolescent victims and letting them bleed out slowly and painfully.

Sara, however, had not slept with Stemmons mere days before his apprehension, and the fact that she *had* slept with the man who had ripped into Marcus Braddock's throat made her stomach turn, and she breathed softly through her mouth, trying to quell a rising bout of nausea.

"Something on your mind, Constantine?"

She squared her shoulders and slammed a mental door on her intruding memories. Of her father. Of Luke.

And of a vampire named Jacob Crouch who'd killed her father, then gotten away with murder.

She could do that, she told herself. She could close it off. Block it away. All of it. She could do it, she knew, because in the end, this was the job she lived for.

"I'm fine, sir," she said, determined that she would be. To steady herself, she skimmed the information about the victim, learning that although he appeared human, he was actually something else entirely.

"A Therian," Bosch said in response to her question. "A shape-shifter. In this case, a were-fox. Considered a para-human for purposes of the Covenant, and violence against a human is the most egregious of crimes."

Which meant that Luke was facing the death penalty. She flipped briskly to the next page of the report, then frowned when she found no reference to a confession. "Sir," she said, making him pause as his hand closed around the door handle. "Earlier you said that the suspect killed the victim."

"I did."

"He left a signet ring behind, but other than that…" She trailed off, her voice rising in question. She hoped that the question sounded merely academic and didn't reveal the wellspring of hope that had bubbled up inside her. A tiny, unprofessional voice that had whispered the possibility that this was all a mistake and that Luke was innocent. That he hadn't done this horrible, unforgivable thing.

"Your point, Constantine?"

She swallowed and told herself that this wasn't personal. It was the job, and she would be asking the same questions even if she'd never seen Lucius Dragos before in her life. "A question of semantics. There's nothing in this paperwork to indicate that the suspect has confessed, and yet you flat-out stated that the suspect killed the victim." She licked her lips. "I was simply wondering why that was. Sir."

Bosch's mouth worked, and Sara couldn't tell if it was with humor or with irritation. After a moment, he answered briskly. "Two reasons. First, we're not constrained by the rules that you're used to upstairs. Due process has a different meaning down here. You'll get used to it. Or you won't, and you'll be requesting a transfer back to Porter's office. That would be a shame, but we'll cross that bridge if we come to it."

Sara swallowed, convinced by the heat in her cheeks that Bosch could see her mortification.

"And second, we have the defendant dead to rights."

Despite the lingering sting of the verbal hand slap, Sara bit back a guffaw. "With a signet ring?"

"With a witness," Bosch said, the words killing her hope as effectively as a knife to the heart.

"A witness?" She flipped through the report, looking for something to back up his statement, both frustrated and relieved when she found nothing. "There's no mention in the file of a witness."

"Agent Doyle's in the process of preparing a formal affidavit regarding the final image that registered on the victim's conscious mind."

"He's—I'm sorry. What?"

"Not the kind of investigative methods you're familiar with, I know. But I assure you that Agent Doyle's skill is not only legitimate, but an enormous asset to this department."

"No kidding," Sara said, still trying to wrap her head around what the investigator could do. "So he just looks into the minds of the dead?"

"Not exactly. If the conditions are right, he has the ability to experience a victim's last emotional moments, and see through the victim's eyes at the moment of death."

"If conditions are right," Sara repeated. "And in this case?"

"They were dead-on perfect. He's our man, Constantine."

Something cold and empty settled over her. *It was true, then. She'd slept with a murderer.* Sex alone she could handle. She wouldn't like it, but she could handle it. But with Luke it had been more than sex. She recalled the warm tingle that had spread through her like the buzz of fine wine when she'd found the tulips on her doorstep. She'd been gloriously happy, awash with possibilities and the eager excitement of a girl starting a new relationship. Now all of that was shattered. And the worst of it was, she'd never seen it coming.

Bosch looked her up and down, and she worked hard to keep her raging emotions from showing on her face. "Call him the accused if it makes you do your job better, but don't forget what he is and what he did."

"I won't, sir. Believe me." Her mortification faded slowly, replaced by a steady, burning anger. "I understand what he is. I apologize. I spoke out of turn."

"Are you under the impression I'm annoyed with you?"

She managed a half-smile and didn't voice the very definitive *yes* that screamed for release.

Apparently she didn't need to. Bosch could clearly see her answer on her face. "You're here because you're quick and you're bright and you ask the right questions. Stop now and I will be annoyed. Now, can we go in, or shall we address the differences in fashion for prisoners here and upstairs? Personally, I find the orange jump-suits L.A. County issues to be rather repulsive."

"Agreed. And, yes. We can go in."

The green light above the door had defaulted back to red, so Bosch reentered the code, then gave the door a tug and stepped inside, holding it open for her to follow. She stepped smartly through the door, her head high, her heels clicking firmly on the cement floor.

He looked up as she entered, and she saw it immediately. That spark of recognition. That quick shadow in his eyes that suggested that his world was tilting along with hers.

She, at least, wasn't locked up.

Not that Luke had the appearance of a prisoner. True, he wore a faded gray T-shirt with "Detention C" stamped across the chest in black letters, but there was nothing about him that seemed bound. On the contrary, walking into that room felt much the same as walking into a conference room, with Luke at the head of the table, slowly surveying those summoned to do his bidding.

Beside her, Bosch's gaze shifted between the two of them, his eyes dull and unreadable. Then he pressed a hand to her back, easing her forward to one of the two chairs on the opposite side of Luke. If he knew that anything other than a murder investigation was taking place in that room, he didn't show it.

Sara was determined not to show it, either.

She pulled out the chair and sat, then took a yellow pad from her briefcase and placed it efficiently on the table in front of her. The investigator's report was tucked underneath, just enough of the page revealed under the pad to signal to Luke that she'd read the report and she knew what he'd done. She kept her pen in her hand, idly twirling it in her fingers as she watched Luke's face. Other than that first flicker of recognition, however, he revealed nothing.

"Lucius Dragos," Bosch said, taking the chair beside Sara. "It's not often I have the chance to sit across from a man with such a notorious reputation."

"Notorious?" Luke repeated, his mouth curving down into a frown. "I didn't know you listened to gossip, Nostramo."

The easy use of Bosch's first name surprised Sara, and she glanced at her new boss, anticipating his reaction. None, however, was forthcoming. Instead, he merely flipped through the papers in his hand. "Belfast, last month," Bosch said. "A werewolf dead in Glencairn Park. Nasty business."

"Wasn't it, though," Luke said, leaning back in his chair, utterly calm in the face of Bosch's accusation. "Turns out Division 3 suspected that same werewolf in the killing of a human politician not three days after being released from PEC custody." He shook his head. "I had a pint with the lead investigator. Not only was I not charged, but the bloke picked up the tab for my Guinness."

"And Talijax Feaureaux? Dallas, Texas."

"Apparently I was in the wrong place at the wrong time. The charges against me were dismissed."

"And Milton Craymore?" Bosch pressed, as Sara sat more stiffly in her chair, the accusations seeming to fly at her like blows.

"Responsible for planning that deadly werewolf raid on the Oslo vampire community center." A slow smile crossed his face as he looked straight at Bosch, never flinching. "Or so I heard."

It didn't matter that the charges were dismissed. She knew, and Bosch knew. It was in his eyes. He'd killed. He'd gotten away with it. And he was proud of what he'd done. Proud of the blow he'd struck. She'd bet her new job that no one had gone to trial for any of those crimes. They'd had the right defendant; they just hadn't found the evidence to prove it.

Beside her, Bosch pushed back his chair. Sara took a deep breath and made sure she had her game face on before looking over at her boss. He was standing, forcing Luke to tilt his head back to look at the prosecutor. It was, Sara knew, a simple trick that had the effect of creating at least an illusion of power. In this case, however, the maneuver didn't work.

Despite Bosch's cool confidence, Lucius Dragos lost none of his power. Instead, he rocked back slightly in his chair so that it balanced on the two rear legs. He shook his head, ruffling the perfect mane of silky black hair. He could not, Sara realized, run his fingers through his hair, as both hands were currently manacled to the arms of the chair. Yet despite that disadvantage and despite the fact that Bosch now towered above him, Luke was in no way diminished. If anything, the two men now seemed equally pitted against each other.

It was, Sara thought, fascinating.

Bosch leaned forward, his hands on the table, his head and shoulders thrusting into Luke's side of the table, getting into his space. Getting into his face. This time, when Bosch spoke, his words were low and controlled without the earlier suggestion of civility. "Let us understand each other, Dragos. You are here because we brought you in. We trapped you. We caught you. We shackled you. And once we dispense with the formality of a trial, we will execute you."

Luke's eyes flicked up, the heat in them banked by a tight control. "You don't win the game until the executioner's stake slams through my heart. Until then, I think the wise money is on me."

The scent of cinnamon filled the air. "Do not for a moment think that this is a game, Dragos."

"I don't play games. I would have thought you knew that much about me." He turned his attention to Sara, and she forced herself to remain steady, to keep her expression bland as those deadly eyes looked into hers. "Perhaps you speak for your companion's benefit?" His eyes lingered on her, and for a moment, one fleeting, dancing moment, she thought she saw a glimmer of regret in his face. Then it cleared, and all she saw was ice. "I doubt she is as familiar with my file as you are, Nostramo."

Bosch nodded toward her, his expression filled with something akin to fatherly pride. "I would suggest, *Lucius,* that you work hard not to antagonize Ms. Constantine. She may not yet know all there is to know about you, but I assure you that she is a quick study. She'll learn, Luke," he said, leaning slightly forward. "She'll learn all about you."

"I look forward to being thoroughly examined," Luke said. He turned toward her, the heat from his gaze curling through her.

She tamped it down, angry at herself for letting that heat warm her for even a millisecond.

"You'd be wise not to underestimate me," she snapped, and left it at that. She wasn't going to get into a verbal sparring match with him. Not now. Not ever.

For a moment, she thought he would answer. Then she felt the press of Bosch's hand on her shoulder. The simple weight of it calmed her, and she drew in a breath, furious with herself for lashing out.

"You are entitled to a representative, Luke," Bosch said, almost kindly.

"I don't require one at this time," he said.

Bosch looked as though he would argue. But in the end, he merely nodded. "Very well. Then let us dispense with the pleasantries and move straight to business. Record on. Interview with suspect Lucius Dragos, vampire. Interview Room A. Present are Division 6 representatives, prosecutors Nostramo Bosch and Sara Constantine. Mr. Dragos, you have declined to have a representative present?"

"I have."

"Very well. Following interview, suspect will be remanded to Detention Block C. Mr. Dragos, you are a vampire?"

"I am."

"You are the sire of the Dragos clan?"

"I am the last acknowledged Dragos, as you well know."

"Of course," Bosch said. "Your ward cannot claim the clan name." He flipped through his notes. "In light of her precarious mental state as a human, Tasha was subject to termination. She received special dispensation in 1790, sparing her life, but forbidding her to propagate or inherit, and requiring you to stand as guardian."

"I'm aware of the circumstances," Luke said, his voice hard. On her pad, Sara scribbled *Tasha,* then circled the name with a question mark.

"A hard-fought battle, if I recall," Bosch said. "I believe there was significant testimony both for and against termination."

"We were both there, Nostramo," Luke said. "I'm sure you recall the testimony as well as I do."

"And while you are here, she is under the care of..."

"She is well watched after now," Luke said, "and successfully survived the Holding all those years ago. Her daemon is bound, and those who fought for her termination can all go to hell." A muscle in his jaw twitched, his hands tightening on the arms of his chair in a visible effort to calm himself. "If you wish to question me about the death of Marcus Braddock, I would suggest you get on with it. I'm growing tired, and it would be a shame if I couldn't give you my full cooperation merely because the sun looms high in the sky."

Bosch hesitated, then nodded. "Very well. Let's cut to the chase. Where were you last night?"

"Isn't that what you intend to prove?"

"Fair enough," Bosch said as the phone at his hip vibrated. He lifted it, reviewed the screen, then set the device on the table, along with the case file, open to the photograph of Braddock's brutalized neck. "Then let me tell you, and you can stop me if I get anything wrong."

Smart, Sara thought. Lead him through the evidence. Let him know how bad it is for him—and with a witness like Doyle, it was very, very bad—and then present the offer for a plea bargain again at the end of the interview.

In the calm, unemotional voice of an experienced prosecutor, Bosch began a rundown of the evidence against Luke, including the investigating agent's conclusion that the injury was caused not only by a vampire, but by Luke himself. "Agent Doyle saw you. Or didn't you know that Agent Doyle is a percipient daemon?"

"Ryan Doyle is many things," Luke said, the tame words a counter to the tone, which clearly called the agent a son of a bitch.

"Agent Doyle's conclusions have been confirmed by the PEC's medical examiner."

Luke leaned back in his chair. "Is that a fact?"

"Division 6 has a record of seven hundred and eighty-six vampires permanently residing in the Los Angeles County area," Bosch said softly. "And yet yours was the DNA we discovered on the victim."

Sara lifted her head, startled by the mention of DNA evidence. Luke, however, remained impassive. Unreadable.

"Text message just came in from Agent Doyle with the lab results," Bosch said. "With your name attached to the file, we were able to rush the results." He leaned casually against the wall. "You should be gratified to know that your involvement piques such interest across the organization. It's almost as if you're a celebrity."

Sara glanced at Luke, searching for some kind of reaction—anger, fear. In her former life, DNA evidence was a serious blow, and she could only assume it was the same here. Couple that with Doyle's testimony, and it looked as if Luke was well and truly screwed.

Luke, however, didn't appear worried. If anything, he seemed amused. And though she didn't know Nostramo Bosch well at all, she could see that he'd noted the amusement, too. And that it was pissing him off.

"I suppose, though, that some of the thanks must go to you," Bosch continued. "After all, until your arrest, we didn't have your DNA on file. And yet you provided a sample to the agents without a court order. I have to wonder why."

Sara worked to keep her features bland, but the truth was that she wondered, too. If Division didn't already have his DNA, why on earth would Luke provide it unless it would prove his innocence. In this case, though, it proved his guilt.

"Would you have been able to obtain a court order?" Luke asked.

"Undoubtedly."

"Then why put everyone to the trouble?"

Bosch ignored the question, instead leaning over the table to face Luke more closely. "Why did you kill Braddock? We'll find out, you know, and in the end it doesn't much matter. Of course, it is possible there was no prior motive. That you met Braddock, you argued, and you killed him impulsively. And that you accidentally left evidence behind. A ring, for example, carelessly forgotten."

Luke flinched, a slight twitch of the eyes. Nothing

overt, and Sara imagined that Bosch missed the reaction entirely as he'd been reaching down for a photograph he now tossed onto the table, this one showing a signet ring with a red-eyed dragon eating its own tail.

Sara, however, noticed, and had to wonder. Because Luke didn't strike her as the kind of man who carelessly forgot anything.

"What I can't figure out is why you returned to your home when you had to know that a swarm of RAC officers would be surrounding you at any moment. Clearly you believed you could escape. But why were you so cocksure? Your Alliance connections? Or some other reason? It's a curiosity, you see. The kind of curiosity that eats at me. So we will find an answer, Lucius. As to that, I give you my word."

He stood then, his posture suggesting the interview was over. Sara pushed to her feet as well, then reached to the table to gather the photographs Bosch had left there. Braddock's cold, dead eyes stared up at her. Luke had done this. A vampire. A killer.

He'd torn Braddock's neck out, drained his blood. And now he sat there, calm and cool despite having committed such a heinous crime. A crime as personal to her as his hands upon her naked body had been. She fought the memory back, unwilling to think about the intimate things they'd done together only one night before he'd gone out and murdered Judge Braddock.

And if she was understanding Bosch correctly, he believed that not only was Luke a murderer, but he had allies within Division 6 who would help him to escape.

The thought sickened her, her reaction all the more intense because the man had gotten under her skin.

"Record off," Bosch said. He turned to Sara, ignoring Luke. "We'll talk in my office."

He headed for the door and she followed.

"I won't say it's been a pleasure, Nostramo," Luke said, his voice controlled and confident. "But I will say that I look forward to seeing Ms. Constantine again. I'm sure our future interviews will be illuminating."

Slowly and deliberately, she turned in his direction. "I look forward to it, too, Mr. Dragos. This case is mine now, and I promise you that I won't rest until the dead have justice."

"I believe you," he said, his expression bland although she hoped her words had kicked him in the gut. "And may I be among the first to congratulate you on your new position."

She started to reply, but Bosch laid a hand upon her arm. "Hire an advocate, Lucius. Trust me when I say that you're going to need it." He keyed in the code and pulled open the door. "Constantine, with me."

CHAPTER 7

"I've read your file, Constantine," Bosch said. They were in the observation room, watching Luke through the glass. "I know today wasn't the first time you've seen an injury like that. For that matter, I'm guessing you still see the torn flesh in your dreams."

She bristled, dragging her attention away from Luke to face her boss. "I've been thoroughly evaluated."

"Like I said, I've read your file." He leaned against the wall, his businesslike expression counterbalanced by the compassion in his voice. "Eight years old and out for an evening stroll with Daddy. Came out of nowhere. Knocked you aside, slammed your head good and hard against a cement bench. Tackled your father. You lost consciousness with his screams echoing in your head, and when you awoke, you found him not fifteen feet from you, dead, his throat opened, and the crime scene remarkably free of blood."

"I know the circumstances, sir. I was there."

"And until this day, you've never known the true nature of the defendant."

"No, sir," she said firmly, forcing her chin up. "That's not true. I've known since the night my father died that the man who did that to him was something monstrous and inhuman. Knowing now that Jacob Crouch was a vampire doesn't change my perception of him at all."

She frowned, something in her memory suddenly worrying her.

"Constantine?"

"Sir, is there any doubt that my father's killer was a vampire?"

"Considering his injuries? None at all."

"But then the court tried the wrong man." Bosch's eyebrows rose, and she continued. "I remember the trial. I remember it vividly. And I also remember Jacob Crouch being led up the courthouse steps in the light of day."

"Ah," he said. "I understand your confusion. Best not to get your facts from late-night television."

"Sir?"

"While it is true that older vampires cannot abide the sun, the young ones have no such issue. Crouch, I believe, was just shy of two hundred at the time of the trial."

"I see." He was right. She needed to erase her preconceived notions.

"It's a slow progression. The skin becomes more sensitive as they age. Eventually, they realize they've reached a stage where they must succumb to the dark.

"Crouch may have walked in the light," Bosch continued, "but he was a vampire. And now you face a similar crime, this time not as a victim but as a prosecutor, now fully armed with the true nature of the murderer. Tell me, Sara. Can you do your duty and seek justice rather than retribution?"

She blinked, knowing he had to ask the question, but hating it nonetheless. She squared her shoulders, straightened her spine, and looked him dead in the eyes.

"I would never allow my personal history to interfere with the way I prosecute a case, or allow my emotions to skew me from the course of justice." She licked her lips, wishing her mouth hadn't gone so suddenly dry. "In light of your concerns, I question why you want me to second chair this case with you."

"Yes," he said. "Of course you do." She waited, expecting an explanation, but none was offered. "I've been monitoring you for a while now, Sara. You have the kind of talent we can use down here. Consider that the answer to your question."

There would be no point in arguing. "All right. Thank you, sir." She followed him into the hall, her pleasure at his confidence in her abilities warring with the need to tell him the truth and recuse herself from the case. Because she had to disqualify herself; in light of her history with Luke, there was simply no other choice. And that, frankly, wasn't something she was thrilled about revealing.

She had no choice, though, and if she was going to be reassigned, she'd just as soon get it over with. "About me working the case, though. There's something else we should discuss."

"Yes, there is. But it can wait until we reach my office."

She nodded, recognizing that he must have correctly interpreted the few glances that had passed between her and the accused. She knew that reassignment was inevitable, yet she couldn't escape the sting of disappointment. She'd meant what she'd said to Luke. And given the chance, she would relish the hell out of taking him down. Would savor the way that reviewing the case and the evidence would harden her heart to this monster who'd squeezed in past her defenses.

She wanted him gone, the sweet memories erased. They were tainted now with the stench of murder, the magic of their night fizzling in the cold, hard light of reality.

A reality that, frankly, broke her heart.

"Any calls?" he asked Martella, not breaking stride as he passed her desk and shifted left into his office.

"Nothing urgent," she said. "I'll send the memos to your desktop."

He grunted an acknowledgment, then gestured for Sara to take a seat. He closed the door, then surprised her by taking the second guest chair rather than sliding in behind his desk. "You're human," he said without preamble.

"Yeah," she said, confused. "I know."

"That presents a theoretical risk in this case," he said, confusing her even more.

She shifted in her seat, using the movement to mentally shift her thoughts as well. Because apparently they weren't discussing her wild night with Luke as she'd expected. What they *were* discussing, though, remained unclear. "A risk?"

"Vampires are unique creatures, even in our world." He picked up a fountain pen, rolling it between his fingers as he talked. "Their life spans are so long that the myths of their immortality might well be considered accurate. And that longevity has made the vampire community very powerful as a whole. A group that is around for millennia tends to achieve a certain strength and bargaining power."

She nodded slowly, understanding his words, but still not seeing where he was going.

"They are exceedingly strong and heal quickly from most injuries. Electrical shock will take them down, of course, and they are stymied by the mineral hematite. The ridiculous stories about holy water and crosses injuring them are just that—stories. But the myths about a stake through the heart or decapitation are stories that the fiction writers of your world managed to get right, at least to the extent that these things will kill. The stake by turning a vampire to ash. Decapitation simply by terminating life and leaving the body behind."

He shifted in his chair. "But I am not trying to educate you on the methods of extinguishing a vampire. Rather, I want you to realize that they have many rare talents. The ability to dissolve into a sentient mist or shift into animal form. Acute senses. Exceptional speed, especially in the mist state. And the power to mesmerize humans."

"Mesmerize? You mean, like hypnosis?"

"Something like that," he said, peering carefully at her. "You're worried."

"Didn't you mean for me to be?" She hoped she sounded businesslike, because the truth was that she was more than just worried. She was terrified. The thought of someone else inside her head, dictating how she should act, all her free will removed, nauseated her.

She thought of Luke, her stomach twisting. She'd been wild with him. Open. They'd shared an intimacy that had, at least to her, seemed like more than sex. If he'd been inside her head...if he'd made her want him...

She honestly couldn't bear the thought.

"A vampire's ability to mesmerize is a concern in this office, yes, but for you it is a minimal one. That's another reason I want you on this case. Your psych profiles show a remarkably high natural defiance to a vampire's power of hypnosis. To all forms of mind control and invasion, actually. That's a rare trait."

"A psych profile is hardly proof positive," she said, even though a tiny bit of the weight lifted from her shoulders.

"True enough. That's why we've had you tested as well."

"Excuse me? Someone's been poking around in my head making me do things?"

"Someone tried." He shrugged. "Several someones actually."

"Who?"

"We have agents whose sole job is to determine the vulnerability of our staff. You passed. Congratulations."

"Forgive me if I don't shout for joy." Although, to be honest, she was extraordinarily pleased. Her feelings for Luke—however much they might now complicate her life—were at least her own.

"The tests are an intrusion, yes. You could even say they are an invasion of your privacy. Or could have been, had their efforts succeeded. But if you said that, I would be forced to once again tell you that we do things differently down here."

"I'm beginning to realize that," she said sourly. "But hold on. Didn't you tell me that if I didn't want the job you could wipe my memories clean? How can you do that if I'm not susceptible?"

"To a vampire's assault," he said, "and to the intrusion of many other creatures with similar abilities. But there are others whose mental powers are stronger. You might not bend to their will, but they could undoubtedly replace or alter your memories."

"Oh." She didn't much like the sound of that.

"Don't worry," he said with a grin. "It's all in the manual."

Her brows rose. "Seriously?"

He leaned over and punched a button on his desk. "Martella, do you have Ms. Constantine's office manual prepared?"

"It's on her desk, sir."

"Take it home," he said to Sara after he clicked off. "Study it. You'll find summaries of basic office procedures, the primary characteristics of all the creatures you're likely to meet during your employment here, profiles of the judges, and a map of Division. It's bigger than it looks, so you might want to keep a copy of the map with you your first week or two."

"Oh," she said again. And then, realizing they'd gotten off track, she turned her focus back to Luke. "You mentioned the defendant's reputation during the interview, along with his Alliance connections. That's not something I'm familiar with." She spoke with calm focus, a prosecutor determined to get a handle on the case, nothing more.

"You're right. The Shadow Alliance is a governing body populated by the leaders of the most powerful groups of Shadow creatures," Bosch began. "Vampires, Therians, daemons, and the like. A parallel in your world might be the Senate. Or better yet, the United Nations."

"Okay," she said. "And Dragos works for the Alliance?"

His smile was almost amused. "Lucius Dragos works only for himself."

She thought of all those cases Bosch had rattled off, and could come to only one reasonable conclusion: Luke was a hired killer. An assassin. And from what she'd seen and read, he was damn good at his work. "No one has ever been able to make a charge stick?"

"Luke is extremely clever," Bosch said, with an admiration that seemed almost affectionate. "He has powerful friends, both in and out of the Alliance. And as we both know, that kind of power can all too often result in a backroom deal, especially when the evidence is weak or nonexistent."

"Those victims," she began, recalling Luke's responses in the interrogation room. "The way Dragos described them and their crimes—was it accurate?"

"Every one of those men could have easily been found guilty within these walls and staked in front of a gallery of witnesses," Bosch said. "Does that make what Dragos did right? Or, excuse me, does that make what we suspect that Dragos did right?"

"Absolutely not," she said. Her mother had been a district attorney, and Sara had been weaned on the idea that the courts meted out justice, not civilians. And though she meant her words—truly meant them—she couldn't stop the tiny trill of relief that fluttered in her chest. Relief that maybe, just maybe, the man she'd slept with wasn't as much of a monster as she'd thought.

Still, those crimes were not on her docket, and there was no point analyzing either them or the man who may have committed them.

"The evidence isn't weak in this case," she said.

"No," Bosch agreed. "It's not." His brow furrowed, his gray eyes going dark with inquiry. "You said you had something to discuss with me concerning you prosecuting this case?"

"Right." She slipped her hand into her pocket, her fingers closing automatically around the ribbon that had once encircled a gift of tulips. "It's just that Wednesday night, after the jury came back on the Stemmons matter, I was at this bar celebrating, and—"

He held up a hand. "We know."

"Oh." She forced herself to keep her chin high, even though she was certain she'd turned six shades of pink. "And you still want me on this case?" A stupid question, since they'd already assigned her to the case, but the words were out before she could recall them. And, besides, she really did want an answer.

"As I've already mentioned, you're going to find that we do things differently here in the basement. Comparatively speaking, the community is small. And when you factor in the life spans of the various Shadow creatures, odds are high that prosecutor and defendant, investigator and suspect have crossed paths before. Such interweavings do not demand an immediate recusal. Not without additional extenuating factors."

"Right. Of course."

His eyes twinkled with what she could only interpret as amusement. "Let me ask you this. Does this—

encounter—in any way impact your ability to prosecute this case?"

She hesitated before answering, because the question deserved honest appraisal, and she tried to ignore the rage she'd felt in that interrogation room, knowing that she'd cozied up to the very thing she tried so hard to keep off the streets. The truth was, she *couldn't* ignore it.

She'd been handed the chance to put a lying, scheming, murdering vampire into a cage. A vampire, she now knew, who committed heinous crimes, then abused his connections to the Alliance to wriggle free from the law. To thumb his nose at the system into which she'd put her heart and soul. No way—*no way*—was she walking away from this opportunity.

Crouch might have escaped justice on a technicality. But Sara would make damn certain another vampire didn't slip through the noose as well.

"No, sir," she said firmly. "It doesn't impact me at all."

He leaned back, then steepled his fingers. "I believe you. More than that, I know that you believe what you say."

She forced herself not to frown, wondering what new path he was starting down. "But?"

"But I wonder if you fully comprehend how inherently different things are down here in the basement."

She couldn't help her smile. "Trust me. I've noticed."

"We have interview rooms and secretaries, along with file sheets smeared with toner because budget cuts don't allow for the replacement of the copy machines.

We have judges and juries, as well as chairs at the counsel tables that desperately need to be reupholstered. We have laws, Constantine, just like you do upstairs. But our laws date back to ancient times, before even the common memory of humans. And when those laws are broken, judgment is swift and punishment is brutal. On the surface, it may look the same. But that is where the similarities end."

She swallowed. "I understand," she said, even though she was quite certain that was a lie.

He reached onto his desk and buzzed Martella. "Has Lortag been brought into the theater yet?"

"They'll be leading him in any minute now."

He clicked off, then stood and gestured for Sara to do the same. "Let's take a walk."

She didn't ask why. He clearly had a point to make, and he'd tell her his purpose in his own time.

They wound through the halls of Division 6, finally reaching an elevator bank that took them even further into the bowels of the building, all the way to sublevel twenty. The doors opened on a concrete tunnel, much like a highway underpass. No signs announced the floor's purpose, and Sara was struck by the thought that if you had to ask, you didn't belong there.

"Come," Bosch said, and with that single word led her out of the elevator and into the tunnel. He stepped onto a moving walkway, and she followed, the black rubber path leading them through the lengthy tunnel and toward a dim yellow light at the far end, its color and strength as out of place as sunshine in the subterranean environment.

As they drew closer, Sara began to hear the thrum of voices, of dozens, possibly hundreds, of people talking among themselves.

She licked her lips, a sense of dread settling over her without warning. For the first time, she saw a sign, mounted to the ceiling and hanging above their path: Authorized Personnel Only. "The public entrance is on the other side of the theater," Bosch said. "As you can hear, we have a full house today."

"For what?" she asked as they stepped out of the tunnel and into the light. But even as the question left her mouth she knew she needn't have asked it. The creatures in the stands had come to watch a show. And today's episode was an execution.

CHAPTER 8

The room reminded Sara of a movie theater, with stadium seating that looked out onto a large screen. The only difference was the large open space between the first row of seats and the high white wall.

A raised wooden platform dominated that space, and as Sara looked, she saw an unusual contraption with tall posts seeming to extend upward from a mobile base. It wasn't until Bosch had led her farther to the left, though, that she was able to get a clear view—*a guillotine*.

She stumbled, her blood suddenly cold. "Sir, is that...?"

"It is."

She swallowed, keeping her mouth shut and breathing in deep through her nose and trying not to imagine a neck being placed on the curve of wood, the blade falling, and—

Oh, God.

She told herself to relax. After all, she'd witnessed executions before—her first only eight months after she'd graduated from law school. The setting, however, had been significantly less theatrical. And there'd been no lopping off of heads.

The witnesses also had been behind glass, and other than the families of the defendant and the victims, the witnesses were for the most part officers of the court. Here, though, the crowd seemed to have been pulled from the street, and now they talked among themselves, their chatter filling the room with an expectant buzz.

Bosch led her to a cordoned-off section and chose two seats next to a giant of a man with ruddy cheeks, a bulbous nose, and inquisitive eyes, which he promptly aimed at Sara.

"Sara Constantine, Chance McPhee."

Chance held out a beefy hand at least ten times larger than Sara's own. "Come to watch me gloat, have ye?" he asked, his voice accented with a soft burr. "Hard fought, this one, but that just makes the victory all the sweeter."

"I'm not familiar with the case," Sara admitted.

"Sara's new to the team," Bosch explained. "She'll be my second on the Dragos matter."

Chance's eyes widened. "That a fact? You need anything, lass, you let me know."

"Thanks. I'll be sure to take you up on that."

"Not this weekend, though," he added with a wide grin. He hooked a thumb toward Bosch. "Don't tell the boss, but I figure I earned myself a few days away from the office. Going back home, I am. Get a little R and R. I'm the current title holder for the two-ton boulder toss, and my wife'll have me head if I don't win the trophy again this year."

"Where's home?" Sara asked, figuring that was safer than inquiring about boulder tosses.

"Scotland," Chance said.

"Chance is a mountain troll," Bosch added.

"Oh." And since she didn't know what else to say to

that, she shifted back to look at the guillotine. "So what did the prisoner do?"

"Turned two humans," Chance said. "A female and her wee lass. Couldn't control the daemon, he says. But that's no excuse. Not under the Covenant. Not once he's been through the Holding."

"A blood ritual," Bosch explained. "It calls forth a spirit—a *Numen*—for strength and assistance in battling the daemon that's released during a vampire's transition."

"I'm sorry, I don't understand."

"You've undoubtedly heard from your human stories that vampires are soulless, evil creatures?"

"Right."

"In fact, their soul does not depart with the transition, but it is subjugated to the power of the daemon that rises when they are made a vampire."

"They're possessed?"

He shook his head. "No, the daemon comes from within. You can think of it as the dark side of the soul. The change frees it, and the daemon seeks to grow, to feed. To become. It wants power, and it feeds on pain. That is why each newly made vampire must undergo the Holding."

"The blood ritual," Sara said, trying to keep it all straight in her head.

"Correct. Through the ritual a vampire is able to suppress the daemon. To wrest control away and restore the prominence of his soul."

"So the daemon completely disappears?"

"Once released, it will never completely be gone. But most vampires can adequately suppress it and are not tormented by the daemon's influence and live almost ordinary lives. Many are bartenders in local clubs. Some night DJs. They blend in. They survive, and even thrive."

"You said most?"

"Some do not prevail at the Holding," Bosch said.

"Those are the rogues," Chance added. "The PEC's got teams that hunt down and kill rogues. Nasty business."

"Is Dragos a rogue?" She had to know, had to understand the man as well as the vampire. "Is that why he killed?"

"Why do humans kill?" Chance asked. "Not every murder can be blamed on the daemon."

Sara licked her lips. "Of course not."

"Dragos is not a rogue," Bosch said. "But I fear that the Holding was not entirely successful with him."

"I don't understand."

"His daemon is exceptionally strong. It seeks release even now, and Lucius Dragos must constantly struggle to keep the daemon at bay."

"But—" She started to ask what exactly that meant, but her questions were cut off by the sudden roar of the crowd. Sara searched for the reason behind the change in the spectators' demeanor. She found it quickly enough—a door had opened in what she thought of as the movie screen, and a woman walked in, her head bowed, carrying a large, square object. She climbed the stairs to the platform, then set the item on an easel that had already been erected in front of a wooden table that Sara hadn't noticed earlier, having been far too interested in the guillotine.

The square was draped in black cloth, and now the woman pulled off the cloth to reveal a portrait of a young girl, about four or five years old. The crowd fell into a respectful silence as the woman stood tall and proud at the front of the theater. "Let us remember Melinda Toureau," she said. "She sleeps now with the angels."

"Melinda," the crowd repeated.

The woman bowed her head, then stepped backward until she was almost pressed against the screen. Once she was still, the door opened again, and this time two men entered. One, the prisoner, wore a black shirt and loose black pants. His hands were crossed behind his back and bound by metal cuffs. His feet were similarly bound, the chain between the two cuffs sufficient only to allow him to walk in a shuffle.

Beside him, the second man was also dressed in black. His outfit, however, was fashioned from leather. And unlike the prisoner, whose proud face looked out at the crowd with absolutely no remorse, the executioner stood anonymous, the black leather hood covering his entire face with the exception of two narrow slits for his eyes.

The executioner tugged at a chain attached to a collar around the defendant's neck, and the prisoner followed him up the rickety wooden stairs to the middle of the platform. The crowd began to whisper and shuffle, and Sara realized her own fingernails were cutting into her palms and made an effort to relax.

"Lortag Trevarian!" boomed the executioner's voice. "You have been convicted of two counts of a Class Five felony in violation of the Fifth International Covenant and sentenced to public execution by head or by heart. I ask the prosecutor, is this so?"

Beside Sara, Chance rose. "The conviction holds," he bellowed. "The punishment just and good."

As Chance returned to his seat, the executioner turned to Lortag. "Have you any final words?"

The prisoner stood stock-still, his face a mass of fury.

"So be it." The executioner turned his back to the crowd and faced the woman, who now raised a tear-streaked face to meet him. "Evangeline Toureau. Would you avenge the death of your child? Or would you watch the same?"

"I will avenge her," she said, her voice weak but steady.

"What say you, then? Death by stake or by blade?"

"By stake," Evangeline said, her chin lifting. "I would take his life with my own hands."

"So be it," the executioner said as a hush settled over the room.

Evangeline followed the executioner to the table near her daughter's portrait. She hesitated only an instant, then turned to the table and chose both a wooden stake and an iron mallet. Then she stood aside as the executioner approached the prisoner and shackled him tightly to a wooden pillar.

"He is yours," the executioner said.

Evangeline stepped forward without hesitation, pressed the point of the stake to Lortag's heart, then slammed the mallet down upon it, making Sara jump with the brutality of the blow.

For one brief moment, fear flashed across Lortag's

face. Then he was gone, reduced to nothing more than a pile of dust.

Evangeline turned to face the crowd, nodded, then descended the steps and marched out, her footsteps echoing in the silence of the crowded room.

Sara's chest felt as though it was about to burst, and she drew in a sharp gasp of air, realizing that she'd forgotten to breathe.

"Constantine?" Bosch asked, looking at her through narrowed eyes. "Are you all right?"

She looked up at him and nodded, because what else could she do? She was used to the near-euthanasia-like executions she'd witnessed, with the prisoner behind a glass wall, and doctors in attendance. The same result, but one hell of a different presentation.

This, however...

The crowd. The leather-masked executioner. The mother wielding the ultimate punishment.

And the sickening sound of the iron mallet pounding the wooden stake into the prisoner's heart.

It was harsh. It was brutal.

And she couldn't help but think that if it had been Crouch up there on the platform, that maybe, finally, the nightmares would end.

"I'm fine," she said, but as she spoke the words, she had to wonder how fine she would be when the time came for her to sit in Chance McPhee's chair.

Because if she did her job right, it would be Luke on that platform, his death ushered in by the applause of the masses, and Sara herself announcing that his punishment was just and good. She told herself she wanted that—he'd killed and needed to pay for his crime. But she couldn't ignore the small part of her that wished otherwise. That fantasized that this was all a mistake. That Luke hadn't killed, that she wouldn't be the one to condemn him to die in this room, and that they could go back to where they'd started with Sara safe and warm in his arms.

Bosch stood, ready to leave the theater, but Sara remained seated, her eyes on the portrait of the child. "What happened to Melinda?" she asked, wondering why the child had not survived. "Is it dangerous for children to turn into vampires?"

"Not in the way you're thinking," Bosch said, pausing in front of her. "Melinda made the transition. Division terminated her."

Sara swallowed. "Terminated?"

"It would have been too dangerous to allow her to live," he said. "Children, the mentally unstable, they do not have the strength to control the daemon."

Her stomach clenched in horror. "But—"

"Let me tell you the story of Michael Blessing. A strapping blond-haired boy with brilliant blue eyes and the cheeriest smile. He got turned five days before his sixth birthday, and Division was not aware of the transition. By the time the authorities learned about his turning, three days had passed. And in the course of those seventy-two hours, his mother and father fell prey to the child. His baby sister, and the nanny, also dead." He drew in a breath. "A child unchecked with its daemon is not to be toyed with."

She blinked back rising tears as she looked once again at Melinda's portrait. "And special dispensation?"

"Very rare indeed," Bosch said.

"But it was granted for Dragos's ward."

"It was."

"And she survived the Holding and got control of her daemon. So it's possible, right? Even for a child or someone like Tasha? Shouldn't they have the chance to fight the daemon, too?"

He drew in a breath. "I understand this is new to you. That you have no frame of reference. But the daemon that rises in a vampire is heinous. Murderous. Clever and cunning and utterly lacking in remorse. Many adults do not make the transition and lose themselves instead to the daemon. They do not survive the Holding—they never manage to control the daemon. They are rogues and, yes, we hunt them down. The position of all Shadow creatures on this earth is precarious. We have strength, yes, but our numbers are small compared to the humans. We self-police because we must."

He turned now to face Melinda's portrait as well. "That child had the rage of hell within her and not the slightest chance of controlling it," he continued. "She was turned, she was staked, and she was avenged." He looked hard at her. "That is the way it is, Sara. That is the way it must be."

CHAPTER 9

Luke paced the metal-and-glass cell. Or he tried to pace, but as he could take only five strides before colliding into a wall, he gained little satisfaction from the mindless motion.

He had never intended to end up caged like an animal, and his own miscalculation frustrated him. Tariq's removal from the active RAC team had been a critical blow, and considering that Luke was now locked in a cell, he took little satisfaction from the fact that Tariq's debt remained unpaid.

He needed another way out.

The possibility of calling upon his usual connections crossed his mind, but Braddock had been a personal matter, and any assistance he requested would come at a very heavy price. Since he had no interest in being beholden to anyone, he preferred to keep that possibility dormant until the need was truly great.

Then again, considering that the prosecution intended to remove him from this plane of existence, perhaps the situation called for desperate measures.

Not that this little detour hadn't been useful—Luke had at least been able to confirm firsthand that the evidence gathered with regard to the death of Marcus Braddock was sufficient to condemn him. His hope that a percipient daemon would be among the first responders had been satisfied, and both the DNA and the ring had played their intended roles. With such indisputable evidence in its pocket, the prosecution would have no need to look for motive. No need to look closer into Braddock's life and uncover that reprehensible creature's connection to Tasha.

She was safe.

Luke had accomplished what he'd set out to do, and that knowledge gave him some bit of satisfaction, though he had to confess to a small trickle of apprehension. While it was true the prosecution could convict on the evidence they held, Sara's involvement skewed his plan. He remembered the way she'd described her tenacity in the pursuit of Xavier Stemmons. She was a woman who demanded answers, and if she went in search of a motive, she might dig deep enough to drag Tasha into this mess.

And that was unacceptable.

"Sara," he murmured, his body tightening from the mere memory of her touch. He'd expected nothing more than a night with a beautiful, responsive woman. A few hours in which he could take his pleasure, savor it, and then walk away satisfied.

She'd turned out to be so much more.

They'd made love with a fierceness born of need, a delicious intensity that was somehow both gentle and rough, giving and accepting. And when they collapsed, sated, in each other's arms, he'd stroked her hair and her dewy skin, relaxing gently against her until they were both calm enough to go again, this time slow and soft and sensual.

For the first time in centuries he'd found himself

wanting to remain by a woman's side. Wanting to talk with her, to laugh with her, and not merely to sleep with her. He'd tried to analyze why, but it was something he couldn't quite put his finger on, and perhaps that alone was it—the mystery of the woman. He didn't know. All he knew was that there was something about the way she laughed. About the way she drew him naked to the window to count the stars. About the way she so casually sipped from his wineglass, then smiled at him playfully.

She'd caught him off guard, eased the constant roar of the daemon in his head, and even managed to make him laugh. And a woman capable of that both fascinated and confounded him.

As the clock ticked on toward morning, she'd stretched out naked beside him and told him about the case she had won only hours before. The Stemmons matter. A serial killer who had raped and murdered young girls. A human coward who lacked control and fed off pain. As she'd described her relentless pursuit of the murderer and the hard-fought legal battles, he'd felt a fervent solidarity. Even then, though, he had doubted that she would accept either his methods or his tools. But he, too, strove for justice. Had, in fact, brought the scales back into balance on more than one occasion. And as he'd held her close, he'd thought of his purpose in going out that night—his intent to find the judge. Find him, and kill him.

The moment he'd let Braddock into his head, he'd regretted it. The daemon within had roared, and he'd stalked naked to her window, his blood hot, his thoughts dark, and his mouth watering for the kill. He'd jerked away when she'd slid up behind him, only to find himself relaxing under her touch. Her proximity calmed him, her scent like a balm upon him. And before he even had time to process the change, he found himself feeling like a man, not a beast.

She had soothed him. And now, he thought, she would free him.

Because in the absence of any other way out of these damnable four walls, Sara was his best hope. A woman who'd melted under his touch and would, he hoped, melt under his will as well.

He allowed himself one small moment of regret, but his plan was sound. He needed a new asset within Division, to be used when the moment was right. And Sara was his first, best option.

A high-pitched beep signaled the opening of the detention block door, a sound that was soon followed by steady footsteps. Luke cocked his head, listening. Three creatures, one surefooted, two oafish, moving in his direction. He returned to his bench, sat, and waited. In a moment, Nicholas Montegue's pretty face appeared beyond the glass wall, flanked on either side by the ogres who guarded the detention block.

Despite his angel face, Nick was both vicious and brilliant. And because of his innocent features, he was a far more effective defense advocate than he would be working with his intellect alone, admirable though it might be. They'd been friends for five centuries, watched each other's backs countless times, and owed each other their lives a dozen times over.

It had been Luke who'd introduced Nick to Tiberius,

and as the vampiric liaison to the Shadow Alliance, Tiberius had sponsored Nick's training as an advocate.

As Luke watched, Nick signaled to the ogres, who unenthusiastically began to disengage the series of locks that held the glass door shut. The glass itself was unbreakable and, like an antenna embedded in a car's back window, was infused with a series of thin hematite filaments. The hematite-reinforced glass coupled with the hematite alloy of the walls meant that escape by transfiguration was impossible. Luke knew; he'd tried.

Escape by less elegant means, however, remained a possibility, and the ogres knew it. The ogre who was not operating the locks raised his weapon, the stake mounted on the crossbow aimed menacingly in Luke's direction.

"Hands," growled the ogre. "Clasp you on head."

Once Luke had complied, the second ogre released the last lock and pulled the door open. He gestured roughly for Nick to step inside, then shut the door and locked the advocate in.

"Twenty minute got you," the first ogre said. The second one grunted and stepped away from the door, then followed his leader out of Luke's line of sight.

Once they were gone, Luke took his hands down and grinned at his friend. "It's not the Plaza, but I've had worse accommodations."

"Goddammit, Luke," Nick spat, utterly destroying any illusion that the angel face reflected an angel's temperament. "Have you completely lost your mind? You want to tell me when the bloody hell you got so damned sloppy? And how the fuck am I supposed to get the goddamn charges dismissed with that kind of evidence peppering the file?"

Tirade over, Nick collapsed next to Luke onto the cement slab that protruded from the wall and served as a bed. "Dammit," he muttered.

"Good to see you again, too," Luke said, chuckling when Nick shifted sideways, his expression caustic.

"I talked to Tiberius," he said. "Braddock wasn't an authorized kill."

"No," Luke acknowledged. "Braddock was mine."

"This isn't going to go over well," Nick said. "You know that, right? Tiberius's already foaming at the mouth. Los Angeles is hot right now, and you, my friend, have just added to his problems."

"The Therians?" The shape-shifters—particularly the werewolves—were a constant thorn in Tiberius's side, and like little yipping dogs, they kept howling that they weren't treated fairly within the Alliance. With few exceptions, Luke had little use for shape-shifters.

"Hell yes, the Therians. What else?"

"Fuck." Luke leaned forward and dragged his fingers through his hair. "How pissed is he?"

"At you? Or at Gunnolf?" Nick asked, referring to the Therian representative to the Alliance. "Actually, forget the question. I'd say he's equally infuriated by the both of you."

Though expected, the answer still irritated Luke. At the end of the day, Tiberius was Luke's ace in the hole. The master vampire had connections. Ties. And markers that could be called in when a situation was dire. So far, Luke had never had to ask Tiberius to step up for him, and with any luck, he wouldn't have to now. But if that option was taken completely off the table, then Luke had no plan B. And Luke was a man who always kept a second out open.

"What's the situation?"

"That's the trouble," Nick said. "We don't know. Intelligence has hit walls. All we know is that Gunnolf's planning another play for Los Angeles. Bastard's determined that Los Angeles will be under Therian, not vamp, control. Like he's got a shot in hell of managing to pull that off."

"The Therians have been trying to oust Tiberius from the key territories for years," Luke said. Centuries, really, with the pissing contest played out over different real estate. New York. Constantinople. Prague. Moscow. London. But with the exception of the long-standing Therian control over Paris, Tiberius—and the vampires—had maintained control over the prime territories.

"Talk is this time they've got the golden ticket."

"You believe that?" Luke said. Less than a decade prior, a covert werewolf team had managed to taint the Southern California blood supply. A lot of innocent vamps had died, but the plan hadn't weakened Tiberius's hold over the territory. On the contrary, Tiberius's support within the Alliance had grown, even as Gunnolf's had fallen, despite the fact that the apprehended team members insisted that the head werewolf had no knowledge of the maneuver. Sadly, the team members had died mysterious and painful deaths while out on bail awaiting trial.

"Hell no, I don't believe it," Nick said. "But as Tiberius's counsel, I can't ignore the risk. The wraith and para-daemon liaisons to the Alliance have been making pro-werewolf noises recently. If Gunnolf manages to make it look like Tiberius's ironclad control over Los Angeles is slipping, the Alliance members might actually vote to shift the territory away from the vamps and over to the Therians."

In other words, Luke thought, Gunnolf didn't have to succeed at whatever he had planned in order to win. He just had to kick up a shitload of dust.

All in all, a fucking nightmare for Tiberius, and a great big glowing opportunity for Luke. Because if he could figure out a way to help Tiberius with the Therian problem, then Tiberius would be more receptive to helping Luke with the little matter of his incarceration. "I need specifics," he said. "What's the word on the street?"

"Not much chatter, actually, but whatever it is, it's going down soon. Hasik rolled into town yesterday." An alpha wolf by the light of the full moon and a royal prick on all other occasions, Hasik was one of Gunnolf's top men. If there was a play to shift control of the L.A. basin from the vampiric to the Therian, then Hasik would be at the heart of it. Already, he'd tried to recruit a number of Tiberius's lieutenants over to Gunnolf's side, then killed them in cold blood when they'd refused to shift their allegiance. As if a vamp would ever be truly aligned with the Therians.

At the time, Tiberius had been looking at an even larger endgame and had decided against sending out the *kyne* to take care of the Hasik problem. Which made Hasik one hell of a lucky werewolf.

"And Tiberius doesn't have any solid intelligence as to what Gunnolf and Hasik have planned?" Luke asked.

"Not a hint, not an inkling."

"That kind of information would be worth something, don't you think?"

"A price beyond rubies, my friend. So would making the Hasik problem go away. Too bad you're a bit indisposed at the moment." Nick leaned back, looking perfectly at home in the sparse cell despite the tailored Savile Row suit. "Which brings us full circle. And so I ask again," Nick said, his voice now deadly calm. "What kind of crazy shit are you pulling?"

"I assume it's safe to talk?"

"I've got an asset in Monitoring. For the next hour, the observation discs will have unexplained auditory interference."

"You trust him?"

"My asset?" Nick asked, his eyes dancing. "Very much."

A woman, then, Luke thought, and let the subject drop. If Nick said he'd taken care of the problem, Luke believed him. And he should have known Nick's associate would be female. With Nick, that was practically a given.

"Now quit stalling," Nick demanded. "You killed Braddock. Why?"

"The man was a son of a bitch."

"So are you, but you don't see me pulling out a stake."

"And for that, you have my gratitude."

Nick stood, his expression troubled. "Dammit, Luke. You've compromised the Alliance. Hell, you've compromised the secrecy of the *kyne,*" he said, referring to the secret society of brothers in arms who undertook certain missions for the Shadow Alliance. Missions without official sanction, and that would be loudly and strongly denied by every Alliance representative.

"I haven't," Luke said, the denial automatic and without conviction. "This mission was outside the Alliance's authority, and the *kyne* are not involved."

"*I'm* involved," Nick said.

Luke nodded. "You are *kyne*," he agreed. "And that bond is strong. The bond of friendship, however, is stronger. Or so I would hope."

"God, you're a pain in the ass," Nick growled.

"It is one of my most persistent failings," Luke agreed.

"What about Tasha?" Nick asked, sighing. "Where is she? Do you need me to check in on her? Did you even consider what this would do to her, you being tossed in a cell? She won't understand."

"I considered it," Luke said. "And I weighed everything before acting. About that much, at least, I would think you would give me credit."

"Luke— I didn't mean. I know you wouldn't do anything to put her at risk. I just— It's just that she relies on you."

"A fact of which I am well aware." Frustrated, he moved to the glass and looked out the barrier at the hall beyond. It was because of Tasha that he was in this cell in the first place. Because of her, and because of his own hubris so many years before.

He should have known better, he thought, as the memories welled inside him. He should never have brought her over.

He'd found her, alone and bleeding, fear clinging to

her like a blanket, and she'd looked up at him, life fading from eyes so like his own sweet daughter's that he'd been unable to think clearly.

Take, the daemon had whispered, and so help him he'd listened. He took, he drank, and when the change came upon her, he became father, teacher, protector. Most of all, he'd helped her fight her own daemon. Helped her bring back the girl within.

A confused, lost innocent who by all rights should have been in heaven with the angels by now instead of walking among daemons. Instead of suffering at the hands of bastards like Marcus Braddock, men who took what they wanted and cared little for the consequences.

Whatever particular arrogance Braddock had suffered under, it was stilled now, as was the man himself. And for that, at least, Luke was grateful.

"Tasha's taken care of," he said softly. "I sent her to New York." He turned back to face Nick. "She's with Serge."

"With Serge?"

Something in Nick's voice caught Luke's attention. "What?"

"I called Serge," Nick said. "Not less than an hour ago. I wasn't able to reach him."

Something cold and unfamiliar settled in Luke's stomach. *Fear.* Serge's journey to sanity had been even more dappled than Luke's. Many vampires—most even—were able to control the daemon, to push it back down, and keep it bound. The Holding was brutal and exhausting and sometimes deadly. But those who survived walked away with the daemon bound. Trapped.

Or, at least, most did.

A few survivors gained control over the daemon, yes, but did not fully bind it. Instead, the daemon lurked beneath the surface, teasing and taunting and begging to be brought out to play.

If the daemon won the battle—if the vampire could not regain control—the vampire became hunted. A rogue. A threat to society.

And if the vampire was able to keep control despite the daemon's taunt, then that vampire lived on the knife-edge. A difficult existence, as Luke well knew.

As all the vampiric *kyne* knew.

So yes, Luke knew the extent to which Serge forced himself to hold on, sometimes by only the thinnest of threads. If that thread unraveled...

"You tried all his numbers? You sent an e-mail?"

"I did." Nick stood and started to pace. "I'll send Ryback over to Serge's penthouse. He's in New York on an assignment. As soon as he wraps, I'll have him go by. I can't imagine Serge would leave Tasha alone, but if he did, Ryback can bring her home."

Luke nodded, unsatisfied. He should be the one going to her, the one bringing her safely back to L.A. Since that was impossible at the moment, he reluctantly agreed, and tried damn hard to push the worry out of his head. No easy task.

Nick stopped pacing and looked at Luke, his expression pensive. "You sent her away, which is something I've never been witness to in all these centuries. And all the way to Manhattan. She could have stayed with me. Even Ryback or Slater would have taken her in, and she'd have been here. Close by you. But you sent her to the far side of the country. I'm not an idiot, Lucius. You're protecting her. But from what?"

From what indeed.

Slow fury bubbled within Luke as he recalled Tasha's words, her tearful entreaties. The terror on her face when she'd described what Braddock had done to her. And as he thought, the daemon stirred.

"He raped her," he said, his voice low and dangerous. He felt his fangs extend, now thick against his lips. "Braddock hurt her. He put his hands on her and he took what he had no right to take."

"And so you took back," Nick said, his voice soft. "From him."

Luke's jaw was set. "Did I have another choice?"

Nick closed his eyes, shook his head. "No," he said. "You didn't." He moved forward and put his hand on Luke's shoulder. "I would have done the same thing."

Luke nodded. "If I didn't believe that, you wouldn't be the one in here representing me."

"This case could get dirty. Everything you've done, Luke—it could come back down on you."

"I know that." The faces of his victims swam through his memory. Killers themselves, dark creatures that had escaped justice for the murder of their kind and humans. That had, because of technicalities or corruption or pure cunning, escaped the system that was supposed to lock them up or put them down. They'd slipped free, and even as the filthy rats were congratulating themselves on outrunning the long arm of the law, the Alliance stepped in with soldiers who operated outside the confines of the system, its sticky fingers able to reach where that long arm could not.

The PEC itself answered to the Alliance, and yet in sanctioning its own brand of justice, the Alliance broke the very covenant that had created it. That violation was justified by the need to protect the Shadow society as a whole, to ensure the secrecy of a world that operated on the fringes of and beneath human civilization.

Luke was a player, and expendable. He had always known that. But his ultimate goal was justice. And, yes, he sought penance as well. Redemption for a past that he had managed to escape. A past that crept softly up to him more often than he would like to taunt him, to urge him to sink down under.

He would not.

He had fought long and hard for the restoration of his soul, and he despised those who willingly succumbed to the daemon, who would not even pitch the battle.

He was *kyne* for a reason and, acknowledged or not, he would stand true.

"If it comes to that, you know I'll protect the *kyne*. But I don't expect an investigation that deep. They have my DNA, and Ryan Doyle has already filed a witness statement. The case is open and shut. There's no reason to dig."

"The PEC doesn't always need a reason," Nick retorted. "And Ryan Doyle will probably take on your trial as a personal crusade."

That much, Luke thought, was true. "I need out of here, Nick," he said, standing. "I have no intention of staying in this goddamn cell."

Nick didn't even bother to pretend shock or dismay. "I'm assuming you're not intending to wait for my brilliant legal tap dancing to acquit you. So what are you planning, and how is my ass going to be compromised?"

"Not you. The prosecutor. She's a human, new to the Division. Her name's Sara Constantine."

"I know," Nick said. "I've started a file. Her legal background's exceptional, but unremarkable for our purposes. Straight A's. Good creds. Solid work history with the county."

"And with Division?"

"Today's her first day on the job, actually. Division ran all the standard tests—she's not mentally susceptible, which is a damn shame—and they've tossed her into the job running. From her file, I'd say she's up for the challenge, which leaves us no lines to tug. Not professionally, anyway."

"But personally?"

"There, we may have caught a break."

He pulled out his cell phone, then slapped it down on the table, a dark image locked on the screen.

"Her father," Nick said, as Luke looked down at the date-stamped crime scene photo of a middle-aged man, his neck ripped open in a manner that was only too familiar. "Armand Constantine. And eight-year-old Sara saw the whole bloody business."

"Ah, Sara," Luke said, his heart breaking for the woman she was, and for the child she had been. He could feel the daemon raging inside him, and he welcomed it. Longed for it to surface if by revealing itself he could rip the life from the vampire who had taken so much from her. "Who did this?"

"Well, friend. This is the portion of our program

wherein we wonder if the universe doesn't have one hell of a sense of humor."

"Who?" Luke repeated.

"Jacob Crouch."

At the name, Luke's head shot up, his attention shifting from the image to his friend. "What did you say?"

"You heard me." He met Luke's eyes, and Luke saw the calculation there. The same thoughts that had swirled through Luke's mind. The same schemes, the same plots. "No guarantees, Luke. You might be her goddamn hero, and if you are we can get one hell of a lot of mileage off the deal. You killed her father's murderer, and she might fall to the ground and kiss your feet. But it could just as easily turn the other way. A vampire killed Daddy. A monster from the dark. And you're a vampire, Luke. Just like Crouch. To Sara Constantine, we may all be monsters."

That was, Luke knew, exactly how she thought of him. A monster who killed. A beast who'd toyed with her heart.

The wound he'd cut was deep, and he would have to work skillfully to heal it. He would be lying, though, if he didn't at least admit that he was looking forward to the process. His plan would kill whatever small thing might have begun to grow between them—he knew that, and regret cut him like a knife—but at least he would see her again. Would touch her again. Would see the soft part of her lips as she came, and feel the slick brush of her damp skin against his own.

He would use her, but the pleasure he gave her would be real. For Sara, he knew, that would make the betrayal all the worse. That, however, was a reality from which

Luke couldn't escape. He had to be free, and he couldn't compromise Tasha's safety because of the whims of his heart.

"I'll make her an asset," he said, then looked up at Nick. "I need you to get me on the street." He needed to see her, needed to put these wheels in motion.

"Do you really think now is the best time? Her first day? They'll be wiring her house with security, issuing her a panic button. You show up, she pushes that button, and the gig is over."

"I have no intention of seeing her tonight," he said, only slightly regretting the lie. He wasn't going to tell Nick about his night with Sara. That much, at least, would remain pure. But without that bit of information, Nick couldn't understand why Luke wanted to go to Sara now. Why, in fact, he believed that she would see him—and that she wouldn't bring the wrath of Division down upon him.

"So, what? You're just interested in taking a stroll around town? See the sights? Catch a movie?"

"Actually, I'm interested in having a little chat with Ural Hasik."

"Hasik might not be in a conversational mood," Nick said, but his mouth curved with understanding.

"I'm sure we can find something to chat about."

Nick stood. "I'll arrange for a furlough."

"Try Judge Acquila," Luke said. "Remind him of Prague, 1874. That tussle between him and a British diplomat regarding said diplomat's daughter."

"Kind of you to have helped him sort it out," Nick said. He aimed a hard look at Luke. "Hear me well, though, Luke. I'll get him to authorize an advocate-escorted furlough for the purpose of reviewing the crime scene with my client. Three hours. And then we walk back into this detention block and they close the cage on you. We'll get you the hell out of here, but you are not escaping on my watch. I want your word."

"You have it."

"I like my privacy, and I'll not have the PEC looking into both of us."

"I'll be outside, Nick, but I won't be free. You know the drill. Escape would be next to impossible. Wasn't it Ferdinand Cristo who broke furlough last summer? His death was not a pretty thing."

"Your promise, Luke," Nick repeated.

"I swear on our friendship and our bond as *kyne* that I will return to this cell." But before he did, he would have his time with Sara. And though his purpose was dark, his heart still leapt at the thought of touching her again.

CHAPTER 10

Ural Hasik slammed through the double glass doors into the Quik-Stop Mart on South Figueroa, his nose twitching. He stopped, then looked around, silently daring anyone to give him grief. A human in a black leather skullcap and an oversized jersey kept his nosy ass looking in Hasik's direction a second too long. Hasik growled, the sound starting low in his throat as he bared his teeth.

The human backed away, almost knocking down a display of breakfast cereals.

Fuck, yeah, you better run away, you worthless piece of human garbage.

He shoved his hands into his pockets and prowled toward the counter, where a skinny wraith of a man was working the cash register.

"Can I help you?" he asked, a definite tremble to his voice.

"You can point me toward the self-service section."

The elderly cashier's eyes went wide. "I—I don't think you want to go down there."

"You're telling me what I want, old man?"

"I just mean . . . Your kind. Down there. It's not—"

"I'm expected," Hasik said, slapping a C-note onto the counter. Then he twisted his mouth into some version of a polite smile, his white canines gleaming under the fluorescents.

"I— Yes. Of course. This way." He stepped out from behind the counter, then shuffled to the back of the store. He paused in front of the door to the walk-in refrigerator through which the glass display cases of soda, beer, milk, and snacks were stocked. "Through there. All the way back. There's a door. Just past the empty milk crates. Code's O-NEG."

Hasik curled his lip in a snarl, just because he didn't like the bastard, then pushed through the cold, the fine hairs that covered his body standing on end. When he reached the keypad box, he punched in the code, then slipped inside as the steel door opened. The corridor was long and damp and twisted down in a spiral pattern until it reached a small stone-hewn room three stories beneath the Quik-Stop. The walls were lined with benches, and on the benches sat at least a dozen pasty-faced bloodsuckers drinking blood through long tubes extending through the stone walls. Hasik bit back a snort of disgust. He might not have their life span, but at least he didn't have to put up with that bullshit.

Two young-looking vampires stepped into the room from the underground entrance that fed into the L.A. subway system and allowed the vamps to come in and feed during the day. They eyeballed him, but he ignored their questioning glances. Not surprisingly, few werewolves ventured into vampire feeding arenas, but these two paid him little heed, moving instead to a kiosk at the far end of the room. As Hasik watched, one slid several coins in, then punched a few keys on a brightly lit pad.

The kid leaned in and read the keypad, then turned to his buddy. "Gotta wait. All the stations are full."

"Damn, I'm hungry. We shoulda come yesterday. Told you I was getting in a bad way."

"Almost time. You'll be fine."

"Way I feel right now, I could suck down a human."

The first kid's eyebrows rose. "Whoa now, man. Don't even think about that. That's some seriously illegal shit."

The hungry kid shrugged. "I didn't say I *would*. I said I *could*. What, you think I faked the Holding? I got some serious control, dude. But, damn, it would be nice to taste something not through a goddamn straw."

"You hear about that Division judge? Throat completely ripped out."

"I know. Bad mojo, huh?"

"Worst. You ever lose control? Your daemon ever... you know?"

"No way, man. Yours?"

A shadow passed over the kid's face, and he shrugged. "Fuck no. I'm solid."

"You'd tell me, right? I mean, you wouldn't try to work that down on your own."

"Shit, man, I told you. I'm good." The kid turned back to the kiosk, now beeping with a seat number, and their conversation died away.

Hasik sneered. Pussies. That's what they were. All that power flowing through them, and what do they do? They bottle it up.

Idiots. Working so hard to tamp down on something that would raise them to the level of gods. Didn't make any damn sense.

Not werewolves. With the rise of the full moon, the beast within burst free, and man and beast were one. It was glorious, and no way would the Weren ever subject themselves to some bullshit ritual. Confinement, yes. The damn Covenant required confinement for the protection of humans. Something else Hasik considered bullshit, but he also didn't want to end up on the gallery stage facing a leather-clad executioner. So yeah, he was willing to watch the moon and go in for confinement. Didn't mean he liked it. And it didn't mean he did it every month...

Shit no. And at the end of the day, he had it one hell of a lot better than the vamps.

Damn, but the little bloodsuckers gave him the willies, and now they were all looking at him, catching his scent, knowing he wasn't one of them.

He bared his teeth, staring them down. He'd killed his share of vamps. Watched the surprise on their supposedly immortal faces as he whacked their heads off. No, they weren't any better than he was. Not by a long shot.

But damn if they wouldn't stop staring.

He shouldn't have come. Should have insisted she meet him someplace else, especially since he'd scanned the whole room and didn't see her. The female vamp. Gunnolf's new squeeze.

Hasik's lip curled automatically. Gunnolf, one of the key Alliance members. Gunnolf, head of the entire Therian community. Gunnolf, Hasik's friend and mentor, and the horny bastard went and hooked himself up with a female vampire. Fucking unbelievable.

Then again, Hasik wouldn't turn down a fine piece of ass like Caris, either.

"You look stupid just standing there." The female voice came from behind, and he whipped around to face her, taking in the short-cropped hair and blood-red lips. She wore a white tank top that hugged her breasts and a diaphanous white skirt that brushed the ground and revealed the curve of her thighs. The outfit of an innocent, but he knew damn well this woman was anything but.

His nostrils flared—he could smell the wolf upon her, the filthy whore. "Mind your manners, bitch," he sneered.

She ignored his menace. "Hard to believe Gunnolf actually trusts you to advise him." Her green eyes narrowed. "Then again, maybe that's why he's not controlling the City of Angels. Yet."

She pressed a hand onto his arm, and he growled, low and dangerous, the sound not fazing her in the least. "You think that's it, wolf-boy? You think you're the reason Tiberius's constantly making your buddy Gunnolf take it up the ass?"

"You watch yourself."

"No," she said, her voice as low and dangerous. "You watch it. You think you have Gunnolf's ear, and maybe you do. But I've got the rest of him, and you damn well know it."

"Meeting here was a mistake."

"I have to feed."

"Stories I've heard about you, I'm surprised you don't find a human. One nobody'd miss much."

The corner of her mouth curved with a secret pleasure, and he wondered if he'd hit the mark. But all she said was, "I'm law-abiding. You got any proof to the contrary?"

"I don't give a shit what you do, so long as you don't screw Gunnolf."

She laughed, the sound light and flirtatious, and right then she didn't seem like a warrior but like a woman. "Too late for that."

Hasik looked around. The other vamps were staring at them. All except one. A white-haired vampire with red eyes who was shifting in his seat, the tube going into his mouth flowing red. Whitey looked up, met Hasik's eyes, then flashed a bloody grin. Hasik turned away. "I don't like it down here."

"Scared?"

"Fuck you."

"Such language," she said, raising an eyebrow and sounding bored. She headed to the kiosk.

He tugged at her elbow. "We talk, I leave, you feed. I'm not sitting here while you do the suck-fest ritual."

For a moment he thought she'd argue, then she nodded. "Whatever you say. I came to this beautiful city to work for you, right?"

"Damn straight. Gunnolf tell you the plan?"

"The basics. Said you'd run me through the full briefing. When do we start?"

"Soon," Hasik said. The plan was beautiful, if he did say so himself. He'd pitched the idea to Gunnolf, and the pack leader had bitten right in. Sabotage that prick Tiberius. Make it look like he couldn't control the vamps in the area. Make it look like they were indulging their daemons and feeding off humans instead of skulking around underground in pussified feeding stations like this goddamn place. "This ain't gonna come out well for your kind, you know?"

Her face hardened. "I never said I claimed them as my kind."

"What the fuck? You're a vamp. So what's that supposed to mean?"

She waved the question away. "Give me the deets, and let's get on with this. I need to feed."

"You know Feris Tinsley?"

"Gunnolf's lieutenant in Los Angeles? I've met him."

"He keeps an office in the Slaughtered Goat, a pub in Van Nuys."

"I know it."

"Meet me there later. I'll brief you."

"Screw that. You tell me now. That's why you came here."

"I came to meet you," Hasik said, standing a little straighter. "I came to make sure I could work with a female." His lip curled. "Ain't ideal, but you'll do. But I don't take orders from you, bitch. You want in on this, you come to the Goat."

He could see the storm clouds brewing in her eyes, a dangerous fury rising that had Hasik taking a step backward.

"We're talking now," she said, but no way was he giving in to a woman. Not even Gunnolf's woman.

"No we ain't. You come to the—"

"*Noooooooooooo!*"

The cry echoed off the stone walls, and Hasik shoved past Caris, searching for the source. He found it in Whitey, the vamp with the red eyes who'd been sucking on a flowing red tube. Apparently Whitey wasn't enjoying his lunch. The albino bastard jerked out of his chair, ripping the tube from the wall.

"Fuck this shit! Fuck this goddamn plastic shit. They got humans back there. Bleeding for us. I want to taste them, dammit. I want to taste the life. This is bullshit. *Fucking bullshit!*"

He lashed out, knocking the girl next to him to the ground, then crouching over her as the two kids Hasik had seen enter looked on with horror on their faces. "You full up, bitch? You full up with blood? How do you stand it? How the fuck do you stand it?"

Something light and fast whipped past Hasik, and it wasn't until she had Whitey down on the ground seconds later, a lethal-looking blade to his neck, that Hasik realized the something was Caris, moving faster than Hasik had ever seen a vamp move. Whitey struggled beneath her, but she held him with ease. "Back off," she said. "Back off right now."

"I can't take it." His face contorted with pain. "How do you take it?"

Caris kept her knife on his neck, then leaned in close. She turned her head slightly, so that she was speaking to Whitey, but looking at Hasik. "You do," she said. "You just do."

♦

Only hours into the job, and already Sara's desk groaned beneath the weight of case files, two three-ring binders, and three yellow pads full of notes. The spoils of a full day's work. Though it might be Friday, Luke's bail hearing was already scheduled for Monday, and Sara had hours and hours of prep work ahead of her.

And yet despite the stack of work on her table, her overburdened thoughts, and her exhausted body, she kept coming back to that one, simple word: *vampires*.

Almost without realizing she was doing it, she pulled her wallet out of her purse, then withdrew the small photograph she kept behind her driver's license. A picture of her and her father on the Pepperdine campus. He looked undeniably professorial in a tweed jacket and holding a pipe, and she'd been trussed up in a dress with an itchy petticoat. They'd come—she and her mother—to watch her father receive an award. Sara didn't know for what, only that a lot of people were applauding for her daddy. She'd made it a point to clap the loudest.

Four days later, her father was dead. His neck ripped open. His blood drained. And her own screams echoing through the park.

She squeezed her eyes shut, willing her mind to replace the horror of that night with happier memories. The smell of tobacco and mint that always laced his jacket. The way he'd stroke her hair when he'd tell her bedtime stories about Caesar's triumph over pirates or Nero's hideous singing. When he talked, the past had come alive for her. Not anymore. He'd become part of history, a daughter's memory.

And it had been a vampire who had taken him from this world. From Sara.

Full circle, she thought, drying her tears with the back of her hand. Today, everything circled around to vampires.

Vampires.

A vampire had murdered her father, leaving his

daughter with only memories and a legacy of night-mares.

A vampire had seduced her, leaving her sweaty and satisfied and clinging to the illusion that she had met a man who was worth something. A man whose kiss had brought her to her knees. A man who'd left flowers along with a silent promise that he would be back.

What a crock.

She pulled the ribbon out of her pocket and twisted it around her finger, cutting off the circulation to the end of the digit. Her naivete disgusted her. Even if Bosch was right and she was insusceptible to a vampire's mental tricks, she'd still fallen under Luke's spell. The potent allure of a confident man who takes what he wants; the decadent pleasure of being the woman he'd desired.

Enough of that.

She released her tight hold on the ribbon, letting it fall to the desktop. Then she used the remote control to power on the monitor mounted on her wall. Martella had shown her how to flip through the camera feeds, and she rotated through the images until she found the feed from Luke's cell.

He stood at the glass wall, his hands pressed to the barrier. Even over the computer monitor, his presence was compelling, a man who didn't merely occupy a space, but commanded it. Now he was quiet, pensive. And though his expression was no more revealing than it had been in the interview, Sara thought she detected a hint of sadness, of worry.

A bubble of concern rose within her, and she immediately quashed it. Of course he was sad and worried. He damn well should be considering the weight of the murder charge against him.

He moved across the cell to sit on the concrete bench that served as a bed, thighs straining against the thin material of the PEC-issued pants. She told herself she was unaffected by the view, insisting that the lazy curl of desire that eased through her was nothing more than residual lust. She couldn't want him, this murderer, this beast. She was better than that. Had more control over her emotions. Over her damn hormones.

Yet she'd picked up the ribbon again, and now her fingers were tying themselves into knots. And when he tilted his head and looked straight at her—at the camera—she felt the heat swirl through her. It shamed her. Infuriated her. Not because of what she'd done with him that night, but because the memory of his hands on her skin still fired her senses, making her nipples peak and her sex tingle.

Even knowing what he'd done—what he *was*—her body still craved him. His hands. His lips. Even the scrape of danger as his teeth dragged over her bare skin.

She wanted it—a vampire's touch—and she despised that weakness in herself. Despised him for being the cause of her folly. Slowly, purposefully, she looked down and opened the file in *Division v. Dragos*. She flipped to the crime scene photo and stared hard at the image of Braddock's neck wound, so similar to the wound she saw night after night in her dreams.

The ripped flesh. The dried blood.

There was no room for lust here. No room for desire or longing or fancy wishes of different circumstances.

This was murder.

Luke had killed. She was a prosecutor.

It really didn't get much simpler than that.

She stood up, then dropped the red ribbon into her office trash can. Time to get to work.

CHAPTER 11

"Sara Constantine," Tucker said, squinting at his phone. "Haven't met her. You?"

"Never heard of her," Doyle said. He was sitting in Dragos's office, the bastard's electronic calendar up on one of the computer monitors. They'd come back to the mansion after leaving the lab, and now Doyle was trying unsuccessfully to concentrate on the screen. No luck. His body was wrung out, every movement akin to pushing his limbs through pudding. And the miners with pickaxes whacking at the inside of his skull weren't helping the situation.

He squeezed his eyes shut and breathed in hard through his nose. "Who is she?" he asked, determined to stay on task. To stay focused.

"Prosecutor," Tucker said. "She caught this case. Martella says we need to be in her office at ten tomorrow, sharp."

Doyle nodded, managing a half-assed grunt.

"Fuck it, Doyle," Tucker said. "Give it up and let's go get you what you need."

Doyle gritted his teeth and shook his head. "Be fine," he managed. "Just gotta sleep it off."

"The hell you do," Tucker retorted. "You've been spiraling down ever since we sent Sanchez and her band of merry men on their way. You think I didn't notice how ripped you looked when we were at the lab? I'm surprised Orion didn't confuse you with one of his corpses and do an autopsy right there."

Doyle lifted his head to tell his partner to fuck off, but found he didn't have the energy.

"Okay. That's it. We're shutting it down." Tucker had been reviewing Dragos's security camera footage, hoping for an image of Braddock. Something, anything, to raise the already stellar evidence to the level of unbreakable. "The geek squad should be doing this grunt work anyway. I'm going to call a tech, get him to haul all this electronic crap to Division, and you and I are going to take a little ride."

"No." He hated that his partner knew what he went through. Hated more that Tucker had been sucked into helping each time Doyle sank deeper into the mire.

"I don't see that you have a choice, buddy," Tucker said, hauling Doyle up from under the armpits. "You're fading fast. When was the last time you had yourself a Happy Meal?"

Too long, and he hated that he needed the hit. Needed to feed.

The weakness in him shamed him. He was only half daemon, dammit; he should be able to wrest more control. Should be able to function without taking, without feeding.

And it wasn't just the weakness that plagued him when he didn't feed. He lost his gift, too. How was that for fucked up? He could see the deads' attackers, but only if he made himself one of them.

No. He wasn't like that. Wasn't like Dragos. He controlled it. Hardly ever took straight from a human. And when he did, he never took it all. Never drained them. Never left the humans to wander as lost, empty shells as some of his kind did.

He had control, after all. Had spent centuries fighting to gain some semblance of control.

So much easier to keep control when he was like this. Weak. Feeble.

So much easier to be human. To be lost.

When he fed, his daemon side surfaced. Claimed. Wanted.

Yes, he'd have strength. He'd have power. He'd have his visions.

But he'd also have the dark fury of a daemonic temper fighting for release.

The constant battle exhausted him. And in his darker moments he even understood why some of his kind lost control. Why the vampires let the daemon take over. So much easier to just stop fighting. To let go. To give in to his own inherent nature.

No.

He'd lived that way once, and he wasn't going back.

He wasn't a thing. Wasn't evil.

He wasn't Dragos.

And if he had to battle his own nature until the end of time to prove it, then that's what he'd do.

His body jerked forward, then slammed back, and Doyle realized his eyes were closed. He opened them, and found himself in the passenger seat of his car, with Tucker stomping on the brake beside him. "What the fu—"

"I told you, man. You're bad off. I carried you out like a damn baby and you didn't say a word."

Doyle glanced out the window. "Where are we?"

"South-Central. Roll down your window."

"Shoulda taken me to a Trader bar. Orlando's. One of the others."

"Fuck that. You know I don't go in those places. You want to go there, then don't get so bad off you pass out on me."

"Shit."

"Roll down your window," Tucker repeated.

Doyle groaned in protest, but lifted his hand, which felt like it weighed about as much as the car he was riding in.

"Never mind," Tucker said. "This will take a decade if I wait for you." He scooted over on the bench seat, leaned across Doyle, and cranked the window down. One sharp wolf whistle and he'd caught the attention of a hooker who weighed at least eighty pounds over the legal limit for spandex. She pasted on a smile, adjusted her tiny skirt and enormous tits, then tottered toward them from her station under a streetlamp.

"Your lucky night, sugar," she cooed. "I'm running a two-for-one special."

"Save it," Tucker said. "I'm just here to watch."

Her brows rose slightly. "That'll cost you extra." When Tucker didn't protest, she turned her attention to Doyle. "What's he want?"

What Doyle wanted was to get the hell out of there. That, however, wasn't happening. Especially not with Tucker next to him playing pimp. He half wondered why Tucker didn't just tweak the whore's brain. Then again, where was the sport in that?

"Do you kiss?" Tucker asked.

The hooker looked affronted. "What? On the mouth? Shit, no."

"That's what he wants," Tucker said. "And he'll pay extra."

"How much?"

"Whatever it takes."

"Yeah?" She looked at Doyle with respect. "That a fact?"

"Get in," he croaked, his voice thin, his lips barely moving as he forced the words out.

Her brow furrowed, and she took a step backward. "That boy's sick. No way I'm getting whatever he's got."

"He's not sick," Tucker said.

"Kiss my ass." She turned and started walking away.

Doyle reached up and clawed at the door handle. He needed it—her—and he needed it now.

"Wait," Tucker called. She turned, hands on her hips and a scowl on her face. "Kiss him," Tucker said, with that look on his face. "Kiss him nice and hard."

She teetered a bit on her heels, then sauntered back to the car, her eyes glassy and slightly confused. "Got a freebie for you, sickie-poo," she said, leaning into the window so that the shelf of her breasts balanced on the window ledge. "Come to Mama."

He did, leaning into the kiss and opening his mouth wide.

Opening and sucking and feeding and—

Oh, fuck yeah ...

Her soul filled him. Nourished him. And, yeah, it roused the daemon inside him.

Right then, he didn't care. The strength flowed back,

and he wondered how he'd ever given it up. How could he have thought to exist without this? Weak as a kitten and docile as a bunny?

This was it. This was *good*. This was power and strength and—

Beneath him, the woman made a mewling noise. Tucker's bond had broken, the soul that remained within her insufficient to accept the suggestion.

He needed to back off. Needed to leave her some. With even a scrap, she'd heal. Wouldn't be hollow. Wouldn't be a shell. A casing for one of the incorporeal creatures to fill.

He knew all that, yet he clung to her, the taste of the power flooding him too sweet to resist.

Beside him, he felt Tucker tug at his arm. Heard him mutter words of protest, his tone frantic, but his words indistinct.

He heard the melodic tones of Tucker's phone, felt another poke, and then—holy fuck—the asshole was inside his head.

Let go.

Doyle did, releasing the whore in an instant, minute scraps of her soul still intact. He rounded on Tucker, his hands to his partner's throat, his blood boiling as he pressed the traitor up against the driver-side window.

"Never," he said, slowly. "You do not *fucking* get inside my head."

"You were...destroying her," Tucker said, gasping for air.

"Who the fuck cares?"

"I thought you did."

That got through, and Doyle released Tucker, shooting back to his side of the car, horrified by what he'd just done. "Tucker, I—"

Tucker held up a hand to stave off the apology. "You together now?"

Doyle took a breath and clenched his fists, fighting, *concentrating,* until he felt his daemon side slip reluctantly beneath the surface. "Yeah," he said, wiping beads of sweat from his brow. "Sure."

"Division called," Tucker said. "Dragos. Furlough. *Now.*"

"Fuck." Doyle closed his eyes, forced himself not to think about that as he wrestled his daemon half into submission.

Tucker peeled away from the curb with one last nod toward the hooker, who'd resumed her position under the streetlight. "She gonna be okay?"

Doyle thought of the strands of soul he'd left her. They'd grow back. But he'd stolen from her. Cheated her. And that left a mark.

"No," he said, as the daemon inside celebrated the knowledge of what he'd wrought. "She'll never be the same again."

♦

"This is bullshit," Doyle raged as he stalked the length of the antechamber. "Fucking bullshit." He was on edge, his daemon half still too close to the surface after his feeding. Couple that with the total fucked-up nature of the situation, and Doyle found himself in a fury that he considered completely fucking legitimate.

At that very moment, behind the thick metal door, Security Section was fitting that murdering fuckwad with mobile detention devices, and as far as Doyle could tell, he was the only one who saw a problem with that little scenario. He lashed out, kicking the door but failing to make even a dent in the metal.

At the far end of the room, Dragos's advocate puppet stood expressionless against the wall, calmly tapping something into a PDA. Doyle took a step closer, his fists itching to bloody up Montegue's all-too-pretty face, but was held back by a firm hand closing on his shoulder.

He turned and snarled at his partner. "What?"

"Chill," Tucker said. "Push it under."

"Chill? Whose side are you on? That animal's gonna be out walking the streets, breathing *my* air. And this asshole's standing over there playing the calm cool counselor, when we all know some serious shit's gone down." He tried to take another step toward Montegue and once again felt Tucker's hand hold him back.

This time, however, Montegue looked up, his face impassive. "Are you talking to me?"

"Don't play games with me, you useless worm. This ain't right and you know it."

"An accused is entitled to an on-site review of the evidence against him with his advocate of choice," Montegue said, spouting a load of legalese crap. "Three hours, fair and square."

"My ass," Doyle retorted. "That ain't a guarantee. Dangerous suspect, risk of flight. All those things have to be taken into account."

"As the judge surely did."

"You pulled strings, cut corners." He jerked his

shoulder out from under Tucker's hand and shot his partner a warning look. The hand didn't return, and Doyle took a step forward. "What have you got on Judge Acquila? What threat did you make?"

Something dark and dangerous flashed across Montegue's pretty face. "I would suggest, Agent Doyle, that you keep your accusations to yourself. Since I'm aware of the enmity you feel for my client, I'm willing to ignore that outburst. But if you once again even hint that I have crossed any ethical lines in representing my client, I assure you that I will make your life miserable."

"Hint? I'll do more than hint, you filthy bloodsucker." A comfortable rage flooded him, and he lunged forward at the same time Montegue did, the two men coming nose to nose before Tucker grabbed Doyle by the shoulder and yanked him forcibly back.

Doyle whirled, hissing, and saw Tucker leap back, hands up in defense, fear flickering in those human brown eyes.

Doyle sagged. "Goddammit." He fired another sneer Montegue's way. "You didn't even give the prosecution a chance to argue."

"Nor was I required to do so. I wonder, in fact, how you came to be here."

"I keep my ears open," Doyle said. "Especially where defendants like Dragos are concerned."

"I'm gratified to know our civil servants are looking out for the public's best interest," Montegue said silkily.

"Underhanded game playing," Doyle muttered. "But you've forgotten who you're dealing with, and it'll be on your head when the bastard skips out on you. How much credibility do you think you'll have in court after that?"

"My client will be returning to custody in three hours. Or are you suggesting that you are aware of a way to disable the mobile detention devices? If so, I suggest you inform Security Section. The failure to disclose such information is, I believe, a Class A violation of the Covenant."

"Fuck you."

Before the advocate had a chance to respond to Doyle's brilliant comeback, the light above the metal door switched from red to green, and it swung open, the hydraulic mechanism hissing. A beefy daemon with a thick, armorlike skin stepped out, followed by Dragos, now clad in the black jeans, T-shirt, and duster he'd worn when Doyle and the RAC team had taken him down.

"Uh-uh. No way." He looked Dragos in the eye. "Strip."

The corner of Dragos's mouth twitched. "Truly, Ryan, you're not my type."

"I'm serious. Take it off. No way are you walking out of this room without me seeing the countermeasures."

"Are you suggesting Wrait is untrustworthy?" Montegue asked, stepping in beside his scumbag client. Doyle sneered. What he wouldn't give to take both of those sons of bitches down . . .

"Bartok alesian rhyngot!"

Doyle rounded on the daemon, got right in his face. "Damn straight I don't trust you. And the next time you've got something to say to me, you say it in English. You understand me, *daemon*?"

"He doesn't speak English," Dragos said. "Just transferred from Division 18 in Paris."

"Yeah? Then how'd he know what I was saying?"

Dragos shot him a bored look. "Subtlety's not your strong suit, Ryan. It never has been. But if you want to ensure you are understood, speak French. Or Daemonic," he added with a thin smile.

"Strip," Doyle said, ignoring both the taunt and the daemon who was still glowering at him. "Right now, or I'm calling Bosch."

"You have no authority to—" Montegue began, stopping short when Dragos held up a hand.

"Let the little boy throw his temper tantrum. I have nothing to hide." He shrugged out of the duster and handed it to Montegue, then thrust out his arms to Doyle. A band of polished silver-gray metal had been cuffed tightly around each wrist. Doyle grabbed Dragos's arm roughly and twisted, looking at the band from all sides. A muscle flickered in Dragos's cheek, but the bastard didn't protest, and, satisfied, Doyle dropped his arm.

He eyed Tucker. "They're solid. No seams. No visible breach points." The hematite bracelets, Doyle knew, prevented Dragos from shifting into animal form or sentient mist. He still had strength and speed, albeit lessened, but wherever he was going, he was getting there on two humanoid feet.

Tucker crossed his arms over his chest, eyed Dragos up and down. "Guy like this wouldn't cut off his own hands to get free of the bands, either. How would he jerk off if he did?"

Doyle barked out a laugh. "True enough, but that

ain't a real risk. Any attempts to alter the body in order to remove the bands, and the stake is activated. So let's see it," he added, turning his attention from Tucker to Dragos. "Show me the stake."

Pure hate burned in Dragos's eyes, and it gave Doyle a nice warm feeling of satisfaction to know that he was getting under the murderous bastard's skin. Dragos's eyes cut toward the pretty-boy advocate, who shrugged. "The agent wants to pretend he's got a big dick, I'm not going to stand here and prove to him how shriveled and tiny it is. Just show him, Luke, and let's get the fuck out of here."

Dragos set his jaw, then reached up to the neck of his T-shirt. Doyle expected him to yank it over his head, but instead, Dragos clenched his fists and pulled, ripping the shirt down the center to just over his heart. He peeled back the raw edges of black cotton to reveal a thick metal band strapped tight around his chest. Over his heart, a circular-shaped portion of the metal protruded slightly from the skin. Underneath the protrusion, Doyle knew, was a piece of wood, cut so that it would, upon being triggered, expand and lock into the shape of a stake. A stake that would instantaneously be thrust into the wearer's heart.

Doyle took a step closer, wanting to see the actual mechanism that had the power to end Lucius Dragos, then stopped as he heard the low growl in Dragos's throat.

"It's set," Montegue said firmly. "He tries anything, he goes outside of the jurisdictional area, he in any way blows the terms of the deal, and the stake deploys. And I don't care if you're satisfied or not at this point. We're leaving." He looked at the daemon then spoke smoothly in French.

Wrait grunted. *"Trois heures. Oui."*

And then, as if Doyle and Tucker weren't even standing there, Montegue and Dragos stepped out the door, and Dragos began the short walk toward freedom.

Doyle waited until the door shut behind them, then he turned to Tucker. "Let's go. And the gods help that bastard if he tries anything. Because I will hammer that stake myself."

CHAPTER 12

The Slaughtered Goat in Van Nuys was the kind of pub you went to if you didn't care about food poisoning, knife wounds, gunshots, or just general bad service.

In other words, the perfect place to kill, quickly, thoroughly, and without too much fuss.

Luke watched the door from the driver's seat of Nick's BMW. The information that Nick had received from Tiberius indicated that Gunnolf's man in L.A., a vile little were-cat named Feris Tinsley, kept an office in the back section, which he habitually visited every evening at twelve-fifteen. Before that, Tinsley spent an hour or two in the main section of the pub, drinking bourbon, eating corned beef sandwiches, and copping a feel off a waitress named Alinda.

Since Alinda was neither appreciative of such affection nor fond of shape-shifters, the elfin female had been more than happy to provide information and assistance when a gorgeous man like Nick had come around asking questions.

Not only had she told Nick that Hasik was due to meet with Tinsley that evening, but she'd agreed to enter the access code on the back door to allow Luke to slip into the back of the pub through the alley. In exchange, Nick would arrange new employment in a new city.

A fresh start for an elf who'd come to the wrong town

and fallen in with the wrong people. Luke considered it a fair trade.

As for the job for which he'd come—killing Ural Hasik—he considered that a fair deal, too.

Luke paged through the electronic file on his PDA, the images of beheaded vampires burning his eyes and boiling his blood. Ural Hasik had used no stake, but had instead left his victims degraded in death, spread out over the ground to molder and rot.

The daemon within growled and tensed, tightening and twisting, alive with fury. Alive within Luke.

"Soon," Luke said. Soon the daemon would have satisfaction.

He checked the clock on the dashboard, put the car into gear, and eased around the block and into the dark alley. He left the car near the street and walked the short distance to the pub's rear entrance.

He saw her immediately. A wisp of a girl standing by the back door, holding a sack of garbage. She wore tight red leggings and a transparent shirt, her small breasts pressing against the gauzy material. Fear tightened her features as she looked up at him. A small pink tongue darted out, and she tossed the sack into a nearby trash bin, then turned back to the door and keyed in the access code.

She opened it, slipped inside, and Luke caught the door before it slammed shut. Smooth as silk.

He waited a moment, giving her time to move from the back section to the front of the pub. Then he pulled open the door and slid inside, easily finding the door to Tinsley's office. Normally, he would have already changed into mist, foregoing altogether the risk of being seen by witnesses or by the target as he materialized silently behind him, knife in hand. There weren't many percipient daemons walking the earth, but one of the most prominent was determined to see Lucius staked, and he was not inclined to give Ryan Doyle more ammunition.

Now, though, with the detention device, transformation wasn't an option. Not only that, he needed to make the bastard talk. Capture. Interrogate. Kill. Which meant his voice would register in Hasik's mind, even if he were able to take the pup from behind. He'd have to remove the body and hide it someplace where it wouldn't be found until the window for Doyle to look into the werewolf's mind had passed. That would shave off time from his furlough, but he had no other option.

Within, the daemon stirred and Luke's skin tingled in anticipation as he moved quietly toward the open doorway. He paused outside the door, his back to the wall, then eased slowly around until he could peer inside.

Hasik sat at a desk, his hulking form dwarfing even the huge stainless-steel monstrosity. "Don't like the bitch," he said, as Luke searched the room for Feris Tinsley. He found the black cat perched on a bookcase opposite Hasik. The cat leaped, transforming midjump into Gunnolf's L.A. minion. The mangy were-cat's crimes against the vamp community were at least as wicked as Hasik's, and Luke eased back against the wall, his mind humming, the daemon roaring with anticipation.

"You just spent a half hour laying out the score for her, and I didn't see her flinch once. She's in," Tinsley said.

"She ain't one of us."

"Gunnolf trusts her."

"Gunnolf's fucking her," Hasik said. "Wouldn't mind that myself, but that doesn't mean I'm gonna trust the bitch. She's got Gunnolf whipped. She shouldn't be involved. Not with this. We're already getting closer to the humans than I want. Now we're adding her kind to the mix? It's too dangerous."

"You're second-guessing Gunnolf? Do you have a fucking death wish?"

"I came up with the plan," Hasik growled.

"And a damn good one. Stage a few vampire attacks. Bloody human deaths. The kind that make the news. Make it look like Tiberius can't control his people."

At the door, Luke squeezed his hands into tight fists, fighting back an eruption of fury.

"Got to hand it to you, Hasik, it just might work. But you listen to me. Gunnolf knows what he's doing. She may be a fucking bitch vampire, but she's also a powerful ally, and you damn well know it. Caris is as tied in to the vamps as you can get. Hell, she used to bang Tiberius."

Caris.

Immediately, Luke pictured the chestnut-haired female with cat's eyes and a tiger's temperament. He tilted his head back, finding the fresh scent of a female vampire. Sharp and woody, like a forest after a rain. She'd been here, in this room, and not so very long ago. Once he had thought her an ally. A good match for his leader and mentor. But then she'd rallied the charge against Tasha, arguing for termination rather than salvation.

Now her defection from the vampiric community and alignment with the Therians was proof that she had only grown more despicable with time.

A slow burn rose within him, and he had to tamp down hard on the daemon, now screaming for release. He wished that she were there, in that room. Because right then he'd happily add her to the butcher's bill, and return to Tiberius with news of not only his enemy's death, but a traitor's as well.

Since she'd already left, it was time to take what he could get.

It was, he thought, time to kill.

He slipped his hand into his pocket and pulled out the key to Nick's car. He tossed it to the far corner of Tinsley's office, where it landed on the concrete floor with a sharp ping. As he'd hoped, both Hasik and Tinsley turned in that direction, away from him. When they did, Luke drew in a sharp breath, snipped the last thread of his control, and let the daemon rage. Then Lucius Dragos burst over the threshold, his knife out and flying.

It arced hilt over blade to land deep in Tinsley's back, and the were-cat fell face forward onto the ground as Luke tackled the burly werewolf. He landed on Hasik's back, an arm tight around the beast's neck. It snarled and snapped and tried to turn to see its attacker, but to no avail, and even as it twisted, Lucius tightened his grip, the daemon within juiced for the kill, satisfaction running high when he shifted, twisted, and heard the sharp *pop* of Ural Hasik's neck.

He jumped back, letting the body sink to the ground, careful to stay out of the beast's line of sight until he was certain the last light of life had faded from the creature. One moment, then another, then safety. No need to move the bodies now. He'd managed a clean kill after all.

He moved swiftly to Tinsley's body, caught the scent of remaining life, and cursed as he saw the limbs twitching and heard the beast's labored breathing.

Careful once again to stay out of the beast's line of sight, Lucius pulled his knife free, then grabbed a chunk of the were-cat's hair. He pulled the head up off the floor and reached around to draw his knife hard across Tinsley's neck. Blood gushed, and Lucius let the head fall back in its own puddle of blood.

Done.

He gathered up Nick's key, took one last look at the bodies, and then Lucius Dragos slid out the door and disappeared back into the night.

◆

"Holy shit," Nick said, after Luke told him about the plot and about Caris's involvement. They were holed up in one of the tombs that Luke had connected to his Beverly Hills mansion via a series of underground tunnels. The tombs that celebrities had built for their egos served Luke's purposes well, and in the mid-1930s, he'd purchased a plot and built his own crypt, which he'd then connected to a half-dozen similar structures scattered over the manicured cemetery lawn.

"Caris," Nick said. "I never would have believed. Tiberius's going to be on the warpath."

"He will," Luke agreed. "But Hasik and Tinsley are

out of the picture, and unless they've already set their troops out onto the city, their plan is trashed. So you tell Tiberius I want a practical token of appreciation."

"That I will. This is one time I think he'll be happy to pull strings."

Luke nodded, almost tasting the freedom.

"I have good news for you, too," Nick said. "Tasha called."

Luke's head jerked up. "She called you?"

"She called *you*," Nick corrected. "I had your calls forwarded to my cell while yours is stored at Division. She's fine. She's in New York still. Says she wants to come home."

"Thank the gods." The relief that swept through Luke almost drove him to his knees. "And Serge?"

At that, Nick's expression grew hard. "She doesn't know where he is."

"God*dammit*." He drew in a deep breath, forcing himself to remain calm.

"It's worse, Luke," Nick said. "The things she said . . . Would he touch her? Would Serge break your trust?"

Bile rose in Luke's throat as he thought of his friend's hands on Tasha's innocent flesh. If Serge was not already dead, he may well die by Luke's stake when they next met.

He drew in a breath, forcing himself to be calm. "Ryback hasn't been to the apartment yet? Tell him that he's to bring Tasha back now. No side trips, no hesitation. I want her back yesterday, Nick. Are we clear?"

"Crystal. I'll tell him." Nick nodded toward the entrance to the tunnel that would lead them back to Luke's mansion, their supposed destination during the furlough. "Let's get back to Division and get you out of that contraption before Doyle bursts in here and spoils our party."

"You saw him, too?" Luke asked.

"Hard to miss that baby-shit-yellow car. I'm sure he's got officers at all your exit points."

"*Known* exit points," Luke corrected.

"Probably expects you to coldcock me and make a break for it," Nick said.

"We still have over an hour before I'm required to return. Why waste the opportunity?"

"What are you planning?"

"Sara Constantine," Luke said, the possibility of seeing her again too tempting to postpone.

"Is that still necessary? You've got Tiberius in your court now."

"Plan B," Luke said.

"Forget it. She's all the way across town. And we talked about this. This isn't the time. Not for her."

"Perhaps you're right," Luke said, not inclined to argue with his friend. "Give me one moment, though. I want to show you something." He moved to one of the two stone coffins in the room and began to shove aside the lid, releasing the thick stench of death. "Look," Luke said.

Nick did, but saw nothing more interesting than stone and dust.

Then he glanced up at Luke and saw the apology on his face, saw his friend's hand moving as fast as lightning.

He had time for only the merest flash of understanding before the hand connected, and black, liquid pain flooded his nose and face.

His knees went weak. The world swam in front of him. And the last thing Nick heard as he dropped into Luke's arms was his friend's murmured apology for doing exactly what Doyle had expected he'd do.

CHAPTER 13

Nick lay motionless at the bottom of the sarcophagus, remarkably at peace for a man who would soon wake in a fury. For that, Luke was sorry, but there was no other way. What he intended must be done alone.

He reached inside the coffin and removed Nick's watch, which had already been set to count down the remaining furlough time. For a moment, he considered also taking Nick's cell phone. After all, he needed to be careful, and Nick's reaction to Luke's betrayal was an unknown—a potential risk to not only his life, but to Tasha's life and the lives of his friends as well. One call, and Nick could report Luke's treachery. One call, and the stake poised over Luke's heart would be triggered.

No.

He turned away, shamed that he could even consider the possibility of such perfidy. He left the phone in the pocket of the friend he trusted with his life, and never doubted that he'd made the right decision.

And then, with one last look at the man in the coffin, Luke slid the stone lid back into place.

Unlike his own crypt, this tomb truly did house the dead, and the scent of death lingered on the thick summer air, reminding him of both what he was, and what he was not.

Like the corpses in this tomb, Luke had once been

human, his life marked by the minutes counting down to the day he lived no more, but instead lay in stasis and began to rot. Such a cruel trick was birth, he'd thought, inescapably tainting that gift of life with the horror of death.

And to him, a young man who had seen his mother and baby sister die in childbirth, who had watched his father fall from another man's sword, death truly was a horror. A cruel taskmaster that came without warning, trying daily to cheat the living out of the gift bestowed at birth.

He had been eighteen when he heard rumors of a dark woman of timeless beauty whose kiss could grant eternal life. He had become obsessed, determined to find her and convince her to bestow her prize upon him. For seven long years he searched, but to no avail. As a soldier in the Roman army, he was afforded very little freedom, his investigation limited to listening to the tales of travelers and interrogating other soldiers returning from duty in the far reaches of the empire.

So futile seemed his efforts, that in time he almost forgot his obsession, his thoughts turning more toward the lusty Claudia, a merchant's daughter with whom he had fallen in love. He had taken her as his bride in the spring, and by the fall harvest she was heavy with child. When, months later, the midwife had placed the tiny Livia in his arms, Luke was deaf to those who urged that she was flawed. To him, she was perfect. He was the one who was weak. For he could never be strong enough or wise enough to fully protect this child, to make her healthy.

She grew slower than other children, each passing

year seeming to drain her body of life. Though careful not to let the child see his fears, he nightly succumbed to the crippling horror that she would be snatched from him. He turned not to his wife for comfort, though, as his own impotence shamed him. Instead, he would wander the wheat fields after dark, the baleful sound of his anguish drowned out by the whisper of the grain in the wind.

Livia knew nothing of her parents' fears, and though often confined to bed, her mind grew sharp and quick. By the time she was ten, sweet Livia had her doting father entirely under her control. Still, the joy that stole his breath when he looked upon the child was snuffed out by the fear that he and Claudia would be forced to bury her before the year was out. Her body, the physicians told them, was breaking down, and despite regular entreaties to the gods, her condition worsened daily. Fate, it seemed, had contrived to allow Luke only a taste of true happiness before ripping it brutally from his hands.

He recalled with perfect clarity the day his life had changed forever. Livia had been confined to bed, and both Luke and Claudia were sitting vigil at her side when they'd heard the thunder of hooves approaching. Luke had stiffened, imagining the rider was Death, come to bear his daughter away.

He need not have worried. Death was not coming then. Would not, in fact, come until Lucius himself invited it in.

The rider was Sergius, who had ridden his horse hard to deliver the news that the streets were filled with rumors that the dark lady had come to Londinium. And though Luke had not thought of his obsession since the months before Livia's birth, to him it seemed as though Serge had arrived on the wings of destiny. For how better to save his daughter than to bar Death from the door?

It had broken his heart to part from her and from Claudia, who had wept and clung to him as he'd mounted his horse. He had held fast, though, promising his wife that he would return presently, bearing Livia's salvation.

The trip south was grueling, and he'd arrived at the city gates sore and hungry, his horse ridden almost to the point of collapse. He had cared not, his thoughts only on Livia, on finding the dark lady who could return his daughter to him. For three days he and Serge had scoured the city's underbelly, following any rumor, any hint of news, but never finding the lady herself.

He'd been on the verge of giving up when he'd located her in a tavern and pleaded his case. She had declined at first, unconcerned, she'd said, about the welfare of his child. He'd persisted, though, determined that he would have what he came for. That he would win the lady's gift and deliver it triumphantly to his home.

His tenacity persuaded her, and in the end, he won his heart's desire. He would like to say that he hadn't fully understood the terms as she relayed them to him, but that would be a lie. He'd understood. There had been no failure to disclose. No dark trick.

The soul, she told him, is not alone in man. There is evil as well. And the evil has a name and a face: *daemon*. In some, it is mild. Calm. Controllable. In others, it rages. Burns. Writhes. But in all humanity, it is there, hidden well in most by the power of their soul to suppress it. To quell and control.

The dark gift releases the daemon, and only the strongest have the strength to battle it back.

He listened. He understood. And he had taken the gift with eyes wide open, arrogant enough to believe that the terms did not apply to him. He was a good man, after all. Kind. He loved his family deeply, and they him. He took the gift not selfishly, but with his child's wellbeing at the forefront of his mind.

Surely, with motives so pure the gods would exempt him from the gift's dark effects or bestow upon him the strength to control the daemon.

Of course, he'd been wrong. The curse *vampyre* had freed the daemon, just as the lady had told him it would. It did not, as human mythology sometimes suggests, allow evil to enter. The evil was already within him, had been there all along. And once he became *nosferatu,* that evil ran free.

He'd become a killer, a monster, and were he given the chance, he would gladly return to that fateful day and sacrifice himself to the normal course of nature, if only to save those he had hurt.

The innocent. The strangers.

And, yes, to save his Livia.

Even now, all these centuries later, his stomach roiled and his blood ran cold when he remembered what he'd done, the torment he'd wrought upon the child he'd adored, the woman he'd loved.

With the daemon riding high, he'd left Londinium for home, intending to fulfill his original purpose and draw his wife and child into his shiny new world. Claudia, however, had been horrified and had thrown herself on him as she tried to keep him from his Livia.

He'd shaken her off violently, having no patience for the foolish woman who would sentence their daughter to a mortal death. With a daemon's strength, he'd thrown her against the stone hearth, and she'd slipped into unconsciousness, her body sagging to the floor.

He'd felt no regret, only a renewed purpose as he'd stalked through the house toward his child. He could smell her, the scent of her teasing his senses. Death waited in the room for her, but Lucius refused to give the vile beast satisfaction. He would snatch Livia from Death's clutches. He would, finally, save her.

She'd smiled as he'd approached her bed, but the expression had faded as he'd moved closer. *"Pater?"* she'd murmured. *"Quis es?"*

He'd told her to hush, then drawn her tiny body into his arms. She'd snuggled close at first, reassured, then pulled away, confused, and complained that his skin didn't feel right. "I will soothe you," he'd whispered, and with her scream echoing in his ears, he'd sunk his fangs deep into the tender, young flesh of her neck.

She'd writhed and struggled, but the daemon had swirled unrelenting within him, and he'd drunk and drunk, the taste of her fear causing him no hesitation but instead enticing the daemon even more. He drank deep, telling himself that he could stop in time—that he could turn her. That he could save her.

And though he felt the whisper of death touch her— though he knew that he was on the verge of taking her too far—the daemon would not stop. *He* would not stop.

He drank his fill, and drew the last spark of life from her.

There would be no renewal for his Livia. No life.

He had stolen it from her, thrusting death upon her even as he'd tried to give her unending life.

He had failed, and as he looked up, confused and sated, her body limp in his arms, he'd seen Claudia silhouetted in the doorway, a knife tight in her hand. She held the blade out toward him, her face a mask of fear and fury and grief.

The daemon within him had whipped into a frenzy from which Lucius had been unable to emerge. Grief, rage, confusion, loss. All pounding inside him. All driving him down, down into the mire. Lost in the call of the blood, Lucius had leaped toward his wife, a part of him wanting to share his grief, another part wanting to snuff out her life because of the harsh way that she now looked at him.

She hurled the knife and ran even before its hilt collided harmlessly against his chest.

He let her go, then turned back and cradled the lifeless body of his daughter. And as grief warred with hunger, he surrendered, fully and completely, to the daemon within.

CHAPTER 14

Sara sat cross-legged on her bed, eyes closed, taking one deep breath after another. She'd been going a hundred miles an hour since before six that morning, and now she felt ripped apart from the inside. Excited, yes. But completely exhausted as well.

She wanted sleep, but Bosch had insisted that the security system in her condo be updated immediately, so she had to wait up for the installation team. Considering what she now knew was out there in the world, she didn't really have a serious objection.

Without thinking about what she was doing, she scooted to the side of the bed, then bent to open the bedside table's drawer. She hesitated only briefly, then reached in and pulled out the Glock 9mm that she'd bought the day her concealed carry permit had been issued. In truth, she hadn't wanted the thing, but she'd been a green prosecutor working a high-profile drug trafficking case, and Marty had insisted that everyone on the team license up and carry a weapon whenever they were away from the criminal justice center.

Sara had dutifully followed instructions, but the moment the case had wrapped, she'd transferred the gun from her purse to the drawer, and it hadn't emerged since. Until now.

Now she took it out and hefted it, testing the weight.

She ejected the magazine, then pulled back the slide to check the chamber. Clear, she slapped the clip back home, then realized that her thoughts had drifted to Lortag. And, more, to Evangeline Toureau.

If that had been Sara standing there, would she have been able to drive that stake home? If her daughter had been murdered? If the defendant had been sentenced to death?

A brutal system, Bosch had called it, and he was right. Yet she had to admit there was a circular beauty in allowing Evangeline to avenge her daughter.

And what if her imaginary Evangeline had met Lortag in a dark alley?

Or if Sara herself had met Jacob Crouch when the Glock had lived in her purse? What would she have done then?

She knew what she would have wanted to do. She wanted to blow his fucking head off.

And it was for that reason that she no longer carried the gun.

Crouch might be dead—his life taken in a twist of fate that had set her younger self to dancing—but there were other monsters out there. *Her* weapon was the system, though. Not a gun. Not a stake. But the courts and the prisons, designed to punish and protect.

And had the system served little Melinda Toureau?

She shivered, not liking the small voice in her head, and frustrated by her inability to accept what Bosch had so casually told her. Intellectually, Sara understood. But her heart still ached for that little girl.

The doorbell buzzed, and she hurried to answer it, smoothing down her Stanford Law T-shirt as she walked.

She peered through the peephole and found herself facing a man with a sagging basset-hound face and eerie yellow eyes.

"Security Officer Roland, night shift leader and domicile protection specialist," he said, flashing his Division identification. She led him and the team inside, showed them around, then parked herself on the sofa with a stack of files. She turned first to her copy of the initial report, once again skimming Ryan Doyle's summary. Though he was thorough, she wanted to go over the details with him in person, and he and his partner were scheduled to be in her office at ten the next morning.

According to the report, Braddock had been a shapeshifter, on the bench for two decades, an advocate before that. He'd been born in the late thirties, but Sara didn't know if that meant he'd died young, or if a shapeshifter's life span tended to be about that of a human's. Several years before he'd retired, he'd been sanctioned for accepting bribes, and there'd been murmurs that he'd engaged in blackmail. He'd made restitution, appeared before a review board, and had been allowed to keep his seat on the bench. She made a note. The crime was old and apparently resolved, but she knew damn well that bribery and blackmail could be a solid motive for murder. More than that, those crimes were often only part of the story, and she intended to have Doyle and Tucker dig, and dig deep.

She'd moved on to the medical examiner's report when Roland shuffled through the room, and she lifted her pencil to catch his attention. "How's it going?"

"Like wine and aged cheese, fine security work takes time."

"How much time?"

"Can't rush perfection," he said, leaning against the wall as he hooked his thumbs in the loops of his jeans. For the first time, she noticed the long tufts of hair that grew on the back of his wrists and poked out from underneath the cuffs of his sleeves. "But we are in the final stretch."

"Fair enough." She started to turn back to her papers, then paused, peering at him. "How long have you worked at Division?"

She watched his face run through the calculations. "Eh, three decades? Four?"

"You know Judge Braddock?"

"Sure. Retired what, three years ago?"

"Impressions?"

The hangdog face went flat.

"I'm new, Roland. I'm just trying to get a feel for the victim."

"Yeah, well, the victim was pretty much an asshole."

She shifted, interested. "How so?"

"Oh, he was good with the law and all that. But wouldn't give what he called a lesser being the time of day. Snapped at support staff. Had himself one supreme holier-than-thou attitude. Heard he got into some trouble awhile back. Bribes, I think. Wouldn't wish him dead though."

"Somebody did."

"Dragos, wasn't it?"

"So it seems," she said, working to keep her voice flat, even though the thought that the man who'd touched her so intimately could have done that horrible thing was still twisting her up inside. "Any ideas why Lucius Dragos would want Braddock dead?"

"Well, I . . ." He paused, as if truly considering the question. "Actually, I can't think why Braddock would even be on a vamp like Dragos's radar. Kinda makes you think, doesn't it? All sorts of stuff going on under the surface all the time. May not see it," he added, "but it's there."

Yeah, she thought. *But what exactly was "it"?*

"Thanks," she said to him, then looked around the room. "So what are you doing?"

"Ah, this. Now *this* is interesting stuff. We got you covered for magical entrance—that's Chiarra," he added, waving in the direction of a woman with glowing purple hands. "No creature's gonna be porting right into your apartment after we're done."

"Porting?"

He grinned. "Beam me up, Scotty," he said, then waggled his overgrown eyebrows.

"Oh. Right."

"Got the seams around your windows and under your doors sealed up nice and tight against mist, too. Don't want any two-cent vamps or their passengers getting in, do we? Especially not when you've got such a high-profile vampire case on your first go out the gate."

"I'm sorry? Two cents?"

"Huh? Oh, no. Two *centuries*. That's about the age when a vamp develops the ability to mist. Gotta grow into it, you know. You hear about a vamp getting prosecuted by the humans, you know he was a youngster.

No older vamp's gonna sit still for steel handcuffs and cages, that's for damn sure."

"And what were you saying about passengers?"

"An older vamp can transform into mist—that's a fact that's crossed over into your human lore. But most humans don't know that they can clutch another person—vamp or human or whatever—and transform them into mist as well."

"Oh." Sara trembled, an image of Luke, his arms tight around her as they both dissolved into mist, suddenly filling her mind. There was something erotic about the thought of being so entwined with him, and she cursed her own inability to move Luke firmly and finally to the "defendant" slot in her brain.

"Glad you're asking questions. Some humans, they're too overwhelmed their first day to do anything but sit back and let the day wash over them," Roland continued. "Don't even bother opening the manual until at least a week in. And never even ask what anybody is. Think it's impolite or something."

"Is it?"

He shrugged. "Yeah, probably so. But I never was a big fan of Emily Post, you know? Figure if you don't ask, you don't learn."

"So what are you?" she asked, taking him at his word.

"Hellhound," he said. "On my mother's side. Never was too clear on what my dad was. Left when I was a pup. But don't you worry. I ain't one of them wild ones."

"Oh." She considered it, not at all sure what to say next.

Roland didn't notice the conversational lag. "So let me go do a round, see where everybody is, and as soon as it's set to go hot I'll give you a better overview and a run-through of how it works. Okay?"

"Sure," she said brightly, still a little hung up on the hellhound announcement. "No problem."

She watched the team work for another few minutes, then realized the rhythm of their movements was rocking her to sleep. She considered snagging a cup of coffee, but as soon as she did, they'd leave and she'd be up all night, exhausted but jittery.

With no better option and no way to rush the team along, she dove back into work. She studied the crime scene photos, trying to picture the scene. A dark night, and a man in a dark suit crossing a muddy park.

She closed her eyes, imagining a mist forming into a vampire, and the vampire bending over Braddock. Knocking him down, kicking him hard in the gut, and then swooping over him. While she watched, the creature bit down, then lifted his face to look directly into her eyes.

Luke.

Her heart pounded, but her body had turned to lead and she couldn't move, couldn't cry out, not even when the image shifted, and it wasn't Braddock that Luke was leaning over, but her.

His amber eyes never left hers as he slid inside her, her hips rising to meet him, wanting to take more of him, all of him. Needing him. Craving him.

His mouth curved with male satisfaction.

You're beautiful.

Don't stop.

He hadn't stopped. He'd touched her, played her, his skin smooth against hers, his lips soft, his words and body nothing but need and passion, lust and longing, and all of it focused on her as he moved in and out, taking and giving, flesh against flesh. He was poised above her, his strong arms supporting his weight as he looked at her with pure, sensual hunger.

A hunger she understood, for it burned within her, too.

Take me. Luke, please, please!

He smiled then, and for an instant, her heart skipped from pure joy. Then the smile widened to reveal the bloody tips of his fangs. And when he drew his head down toward her neck, she screamed.

"Ms. Constantine! Sara!"

She opened her eyes to find Roland shaking her shoulder, and she sat up, damp with sweat and completely mortified. "Sorry. Sorry. I fell asleep. I'm okay. Sorry."

He smiled good-naturedly. "It's normal."

"Sleep?"

"The nightmares. I do this for all the humans on staff. Gives me special insight, you know?" He grinned, yellow eyes flashing. "Consider it a breaking-in period."

"Right." She rubbed her hands over her face, then started when he shoved her phone in her face. "When you didn't wake up, I answered it. Says she's Emily. Says it's important."

She fumbled for the phone, clicked it over from mute to talk, and had barely managed a hello when Emily laid into her.

"Who the hell was that?"

"Security," she said. "Division 6 takes security very seriously." She ran her fingers through her hair and stood up, hoping that the movement would shake the image of Luke from her mind. She no longer had to worry about falling asleep. The nightmare had at least taken care of that.

"Wow," said Emily. "Guess Homeland Security really does begin at home. Marty told me about your promotion. I'm so proud of you. Insanely jealous, but also proud. And I miss you already."

"Listen, Em, I would say I miss you, too, but I saw you this morning. If you want me to give you a rundown of my first day, we could meet for a quick lunch tomorrow. Right now I'm totally wiped, and—"

"No, no," Emily said. "I mean, lunch is fine, I'd love to. But I'm not calling to congratulate you or gossip. I got called in tonight, Sara. Marty, Porter, the whole office. And I said I'd be the one to call and tell you."

"Tell me what?" Maybe her brain was still sloshy, but Emily wasn't making sense. Sara didn't work for the District Attorney's Office anymore, so why on earth would they notify her of a meeting? "What's going on?"

She heard Emily suck in a breath, felt the hairs on the back of her neck prickle. "Emily," she prodded.

"He escaped," Emily said, her voice flat. Dull.

"What?" Sara asked, her mind automatically flashing to Luke. "What are you—"

"Stemmons," Emily said.

Sara's knees went weak and she sank back onto the couch. "Don't be absurd. They transferred him to Corcoran this evening. He's in solitary by now, and good riddance to him."

"You're not listening," Emily said. "He got out."

"That's not possible."

"He had help, apparently. Both guards are dead."

Sara closed her eyes, imagining those poor guards riddled with bullets. "There was nothing in his profile to suggest he worked with anyone," Sara said. "Did he have a shiv? Hire a gunman?"

"No gun," Emily said. "Their throats were ripped out."

Sara's head swam. "Wait. Their throats?"

"Massive blood loss," Emily said. "Only get this—"

"No blood at the scene," Sara finished. "Has Porter contacted Nostramo Bosch?"

"Who?"

"My new boss."

"Oh." Emily paused. "I'm not sure."

"Tell him to, okay?" For that matter, Sara thought, she'd do the same. Because from what little she'd heard, they'd either completely missed the fact that Stemmons was a vampire, or he had help from the fang gang.

"Sure," Emily said. "You wanna tell me why?"

"The MO matches a Division matter," she said. "That's all I'm allowed to say."

"I'd tease you for that if this wasn't so serious."

"Task force?" Sara asked.

"Already in place. If this is crossing jurisdictions to bring in Homeland Security, then Porter's probably going to ask for you to be part of the team."

"I'm in the second Bosch okays it," Sara said. "We know Stemmons has at least two hidey-holes we never found. He'll rabbit to one of them."

"Yeah, we've notified the school district. All the principals in the L.A. area have already been contacted, and the police are set to do extra patrols around schools and public parks."

Sara nodded, wishing there was more they could do, but gratified to see how quickly the wheels had been put into motion. Over the course of four months, Stemmons had abducted, raped, and brutally killed seven girls between the ages of nine and fifteen. The girls were all blondes or redheads, with green eyes and tall, lanky builds.

Stemmons was smart and hungry, and Sara knew damn well he wouldn't stop. He'd kill again, and soon.

"Hopefully our intelligence on the locations is correct," Sara said. "It's going to be like looking for a needle in a haystack."

"We know who he is now," Emily said. "That's huge. He can't move around like he used to. His picture's everywhere. We'll get him, Sara. He can't hide forever."

"Thanks," Sara said, then felt stupid for saying it.

"You're okay?" Emily asked.

"I'm fine," she said, trying to decide if she really was. "No, I'm not. He'll kill again, Em. It's what he does."

"I know," Emily said. "We'll catch him."

"We better."

After she hung up, Sara frowned. All those dead girls, and now more little girls were out there, big red targets painted on their backs, and they didn't even know it.

With a sigh, she moved to the balcony and pressed her hands to the glass. Porter had been right. Before today, she hadn't known that vampires and daemons and shape-shifters existed. The creatures that lived in the dark, Porter had said. The things that crept out of nightmares.

Maybe so, but Stemmons was more of a monster than any she'd met in Division.

And what did it say about her that she'd gone to bed with a man she should have seen as a beast? That even once she knew of his crimes, she still couldn't keep him out of her head? Could still imagine the soft caress of his hand upon her skin?

He'd stood right there on this balcony and held her, looking out across the night with her, his arms engulfing her, his touch completing her.

He'd filled her, and that night—now locked tight in her memory—he'd been a man, not a monster.

♦

Xavier Stemmons stood in the dark, the swing set behind him casting eerie shadows in the light of the moon.

Now the playground was empty. Soon, though, the sun would rise, and they would come. The young girls with their soft bodies and beguiling eyes. They were youth; they were life. And he'd taken what they offered, drawing their essence in, capturing their light.

He realized now what a fool he had been.

It was their blood that was key. He should have consumed it, not merely drained it. Taking their life gave satisfaction, but only by taking their blood would he rise up. Would he *become*. Would he be freed of earthly bonds.

A god.

Without the blood, he couldn't rise like the Dark

Angel who had swooped in to rescue him. Who had delivered him from the fools who had sought to confine him, to constrain his gifts.

He breathed in deep of the chill night air, remembering the way she had burst into the van as the second guard had been about to lock the door. She'd moved with inhuman speed, so fast that the guard never even had time to reach for his weapon. With one bold stroke, she'd tumbled him to the ground, moving so fast Xavier hadn't even seen her fall upon him. Hadn't seen her sink her teeth into the guard's neck.

He'd seen only the result—the guard, dead on the van's floorboard, and the blood on her mouth as she'd smiled at him over the body, her eyes soft and sultry, her grin wicked.

The first guard—the driver—never came, and Xavier assumed she'd taken care of him first. Left him collapsed over the steering wheel, his neck gaping open, his life now in her belly.

She'd crawled toward him, a lioness hunting her prey, and for a moment he'd felt the cold pangs of fear. For a moment, he'd understood why the girls had cried out. They hadn't understood what he'd wanted from them, and they'd been afraid. Afraid as he was, even then.

Like his little girls, though, his fear was misplaced. She sought not to take his life, but to raise him to a higher level. She saw the depths of him, she said. Saw his great potential, and promised him not death, but everlasting life. Life, power, *light*.

Draw the light, draw the blood, and feed the angel.

She'd explained it all so beautifully. And now he knew what he had to do.

Now he knew the true nature of his work.

Satisfy the angel—do her bidding—and she would render upon him the glory of the world.

He spread his arms, embracing the night and imagining the satisfaction of the coming days.

He had freedom. He had life.

And he had purpose.

Xavier Stemmons was a man with renewed vision.

Free, and ready to drink deep of the light of youth.

CHAPTER 15

Luke steered the BMW with his knee as he rummaged futilely in the glove box, cursing Nick for not keeping even a pint of goddamn synthetic in the car.

Frustrated, he sat upright, his stomach clenching with the hunger, his blood burning with need. The fight with Hasik and Tinsley had sapped his strength, and he was cursing his lack of foresight. The daemon stirred more when the hunger was upon him, and without the strength to fight, the daemon rose and stretched and came out to play.

No.

With a low growl, he clutched the steering wheel and concentrated on driving. The more focused he kept his mind, the less his physical needs would intrude.

He saw the exit for downtown in the distance and crossed neatly over three lanes of traffic. Even at midnight, the traffic was dense, especially on a Friday, when the humans who lived mostly during the day came out to join all the creatures of the night.

He parked on the street across from Sara's building, then looked up, easily finding her balcony on the thirty-sixth floor. Were it not for the bands on his arm, he could have transformed, then arrived at her back door on windswept wings. Quick, simple, clean—and utterly impossible given his present circumstances.

Which left him to more mundane, human-oriented methods. Like the elevator. He would be revealed on the building's security footage, but that was a risk he would have to take. If all went as planned, Sara would be firmly aligned with him, and there would never be a need to pull the footage.

He moved toward the entrance, then stopped as the elevator doors within the lobby slid open. With a small hiss, he stepped back, his eyes fixed not on the faces of the pair now leaving the elevator, but on the badges clipped to their shirts.

Division 6—Security Section.

Damn.

He melted into the shadows, waiting until they exited the building, and as they passed by, Luke slipped in. A woman was on the elevator now, the doors beginning to slide closed. He called out, flashed a smile, and she leaned forward to hold the doors open.

He slid in, smelled the slow rise of desire as her eyes dragged over him. Inside him, the daemon stirred, awakened again by the burn of hunger in his blood and the need radiating off the woman beside him.

So easy, he thought, his head pounding and his fangs tingling. So easy to take. To feed.

The hunger pushed at him, growing stronger with the daemon's urgings, and resistance was hard-fought, painful. He kept his mouth shut and took in a breath through his nose, the simple act of drawing in air reminding him of the humanity he'd worked so hard to restore.

He did not harm the innocent. Not anymore.

And no matter how hard and how fast the hunger

came upon him—no matter what danger he could pose to Sara should he meet her when the hunger was at its most keen—still, he could not partake.

Not even a morsel.

Not even one tiny, delicious taste.

He couldn't.

He wouldn't.

"Thirty-five," he growled, ignoring the fear that now flashed in the woman's eyes. The way she backed away. "Punch the button for thirty-five."

She did, then pressed herself into the corner as Luke fisted his hands, willing the daemon back down, down, down.

Letting the hunger pass. Fighting not to lose himself.

The doors opened and he burst into the hall, slamming his fist through the drywall, trying to wrest control. Behind him, the woman jumped forward, her hand slapping hard at the button to close the elevator doors.

Good.

The sooner she was gone, the sooner he could see Sara.

Even her name calmed him, and he conjured her image, the mere thought of her soothing him, pushing down the last remnants of the daemon.

He stood there, breathing deep. Once he was certain that control had returned, he moved through the halls until he reached the condo directly beneath Sara's, 3519. He moved to 3521, and rapped sharply on the door. After a moment, he heard the low grumble of a human awakened from a deep sleep. The man who opened the door was tall and lanky and clad only in boxer shorts and a ratty flannel robe. "What the fuck?"

"Inspection," Luke said, mentally reaching in to twist the man's thoughts. "Nothing to be concerned about."

"Oh, well, if that's all."

The man stepped aside, and Luke moved through the condo toward the small balcony, even as the man rubbed his fingers through his hair and stumbled back into his bedroom.

On the balcony, he took his bearings. Sara's apartment was up one floor and over one unit. Easy enough to access. He climbed onto the railing, then it was a simple matter of leaping up and over.

He landed with a small thud on her ridiculously small balcony, then pressed himself up against the wall, out of sight of anyone who might be looking toward the door that, he was delighted to see, hung open.

A male voice drifted toward him—"That pretty much wraps it up"—followed by Sara's rich, "Thank you for doing this. I feel safer already."

Concentrating on remaining in the shadows, he eased forward until he had a view into the room. A group of security drones were filing out, and he caught the distinct whiff of hellhound coming from the creature talking to Sara.

As the hound pressed a small black control box into Sara's hand, Luke knew that he had no time to spare. He took one step closer to the open patio door and slipped inside, unseen.

♦

"So what you've got here is your standard portable control box," Roland said, tapping the black box that was about the size of a garage door opener. "Exactly like what we've installed by the front door, but it's portable."

"I figured that out just from the name," she said, unable to resist.

"You got a wit, kid. A genuine laugh riot. Now you wanna pay attention?"

Her lips twitched, but she nodded and focused on the box.

He indicated a row of buttons along the top labeled with the numbers zero through nine. "You use these buttons to key in your code when you set or deactivate the alarm. Pretty easy," he said, "so long as you don't forget your code."

She tapped her temple. "Got it."

"Good. And this little baby," he said, pointing to the red button situated right in the middle of the box, "is your good old panic button. Anything hinky goes down, you give it a push and you'll have all the muscle in the PEC at your side in seconds."

"How?"

"Whassat?"

"How would they get here in seconds? All that stuff you were doing to my apartment, wasn't that to make it so that folks couldn't get in like that?" she asked, adding a snap at the end of the question for emphasis.

"I like you, kid. I really like you. Good question. Shows you were listening. Remember how I said no one can port or mist into your apartment when you've got the system active? Well, you punch that button and all bets are off. Total deactivation, and at the same time, the cavalry comes running."

"Wow," she said. "That's impressive."

"We aim to please."

He crossed the room to close her balcony door, then returned to the front hallway. "You arm the system the second I'm gone," he said.

"Promise."

He gave her one last grin, then pulled the door shut behind him. She keyed in her code, saw the light on the panel switch to green, and smiled. Her own little fortress. Who would have thought?

And now, finally, she could go to bed.

She kept the control box with her, intending to keep it on her bedside table. She felt a tiny bit foolish doing it, but Roland had told her to. And the truth was that she couldn't deny the fact that she was antsy. Stemmons's escape, the truth about her father's murder. It all came together to make her edgy and out of sorts.

She hooked the box onto the waistband of her yoga pants, then reached inside her T-shirt to unfasten her bra. She did a Houdini move and pulled it out through her sleeve, then hung it on her bedroom doorknob. Without bothering to turn on her bedroom light, she headed toward her dresser, tugging off her earrings as she moved.

She'd put the tulips from Luke in a vase, and now she set the earrings in a crystal dish next to the flowers, forcing herself not to reach out and stroke the soft petals. She remembered the romantic thrill she'd felt when she'd discovered the flowers on her doorstep, the care she'd taken in arranging them just so. She'd fallen asleep that night gazing at them, feeling warm and cherished.

Even now, her body tingled when she looked at the

vase, her skin recalling the feel of his hands, her mouth recalling the taste of his skin.

She told herself she didn't want those feelings, those memories.

And that meant she didn't want the damn flowers.

Determined, she grabbed the bundle with both hands and yanked the stems straight up out of the vase. She dripped water over her dresser and floor before dumping the lot of them in the wastebasket beside her bed.

She looked down at the flowers, still vibrant, and told herself she'd done the absolute right thing.

With exhaustion dogging her every step, she unclipped the panic box, then wriggled out of her pants. She let them fall into a careless heap on the floor before she stepped over them and put the box on her bedside table. She needed sleep desperately, and neatness was the last thing on her mind.

Clad in T-shirt and panties, she slipped under the covers, sank deep into the overstuffed down pillow, and finally—*finally*—drifted off to sleep.

The night surrounded her, caressed her, and, yes, taunted her. The dream was coming. It came when she slept, and Sara knew that it would come now.

Except she wasn't asleep, so how could she dream? She was awake. Very awake, and aware of everything around her. The crunch of the gravel walking path beneath her shoes. The warm pressure of her daddy's hand engulfing hers. The moon that shone high in the sky.

And the faint but terrifying way that the trees seemed to be laughing as the two of them walked.

"Daddy?"

"It's nothing," he said. "Just the wind."

It wasn't the wind, though. It was Death. And Death swooped down on her father, fangs bared, face twisted with malice.

"Nothing you can do little girl. Nothing at all."

She wanted to fight, to pound, *to kill,* but all she could do was stand there, feet planted, body cold. Death rippled and changed. First Crouch. Then Stemmons. Then something faceless and formless. Something that latched onto her father's neck, releasing a fountain of blood. Warm and sticky, the liquid poured over her, and eight-year-old Sara did the only thing she could do—

She screamed and screamed and screamed and—

"Sara!"

Gentle hands. Holding her close. Murmuring her name.

"Wake up, Sara. It's a nightmare. A dream. You're safe. I've got you."

Luke?

She knew that voice. Knew that touch, and without thinking, she clung to him, pressing her face into his solid chest, losing herself in the strength he offered.

Luke was there.

She was safe.

CHAPTER 16

"Sara, hush. Hush, it's safe. You're safe." Her hands fisted in the thin cotton of his shirt, her body heaving as she sucked in air, growing calmer as he whispered soft words, even as he wanted to lash out in impotent fury at whatever horrible thing inhabited her dreams.

Remnants of sleep clung to her as he stroked her back, her hair, every touch sweet torture. The scent of fear that had engulfed her was fading, replaced now with comfort and faint tendrils of desire, and he knew it would be easy—so easy—to take exactly what he'd come for. *Sara.*

His body thrummed with the knowledge that he could have her, the allure all the more powerful because he knew that she still wanted him. Wanted his touch, his caress. Wanted to forget the nightmare from which she'd awakened and lose herself instead in pure sensual pleasure.

So easy.

He couldn't have planned it any better if he'd tried. Yet he hesitated, wanting to savor this moment, this one snapshot in time where she was once again with him, without guile or pretense, but because in his arms was where she wanted to be.

Her hands relaxed, her palms splaying out across his chest, her fingertips brushing bare skin where he'd ripped the shirt down the middle. The shock of her touch sent ripples of pleasure through him, and he tensed, fighting the urge to thrust her back onto the mattress and claim her mouth with his, not because that was what he had planned to do, but because right then he would go utterly mad if he couldn't touch her. Couldn't taste her. Couldn't lose himself inside her and pretend that nothing else existed and it was simply Luke and Sara, and screw all the rest of it.

"Luke..." Her voice, soft and dreamy, teased his senses. She nuzzled close, sighing, and something he identified as happiness bubbled up inside him, only to burst as she pulled back, the sweet fragrance of desire drowned out by the bitter stench of fear.

Her fingers, once soft, hardened as they shoved him away, and she scrambled backward until she was crouched on her pillow, the panic box from her bedside table now tight in her hand. The hem of her T-shirt barely covered her panties, and he could see her bare thighs, muscles tense and ready to leap.

She was breathing hard, her chest rising and falling in an effort to control her fear, and he held up a steadying hand, hoping to calm her down.

"Sara."

"No," she whispered, and right then he knew that he would have preferred that she scream at him. A scream was anger and rage. But this soft whisper held disappointment. And fear.

This time, the fear was directed at him, and the knowledge that he was the thing that now made her cower was almost enough to make him forget his mission and leave.

Except Luke never walked away from a mission.

More than that, though, he couldn't bear the thought that she was afraid of him. Whatever else there was between them, he didn't want it to be that.

"Why are you here?"

He needed to move closer, to try to calm her. Needed to do all those things he'd planned before he'd stepped into her apartment.

He stood up, determined to do exactly that, yet somehow unable to find the will to take the first step. In front of him, he caught a glimpse of red and looked down to see a dozen tulips dumped carelessly into her wastebasket.

In his long life, he'd suffered many an injury, and yet none cut so deep as the knife that Sara had just thrust into his heart. He bent to pull out a flower, then caressed the soft petal with his thumb.

When he looked up, she was eyeing him warily. "You don't have to fear me."

"I think I do." Her finger shifted, covering the panic button. Luke stiffened, waiting, knowing he should leave, should run. But he stayed, subjugated to her will, his life in her hands.

Slowly, she moved her finger away.

Slowly, he began to breathe.

"What are you doing here?" she asked again. "You're in jail. I watched them cart you down to the detention block. I watched you," she added, "in that cracker box they call a cell."

"You watched me?" The realization pleased him to an absurd degree.

"You're my damn defendant," she said curtly, not

meeting his gaze. "Of course I watched you. And now I want to know why you're here and not there."

"I'm here to talk to you."

"To talk to me?" Her voice rose with incredulity. "About what? The weather? No, wait. Maybe we can talk about local bars. Bars where badass vampires go to pick up prosecutors. Seems to me that would make one hell of a conversation opener." She snapped off her words, as if embarrassed that she'd shown her hand.

"No," he said, determined that she know the truth. "There was no ulterior motive between us. I saw you in the bar. You pleased me, and I wanted you. Hungered for you even as I do now. I took only what you were willing to give."

Guilt washed over him, because though his intentions that night had been innocent, now they were anything but.

"Don't," she said, shaking her head, her eyes sad. "Don't come here with sweet words and try to twist me up in knots. It won't work."

"Do you want me to go?" The words were out before he had considered them, and he stood frozen, waiting for and fearing her answer.

"How did you even get here?" she asked, and he relaxed ever so slightly and took a single step toward her even as he reached up and opened his shirt, revealing the detention device.

"Advocate-escorted furlough," he said. "And this band ensures that I do not run. I did not break out of jail, Sara, but I did abandon my escort."

She licked her lips, a simple motion he found unbelievably sensual. "Why?"

He took another step toward her. "To see you."

She shook her head. "You shouldn't be here."

"And yet who would have comforted you had I not come?" Another step, and he was able to sit on the edge of the bed, the tulip still in his hand. "What were you dreaming?"

She met his eyes, hers defiant, yet still wary. "Of monsters."

"What kind of monsters fill your dreams, Sara?" He would slay them if he could. Kill the monsters and free her from the horrors of the night.

She watched him, her hands tight on the blanket, her mind calculating. He tilted his head, his nostrils flaring, and was relieved to find that the scent of fear was fading.

"Sara?"

"He escaped," she said. "The serial killer I told you about—the one who murdered all those little girls. He escaped. More than that, he had help. The kind of help that walks at night and sucks blood—maybe you're familiar with the breed? And now he's gone and by now he probably has the next girl picked out. And it's pissing me off," she said, voice rising and tears welling. "Really pissing me off that I did everything right. *Everything.* And still he's free. He's evil, and he's out there, and he's going to kill again."

Luke tensed, his body going cold. "Are you in danger?" It was a foolish question. No matter how she answered, he would consider her in need of protection until Stemmons was caught.

"I'm okay," she said, her hand reaching out to cup his before she quickly jerked it back. Even so, the brief touch eased him. Her actions did not match her words, and for that reason he was still in the room. Still basking in the pleasure of simply being near her.

"I almost wish I were in danger," she added, the sentiment making him grow cold. "I can defend myself against the things that creep in the night. The victims, the girls, they don't know what he is."

"I would destroy him," Luke said, the thought of a man who preyed as Stemmons did on young girls sickening him. "If I could find him for you, I would gladly destroy the beast."

"You'd kill him," she said, her voice flat.

"I would," he admitted. "With no hesitation, and no regrets. Does that offend you?"

Once again, she licked her lips, her gaze drifting from him to the table beside her bed. "It offends the law," she said simply.

"Your system isn't a panacea, Sara. Sometimes the law is insufficient to render justice."

She tilted her head, looking at him with grave intensity. "Is that why you killed Braddock?"

"What? Have I so quickly been tried and convicted?"

"Luke." Her voice was hard.

He shook his head. "I would not deny you the pleasure of doing your job."

"Dammit, Luke—"

"But let me ask you this," he said. "Did the system find justice for your father? For the wife and daughter he left behind?"

She paused, her expression darkening, and he feared she wouldn't answer. "No," she finally admitted. "But the system isn't perfect."

"Then why live within its strictures?"

"Because there are lines, Luke. And someone has to draw those lines. The courts do that. Not me. Not you."

On the contrary, he had drawn that line on many occasions, and still believed himself justified in doing so. That wasn't a debate for tonight, however.

Still...

"Your father's killer," he began, "was found dead not long after he was released?"

"Left for dead in a park," she said.

"And does *that* offend you?"

"No," she said, without hesitation. "He took my father from me. Whoever killed Jacob Crouch is a goddamn hero."

He suppressed a smile. "Perhaps we are not so far apart after all."

She shook her head. "Just because I celebrated doesn't make it right. He was my father," she said with a hitch in her breath. "I'm not supposed to see clearly."

"Tell me about him," Luke said gently, both because he wanted to soothe her and because he wanted to know her history, wanted to know from where she'd come.

She met his eyes, but did not speak. He held his breath, longing to hear her words. To know that she had moved past fear and hurt and had, if only for a moment, found the place where it was only Luke and Sara.

"He used to tell me stories when I got scared," she said. Her expression remained flat, fixed. And just when he was about to give up hope, a soft smile touched her lips. "He'd hold me and spin tales about anything that came to mind." She relaxed as she spoke. "Since he was a history professor, what came to mind was usually an obscure story about a forgotten Roman general. When I was little, the stories lulled me back to sleep. When I was older, I'd pretend to have bad dreams just so I could stay up late and listen to him."

"I had a daughter once," Luke said. "I would do the same for her. Soothe her with stories until she fell asleep in my arms." Automatically, he reached into his pocket, his fingers seeking the gold-coiled serpent ring he'd given Livia on her fifth birthday. Even through his daemonic haze, he'd thought to keep it, a reminder of the family he'd once had and a talisman from which he could draw strength to soothe the daemon. He had not been without it since that fateful day, but it was gone now, wrenched from him and put into an envelope with his other personal effects.

The softness in Sara's eyes worked like a balm against the sadness that had welled in his heart. "I bet she was very pretty."

"That she was," he said. "And with the sweetest disposition."

She started to ease toward him, then stopped, carefully planting herself on the far side of the bed from him. "Luke—"

He lifted the tulip, wanting to silence her, not wanting to hear that he needed to leave, especially since all he wanted to do was stay. "I'm sorry you didn't like the flowers."

Her cheeks bloomed pink. "I liked them."

He glanced at the wastebasket.

She lifted an eyebrow, amused. "That? That's because I didn't much like *you*."

"And now?"

She swallowed, hesitated. "Don't press your luck," she said, but there was no way she could hide the scent of her arousal or the way her nipples peaked beneath the thin T-shirt.

He inched closer to her, a single pillow the only barrier between them. He took it and tossed it onto the floor.

"You can't be here," she said, but she didn't retreat.

"But I am." He reached out, wanting to touch her. Knowing this was why he'd come, this sweet seduction. This wasn't about plans or plots or exit strategies. It was about Sara. The woman kneeling before him. The woman leaning in, ever so slightly, but enough to fill his heart with hope.

"You touch me, Sara, in ways that it would be better that you did not. I know I should leave—know even that you should push me away. And yet I cannot stop."

He reached out, brushing a hand to her cheek. He'd planned this, yet there was no lie in his movements, no deceit in his desire.

The tempo of her heartbeat increased beneath his fingers, and he thought of the blood that flowed in her veins. Sweet, delicious, like the woman herself. He thought, and he wanted, and the hunger that he had been fighting for hours surged within, the daemon crying for release.

He beat both back down, subordinating them to his desire, now a living, breathing thing. "Sara," he said, voicing the only word that came to mind. "Please."

♦

Luke eased closer, and now he was right in front of her, mere inches away. So close she could reach out and touch him, if only she wanted to.

She told herself she didn't want to.

Since she didn't seem to be listening to herself, she scooted off the bed, taking the control box with her as she stalked into her living room.

"Sara." He was right behind her.

She moved her lips, managed to form words. "I can't."

"You can," he said. She saw her own lust reflected in the hard planes of his face. Lust, and something else. A hunger that both frightened and excited her.

She swallowed, fever gripping her body as he moved closer still. "You need to go."

His smile was slow and full of promise. "I still have time."

"I won't risk my job for you." Her mouth was dry and she wanted to put her hand on his chest and push him back a step, if only so that her mind would clear of the buzz he was generating. Her body might not care what he was, but she did. He was the defendant. He was a murderer; she was certain of it. And she was the one who would seal his prison cell tight.

"Leave," she said, forcing her chin up. "Leave now."

"No."

"No?"

"You don't want me gone."

"Yes." The word came out weak, so she tried again. "Yes, I do."

"And yet here I stand, when you need only push one small button to summon the power of the PEC to drag me off." His eyes dipped down to the control box in her hand, and then back to her face. "If you wanted me gone, I wouldn't still be standing here."

"No," she whispered, but there was little conviction in the word. "I'll do it. I'll push the panic button."

"No, you won't."

"Why not?"

"Because you're not panicking." And to prove it, he brushed his palm softly over her nipple, sending fingers of fire shooting through her. Making her even more wet. Making her crazy.

She squirmed, her back against the wall, trapped between it and this man. She needed to get away, to get free. Because this wasn't right. He was everything she despised. A killer. A liar. A criminal.

A vampire.

And yet he was there, touching her, wanting her. And damn her all to hell, she wanted him, too.

"Go," she said, because if she didn't say it, she would truly be lost.

He only grinned, then brought his mouth in close to hers. "No," he whispered, the single word barely more than a brush of air across his lips. She felt her body tremble, and she stifled the little moan of pleasure that bubbled up when his lips grazed her cheek, her ear, her hair.

"Sara," he whispered, and pulled her close, his large hands splayed out against her back, his erection pressed hard against her.

Ready, so ready.

"Luke," she managed. "No."

But he merely smiled. "Quiet now. My time is ticking

away." Before her sluggish mind could process, he took her mouth in his. And though she knew she shouldn't—knew she would kick herself black and blue later—she lost herself in the kiss, her pulse tripping as his busy hands slipped inside her shirt and over her bare back. Her breath hitched as his lips danced down along her neck even as he murmured soft words that seemed to shoot straight through her, making her warm and wet and ready.

"Sara," he murmured. "By the gods, Sara."

She melted beneath his words, her mind knowing only a desperate, urgent desire. She let the control box tumble to the ground, then thrust her hands into the back pocket of his jeans and urged him closer, until she was trapped tight between the wall and this man who wanted to consume her.

So help her, she wanted him to.

His hand grasped the hem of her shirt, tugging it upward, and she lifted her hands in assistance. As soon as the shirt was tossed aside, he grabbed her wrists, holding them above her head as his mouth dipped to her breast. His tongue teased her nipple before pulling away, the sensation of cool air on damp flesh intensely erotic, and she writhed with need, silently begging him to touch her, to finish what he started.

He needed very little encouragement. She wore only panties now, and he bent low, dropping to his knees in front of her.

As she gasped, he pressed his hands to the inside of her thighs, the pads of his thumbs playing with the elastic of her panties, teasing her mercilessly. His mouth soon joined in the torment, his fingertips drawing her panties down so that his tongue could lave.

She buried her fingers in his hair, clutching him for support as her legs trembled and her knees threatened to no longer hold her. "Luke," she murmured, wanting to feel the press of his body against hers. Wanting to feel his lips, his tongue. Wanting to taste him and tease him. "Luke, please."

She eased him up, then took his mouth hungrily in hers. She hooked one leg around his waist, locking him in place, wanting him, all of him.

"Please," she whispered, fumbling for his fly. Beneath her hand, his erection strained, and he growled low in his throat, the desire she heard making her even more wet. More ready.

"Sara," he whispered, his voice raw, and yet still soft. Still tender.

And then, suddenly, it wasn't.

She felt the change in him instantly. A stiffness in his back. His hands holding her rather than caressing her. He'd shut down, and she didn't understand why.

Alarmed, she pushed back against the wall, a thousand recriminations running through her head. *What was she thinking? Was she insane? Had the craziness of the day fried her brain?*

But all those thoughts vanished when she saw his face.

When she saw his fangs.

Her hand flew to her mouth and she fell to the ground as her feet slid out from under her, her hand closing over the control box.

"Sara," he said, moving away, his hand held out in supplication. "No. I wouldn't. I didn't—"

It didn't matter. She looked at him, and she saw the beast that had killed her father.

Her own scream ripped from her throat as she fell back into her memories, her last coherent thought to press her finger down—hard—and trigger the alarm.

CHAPTER 17

She shivered, couldn't stop shaking, the cold threatening to consume her.

He'd changed, become a monster.

Right before her very eyes, he'd become the thing she most despised.

Then he'd run, ripping open the patio door, leaping from the balcony into the thick, black Los Angeles night.

A gray mist filled the room, and even as her foggy brain registered that the mist must be the security team, Sara scrambled to her feet and stumbled toward the patio. Hands on the railing, she breathed deep and looked out over the dark, empty night, her eyes searching futilely for Luke. *He deserved it. Whatever happened to him, he deserved it.*

He'd been playing her. Manipulating her.

And if he was dead, well, she told herself that was absolutely fine with her.

She told herself that, but she didn't entirely believe it. Not when she remembered the way he'd held her and calmed her. And not when she remembered the shock on his face when he'd bared his fangs. The horror and self-loathing in his eyes.

She wanted to trust him. Dear God, how she wanted to believe he'd come for no ill purpose. Her mind was in a jumble, though, and right then she didn't know what to believe.

"Constantine." The deep voice held a hint of a Slavic accent, and she cringed as someone draped her favorite afghan over her shoulders. She pulled it tight around her, suddenly realizing she was clad only in panties, then turned to face a creature—a man?—that seemed to be formed entirely of pitch-black smoke beneath a filthy gray cloak. She looked into the creature's face, into the dark pits that served as eyes, and knew that nothing Luke ever did could spook her as much as this being, whatever it was.

"The dwelling is clean," it said, in a voice that chilled her to the bone. Behind it, three similar creatures, all clad in the same monklike robes, glided through her apartment. "For what purpose did you summon the Shade?"

If she'd known what she was summoning, she certainly wouldn't have. As it was, though, all she could do was shake her head. The Shade studied her, the inspection leaving her so cold she was certain she would never feel warm again. Then it passed by her, gliding to the balcony railing. Its hand, she noticed, sat not *on* the stone railing, but instead settled inside it. A specter. A ghost. Formless. And, she was certain, desperately dangerous.

Once again it turned, and she trembled as small creatures—specters themselves—skittered through the depths of smoke inside the Shade's robes. Maggots, rats. The scavengers of death.

"It fled," the Shade said. "That which scared you. It slipped back into the night."

"I—" She licked her lips, then swallowed. Wanting to answer, but not knowing what to say.

The truth? That was certainly her usual MO. But then why weren't the words tumbling out?

He'd attacked her, after all. Almost bitten her. Almost ripped her neck out the same way that bastard Crouch had attacked her father, draining the life from him and leaving him in a heap in the mud while an eight-year-old girl whimpered.

So why wasn't she pointing in the direction he'd jumped and screaming for these creatures to find him and drag him back to hell where he belonged?

Because when he broke away, Luke had been in hell already. She'd seen it in his eyes. Crouch had killed, but Luke had pulled away rather than harm her.

More than that, she'd seen the expression on his face. Horror. Absolute horror.

"Sara Constantine." The Shade's deep voice thrummed within her, like a heavy bass beat. "I ask again. For what purpose did you summon us?"

She didn't answer. *Couldn't* answer. Couldn't condemn Luke with the truth. And yet despite the pain in her heart, she knew that she couldn't completely trust him, either.

♦

Something was prodding him.

Luke blinked, then sputtered, surprised to find himself floating in inky black waters. Surprised even more to find himself looking into two concerned brown eyes.

"Oh, wow. Holy crap. Hold on. Hold on." The

woman couldn't be more than twenty-three, her wild mass of blond curls pushed back with a headband, the panic coming off her in waves. She wore bright blue workout clothes and held a pool skimmer on a long handle. *The pool.* He remembered the elevator panel: Fitness Center/Pool Deck. Fourth Floor.

He'd jumped. Thirty-two stories down to the pool deck.

No wonder his head was throbbing.

"Can you grab it? Come on. Grab it, okay?"

He did, his fingers screaming with pain as they closed around the cool metal of the pole. She tugged, and he tried to move his limbs, tried to help, but there was no help to be had. His limbs were utterly unwilling to function.

His mind, however, was firing back to life, the lingering scent of Sara's hair dancing on the edge of his memory, along with the fear he'd seen in her eyes. A terror that had done more damage to him than any stake ever could.

"Did you jump? Did you fall? God, how high were you? Damn you landed hard! I heard it from all the way in the gym, and then there you were." Her arms were under his, tugging him toward the steps. "God, oh God. You're a mess. I gotta get my phone. Gotta call someone. You need a hospital. Your leg, you know, it really shouldn't look like that."

She shifted to leave, but he managed a small sound, and she stopped. "Huh?"

"Stay." *Blood.* He needed to heal, and the hunger was on him like a living thing.

"I'm not gonna leave you. Honest. But I gotta call

someone. You need help, and there's no one else here. Never is in the middle of the night."

"Time," he said, his voice little more than a whispered croak.

"Huh? Oh." She twisted around to look at a distant clock, revealing a long, taut neck, and he trembled, knowing what he had to do and hating himself for it. She turned back and told him the time, her own words sealing her fate. Because time was running out.

He had no other choice. No other options.

He could feed. Or, he could die.

"Look," he whispered.

She leaned closer, her brow furrowed. "What?"

"Look," he repeated, then turned his head to meet her eyes. He was tired, weak. But his will was strong. And this girl had no barriers, no natural defenses. He slid inside—the hunger firing even more as he did—and made her mind his own.

"Closer," he said. She whispered the word in response, then leaned toward him, turning her head to expose her neck.

His body tensed, anticipating. His fangs extended as the hunger craned up inside him, sniffing. Marking territory. Moving in for the kill.

Come to me.

There was no longer a need to speak. Their minds were one, and she slid into the water, curved herself against him. He could smell her skin, could see her blood pumping in her vein, and though he told himself he did not want this—that he'd forsworn what he was about to take—his senses were primed. Ready. Keening with need.

He shut off his mind. Shut off the recriminations.

Instinct took over. The pure, clean instincts of a predator. The desperate, dark instincts of the beast.

Her skin was firm and tasted vaguely of salt and chlorine. Then his fangs pierced the dermis and the arterial wall, and the blood began to flow, warm and sweet and full of life.

He wanted this, this sharing. This *connection*. Praise the gods, he wanted this desperately—but not with this woman. *Sara*. He wanted her in his arms, intimately enfolded in them. Their bodies pressed together, his mouth on her neck.

He groaned, drinking deep, his cock hardening with need, responding to the woman in Luke's head and not the woman pressed close against him.

He'd been so long, so very long, without the intimacy of a true feeding, and as he drank—as he healed—he let his mind linger where it should not. On fantasy and fiction. On Sara, warm and alive beneath him, her blood calling to him, her breath on his skin, her lips whispering his name.

She healed him. Her blood, making him whole. Bones knitting, bruises fading, strength returning.

Sara.

His mind called to her. Sought her—

Annie.

—and then slammed back when he found not the woman he craved but the woman he'd taken into his arms.

Annie.

The thought was weak. Fading. Her strength dissipating even as his own grew.

My name is Annie.

With a jolt, he broke the mental connection, then gasped as he drew away and saw the damage to her neck. To her.

Her body was fading along with her mind, and he blocked the images. Of Annie. Of Livia. Of Sara.

He had to act quickly, had to stay in control.

She looked up at him, eyes wide in her pale, gaunt face. He needed to leave. It was nearly time. He had to get back, for Tasha, for the *kyne*. He had to leave.

And yet, could not.

"Annie," he said, shaking her shoulders. "Look at me. *Look at me.*"

"Sara?" she whispered, the word like air through dry lips that barely moved. "Who is Sara?"

"Only you," he said, meeting her eyes. "Right now, it's only you."

He brought his own wrist up to his mouth, then bit down, opening a vein. He pressed the wound to her mouth. "Drink," he said, then held her head as she suckled him, stroked her hair as one might a child nursing from its mother. "That's the way. Not too much, you must be careful."

Too much blood, and she would not simply heal, but would fall in tune with him, giving him access to her fears, her hopes, her desires. Even more, and the curse *vampyre* would embrace her. He would have neither for her, so he watched her carefully, and the moment a hint of strength returned—the moment he was certain she would last at least as long as it took for help to arrive— he pulled his wrist away.

"More," she said.

He didn't answer. Instead, he rose up out of the water, the girl in his arms, and carried her to a deck chair. He took a towel from a nearby trunk and spread it over her, gratified by the steady, strong beat of her heart. He brushed his fingertips over her cheek. "Sleep now. Sleep, and heal."

She drifted off, and he stood, saw the time, and swore.

Think, dammit, think.

He tilted his head, looking up toward Sara's balcony. Perhaps, he thought, there was hope after all.

CHAPTER 18

Nick woke in the dark with a raging headache and a boiling anger. It had been one hell of a long time since he'd been clocked—longer still since he'd been taken by surprise—and he wasn't sure who he was angrier with, himself or Luke.

His head pounded and he amended that thought. *Luke.* He was most definitely angrier with Luke.

He shifted, trying to get his bearings, his vampiric eyes adjusting to the pitch black of the tight receptacle into which he'd been dumped.

"Damn the bastard," he murmured as he kicked up, the bones of some human cracking beneath him as he used the strength in his legs to push the top off the sarcophagus. It fell to the floor, the reverberating crash of stone against stone cathartic.

His friend had put him in one hell of a sticky situation. "Goddamn arrogant fool."

"I'm guessing you're referring to Dragos, and not whoever you're sharing that sarcophagus with." Ryan Doyle's gritty voice greeted Nick as he grabbed the sides of the coffin and pulled himself up. He tightened his grip, forcing himself not to leap out and close his hands around Doyle's neck.

"Get the fuck out of here," he said, with admirable calm. "You've got no right to intrude on an advocate-escorted furlough."

"Got a point," Doyle said, then made a show of looking around. "'Cept I don't see you escorting anyone. You see anybody else in here, Sev?"

"Not unless dem bones gonna rise again." Agent Tucker took a step toward Nick, then flashed a smug smile as he peered down into the coffin. He looked back at Doyle. "Nah. They don't look the type."

"Nice job, Counselor," Doyle said. "Lost your client, and now the sorry SOB's going down." He punctuated the remark with a shit-eating smile that had Nick leaping from the coffin to land a rock-solid punch on Doyle's smug, sorry-ass face.

"Motherfucker!" Doyle said, flying right back on Nick, eyes red, veins bulging, skin shifting to a slightly greenish hue.

And every ounce of that famous temper pumping right beneath the surface.

"Whoa, whoa, whoa!" Strong arms grabbed Nick's from behind, tugging him away from Doyle, who looked about to explode. "Let's settle down, boys."

"Let. Me. Go." Nick could break away, no question about that. Tucker was strong, but he was only human.

"Don't even think about it," Doyle growled, those red eyes tight on Nick's face. "Maybe you can take my boy, and maybe you can't, but I know you can't take me. Think you learned that lesson years ago."

Nick shook his arms free from Tucker's grip, stood tall, his hands fisted at his sides. "Things can change over the centuries, Doyle."

"Things, maybe. Not people. Not vampires." He flipped open his phone, pressed a speed-dial number. "And certainly not Dragos. Learned that centuries ago, too." The phone was set on speaker, and Nick heard the electronic buzz as it rang at the other end, then the computerized voice requesting identification.

"This is Agent Ryan Doyle, badge number 1026C, reporting violation of furlough by suspect Lucius Dragos. Requesting activation of mobile detention measures and immediate termination of subject Dragos."

"Goddammit, no!" Nick yelled, leaping forward again.

"Acknowledged and analyzing. Please hold for verification of subject termination."

CHAPTER 19

Sara raced through the halls of Division, part of her wondering what the hell she was doing, and another part fearing she was going to be too damn late.

"*No,*" she yelled into the phone at the Security Section desk drone. "Constantine. With a C, dammit, and I'm prosecuting this case with Nostramo Bosch. You engage that security device and I will have your ass in a sling."

"A termination request has been input," the drone said.

"And I'm overriding it, dammit." She didn't have a clue whether she had authority to do that, but she damn well intended to make the argument. She hurried onto the elevator and pressed the button for sublevel nine. "Just wait for me. Don't do anything until I get there."

No answer.

She pulled the phone away from her ear and stared at it. *Call failed.* No signal.

Dammit, dammit, dammit.

She jammed her thumb on the elevator button, as if that would make the thing move faster, but she couldn't simply stand and do nothing. Dear God, what if they did it? What if they killed Luke?

She closed her eyes and forced herself to breathe, remembering the way his voice had sounded when she'd answered the phone in her apartment only minutes earlier. She'd already dismissed the Shade—claiming a nightmare and a foolish impulse to push the panic button—and she'd been sitting on the floor, her back to the glass, trying to figure out what had come over her. Why she'd let Luke stay.

Why she'd let him touch her like that.

"Sara," he'd said. "I need help."

She'd remembered the way his face had hardened, the way he'd bared his fangs, and she'd almost hung up.

"Wait," he'd demanded, and so help her, she had.

"What is it, Luke? What could possibly make you think you have the right to call me now?"

"No right," he'd said. "No expectation. Just hope, Sara." He needed intervention, he'd said. The fall to her pool deck had injured him, and there was no way he could return to where he'd left his advocate before Security Section activated the stake around his heart.

"I'm going back to Division," he'd said, "but even that's no guarantee. I need help, Sara. Will you speak for me?"

She hadn't answered, her mind too filled with the remnants of both fear and longing, but after she'd hung up, she'd dialed Division.

She told herself that she was stepping in because she wouldn't see a man condemned without a trial, but she knew it was a lie. He'd touched something within her and she had to know why. Had to understand more fully this burning within her. A burning for *him*. This vampire. This murderer.

The elevator doors slid open and she raced through, pounding the redial button even as her eyes scoured the hall for someone with authority. But down here, where Security and Detention were accessed through long concrete halls, there was no one but her. "Is he there?" she demanded the moment the drone answered the call. "Is Dragos there?"

"He arrived," the drone said.

"Then you damn well better make sure he's not ash by the time I get there," she said, and when she finally burst through the door, there he was. Standing right in front of her, dark and dangerous and smolderingly sexy. She gasped, in both surprise and pleasure. Not only because of the heat she saw in his eyes, but because he was looking at her with a combination of gratitude and longing so intense it weakened her knees.

"Ms. Constantine," he said, his voice a caress. "You came."

"I—" She swallowed, the sensual maelstrom building within her almost overwhelming her. She turned away, afraid he'd see too much on her face, and focused on her nemesis the security drone, a tiny creature with bulbous eyes and a high-tech headset.

"Ms. Constantine," the drone said with a small nod.

"Call Leviathin if you have to, but if Dragos is here, termination serves no purpose."

His lips pursed as he tapped something onto his computer, then leaned in close to a monitor. "Director Leviathin concurs," he said, and Sara had to grab onto the table to not sag in relief. "Termination denied."

She allowed herself one deep breath, then squared her shoulders and looked at the officer standing with Luke, Officer Quai according to his name tag. "Get him out of that contraption," she said. "And then give us a minute.

I need to talk to him before you take him back to his cell."

As she watched, Quai went about his work, unfastening the clasp between the two binder cuffs at Luke's wrists and securing one to the wall before instructing Luke to pull his now-free arm out of his coat. Then he had Luke shift and repeated the process with the second arm.

Quai laid the long black coat on a nearby metal desk, and the sight of Luke without his coat caught her attention in ways that had her feeling decidedly unprosecutorial.

In her apartment, he had not taken it off, though she'd been stripped almost bare. The memory teased her, and she watched with unabashed fascination as Luke now stood in shirtsleeves, his biceps straining under black cotton.

He was powerful.

He was dangerous.

And tonight, he'd held her close, comforting her, protecting her even in her dreams.

"Keep looking," he said, making her jump. "Perhaps you'll see something in me you didn't see before."

"I was thinking," she said. "Not looking."

"About me?" That generous mouth barely moved, but even so, she had the impression that he was smiling at her. Once again, she had to push back a wave of surprise at the utter incongruity of it all. He was in prison, for Christ's sake. His shirt pulled up to reveal an achingly familiar torso, over which was strapped a device that could have killed him only moments prior. Yet he was standing tall and commanding, the room filled with the essence, the power, of Lucius Dragos.

"Ah, then," he said, knowingly. "It was about me."

To her utter mortification, Quai took that moment to swivel his slightly orange head around. His large eyes narrowed as he looked at her, and she transferred to him the glare she'd earlier aimed at Luke. He immediately turned back and concentrated on removing the metal band from Luke's chest.

"As a matter of fact, I *was* thinking about you," she said, delighted to see surprise flicker in his eyes. Well, why not? Two could play the one-upmanship game. "I was thinking that I should avoid talking to you."

"Is that so? Any particular reason?"

"Me prosecutor. You defendant. And a defendant with an advocate." She upped the sugar value of her smile. "I'm afraid I can't talk to you without your advocate present."

"So far, I'd say you're failing miserably at that task." She had the impression that his lips quivered, but his expression hadn't changed.

She wanted to laugh, but bit back the urge. "I guess I'll have to put more effort into it. Probably easier once you're gone. Out of sight, out of mind."

"I sincerely hope that is not the case," he said, with such heat in his voice it made her knees go weak.

Quai stepped back, having released Luke from his binds, though one ankle was now bound to the thick concrete by a short length of heavy metal chain. "Give us a moment," she said, in a voice that broached no argument. Quai nodded, then stepped out, the security drone following behind.

"Sara," Luke said the moment the door closed behind them. "Thank you."

"No problem," she said, keeping her face bland and hoping he couldn't see beneath the mask. "I wasn't going to have my first big trial at Division ripped away from me just because the defendant went and got himself staked."

"I can see how that would be an inconvenience to you."

She stifled a smile, then almost immediately turned serious. "Luke, you jumped from the thirty-sixth floor. I've read up, and there's no way you could just walk away from a fall like that. Not when you couldn't transform."

A muscle twitched in his cheek. "Do you have a question for me, Counselor, or are you merely stating facts?"

"I want to know how you survived. Look at you." Lord knew she was looking hard enough at him. "You're perfect. Not a scrape, not a bruise." She moved closer. "How, Luke? How can that be?"

"You know what I am, Sara."

"You fed." She closed her eyes. "Oh, God..."

"Sara." His hand clutched her around the wrist.

"Tell me." She looked up, saw the pain and regret on his face. "Tell me now before I find out some other way."

"I fell to your pool deck," he said. "And, yes, I was injured." He looked hard at her. "The damage could have healed with time. But I did not have time."

"The furlough," she said, and he nodded.

"Do you know what heals a vampire, Sara?"

"Blood," she said, then closed her eyes.

"There was a girl."

"Oh, God."

"Sara."

She shook her head. "Give me a second. Give me a second to get my head around this." She forced herself not to close her eyes. Not to imagine him, mangled and broken beside the pool. And, God help her, she forced herself not to wish that it had been her at his side to help him heal. "Is she alive? This girl?"

"Yes. She will be fine."

Something in his voice caught her attention. "Tell me."

"The hunger was upon me," he said, and she recalled the raw need she'd seen on his face before she'd punched the panic button. "I had...lost control, was still in the throes of that need, that hunger, when I drank from the girl. Annie." He drew in a breath. "I took too much," he said. "Took her to death's door."

"What did you do?"

"A vampire's blood heals," he said. "I gave. She drank."

He closed his eyes, and for one single, shame-filled moment, Sara despised the woman, this girl who had shared something so horribly intimate with Luke.

Disturbed and embarrassed, she looked away, not wanting to picture him cradling the girl, helping her, keeping death at bay. She tried to focus on his file, on all the people he was suspected of killing. The list was long and colorful, yet it was this girl who filled her thoughts.

"You were almost out of time," she said. "Why save her?" Why save one girl when he'd so boldly killed so many others?

"Because she was innocent," Luke said, and for a moment, a brief, fleeting moment, Sara had a glimpse into the heart of the man.

"Will she . . ." She tried to imagine the horror of being thrust into that world, feeling the daemon rise. Of becoming the very thing that had killed her father. "I mean, will she be a vampire, too?"

"No." The word was quick and sharp and said with such force that she took a step back. "I gave her only enough to keep her safe until help arrived. I would not turn her. I—" He broke off, and though his voice remained steady she saw the pain on his face, and she wondered.

"Luke," she said, stepping forward, wanting to comfort even though she didn't understand. Her fingers brushed his, the contact enough to fire her senses, and then the door burst open.

She jumped back, guilty, as the most gorgeous man she'd ever seen in her life got right in her face.

"What the *fuck* are you doing with my client?"

"Nicholas . . ." Sara didn't miss the warning in Luke's voice. Neither, apparently, did his advocate.

"Dammit, Luke—"

"No," Luke said. "I chose to speak to her on my own. I'll not have my judgment questioned."

The advocate stood stock-still, clearly not liking the situation. "We'll talk about this later."

"I have no doubt," Luke said. To Sara, he added, "My advocate, Nicholas Montegue."

"So I gathered."

Nicholas turned his attention to her. "Whatever you

talked about—whatever he told you—it was said without his advocate, and it's out of bounds. Are we clear on that?"

She stiffened, her arms crossed across her chest. "Thank you for the lesson, Mr. Montegue. But I assure you I know the law."

"In that case, you know that I'm entitled to a moment alone with my client."

She nodded, agreeing with Montegue's words, but her eyes were on Luke.

"We will speak again," Luke said to her. She nodded, then stepped from the room, and realized her lips were curved with anticipation.

CHAPTER 20

"Are you not afraid of the dark?"

Xavier shivered, the Dark Angel's breath on the back of his neck like the whisper of a goddess.

"My Angel," he said, bending his head low to show his submission. "The dark gives me strength."

She laughed, as if delighted with his answer, then moved around the swing set to face him. Her beauty stunned him, her eyes compelling. Radiant eyes that he would follow forever.

But it was her fangs that he desired. He would become as she was—she'd promised him so. He had only to prove himself worthy, and then he would be able to take their light with a kiss. A special kiss to the neck, and their light would be his.

He shuddered in anticipation.

She lifted her wrist to her mouth then tore her flesh. "Drink," she said, thrusting her arm toward him.

"My Angel," he said, his heart leaping. "You would change me?"

"I would make you strong," she said. "The change you must earn. Now drink."

She didn't have to ask again. His mouth closed over her wrist and he drew in the sweet, tangy taste of her blood. He drew it in, and felt the power thrum through him. So much power in her, and soon, when he'd proved his worth, that power would be his, too. His to control. To wield.

He would be invincible. A true creature of the night.

And they could never again stop him from taking what he desired.

"If the dark is your strength," she asked, swaying slightly as he drank from her, "then why do you hunt during the day?"

He drew away, his mouth tingling, his head bowed deferentially. "The females," he said, trying to explain. "The ones who fill me up. They don't come out at night." He laughed, suddenly amused by his words and the situation. "There are monsters at night, you know."

She smiled, showing her fangs as she laughed. "Where do they live? The young ones. The ones afraid of the scary, scary dark?"

"All around," he said, his finger pointing to the darkened houses. "There is a ripe one lives there," he added, pointing to a pretty house on the corner. A pretty house for a pretty girl.

"Then watch," she said. "Watch and see."

Before his eyes, she dissolved, her body fading into a pale white mist that matched the color of her gown. It moved over the park as fog then disappeared into the house, creeping through cracks and crevices. Only moments later, it returned, riding low over the ground, then rising as a whirlwind in front of him.

The whirlwind slowed, the mist took form, and Xavier found himself looking again at his Dark Angel, a sleeping girl clutched tight in her arms.

"She's for you, Xavier."

He couldn't speak, so deep was his craving, and she laughed, understanding.

"Wait, wait. So hungry. So desperate."

She bent her head to the child's neck, and the girl's eyes opened in terror, her gaze fixed right on him. Seeing him. *Knowing him.*

He pressed his hand over her mouth as she began to scream, but with that moment of clarity, reason abandoned him. He knew only the craving. The hunger. The need.

"Mine," he said like a thing possessed, and he took her and fell to the ground with her, closing his mouth over the wound the Angel had made for him, then drawing in the life. The light.

CHAPTER 21

"I came here planning to punch you in the face," Nick said, his perfect face twisted in anger. "Although I was considering postponing my assault, however much you may deserve it, as I've got something more pressing to talk with you about."

"My relief knows no bounds," Luke said.

"Oh, what the hell." And then, before Luke could anticipate it, Nick's fist shot out and slammed into his nose. Bone and cartilage shattered. Blood oozed down the back of his throat.

And somewhere deep within Luke, the beast reared its head and growled.

Luke forced himself to be calm. Forcing the anger back down where it belonged, taking hold of the chains and twisting, trying to choke the life from the beast. And only when he was certain that he could control it did he look up at his friend.

Nick took a step forward. "You locked me in a coffin. And I had to wake up to Ryan Doyle's ugly face."

"About that, I truly am sorry. No one should have to suffer that way."

"Dammit, Luke, after everything we've been through, and you pull this shit? Play anyone else you like, line up your pieces however they make sense to you. But you do not play me. Not me. Not ever. We clear?"

"We are." Luke understood Nick perfectly, which wasn't the same as acquiescing, but he didn't feel compelled to point that out. "Now tell me what's gotten under your skin." He needed to speak to Nick about the escaped serial killer and the vampire who had helped him, but that conversation would have to wait. Something was up, and Luke quelled a growing sense of unease as he waited for his friend to speak.

"Ryback called," Nick said, as dread latched its claws into Luke. "Tasha wasn't in the apartment."

"There's more," Luke said, a slow, boiling fury replacing the dread. "Tell me."

"He found goblin blood."

Dear gods, Tasha. "You tried her cell?"

"I did. No answer."

"You go there," Luke said, his voice tight with fury. "Use my jet so you can travel by day, but go there, find Serge, and find out what the fuck has happened to my ward. And get my bail hearing moved up. I cannot be in here with Tasha lost in the world. She's a child, Nick, trapped in the body of a woman. She needs protection. She needs me." He looked hard at his friend. "Do whatever you must to make it so."

"I will," Nick said, "though your actions tonight might make that more difficult." Luke lifted his brow in question. "Constantine's pool deck," he continued. "Caught the news as I was coming here. The human cops have swarmed the place. Apparently some girl had the blood sucked out of her."

"Terrible thing," Luke said.

"Dammit, Luke, you had to go and feed?"

"As a matter of fact, I did."

"It's a crime to suck the life from a human," Nick said mildly. "Or hadn't you heard?"

Luke shot him a look that had his friend recoiling.

"If the prosecution connects the dots, that's not going to help your case on bail."

"The prosecution already knows," Luke said, then waited for Nick to connect those dots.

It didn't take long. "Dammit, Luke. You told her? A gung ho prosecutor with something to prove? She might make a fine asset, Luke, but don't let the game turn into something more." He cocked his head, as if rearranging a puzzle in his mind. "Oh, no. *No.* Don't go there. She's the prosecutor. *Your* prosecutor. Whatever fantasy you're clinging to, you need to let it go."

Ironic, thought Luke, that his friend could find that one sliver of hope despite all Luke's efforts to hide it. "Don't worry," Luke said. "I know who and what she is." What she was, he thought, was dangerous. A woman who would imprison him. The same woman who freed him. Who calmed the daemon within.

Nick eyed him warily. "You know who she is," he repeated. "But don't forget who you are, too. Who you are, and what you do."

"I have not," Luke said, and the knife in his voice drew Nick up short. He drew a breath, calming his temper. "She will say nothing."

"No," Nick agreed. "She won't. Thank the gods your moment of idiocy was between you and her alone. She can't use any of your conversation in court, so I guess that's something."

Nick checked his watch. "I've got a call in to

Tiberius, and I'll see what I can do about moving the bail hearing up before I go."

"Good," Luke said, his mind on Tasha. On the goblin's blood. "I need to know what happened. My enemies? Serge's?" He met Nick's eyes. "Most of all, I must know that she's okay."

"I know," his friend said, as the ogre appeared at the door. "Right on time."

Luke's mind turned to Sara, surely as worried about Stemmons's victims as he was about Tasha. From within this cell, there was little he could do. But perhaps he could help in some small way.

"Wait," he said as Nick stepped out of the cell. "There's one more call I need you to make."

CHAPTER 22

The ground shivered beneath his feet, as if the dead were trying to rise, beating their way through the dirt and the mud, flesh clinging to their moldering bones as they clawed their way up, up, up to the sunshine.

And wasn't that the surprise, Serge thought. You claw your way out of hell, only to get burned in the end. What a world. What a goddamn, depressing, fucked-up world.

All around him, the walls shook, and while he rather liked the fantasy that his own personal walls of Jericho were tumbling down, in fact he could blame the noise and the dust only on the New York Transit Authority. But since the MTA had donated the abandoned train tunnel in which he currently resided, he couldn't quite work up the enthusiasm to curse the blasted subway that ran only a few feet from his barren, concrete walls.

Not that the MTA was aware of its magnanimity. Serge had acquired the property in a decidedly nontraditional manner, and had thus far enforced his claim by bending the will of weak-minded humans. Granted, there were a few flaws in his overall plan, and one day he fully expected to meet a human who was not amenable to his particular methods of persuasion.

But until that unfortunate day, he was quite content

to hold on to this charming Park Avenue address. A small pied-à-terre to complement his uptown high-rise.

A place where he could go when he began to see the world through the eyes of the daemon. Where he could recover after a mission as *kyne*. Where he could call upon the *Numen* to release the flames and the blood that would bind the daemon once more. Because no matter how sophisticated he might look in a three-piece silk suit, the condo board had a tendency to frown when you opened a portal to hell in your living room. New York was funny that way.

Dear gods, he was losing it.

He pressed his hands to the sides of his head and pushed, letting the pressure build. He'd killed men with those same hands in that same method. Could he press hard enough to end his own life? To end this now? All of this? And most of all—goddammit—the urge to claw his way back up to street level, get his ass back to his condo, and fuck the brains out of the girl whom his best friend had entrusted into his care?

No, no, no.

He'd left. He'd brought in a goblin to stay with her, and then he'd left.

At least he'd had the presence of mind to call for Graylach. The creature was a fat, lazy slob, but he'd watch the girl. Keep her company. And as goblins found the human form utterly unattractive, he'd be immune to Tasha's allure.

A damn good thing, because she was certainly trying Serge's patience. He wanted. *Wanted.* And the daemon wouldn't be denied.

The steady jangle of the signal bell came just in time

to save Serge from pacing another lap. He hurried to the door—thick wood with ornate carvings he'd acquired from a nearby church two decades prior—and pulled it open. The woman standing in the dank tunnel looked sickly in the grim yellow light that barely illuminated the subway engineering tunnel. But when he pulled her inside, he couldn't say that the incandescent lighting of his hallway favored her much better.

She had fuchsia hair that had been coated with so much gel it stood out from her head like railroad spikes, and most likely with as much strength. Her skin was so pale her freckles appeared to float in front of her, as if leading the way. Dark shadows rimmed her eyes, accentuated by the thick line of kohl. She wore a white tank top with no bra, through which he could see quarter-sized brown nipples on breasts that would have been more appropriate on a thirteen-year-old. Hiphugger-style jeans shifted on her body as she moved, as if trying to find some actual hip to in fact hug.

The girl was so utterly emaciated that she could have passed as a runway model, a breed of women Serge found uniquely unattractive. He couldn't recall the specific date when women had collectively begun to despise their natural curves, but he rued that day nonetheless.

"I'm here," she said, and took another step into his foyer. "God, what a nightmare that was. Least you tossed out some good directions. But I gotta say, this place is pretty damn frosty."

"I'm thrilled you approve." He had once spent an entire week acquiring and installing the flagstones that led from the entrance into the living area. He had done it because it pleased him, though no one else would see the stones. To know that this creature was sharing even an iota of the pleasure he'd felt seemed almost more obscene than the reason he'd called her to him in the first place.

An army surplus-style backpack dangled from one anorexic arm. The inside of her left elbow was bruised from fresh puncture wounds. If it was sore, she showed no sign.

"So, anyway, like, here we are," she said, swinging the bag off her shoulder. She reached inside and pulled out a long coil of plastic tubing, along with a needle and an empty IV bag. "You into suck or puncture?" she asked. "Oh, and I guess John-O told you my rates, right? And I don't do more than two pints. Makes me too damn woozy, you know?"

Considering that he doubted she had two pints of blood in her entire tiny body, he certainly did know.

"I suck," he said, making her smile. "And we can set up in the backroom." He waved a hand, pointing her toward the heavy steel door.

"Whoa, Nellie," she said, as she stepped inside, and he knew that she was looking at the manacles chained to the walls. "You can really get the kink on in here, huh?"

"I can indeed," he said, following her more slowly, letting the anticipation build. "I've found it's safer this way. You don't mind if I am bound?"

"Hey, you jump all over that safety thing. That's fine with me. I just do what the client wants. But let's be straight here, ya know? I make my living selling this," she said, gesturing to her body. "Pretty much any way you want it. I don't do drugs, and if you want a fuck, you gotta put some jammies on your hammie. But that's about as safe as I get, you know? I mean, hell, if I wanted to play it safe, I coulda got a job waiting tables. Let some wanker grab your tits, and he'll double the tip, too."

"You don't have any tits."

She snorted, then slapped her thigh. "Aren't you a funny dude? Funny bloodsucker. Heh. Maybe you oughta do stand-up or something?"

"I'll look into it right away."

"So what's your deal, anyway? This some sort of religious thing for you? I mean, I know the whole vampire cult thing's all the rage, but I mean, gross me out on the drinking human blood."

"It's extremely nutritious, I assure you. And no, it's not a religious thing." He tilted his head, examining her even as she examined her nails. "Has John-O never told you about your clients?"

"What? Other than you guys are all freaks?"

"Yes," he said dryly. He suppressed a shiver of pleasure at the thought of tasting her, the feel of her blood flowing over his tongue. His cock twitched in anticipation and he couldn't understand his need to engage in this pointless conversation. But if he didn't, the daemon would be harder to restrain, harder to control, and he was barely hanging on as it was. "Other than that."

"Nah. He just says it's more interesting than selling plasma. Pays better, too." She glanced at the wall, at the manacles that dangled there. "So, like, is that for you or for me?"

"For me," he said, amused by the mix of relief and disappointment that danced across her face. "Unless you'd like the honors?"

A brief hesitation, then she shook her head. "Better not. Wouldn't want you to lose your natural rhythm, what-o?"

"What-o, indeed."

With her rather eager assistance, he was soon stripped naked and manacled to the walls. Steel cuffs, and strong. But not too strong. He wanted to be bound—to keep the *faunt* who came so trusting to his door safe.

And yet there was a part of him...

Well, that part insisted on steel and not hematite. Less sport, perhaps. But the potential for so much more satisfaction.

"So, like, you got no free arms. How you going to hold the tube?"

"The tube?" He was spread-eagled on the wall, arms and ankles bound tight. Certainly no threat to anyone at the moment. And still the girl licked her lips, took a tiny, apprehensive step backward.

"Yeah." She held up the plastic tubing, the bag, and the needle. "Whatcha gonna do? Just clench it between your teeth?"

"I'm sure the experience would be delightful, but that is not where I find my pleasure." No, he found it in the flesh. The skin beneath his mouth. And that sweet moment of hesitation before the flesh was punctured and the blood ran free.

It was forbidden, of course. What he wanted. To puncture a human...it was a crime, and yet he wanted it still.

"So what you thinking about?" she asked, looking at his crotch, where his cock had sprung to attention, quite in anticipation of the main event. "What's getting you all hot and bothered?"

"You are, of course," he said.

"Yeah?" She strutted toward him, then pressed her finger to his lip and drew it down, down, down, then flicked the end of it hard on his cock. He winced, with both surprise and pleasure—and knew then that he would have this one.

She laughed, satisfied, and danced back away from him, her expression teasing.

He could tease as well. "Let us play a little game."

"Yeah?"

"Drop the bag. Drop the tube. Drop the needle."

She did.

"Now come to me."

She took one step, then hesitated, her eyes narrowed. "John-O said I shouldn't—"

"Am I not strapped to a wall? What harm can come from indulging a bound man?"

"Well..."

He met her eyes, looked deep...and let his will be done.

"No harm," she said, easing closer, the seductive smile ridiculous on her pixie face and brightly colored hair.

"No harm," he agreed. "Come closer."

She did, pressing herself to him, one hand closing around his shaft. She stroked him in a slow, practiced motion that had him groaning, fighting the urge to let her finish. But no. He had other plans for her, and in a low voice, he told her.

She looked at him, and for a moment he thought the

hold would snap. Thought he would have to change into mist, transform to chase her down. He didn't want to. The shackles, though illusory, kept the daemon at bay. A reminder, he supposed, that he'd once won. Once upon a time, he'd beaten the daemon back fiercely.

Besides, he got off on it. On being exposed to them. Vulnerable to them.

Because he *so* wasn't vulnerable.

This one, though. This one wasn't cooperating. Instead, she was squirming in his arms, fear in her eyes. The fear that came with understanding. In finally realizing what he meant to do.

He'd told her, of course. But until this moment, she hadn't believed.

Concede.

She sighed, long and languid, as the suggestion filled her mind. Then she tilted her head to the side, exposing her neck for him. So white, so smooth. Like marble, and yet not. Pliant and delicious and *living*. Pumping with life. Pumping with blood.

He breathed deep, letting her scent envelop him, letting the pressure build within until he was certain he would come when the first drop of her blood touched his tongue. And then, when he could stand it no longer, he sank his fangs deep into her throat, his entire body convulsing with pleasure as the blood began to flow.

Ecstasy.

This was it. What he needed. What he'd been craving.

But it still wasn't enough.

He needed to taste the tang of fear in her blood. Needed it to bring him out, to pull him through.

Had to have it.

Now.

The bond between them snapped, and the instant it did, she screamed. And inside Serge, the wakening daemon stretched and preened and took one step closer to freedom.

CHAPTER 23

"You banging him?"

The words, cold and harsh, seemed to slam up against Sara as she moved through the Division hallway toward her office. She whipped around to find herself facing a lanky man—she assumed he was a man—with a craggy, weatherworn face and the kind of broad shoulders that suggested tight muscles and latent strength hidden beneath the ill-fitting clothes. He walked with a swagger that suggested an old-time sheriff, and his eyes were cold and flat.

"Oh, wait," he said, stepping up and getting in her face. "You're a human. Not really his type. So maybe you just like his pretty face. Or maybe you're just stupid enough to do the bastard favors."

Nothing about his appearance sparked her recognition, and yet she was certain she knew who this man was. "Agent Doyle, I presume?"

"In the flesh."

"You always skip the introductions and go straight for the insult?"

"Only when it's appropriate."

Because his insult skirted very near the truth, she took the time to consider her response, disguising her discomfiture with a sharp assessment of him and his companion. Whereas Doyle had a no-nonsense vibe about him, his partner, Severin Tucker, lived up to his rep as an easygoing ladies' man. Or his appearance did.

"I'm tired, Agent. I've barely slept. And in case you didn't get the memo, Dragos's bail hearing's been moved to tonight."

She still couldn't believe *that* bit of news. Apparently Luke really did have connections, because the word had come down all the way from Leviathin that the hearing was being bumped up. Lovely. Maybe she'd sleep next month.

Doyle's eyes cut to Tucker, who shook his head. Barely a millimeter, but Sara caught it, and she understood.

"Sorry, boys." She tapped her head. "Can't poke around in here." She aimed a sweet smile at Tucker. "I've heard about your special skills."

"I've heard about yours, too. Figured I had to try, anyway. No offense?"

She crossed her arms over her chest. "That depends. You two going to keep riding my ass?"

"Why don't you tell us what you were doing sprinting to Division in the middle of the night? Especially after what he did to that girl at your pool?"

"I didn't know about her at the time," she admitted. "How did you find out?"

Doyle moved away, then leaned casually against the wall, giving off the appearance of a benign man having a simple conversation with a colleague. But there was nothing benign about Ryan Doyle. She could see the danger bubbling beneath the surface. She imagined that edge made him an exceptional investigator—not to mention a tireless opponent.

"Human police band. The address popped as yours."

"All right," she said, because so far he was making perfect sense. "But there's still no straight line that connects me and Annie and Lucius Dragos."

"The hell there isn't." He reached out his hand, and Tucker slapped a PDA into it. He passed the PDA to Sara.

She peered at the small screen, then let out a small gasp at the image of Luke, battered on the steps of the pool, and Annie moving in close to him.

"Smile," Doyle said. "That fuckwad's on candid camera."

"Got him dead to rights on this," Tucker said. "Drawing from a human. Feeding a human. Big no-nos for vamps. Brings the daemon too close to the surface."

She lifted her gaze from the image, remembering the hint of the daemon she'd seen on Luke's face before he'd fled her apartment.

"Evil bastards," Doyle said. "Tricky, too. Daemons know how to play. How to tease. Even how to lay low. And don't be so naive as to think a vamp's ever really got his daemon under control," he added, his color rising. "That may be the politically correct party line, but it's a bunch of bullshit, and everyone in the Shadow world damn well knows it. The daemon can't be controlled—*won't* be controlled. And when it comes out, it's like a visitation straight from hell."

Sara shivered, then realized she'd been hugging herself. Tucker, she saw, had moved closer to his partner, who shook his head violently, then turned away. *Personal,* she thought. The daemon might be real, but it was also damn personal to Doyle.

"So how did you get this? There aren't security cameras on the pool deck."

Tucker snorted. "Two vamps live in your building. You think the PEC doesn't have some surveillance of its own?"

She frowned, her gaze dipping back down to that image. An image of Luke, with his mouth on Annie's neck.

She tore her eyes away, ignoring that fresh burst of absurd jealousy, the same that she'd felt when he'd told her the story. Dear God, he was *feeding* on the girl. Sara didn't want that. How could she want that?

"So you'll use this, right?" Tucker asked. "At the hearing?"

"Of course she will," Doyle said, looking at her hard. "I'd say this is some pretty solid proof that Dragos is a danger to the community. Wouldn't you, Counselor?"

She hesitated, weighing her options.

"It is," she finally said. "And yes, we'll use it." She told herself that she wasn't crossing any lines by doing so. After all, Doyle had learned about Annie and Luke all on his own, and none of what he learned was within the purview of the off-the-record conversation she'd had with Luke.

Still, she felt a twinge of guilt. With a great deal of mental force, she quashed it. She needed to remember who she was—the new human prosecutor on a high-profile case. Her boss was expecting a seasoned advocate. One who knew how to play the game, not shrink back at breaches of etiquette.

And she was that girl. She hadn't made it to the top of

her law school class without a competitive edge. And she had a feeling she wouldn't have been selected to work at Division without that trait, either.

If Montegue wanted to argue that Luke had fed off Annie to save himself, then Montegue could damn well raise that as an affirmative defense.

She ran her fingers through her hair and nodded toward Doyle's PDA. "Okay. Good. This goes a long way toward establishing the element of danger to the community. But risk of flight's harder. He came back to Division of his own accord."

"With a stake strapped to his chest."

"True," Sara acknowledged. "But it'll be there during his bail term as well."

"So we put on evidence suggesting that given more time he would have found a way to remove it. Three hours wasn't enough. But three days? Three weeks? A guy like Dragos, he must have connections that could pull that off."

Sara nodded. "Right. So we suggest to the court that he's looking to shake loose of the countermeasures. Couple that with the evidence about Annie, not to mention the signet ring, the DNA, and your vision. With all that, I think the court will surely deny bail."

Doyle leaned back, his hands shoved deep into his pockets. "Huh."

"What? You disagree?"

"Nope. We're good. Just surprised is all."

"By?"

"You. Didn't figure you had the balls to go after him."

She lifted her brows. "And I didn't figure you had the balls to admit you were wrong, so maybe we're even. But speaking of balls, you ever come at me in attack mode again, Doyle, and I will nail *your* balls to the wall." She smiled, wide and flirty. "We're clear?"

He let out a guffaw, just as she'd expected he would. She'd spent years with hard-ass detectives, and she knew a thing or two about the care and feeding of same.

"You're not a pushover," he said. "That's good. You last a month in the basement, I'll buy you lunch." He stuck out his hand.

She closed her hand over his. "You're on."

♦

"My eyes are going to fall right out of my head soon," Sara said, looking up from the papers spread across her desk as J'ared floated in. No last name, simply J'ared, and he was a poltergeist who had, in a move that had caused a terrible rift in his family, decided to forego the family tradition of prankstering for a more subdued career in the law. It was to Sara's great credit, she thought, that she'd taken that announcement in stride.

"I know a daemon who did that," J'ared said. "The eye thing, I mean. Big hit at parties. Huge." He glided to one of Sara's guest chairs and sat down, which was to say he hovered a few inches above the seat and tucked his legs under him. Or appeared to. As he'd explained earlier that day, his actual form was visible only to poltergeists. Other creatures visualized him in a form similar to their own.

She wasn't entirely sure how he was able to read and write, since the hands she saw had no substance, but apparently her understanding of metaphysics was faulty, because he was more than able to curve his fingers around a pencil or tap out a sentence on a word processor. More than that, his tapping was brilliant.

His family might be mortified by his choice of profession, but Sara was thrilled to be working with him. Though she'd met him only that morning, Martella or Bosch must have given him a heads-up, because she'd been greeted by two stacks of paper on her desk, both provided by J'ared. On the left, a draft brief in support of Division's Opposition to Defendant's Motion to Set Bail. On the right, all the case law relevant to both the motion and the opposition.

All in all, a huge help, and she'd dug right in, the rhythm of the law helping her find her center and cling to the familiar in a decidedly new world.

"You'll take care of filing our briefs and making sure the evidence is labeled and organized?"

"Sure," he said, tapping out a note to himself. "Now we just need—"

A sharp knock interrupted them, and Sara looked up to see Nostramo Bosch standing in the doorway. "A human child was discovered in Echo Park a few minutes ago."

"Stemmons?" she asked, her chest tight with dread.

"Apparently so." Bosch said. "An Alliance Seer has confirmed his scent."

She was already up and at the door. "A Seer?" she asked. From what she'd read the creatures were extremely rare, and there were none on the Division 6 staff. "Is that usual?"

"It's not," he said, "but if the Alliance wants to send help, we'll hardly turn them away. This is a county/Division matter because of the evidence that vampires assisted Stemmons's breakout," he said as they moved swiftly down the hall, Martella in step beside them. "You've been assigned to the joint task force because of your history with him. But keep a care. The cover story is still Homeland Security."

"Yes, sir." Her mind was already spinning. "If vampires helped him escape, they're probably still with him, and the victim may have seen one of them. I'd like Doyle to come along, too. With any luck, his visions can help."

"Make the call," he said to Martella as he and Sara stepped into the elevator. "Have Agent Doyle meet us at the scene."

"Yes, sir," the secretary said as the doors closed and the elevator whisked them away. On the drive, Bosch gave her the relevant details: ten-year-old female abducted from her home. No witnesses.

The news, and the dry recitation, about broke Sara's heart. But it was the sight of the little girl herself, pale as paper, eyes open in terror, that had sharp tears stinging Sara's eyes, and a flood of pure rage boiling through her head.

Her neck had been ripped open, which wasn't Stemmons's traditional MO, but since the Seer had confirmed his scent, Sara had to assume that the vamps were teaching him a thing or two.

Her hand ached suddenly, and she realized she'd been clutching her fist. She forced herself to relax, to let go of the wave of disgust that was keeping her rooted to the spot.

Goddammit.

"Sir." A tall creature who gave every indication of being nothing more than a skeleton covered by a thin layer of skin approached Bosch. "I am Voight, a Seer. I have a preliminary report."

Bosch nodded and he and Sara stepped aside with Voight. "We've analyzed the residual essence at the escape point, and there's no question that Stemmons was assisted by a single vampire, but the signature isn't reading clearly and we can't even determine if the vampire was male or female."

"Can you tell if that same vampire was here?" Sara asked.

"We can," Voight said. "We're picking up the same signature."

"We need Doyle," Sara said. "If the girl saw the vampire..."

"Has Agent Doyle reported to the scene?" Bosch asked. The question, however, was mooted by Doyle's appearance across the playground. He scanned the scene, slipped under the county crime tape, then crossed quickly, with Tucker at his side.

"What the fuck?"

"A task force matter," Bosch said. "Constantine thinks your skills would be useful."

His eyes cut to the child's body, now surrounded by the human police and medical examiner. "Too crowded."

"We'll clear the crowd," Bosch said.

"It's bullshit," Doyle said. "She's human."

"She's a little girl," Sara countered.

Doyle's face tightened. "You got any idea how fucking hard it is to do what I do? How much it drains me when I do it often? What seeps in around the edges when I'm weak?" His lip curled up in a snarl. "You ask me to do this thing, but you don't know the cost, Constantine. You don't fucking live in my world."

"What about the cost to that little girl?" Sara asked, refusing to be intimidated.

"She's human. Killed by a human. It's not my world. Not my problem."

"A vampire helped Stemmons kill her, Doyle," Sara said, getting right into his face, because if it hadn't been for that damn vampire, then Stemmons wouldn't be out preying on little girls. "*That's* your world."

He kicked the ground. "Fine. Fuck. Clear the goddamn scene."

Bosch and Tucker took charge, with Bosch urging all extraneous personnel to leave the scene, and Tucker using his unique skill set to move the process along.

When the crowd had dwindled and only a few humans remained nearby—their minds ready to be wiped by Tucker—Doyle bent over the body and placed his hands on the little girl, one over her head and one over her heart. His body went slack, his eyes glassy.

"How long?" she whispered to Tucker.

"Depends," he said. "I've seen a hundred of these things, and they're all different. It's the curse of being partnered with a Percipient. They ship him all over the damn globe when they got a fresh one."

"You, too?"

Tucker's expression was grave. "We're partners. Don't always make it in to the scene in time, though," Tucker added, looking at his partner. "Doyle's got a thing about wormholes. Won't go that way. Says they lead straight through hell. Doesn't matter how hot the case, he'll only travel by PEC transport. So sometimes the aura fades." His expression turned wry. "This one looks fresh, though."

Sara hoped it was. She wanted answers, and right then, Doyle seemed like the best bet. Small convulsions wracked his body until, finally, Tucker grabbed Doyle's shoulders and yanked him free of the girl.

Doyle looked up, his face pale, his eyes glassy, and Sara realized her hands were clenched at her sides. "Female," he said. "The vamp bitch is female." He eased backward, shaking his head. "All I could get. Hem of a dress. Impressions from the kid."

"Shit," Sara said, realizing how much she'd been hoping for Doyle to ID the vampire, give them some lead, some clue, something. Because she knew time was running out for the next little girl, and if they didn't hurry, she'd soon be standing over another pale, sweet face.

"Constantine!" Marty called to her from across the crime scene. "We got a lock of hair."

Shit. She hurried over, peered into the evidence bag at the curl of auburn hair held together by a golden ribbon. "Under the body, just like before."

She looked up at Bosch. "He kept them—the girls. Took two or three at a time and kept them in cages. Then when he'd kill one, he'd leave a little clue as to the one he was going to do next. Hair. A favorite toy." She closed her eyes, swallowed hard. "One girl, he left her tongue."

"Son of a bitch," Bosch said.

"He's got the next one in a cage," she said, her stomach in knots. "And unless he's changed the way he operates, he's already got the one after that picked out."

CHAPTER 24

"Tasha!" The elevator doors opened directly into Serge's forty-seventh-floor penthouse apartment, and Nick's voice echoed over the polished marble. The foyer led into an extravagent living room, a semicircle with walls of specially manufactured tinged glass from which Serge could look out over the night, then flip the finger at the rising sun through the impervious glass.

The chemistry upon which the glass was made was unstable, as Serge well knew. Yet even so, he faced the dawn each morning, thumbing his nose at fate.

So far, fate had not kicked back, but it would not surprise Nick to one day step inside the apartment and find a pile of ash by the windows, the deadly sunlight having accomplished its purpose.

Today, thank the gods, was not that day.

In fact, he found nothing at all, and wondered if perhaps that was even more disturbing.

"Come on, Tasha," he called. "It's Nick. Come on out for me."

He waited for her reply. A soft whimper, a terrified yell, even an irritated wail that she'd been left all alone. But the apartment remained quiet, and the fear in Nick's gut bloomed red.

Determined, he stalked through the place, peering

into all the rooms, looking into all the closets, under the beds. Any place a scared girl would hide.

He didn't find her. More telling, he didn't find any of her dolls.

The goblin blood, however, was exactly where Ryback had said, its vinegar scent still pungent.

"By the gods," he whispered. "What the hell happened here?"

He'd been to Serge's subterranean abode only twice, the first time accessing the underground corridors through the basement of the high-rise, and the second through a descent into a subway tunnel. They'd hopped the tracks, then entered the maze of tunnels through a maintenance door. With the sun now shining brightly, Nick had no choice but to take option one and hope that he could find his way through the putrid tunnels to the oasis that was Serge's hideaway.

More, he hoped that Serge would be there when he found it.

The basement had not been designed to connect to the city's labyrinth of tunnels. And, indeed, it was not Serge who had forged the way. That task had fallen upon the misbegotten of the city, the destitute and homeless who searched for a place other than the street to sleep. How they had discovered the thin stone wall behind the industrial washing machines in the basement laundry room, Nick didn't know. Someone had, though, and had chipped away, creating a narrow passage that could be accessed by shifting the machine slightly to the left.

Someone, possibly Serge, had finally become frustrated with the frequent movement of the appliance and had pushed it permanently aside, then situated a draped table in front of the access point. Ostensibly a place for residents to fold clothes, the table provided a permanent doorway for anyone who crawled beneath and pushed aside the drape.

It was, thought Nick, the kind of portal to hell that enlivened children's nightmares. The place where they would disappear. Where the monsters would grab them.

He moved quickly inside the tunnels, passing these humans, these people who would look upon him either as monster or as savior. Had Serge turned any of them, he wondered? Had he made these gutter rats into their kind?

The possibility disgusted Nick. Serge would say he was a snob and, in fact, he would be right. Because there was a beauty to what they were. *Nosferatu.* Creatures born of night and filled with night.

They suffered, yes. And those who lost the battle within could spend eternity lost in torment. But if the battle could be won—if the beast could be tamed—then the world seemed to exist for their delight, the most powerful and feared of all the Shadow creatures. With strength and grace and abilities like none other.

It was intoxicating.

It was, he thought, divine.

And had it not been divinity that he had searched for, all those years ago in Venice? Had he not sought the face of God through his studies? Through examination of the stars? In the very art of his ancestors?

He shook his head to clear his meandering thoughts. He did not often think on his nature, as he did not want to tempt fate. Become too complacent—too arrogant—and the daemon would rise up and try to wrest control.

That had happened with Serge, he was certain.

His daemon had burst forth. The only questions now were how many had it killed, and how much of Serge was left.

Rats scurried around his feet, and he trod carefully on the metal flooring. The way was narrow in places, but when the tunnel widened, he could see people huddled together over Sterno cans, their eyes white behind filthy faces.

One foolish man stepped into Nick's path, a metal shiv held at the ready. " 'at you doin' down hae?"

"I'm out for a stroll," Nick said. "You'd be wise to go your own way."

"Smart man. Fancy man."

"Deadly man," Nick said, and bared his fangs.

That was all it took, and the man scurried away like the rats Nick had passed earlier. He didn't stare in awe and wonder. Didn't snarl and claim Nick was a monster. He turned and ran.

And that, Nick thought, was telling. These people had seen a vampire. Knew what one was, and what one was capable of.

He stopped, for the first time really looking at the people huddled together, their eyes fixed on him. He lifted his chin, sniffing the air, finding their scent. Heroin and sex. Blood and vomit. But they would know, and they would tell.

He took a step toward the closest one, and she scooted backward, her halter top falling open to expose a flaccid breast. "Get away, get away, get away."

"You know me?"

"I know like you," she said, then spat at his feet. "Got the evil in you, you do."

He cocked his head. "What do you know of it, woman?"

"Tossed her out. Out of his big house. Hell house, underground, just like the way to hell. Find her, and she's all broken and can't fix her, just like that egg boy."

"Egg boy?"

"Humpty," she said. "Egg boy."

"Ah, yes."

"Just wanted to get her groove on, that's all she wanted. Just trying to get by, get high."

He stepped closer. "Move."

She hesitated, and he curled his lips. That sufficed, and she scuttled sideways, revealing a mound under a tattered, filthy blanket. He bent closer, saw bugs scatter as he reached to draw the cloth away, then found himself staring at an emaciated young woman with a mass of dark, curly ringlets. She was pale and motionless, and the scent of death was upon her.

"Where?" Nick asked. "Where does he live? The one who did this thing?"

The woman stuck out a thin arm and pointed to the left fork of the tunnel. "He's a fiend, he is. Rip your heart out as soon as look at you. Toss 'em away, all our pretty girls. Just trying to get by. Just trying to get a fix."

He left her prattling on, her words echoing eerily in the metal tunnel.

He found Serge's door easily enough. There was no mistaking it. The polished, ornate oak, completely devoid of graffiti. Because who in the tunnels would be fool enough to deface the monster's doorway?

"Serge! Open up!" Nick pounded, ignoring the eyes that peered out from the dark. "Dammit, Serge, open the fucking door."

Nothing. No sound. No noise. Nothing.

"Fuck." This time, the curse was whispered, and said more to himself and the door than to anyone inside. "Too bad. It's a damn nice door." And with that, he reared back, kicked, and sent the heavy oak door flying across the flagstone-paved entrance hall.

His eyes told him the place was empty. His nose told him otherwise. The pungent, enticing scent of blood hung in the air, laced with fear and a little piss and shit just to give it that nice round edge.

"Bloody hell, Serge," Nick whispered, moving slowly through the place. "What the fuck are you into?"

He heard it then—a single, low grown that had him racing to the far door that led into Serge's private play-room.

Serge was there, naked and prostrate over a huge broken mirror. Deep gashes marred his arms and legs. Fresh, Nick knew, as they hadn't yet begun to heal.

"Serge."

His friend twitched, but didn't look up.

"Serge, look at me."

He turned, and Nick saw the daemon in his eyes warring for control. And the horror of what he'd done—what he *would* do—etched on Serge's face.

"Can't get it out. Can't bring the *Numen*," Serge said, taking a shard of glass and digging it deep into his arm.

The blood ritual.

Even now, Nick felt the cold, hollow grip of fear. The terror he'd experienced when he slid into the netherworld for that ultimate battle. And the sinking knowledge that he could even then lose the battle despite the *Numen* at his side. And if he did, he would be forever trapped, the daemon Nick evolving, while the other Nick dissolved into nothing.

In front of him, Serge howled with pain, but didn't stop mutilating his skin. "Come, you bitch! Get it the fuck out of me. Push it back!"

"Serge. *Serge!*" Nick knelt beside him, grabbed his shoulders with one hand, and with the other took the bloody glass. "You're you. You're still you. It's working. You're fighting. You don't need her yet. You're pushing it back. I can see it. You're pushing it back."

"No, no, no." With a terrible, heart-wrenching squall, Serge looked up, met Nick's gaze with drunken eyes. "I lost it. It killed her."

Nick stiffened, a cold terror racing through him. "Who?" he asked carefully, afraid that Serge had spilled Tasha's blood. That he had staked her, and that she was no more. "Focus," he said, shaking his friend. "Tell me. Who? Who did you kill?"

"The girl with kaleidoscope eyes," he said, his smile crooked and his voice singsong. "Came here selling herself. A *faunt*," he said, referring to the humans who sold their blood to feed vampires. The word sent relief coursing through Nick. *Not Tasha.* Thank the gods it wasn't Tasha.

"Wild hair," Serge was saying, which meant that this

girl wasn't the one Nick had seen in the tunnel. "Practically pink. Chatty. Liked her, too. Killed her anyway. Didn't like the rest. Didn't even know them."

Nick closed his eyes, trying not to imagine the damage a powerful vampire like Serge could cause. "How many?"

Pain flashed in the daemon-red eyes. "Don't know. Just killed them. Found them, and had them."

"Fight it back," Nick said, his body tensed for a fight, his words wary. "Kick it back to hell where it belongs."

"I am in hell," Serge said.

"There you go," Nick said, and earned a slow smile from his friend. "That's it. Come on back. *Fight,* dammit. *Fight.*"

"Want to," he said. "Getting harder every day." He reached behind him, and from the mess of blood and glass managed to produce a wooden stake. He thrust it at Nick. "Take it. Use it."

"The hell I will."

"Dammit, *end me.*"

"*No.*" Nick snapped the stake in two. "Listen to me."

"Son of a bitch. You goddamn, fuck-faced fool." The daemon was coming out, riding the crest of Serge's anger. Well, fine, Nick thought. After all of this, he was gunning for a fight anyway.

"Listen to me," Nick repeated, but he knew Serge wasn't listening anymore. He was sinking inside himself, and something else was coming up.

Nick wasn't going to let it get there.

Without warning, he hauled back and punched Serge in the face. His startled friend howled, then pounced, but Nick was ready, leaning back so that he had leverage, and then kicking out and catching Serge hard across the throat with the sole of his foot. Serge staggered back, blood in his eye, and came forward again.

"Enough," Nick growled, as Serge barreled into him, knocking them both on the ground. "I won't kill you, no matter how damn much you provoke me."

"Fuck you, Nicholas."

"No, fuck you." And he reached down, grabbed his friend's naked balls, and twisted.

The effect was pretty much what he'd anticipated. Serge dropped like a stone and clutched his crotch, which gave Nick the opportunity to get back to him, crouch down, and place half the broken stake right at his buddy's temple. "It won't kill you," he said, "but you won't be the same."

"Knock my brains out, and at least I won't know what I'm doing." The pain that colored Serge's voice had Nick lowering the weapon.

"You're back."

"You twisted my nuts into a knot, damn you. You think the daemon's gonna hang around for that kind of torture?"

"You clear? Good and clear?"

Serge looked up, met Nick's eyes, then shook his head no. "But I'm steady. I can fight. I *can*," he added, in response to Nick's doubtful expression. "Dammit all, it's been building. Growing in me. Taking over. Fucking nightmare. Fucking goddamn life."

"You should have told us."

"What? Hey, dudes. Losing myself here. If I fall, don't piss too hard on me?"

"You should have told us," Nick repeated.

Serge sighed. "I know." He ran his hands through his shoulder-length hair, sweeping it back out of his face. "Dammit, I know."

"Where's Tasha?"

"You think I'd let her see me like this? I got Graylach to stay with her."

"The goblin's dead, Serge. It's dead, and Tasha's gone."

He could see the shock flash in Serge's eyes. More, he could see the flash of opportunity—the daemon taking a tentative peek out once again.

"Focus for me. Focus, damn you. Where is she? Did someone know she was staying with you? Someone who'd want to hurt Luke?"

"I don't know." He pressed his hands to his skull. "I don't know. I left. Had to keep her safe."

"Safe?" Nick repeated. "Safe from what?"

Pure pain glowed in Serge's eyes. "From me."

He drew in a breath, then clutched his head even tighter. "By the gods," he whispered. "Lucius. He will have my life for this."

"No," said Nick, standing up and looking away from his friend as compassion warred with disgust. "Right now, I don't think your life is worth the debt."

◊

Luke buried his rage—his fear—under an icy calm, knowing that if he lost control now he would be hard-pressed to ever get it back.

"You cannot feel her at all?" Nick asked. "There

is no blood connection between you? Not even the slightest?"

"You know there isn't," Luke said. It was one of the reasons that the Covenant prohibited the turning of the addled. With any other, he would be able to seek them out, discern their feelings, come close to actually reading their mind.

With a mind such as Tasha's, though, that was not possible.

"*Dammit.*" Luke grabbed the edges of the small sink in his cell, fighting once again for control, feeling it slipping away. "The dolls," he said, forcing his mind to think clearly. "You said that her dolls were gone?"

"All of them. Her clothes, too."

He considered the fact, focusing on the scenario, pushing emotion out of the mix so that he could think clearly. Because unless he was clear, he couldn't find her. "A killer would not take such things."

"There'd be no reason," Nick said, agreeing. "Neither would someone holding her to send you a message."

"And where is the message?" Luke asked. "There is none, because it is not my enemies who have her."

"She left on her own," Nick said, nodding. "But that's not a whole hell of a lot better."

"No," Luke agreed. "It isn't." She may have left Serge's of her own free will, but so far she had not contacted Nick again. And to Luke's mind, that meant trouble.

"She would have come to Los Angeles," he said.

"To you," Nick said. "Of course."

"And we know that Caris is in town."

"Fuck," Nick said. "You don't think—"

"I think it's a possibility," Luke said. "Payback for my taking out Hasik and Tinsley. For fucking up Gunnolf's little plot." Nick had briefed Tiberius, who had in turn paid a visit to Gunnolf. For now, Gunnolf's plan was on ice, and as Tiberius had agreed not to inform the rest of the Alliance about Gunnolf's treachery, Tiberius had acquired a powerful political marker. As had Luke.

"You think she'd know it was you?"

"Tiberius knows it was me, and I'm sure she still has sources within his organization. But even if she doesn't know, I wouldn't be surprised if she'd snatch Tasha simply out of spite. Damned ancient history." Back when Luke had turned Tasha, Tiberius had spurned Caris's argument that the girl shouldn't be allowed to live. The vampire master had thrown his weight around, supporting Luke's plea for special dispensation. At the time, Caris had been furious, and he knew that she still blamed Luke for the wedge that had been shoved between her and Tiberius.

"If that traitorous bitch really has laid a hand on Tasha, she'll soon feel the sharp end of a very hard stick."

"We have to find her first," Nick said.

"I know. I want you on the street. Find out where Caris is holed up."

"In case you've forgotten, you have a bail hearing in a few hours. A hearing that I had to do a particularly complicated tap dance to get moved forward."

"Then get Slater," Luke said. "Tell him it's a favor to me."

"Will do," Nick said. "If Caris is still in town, we'll find her."

"Tell him I want a location by the time this hearing is over. I haven't seen Caris in decades. I think it's time to renew an old acquaintance."

"What about Serge?"

Luke sagged. "He is more than *kyne,* Nicholas. Of all of us, Serge is the only one I can truly call brother. But if he did this...if he touched her..."

He closed his eyes, a barrier against the horror of his friend's betrayal, and incongruously, he thought of Sara. Sara, searching for justice in a world where it was so rarely found. Sara, in whose arms he had forgotten, for just a moment, the sharp edges of the world in which he walked.

CHAPTER 25

The Los Angeles branch of the International Order of Therians was housed in a refurbished 1940s historic mansion on South Highland Boulevard, two blocks from the local Starbucks. Doyle and Tucker had stopped in for a caffeine hit before heading on to their scheduled interview with Ytalia Leon, the organization's acting president. So far, the coffee had been the best part of their day, as the investigation was turning up a big, fat zero.

Specifically, their inquiries into Braddock had revealed a dozen or so colleagues who thought the shapeshifter was a royal prick, but nobody was spouting specifics other than the bribery and blackmail charges, and at least to Doyle's way of thinking, that was old news.

"Our man's either very good at keeping secrets," Doyle said, "or Constantine's got us running in circles." The prosecutor had insisted they dig, so they were digging. And while Doyle agreed with her in theory that bribery often cloaked a multitude of sins, so far the theory wasn't panning out.

Tucker flipped through his notes. "Sanctioned for taking bribes. A few allegations of blackmail. Some undisclosed financial accounts. Yeah, I'd say the guy was a natural on the secret front."

The steady *clip clip* of heels on wood echoed down the hall, shutting off further speculation. A moment later, the sound was followed by a petite woman with short red hair, an angular nose, and sharp, small eyes. Following her was a young woman with long straggly hair and a face bent perpetually toward the floor. She shuffled to a corner of the room and began to sort a stack of papers into neat piles. Ytalia ignored the girl, but focused exclusively on the agents, her hand extended in a formal greeting.

Doyle took it, gave it a firm shake, then indicated for her to sit. He mentally flipped through her file, remembering that Ytalia was a were-coyote. *Yeah,* he thought. *That fit.*

"You wish to discuss Judge Braddock?"

"That's right," Doyle said, noticing that on the far side of the room, the younger woman stiffened.

"I'm happy to help in any way I can."

"You were his secretary when he was on the bench, right?"

"That's right. And after his retirement, he was very active in the Order. In the fight for equal rights for all were-creatures. He was a most vigorous advocate for our cause, and we're all extremely distressed by his unfortunate demise."

"Yeah, murder's a bitch."

She peered down her nose at him. Beside him, Tucker cleared his throat.

"We've talked to quite a few people, ma'am," Tucker said, "and the picture we're getting is interesting, to say the least."

"The man is dead, sir. I'll not have you besmirching his good name."

"Did he have a good name?" Doyle asked. At Ytalia's glare, he spread his hands. "Just asking."

"The judge had some vices, it's true. But he worked very hard to overcome them. He should be honored for his fortitude and determination. Not vilified."

"What vices, exactly?"

"Is this relevant?"

"Everything's relevant in murder."

She sighed, then shifted so that she was speaking more to Tucker than to Doyle. "He was...proud of his position. He had worked very hard to rise so far, and while he deserved the honor, I think in some ways it went to his head."

"Sure," Tucker said, nailing the role of good cop with such precision that Doyle was sure an Oscar was in the boy's future. "Who wouldn't get a swelled head?"

"Exactly," she said, clearly pleased to have found an ally. "And that is exactly what happened. That power... well, it can be heady."

"He took bribes. He used his position to blackmail," Doyle said.

"He did, he did." She looked positively miserable at the admission. "And he recognized the error of his ways and worked hard to overcome it." She leaned forward, speaking earnestly to Tucker, whom she obviously saw as the more reasonable of the two. "And he did overcome it. He really did."

"All that heady power," Doyle said, "it push him toward anything other than blackmail?"

Her back stiffened. "I don't know what you mean."

"Just thinking aloud," Doyle said, but he was focused more on the girl—who'd become frozen in the act of sorting papers—than on his witness.

"Even rumors," Tucker said. "We're looking for a motive here. Maybe his killer got it wrong. Heard something untrue, but acted on it."

"Well, I don't know what," she said, turning back to Tucker. "The judge was a good man at heart, and nobody says otherwise. Certainly not around here. He did some rousting in his youth—packs of were-creatures tearing through the nicer neighborhoods, stirring up the humans. It's ridiculous, and of course it's frowned upon. Frightens the humans something awful, but there's no real harm. And of course he was sanctioned for it. But that was ages ago. Long before he was ever put up for the bench."

"Even whispers," Tucker pressed. "Irate phone calls. Anything."

"Nothing," she said. "Nothing." She shook her head. "I can't believe he's dead. I simply can't. It's not like him. He'd worked so hard to clean himself up. He was even dating again. Seeing a nice young woman, he was. Too young for him, if you ask me, an elder statesman such that he was. But still, he seemed smitten."

"Got a name?" Doyle asked.

"Oh, no. I don't. He never brought her here. I heard about her, of course. Saw her in his car once. Just a glimpse. I'm sorry."

"How about Lucius Dragos?"

"The vampire?" Her nose crinkled, and Doyle's estimation of the woman rose a notch.

"Did Braddock have any business with Dragos? Any of the blackmail or bribery schemes touch on him?"

"Not that I'm aware."

"Did he keep any papers here?" Doyle asked. "We'll need to take them back to Division for review."

"Just the file that the Order maintains on all the Therians." She stood up, as if grateful for something to do. "I'll run and get it for you."

She slipped out, and Doyle stood up and started walking casually around the room, ending up at the table with the girl. "Got a pile of work there, kid."

She nodded, but kept her eyes down.

"How old are you?"

She lifted her head. "Sixteen. My mother works here. I've been coming here for years and years. They gave me a job last year. I do the filing."

"Sounds like a good job. What's your name?"

She blushed ferociously. "Shana."

He pulled out a chair and sat down. "Nice to meet you, Shana. I'm Doyle. You know Judge Braddock?"

She swallowed, then nodded once.

"What do you think of him?"

A shrug. "I don't really think of him, you know?"

"Like the guy? He friendly?"

She focused on her papers. "Sure. Yeah. Whatever." She looked up. "He's dead now, right?"

"That he is."

She held his eyes for a moment, then looked back down at the tabletop. She didn't say a word, but Doyle would have sworn the girl smiled. Not that he got a chance to ask, because Ytalia was returning, a small box in her arms.

Doyle moved toward her, ignoring the pursed look of disapproval she shot his way as he moved away from the girl.

"Is that all?" she asked.

"I think that about does it," Doyle said. And if Tucker's open mouth was any indication, the wrap-up was a surprise to him.

"What are we doing?" Tucker asked once they were outside the building, the box in the Catalina's trunk, and the two men leaning against its polished mustard-yellow body.

"Waiting," Doyle said, an activity that took another ninety minutes and included sending Tucker on a Starbucks run. He'd just returned when Doyle saw what he was waiting for—Shana, leaving by the side door and walking away from them down the sidewalk.

He hurried to catch up, leaving Tucker and the coffee behind. "Hold up there, kid."

She slowed, looking back over her shoulder, and frowned. Then she kept right on walking. He fell into step beside her.

"Anything you want to tell me?"

"No."

"The man's dead. He can't hurt you now."

She stopped, facing him with wary eyes. "If he's dead, what does it matter?"

"Goes to motive," he said. "Hard to put a killer away if you don't know why he killed. Even with solid evidence." At the same time, if Doyle's suspicions were correct and Braddock had been secretly boinking little girls, he was going to come off as even more of a son of a bitch, and end up making Dragos look better by comparison. Shit. That was one hell of a fucked-up trade-off.

"I'm glad he's dead," the girl said.

"Why?" Doyle asked, certain he knew the answer.

"He told me not to tell. He told me I'd get in bad trouble."

"He can't get you into trouble now."

She looked down at the sidewalk. "I was thirteen," she said, her voice so soft that he could barely hear it, even with his preternaturally keen senses. "I kept his dirty secret," she said. "But I don't have to keep it anymore if I don't want to."

"No," Doyle said, fighting to stay level. Now wasn't the time for the rage to rise. He needed to be calm. Needed to not scare the girl. "Tell me what he did, Shana. What did Marcus Braddock do to you?"

"He hurt me," she said, her voice flat. "He raped me."

And then, with Doyle gently prodding the truth from her, Shana told him everything.

◊

The prep meeting for Luke's bail hearing was in thirty minutes, but instead of heading to the conference room, Sara took the elevator to sublevel nine and found herself urging a foul-smelling ogre to escort her to the prisoner's cell.

"Meeting you set, open we the door."

"Either you let me in now, or I'll get Mr. Bosch down here. Your choice."

The ogre grumbled, but he stood. He slid a stake into a holster above his beefy hips, then grabbed a battle-ax. "Go we now."

The detention block consisted of a series of glass-walled cells, and Sara kept her eyes straight ahead as they passed cell after cell occupied by a variety of scaled and furred creatures that shouted inventive sexual suggestions at her, alternating with pleas for release.

She didn't relax until they reached the end of the walk and Luke's cell.

"Sara," he said as she approached, and the pleasure she heard in his voice was enough to make her tremble.

"Was it you?" she asked, after the ogre had locked her in the cell with Luke. "Did you ask the Alliance to send a Seer?"

"I can't stomach the thought of a child killer walking free, so I asked Voight to give what assistance he could. Was he able to learn anything about the vampire who helped break Stemmons out?"

She swallowed thickly, thinking of the child's large eyes and bloodless face. "He's killed again. Ten years old. We've identified the body. Betsy Todd," she said, her heart breaking for Betsy, for her parents, and for the next child who Sara feared was already dead.

Luke stood for a moment, his body tense, his jaw tight. He clenched his fists at his side, then stalked to the wall of the cell. He thrust back, and punched hard, so hard Sara swore she felt the room shake. When he stepped back, a spiderweb of cracks radiated out from the spot where his fist had landed.

He was anger and energy, but she didn't hesitate. She

went to him, pressed her hands on his shoulders, and softly whispered his name.

He was silent for a moment, and she could feel the tension in his body, his muscles corded like wires. "My daughter was ten when she died," he said, his back to her. "Do you remember what I said? That I would kill this man for you?"

"I do."

"And now?" he asked. "Would you still keep me from that task?"

She turned away, not willing to answer him, not sure she could answer honestly, because she did want Stemmons dead. So help her, she wanted him dead and rotting and burning in hell. "It's a moot point," she said. "You're in here, and he's out there, some vampire working with him, and time is running out."

Luke turned to her, his body relaxing slightly, and the effort to make it so reflecting in his eyes. "What has Voight told you?"

"He said he couldn't get a clear read at the escape point, but he was able to confirm that it was the same vampire there and with Stemmons at the crime scene. And he confirmed that there is only one vampire helping Stemmons."

"Nothing else?"

"Not from Voight, but Doyle took it to the next level."

"Ryan Doyle," Luke said, his features tightening.

"There's a history between you two."

"There is," he said, but he didn't elaborate, and she didn't push.

"He learned that the vamp with Stemmons is female."

"Female," he repeated, and something in his voice made her frown.

"Does that mean something to you?" He hesitated, and she stepped closer. "Dammit, Luke, if you know anything—*anything*—that might help us, you had damn well better tell me."

He lifted his eyes to hers and then slowly, very slowly, he nodded. "There are things at play that you do not yet fully understand. Rivalries. Political positioning."

She frowned. "And this is relevant how?"

"The vampire and Therian communities are old enemies," he said. "And I've learned that a Therian plot to paint the vampires in a bad light has been foiled."

"What kind of plot?"

"The Therians intended to kill humans. To make the kills appear to be the work of vampires."

Sara hugged herself, thinking of the bite marks on little Betsy's neck. "Go on."

"The primary instigators have been stopped, but one remains at large. A vampire. A traitor to the race who has aligned herself with the Therians."

"Herself," Sara repeated. "A female."

"Her name is Caris," Luke said. "Take care not to underestimate her."

"And you think she could be involved with Stemmons?"

"I think the pieces add up. Tell me," he said, "how did Stemmons kill Betsy?"

"A neck wound," Sara said slowly. "Not his usual MO."

"But Caris has reason to increase the number of vampire attacks around town. Or at least to make it appear that they have increased. And the more offensive, the better. She wants to finish what her team started. And she wants to thumb her nose at the vampire community for foiling the Therians' original plans."

"How can we find her?"

"I don't know," he said. "Yet."

Sara nodded. "Thank you." This was a solid start. She could find this Caris, and with any luck, they would find Stemmons and the next child, too.

"I need to go." A humorless smile touched her lips. "I have a hearing to prepare for."

"You'll forgive me if I don't wish you luck."

She smiled and was reaching for the button to summon the ogre when his voice stopped her. "Tasha is missing."

She turned, saw the flash of worry on his face. "I'm so sorry. Can I help?"

He reached for her hand, and she gave it. "You help simply by asking."

"I could speak to Missing Persons," she said, wishing she had a cure, a fix, some way to wipe the worry from his face. "I don't know if the PEC has a section like that, but I have friends in the LAPD. They could—"

He pressed his palm to her cheek, the touch affecting her more than it should. "Thank you. All I ask is that you contact Nick. Tell him I need to speak with him before the hearing."

"All right. Of course I will." She hesitated, thinking about propriety and her position and the whole damned mess. She didn't care. She leaned forward and brushed a quick kiss over his forehead. "I really am sorry," she said. "I'm so terribly sorry."

"Sara," he said, heat flaring behind the pain in his eyes.

She stepped back, her hands shoved into the pockets of her suit jacket, not quite believing she'd just leaped gleefully over that line. "We've been investigating Braddock," she began, thinking of the report she'd just received from Agent Doyle. "Luke, did he harm Tasha?"

He drew in a breath, then slowly released it. "Welcome back, Counselor."

She flinched, but held her ground, staying silent as he moved back to the concrete slab that served as a bed.

"Unless I am mistaken, this subject is forbidden without the presence of my attorney."

He was right, of course. "In that case, you can speak freely without fear of your words coming back to bite you." She tried again. "Is that why you killed him? Revenge for Tasha?"

He smiled thinly. "I have never admitted to killing the bastard, though I do not deny an intense joy that he is in fact dead."

She thought of his file, and knew how easily denial could come to his lips. He'd been briefly suspected and then cleared in dozens of deaths, all vigilante-style killings. All men and women who society would likely say deserved to die.

Too many for it to be coincidence.

And he had powerful Alliance friends.

She couldn't condone the acts or the deaths. Vigilante justice, she thought sourly, was not justice at all.

And yet . . .

"I turned nine about the time Jacob Crouch was freed," she said. "And I remember my mom went on and on about the system, and justice, and how sometimes bad people slip through the cracks, but without the system, chaos would run wild and anarchy would take over."

"Your mother sounds like a woman with strong beliefs."

"You could say that. She was an assistant district attorney. She lived and breathed the system."

His mouth twitched as he stared at her. "Imagine that."

"Yeah. I definitely inherited a few traits." She drew in a breath. "Her resolve never faltered. Even when Crouch went free."

He got up off the slab and moved toward her, then sat on the concrete beside her. "And yours has?"

She thought of the fantasies she'd had about killing Crouch, about taking down Stemmons. She didn't want to answer, but the question was fair, and she wanted them to understand each other. "No. But in my mind—" She shook her head. "I would never do it, though. Justice is found in the law, not on the streets."

"But with Crouch, the system got it wrong," Luke said. "And when he was killed, the world self-corrected."

"I still go to bed every night thanking the person who shut that monster down. And sometimes I hate myself for that."

"You shouldn't," he said. "Crouch got what he deserved."

"No," she said. "He didn't. What he deserved was to be tried and convicted. Everything else..." She trailed off. She couldn't justify that next step. Couldn't justify the way her fingers sometimes itched to pull the trigger. Or the way she celebrated Crouch's anonymous killer.

She couldn't justify it, but she did understand it. That urge—that need—to avenge someone you love. "Luke," she began, softly, hesitantly, "what did he do to Tasha?"

He stiffened, silent, and for a moment she feared he wouldn't answer. Then he stood, crossed the room and faced the hard stone wall.

"I witnessed nothing," Luke said, but the sharp edge to his voice told a different story.

"Did he come to her? Seduce her? Take advantage of a girl who didn't understand, not really, what he wanted? What was happening to her?"

"Sara—" His voice held both warning and pain.

"Mitigating circumstances, Luke," she said, moving forward and pressing her hands to his shoulders. "If there are circumstances, you need to raise them in court."

"Will you stand now as my defense attorney?"

"Dammit, Luke, let me help you. My goal is not a stake to your heart. I'm looking for the truth."

"Truth is often elusive, and some debts are best paid outside the bounds of the law."

Her chest constricted, knowing that she'd just heard as close to a confession as would ever cross his lips. *He'd killed Marcus Braddock.* And yet she didn't want him going down. Not if there was a defense, a way to save him. "If he was harming Tasha..." She trailed off, giving him an opportunity to speak, to latch on to the defense. He was silent.

She rubbed her fingers on her temples. "Luke, please. Tell me what happened. Don't go down hard if you don't have to."

"I have nothing to say." He turned to face her. "And anything I have said here today cannot be used against me at the bail hearing."

"No," she agreed. "It can't. But if you work with me, maybe we can get the charges reduced, even dismissed. At the very least, we can get you out on bail."

He turned around, and she was surprised to see that he was smiling. "I have the utmost faith in your system," he said. "This evening, I will have bail."

She crossed her arms over her chest. "Don't count on it, Luke. I play to win."

"A wager, then," he said, both heat and amusement tainting his voice. "If I am released, I want you in my bed."

"You won't win," she said, though she couldn't deny that part of her desperately, deeply, hoped he did.

♦

The girl lay on the floor, ripe and ready. Fourteen years old. This one long and lean. An athletic build, with strong hips and breasts that were just beginning to ripen.

Delicious.

The girl stirred slightly in sleep, and Xavier pressed a hand to her forehead. "Calm now," he said, his caress soft. Soothing.

It wouldn't do for her to fear him, not when she was giving him the gift of blood. The gift of becoming.

Across the small basement room, his Dark Angel stood watching, her gaze fixed on the girl's face. "Drain this one, and the light will surely fill you."

He bowed his head in deference. "Will you feed, too, Angel?"

"I feed," she said. "You feed." Her mouth drew into a thin smile. "We will have a feast."

Beneath him, the girl stirred; the drugs were wearing off. Good. It was better when they were awake. Asleep, and they seemed dead. Awake, and he could watch the life flow from the child to him.

He stroked her neck with his fingertip. "Wake up, wake up. It's time for the gift. Time for the light."

He turned his head, looking at his Angel. "This one is all for me?"

She laughed, delighted. "How will you make the wound?"

It was a problem. His teeth were not sharp like hers. Not yet. Not until he proved himself worthy. And though he could rip and tear at her flesh, that would spoil the beauty of the soft, sweet skin.

He moved to the table for his knife. It had served him well so many times before. It would serve him again. Open the wound, and close his mouth over the sweet flow of life.

But it would drain out too quickly. He needed another, and the cages were empty, the hunt not complete.

"We will hunt after?" he asked.

She laughed. "So eager."

"I seek only to please you." He kept his head down, wanting to ask about her plans for him, but not sure that he should. In the end, though, he couldn't keep silent. "Am I worthy? Will you take me with you to your side?" He wanted to be like her; he wanted to feed only on the blood. On the light.

She laughed, then twirled, her skirt flowing outward. "Some of my kind are worthy. Some waste their gift. And some should never have been turned at all."

"And me?" he asked, praying she would find him worthy.

"You," she said, "are meant for wondrous things. Special. So special." She glided toward him, circled him. "Tell me, Xavier. Do you know the one who bound you? Who called your genius criminal?"

"I know her," he said. "A bitch prosecutor." He looked up, afraid he'd gone too far, but the Angel was only smiling at him.

"She is horrible. Takes things that do not belong to her."

"My life," he said. "My freedom." But he had his freedom back now, and the bitch prosecutor didn't matter. Only the girls mattered, and this one especially. This one who even now stirred at his feet. "It's time to get started," he said.

"Then do not hesitate."

But he did, because the girl was not enough, and he needed to know. Needed to be certain another would come. Another would fill him. "And after?" he asked. "When the light is gone?"

"Then we will hunt again," she said, satisfying him.

And with the greatest anticipation, he pressed the knife to the child's throat, and listened as the scream came, yanking her back from the depths of sleep.

CHAPTER 26

The hearing was not going well. She'd put on more than enough evidence to show that Luke had connections—serious connections of the type who could wrangle a way to remove the detention device. She'd presented evidence of guilt—the DNA, the ring, Doyle's testimony. And she'd even been allowed to provide evidence of Luke's notoriety—the kind of evidence that would never have been allowed upstairs—to show that he was a danger to the community.

She'd done everything right, and still she was losing. She could see it in the way the judge shifted and turned on the bench, his beady bird eyes seeming to look past her evidence to a conclusion he'd already established.

"I'm sinking," she said to Bosch.

"You're putting on the best case you have," he said, which didn't make her feel better. This was her first hearing in her new job, and she was sitting at the counsel table with her new boss. She wanted a win, dammit, and the only way she could think to get it was to play her trump card.

She looked over at the defendant's table—at Nick, sitting there looking smug, and Luke beside him, his manner, his appearance, his very essence both screaming of importance and warning of danger. She told herself this wasn't about him—about them—and then, because her feelings for Luke should never have affected her prosecution of the case, she stood up, finally resolved.

"Your Honor, the prosecution moves to introduce video footage of the pool deck of the Broadway Towers taken late Friday night."

Now Montegue surged to his feet. "Objection. Your Honor, may we approach?"

The judge turned one of his beady black eyes on Montegue. The gryphon—with an eagle's head and a lion's body—was huge and imposing, and could maintain order in his courtroom with nothing more than a glance. "Approach? But there is no jury present."

"No, but the gallery is full, and Ms. Constantine is about to lead us into mine-filled waters."

The feathers that covered the judge's face ruffled, but he agreed.

"This is completely unacceptable," Montegue continued. "Counsel is addressing an area that must be treated as off the record."

"Your Honor," Sara said, "that isn't exactly accurate. My conversation with Mr. Dragos is off the record. But Agent Doyle acquired the same information entirely independent of me or Mr. Montegue or Mr. Dragos."

The judge considered for only a moment, then nodded at Sara. "Proceed."

A little trill of victory shot through her, only to be quashed by Montegue's harsh words as they walked back to the counsel table. "There is the letter of the law, and then there is the spirit, Ms. Constantine. I think we both know that what you've done skirts propriety. At the very least you should have given us notice that you intended to piss on the good faith that Mr. Dragos and myself showed to you."

She swallowed a bubble of guilt. "My client is the PEC, Mr. Montegue, and I haven't done anything except protect its interest to the fullest extent of the law. Without, I might add, overstepping the bounds of that law."

She sat down calmly enough, but considering the firm hand that Bosch placed on her shoulder, she had a feeling that her irritation was showing. She *hadn't* crossed a line. Not really.

Yet she couldn't discount the fact that it felt as if she had.

"Your Honor," she said. "The prosecution calls Agent Ryan Doyle." Doyle would introduce the evidence, and through him, she could turn the court's attention to the fact that Luke fed on Annie.

Before Doyle could approach, though, Montegue stood again. "If it please the court, my client will testify to a Directive 27 violation and ask that the court entertain evidence on an affirmative defense at the close of the prosecution's case."

The judge's head bobbed. "Directive 27?" he repeated as a murmur flowed across the gallery.

"Yes, sir. A human woman. Mr. Dragos both fed off the female, and fed his blood to her." He turned and flashed a bright white smile at Sara. "A stipulation, Counselor. Just to make sure we're out of here by the dinner hour."

"If you really want to be out by dinner," she said sweetly, "then drop the affirmative defense."

"We shall all dine in a timely fashion," the judge said, "as this court is ready to issue its ruling."

Sara glanced over at the defendant's table, caught Luke's eye, then ripped her gaze away. She stood with Bosch at her side and waited for the ruling.

"Bail is granted," he said, "in the amount of five million dollars."

A murmur ran through the crowd.

"The defendant will be required to wear the standard mobile detention device," the judge continued. "And in light of the Directive 27 stipulation, the defendant will also be fitted with a bloodletting impediment." He slammed his gavel on the desk. "So ordered."

As soon as the judge had left the courtroom, Sara leaned toward Bosch. "Bloodletting impediment?"

"A secondary detention device," Bosch explained. "This one will trigger if Dragos takes blood directly from a human again."

As she gathered up her papers, Bosch shifted beside her, and Sara thought she caught the subtle scent of cinnamon. "Under the circumstances, the possibility of Lucius staying in jail while the case came up was slim. But you gave them a hard battle, and proved yourself an asset to the team. Good work."

She pasted on a smile, accepting the compliment along with a smattering of "you did good" and "you'll nail his ass in trial" from well-meaning onlookers, some of whom she recognized as other prosecutors in her office.

When she finally did slip through the door and into the hall, she sighed. She may have lost her first hearing, but it was only one battle.

In the grand scheme of things, the battles meant nothing. The only thing that mattered was the war. But since the resolution of that war could see Luke staked, she had to admit, if only to herself, that for the first time in her career, she didn't relish the battles yet to come.

CHAPTER 27

"Batorak metoin shrebat."

"If you're asking me if it's comfortable," Luke said in French, as the weight of the new mobile detention device once again pressed against his flesh, "the answer is a resounding no."

The daemon pressed a hand to his shoulder. *"Bon chance,"* the daemon said, switching from Daemonic to a language Luke could understand.

"Merci." Luke inclined his head as his fingers manipulated the tiny white buttons, buttoning the shirt Nick had brought him to replace the T-shirt that had been shredded once in this very room. A black tray sat on the table in front of him, and he retrieved his wallet and cell phone, then carefully picked up the tiny gold serpent ring. Were it not so small, he would slip it onto his little finger. But Livia's hands had been tiny, and the ring didn't fit. As was his habit, he slipped it deep into his pocket, then reached in, checking to make sure it was in place.

Now ready, he turned to Nick. "Counselor, shall we depart this place?"

"It would be a pleasure," Nick said. They moved through corridors and down elevators, ignoring the stares and whispers of those who worked within Division.

As they approached the elevator, Nick handed Luke a small memory card. "Caris," he said. "Best we can tell, she's been holing up here. You've got the address on there. Known recent associates included, too. Standard encryption. Details in the file."

"Excellent."

"You really think Caris would align herself with a human?"

"If it serves Gunnolf's purpose—or her own—then yes."

"And it does," Nick said. "Tasha even fits Stemmons's profile. Young girls. Red hair, blue eyes. She's older than he took in the past, but she looks young."

"Caris won't care about that," Luke said. "But Stemmons will, and she'll want him cooperative."

"And if she brings Tasha into the mix, she serves Gunnolf's purpose even while cutting you like a knife."

"And Tasha has become both a pawn and a prize." He drew in a hard breath, certain Caris would not hesitate to take the opportunity to destroy Tasha. To use Stemmons and his blade to cut down the innocent child that Caris believed should never have been allowed to live.

"I'll go with you," Nick said as they stepped onto the elevator.

"No. She's mine." After battling back his daemon so hard and so often, letting the beast run free would be a pleasure.

Nick hesitated, his gaze dipping only momentarily to the device strapped to Luke's chest. "All right," he said. "But be careful. Caris isn't one to be trifled with."

"Neither am I," Luke said. "What word do you have

from Tiberius? I'm not inclined to return to this place after we leave, and I'm less inclined to keep this device strapped to my chest."

Nick's face shifted, going hard. "About that, we have a little problem."

Luke turned, wary, the daemon starting to writhe within.

"Tiberius said to tell you that you did good work with Hasik, but that his hands are tied."

"Politics," Luke said, spitting out the word, forcing himself to keep his rage under control. "I need out of this contraption, Nick. And Tiberius needs me on his team."

"He does. But with his control over L.A. so strained, he's not willing to take chances. I'm sorry, Luke," Nick said. "You're on your own with this one."

Luke gave a sharp nod, clinging to control.

"It's not over, Luke."

"I know." He ground out the words, then drew in a cleansing breath, forcing the daemon down. He thought of Sara, imagined her beside him, and felt the calm flow through him.

He shoved the daemon under with abrupt finality. "I'll find a way."

"I don't doubt it," Nick said as the doors slid open and he stepped out into the lower-level reception area.

"Mr. Dragos!"

He turned to face the reception desk, where a young woman with a blue braid wrapped into a cylinder upon her head waved frantically at him.

"I'm supposed to ask you to stay."

"I believe the court has spoken otherwise."

"Huh? Oh! No, gosh. Not for permanent. But Ms. Constantine wants a word with you and Mr. Montegue before you go."

"I see," Luke said, impressed by the calm in his voice despite the fact that the mere mention of her name made his blood flow warm.

Nick, he saw, was watching him. "Tell Ms. Constantine that my client has enjoyed the PEC's hospitality long enough. If she needs to speak to either of us, she has my contact information."

"Nick."

"I am still your advocate," Nick said. "And if you wish me to remain in that capacity, you will follow my advice." His expression softened along with his voice. "Luke, the path you want to walk leads nowhere."

Luke knew that well enough, yet he refused to accept it. Impossible though it might seem, he would find a way to make Sara his.

"I will speak to her," he said, his tone broaching no argument.

"You need to back away." There was both warning and compassion in Nick's voice. "Leave it, and leave her."

"She compels me," Lucius said. "I cannot shut her out any more than I could willingly harm her." He stood still, trying to conjure the words that would make his friend understand. "She soothes the daemon," he finally said. "Tell me that you do not understand. Tell me honestly that were you in my position you would walk away from her. That you could walk away."

He saw the pain pass over his friend's face. The memories of Lissa, the woman who had once soothed Nick beyond all others. Who had hurt him beyond all others, too.

"We will speak about this later," Nick said, but the edge had left his voice.

"I have no doubt," Luke said.

The elevator opened, and Sara stepped out, her cheeks rosy from having rushed. Their eyes locked, and he felt it. A sensual tug he associated only with her. A hard jolt to his senses that had his body firing and his imagination traveling to forbidden destinations.

She held his gaze. One moment. Another. And then she looked away, but not before he saw it on her face— *desire.*

He saw it, and he cherished it.

Mine, he thought, and knew that no matter what else transpired between them, there was a truth in that one simple word.

She walked with exaggerated purpose toward him, sliding her palms along her skirt as if they were damp. "Mr. Dragos. Mr. Montegue. Thank you for waiting."

"My client is pleased to cooperate with any and all reasonable requests posed by the prosecution, Counselor. We hope, of course, that the favor will be reciprocated this time."

"I...of course," she said, but her voice was distracted, and her eyes were on Luke. "Oh, hell. I was hoping to speak to you. Privately," she added, glancing pointedly at Nick.

"Of course. Nick," he said. "A moment, please, with Ms. Constantine."

Nick sighed, long and put-upon. "We've had this conversation, Luke. As long as I'm your advocate—"

"You're fired."

Nick's expression couldn't have been more startled if Luke had dropped his pants and mooned him. "What?"

"You're fired," he repeated. "It's a simple concept resulting in the termination of any business relationship between us."

"Don't do this, Luke."

"Don't fight me, Nicholas." He turned to the receptionist. "Do you have access to the relevant databases? Can you make a notation that Lucius Dragos is no longer represented by counsel, but is proceeding *in pro per*?"

"I . . . um . . . I . . ." She glanced frantically toward Sara, who nodded.

"I'll take responsibility," Sara said, the laughter in her voice delighting him. "Go ahead. I expect you'll be adding Mr. Montegue back to the database after Mr. Dragos and I conclude our conversation."

Luke chuckled. "I like the way you think, but no. Mr. Montegue and I have reached the end of the line. Irreconcilable differences," he said, with a brief nod to his friend.

"This isn't over," Nick said, his voice a taut wire, ready to snap.

"I expect no less from you," Luke said. "But for now, it is."

Nick tossed his car keys into the air, caught them. "Fair enough, my friend. But find your own ride home."

And with that, he slipped through the doors and into the PEC parking garage.

Luke turned his attention to Sara. "I think he's upset."

"Imagine that.

"I wanted to say thank you. For the information about Caris."

"Have you found her?" He almost feared that Division had—he wanted the sweet pleasure of ending her himself.

"Not yet. The investigators are following a bunch of leads." Her mouth quirked up. "I've been a little busy with a hearing, so I'm not completely up to date."

He glanced over her shoulder, saw that the receptionist was trying to watch them without being obvious. "I must go," he said, fearful that Division would soon have the same information about Caris's whereabouts that he held in his pocket. "But I believe there is the matter of a wager between us. I will collect."

She shook her head. "Luke, please. Don't. Don't press me."

"Why not?" He moved closer, drawn in by the heat of her, the desire that emanated from her. She was denying him, yes. But her heart wasn't in it.

"Because I want to," she admitted, her voice small but her words running through him like a song.

"Sara—"

"No." She shook her head, her voice firm, and he sensed the resolve within her. "Whatever this is between us, Luke, I won't encourage it. I wish— Never mind. But we can't, and please don't push me on it."

"I cannot agree to that," he said, "but neither can I argue about it now."

She tilted her head, her brow crinkling with worry. "Tasha?"

"I must go."

She reached for his hand, and the touch almost did him in. "I remembered what you told me, about having a daughter long ago. That's what Tasha is to you now, isn't she?"

"Sara..." Her name came out raw, gravelly with need. He wanted to pull her close, to have her soothe his fears. To lose himself in the simple pleasure of having her beside him.

He could do none of that, and he hated the circumstances that had brought them to this impasse.

He reached into his pocket, his fingers finding Livia's ring. He wanted to draw comfort from it, but comfort didn't come. He feared that now that he'd met Sara, he would be soothed only by her touch.

"You'll find her," she said gently. "But Luke," she added, her voice now sharp with warning, "when you do, don't run. It will be worse for you if you run."

Despite his better judgment, he cupped his hand to her cheek, enjoying the shocked expression on the receptionist's face. "My darling Sara," he said. "Considering the PEC would have me dead, I cannot imagine how it could be worse. But I appreciate your warning nonetheless."

He stepped away from her, moving toward the door. "We'll speak again."

"Ms. Constantine?" the receptionist called. "Mr. Bosch's assistant is on the line." She held the phone out for Sara, and Luke stayed put, listening.

"There's been another child found," a woman said, her smooth voice marred with regret. "The task force requests that you go immediately to the scene."

When Sara hung up, Luke was by her side.

"I'm going with you."

"The hell you are."

But he would broach no argument. "You may work with me or against me, but I am going, and I'm going with you."

◆

"No way," Doyle shouted, his finger stretched out to point at Luke. A finger that was about to be broken if the para-daemon didn't get it the hell out of Luke's face. "No fucking way."

Sara stepped between them. "He stays. He helps."

"He's a murderer."

Sara stepped up, getting right in Doyle's face, a sight that warmed Luke's heart. She pointed to her left, toward the adolescent body, now splayed out in death, over which the techs were doing their job.

"Do you have any reason, Agent, to think that Dragos committed this crime or any crime related to this murder? Do you? Because I don't. But I damn sure want to find out who did, and if I think Dragos can help, then he stays. And he stays on my authority."

"You're on thin ice, Constantine."

"Then it's a good thing I know how to swim, isn't it?"

The look Doyle shot Luke was one of pure hatred. Then he stalked away, leaving Sara seething. She looked up at Luke, her face flushed. "Dammit," she said. "All I want to do is find him before he kills the next victim. I don't need the rest of this bullshit."

"You said he kept all the victims caged? I need to get close to the body." He needed to see if the little girl had

Tasha's scent on her. If they'd shared a cage. And he needed to search for another scent of Caris.

"All right," she said, looking at him sideways. "But I'm sticking my neck out on this, Luke. Don't prove Doyle right."

"Never."

By the time they reached the body, the Division staff had cleared out most of the county workers, and Severin Tucker and a few other agents that Luke didn't recognize were adjusting the thoughts of the few who remained. Sara spoke with Bosch, who turned, stared at Luke, and then gave one quick, curt nod. She cocked her head and Luke joined her. "Two minutes."

"I won't need any more."

He bent over the naked body, focusing only on the smell, forcing himself not to think about the loss, the youth, the horror of this young life ripped away so brutally.

The memory of another time and another place rose within him. Livia laughing, calling his name. He shoved it down. He couldn't go there. Not now. He needed to keep control. Needed to keep the daemon in check. Tasha's life hung in the balance. Lose control, and he could lose her.

He lifted his head, nostrils flaring, breathing in deep the scent of the night. Of raw earth. Of grass. Of the child herself, and the pungent odor of death taking hold.

And just when he was about to give up, he caught it. A familiar fragrance like lavender in the fields. Innocence and beauty. *Tasha.*

He turned, finding Sara beside him. "Tasha."

Sara's eyes went wide with understanding, and she

grabbed his arm, tugging him back away from the crowd. "Tasha?" she repeated. "You came here because Stemmons has Tasha?"

"I feared that Caris had taken her." He drew his hands through his hair, trying to think. So far he had no scent of Caris, and he began to walk the perimeter of the crime scene, searching the night for her woody scent.

"And you didn't tell me? Dammit, Luke, how long have you suspected this?"

He stopped, stared down at her. "Does it matter now? Your monster has Tasha, and unless I've missed my guess, Caris is with her."

She fell in step beside him. "I went out on a limb for you, and—"

He held up a hand. "There."

"What?"

They were at least twenty yards from the crime scene, but there was no mistaking the scent. She'd been there. The vile bitch had stood on that exact spot, and not very long ago, either. "Caris." He turned to Sara. "I must go."

"Go?" she repeated, looking back toward the body. "Go where?"

"Silver Lake," he said, referring to the information on Caris's whereabouts that Nick had passed to him as they were leaving the courthouse.

She hurried to keep up with him as he rushed toward her car. "Why?"

"She's there," he said tightly.

"Tasha?"

"Caris," he said. "And with any luck, Tasha, too."

"Then we need the team. We need—"

He stopped, taking her arm. "I need your car, Sara. I do not need the team. And I can't have you accompanying me."

"I don't care what you need. I'm going with you."

"She is dangerous."

"So are you," Sara countered.

"I'll not argue about this."

"Good. But my car has an ignition lock, and since you don't know the code, you're going to be wasting a lot of time if you don't take me with you."

He stopped, his focus utterly on her. "Why?"

It was a question she couldn't answer, because she hadn't been thinking, only reacting. She knew why he was going—what he would do to Caris if he found her. But she couldn't fight him on this. "It's Tasha," she said, simply. "And she's important to you."

As she watched, he closed his eyes, then swallowed. When he looked at her again, he was all steel. "You come," he said. "But you stay in the car."

Even in the middle of the night, it took them twenty minutes to get from North Hollywood to Silver Lake, and Luke was cursing when he ran the car up over the curb and plowed to a stop in front of the house. He aimed a single finger at her. "Stay," he said, and she swore that she would, a promise she immediately found hard to keep.

She knew almost nothing about Caris other than the brief dossier Martella had run for her after Luke had first mentioned the name. There'd been little information. She was a former lover of Tiberius, the vampiric liaison to the Alliance. They'd had a falling out a few years prior. Rumors were thick, but the most likely suggested that she'd hooked up with a werewolf, which screamed of the political intrigue that Luke had told her about. The bottom line, though, was that Caris was a vampire, and she'd apparently hooked up with scum like Stemmons. She was killing, and she was dangerous, and she wasn't constrained by hematite bands.

So, yeah, Sara was worried.

She waited, her eyes on the house. The quiet house. The way-too-quiet house.

Hell.

She opened the door, not at all sure what she was going to do. She knew she had to see what was going on in there. And as soon as she did, the front windows shattered, and she saw Luke silhouetted in the void.

"Luke!" She raced toward him, not thinking of the danger until she'd burst through the front door. But there was no danger. There was only Luke in a fury, a chair thrust high over his head as he hurled it through the darkened room at the far wall, where it shattered into pieces. "Luke, stop!"

He turned, eyes wild, his face contorted. She stopped, eyeing him warily, realizing quickly that the house was empty. Tasha wasn't here. Neither was Caris.

He'd run out of hope, and the daemon was furious.

"We'll find her," she said, moving toward him, this man who had once held her so tenderly, who now burned with the loss of one he loved. She understood the depth of his rage; she felt it herself every time she thought of Crouch and of the father he'd stolen from her. Tasha, however, wasn't yet gone. "We'll find her," she repeated, and this time she moved in close, ignoring the prickling of fear to cup his face in her hands, letting him know that she was there, and, yes, that she understood.

Slowly, she felt the tension ease from him, and as he collapsed to his knees on the floor, she went down with him, cradling his head against her chest. "Sara," he whispered. "I thought she would be here."

"We'll find her. I bet Division has a lead. We'll follow it up. Luke," she said, her heart breaking for him, "we'll do whatever it takes."

She tipped his face up to hers and waited until he met her gaze. The beast was there, trembling beneath the surface, but Luke was in control now. Barely. Sara felt a shiver of fear but didn't release him. She stroked her fingers over his cheek.

"We will find her," she promised again. And had never meant anything more in her life.

CHAPTER 28

"Someone who works at the Slaughtered Goat might know where Caris is," Luke said to Bael Slater. "Any lead, I want you following it."

"No problem." The huge vampire leaned back, the small chair creaking under the strain. They were in a small bar near Division where Luke had gone after Sara had returned to the office with the team. "Division's got nothing, huh?"

"They don't have shit," Luke said, taking a sip of Glenfiddich. "I'm going back to the crime scenes. Try to pick up a scent."

"Didn't Division already tug on that line?"

"The vamps on the team are at least four centuries younger than me," Luke said. "Their senses aren't as well honed."

"Long shot," Slater said.

"At this point, even the long shots are worth following."

His friend stood. "I'll be in touch." Luke started to stand, but was startled by the sharp ring of his phone. He snatched it quickly from the pocket of his duster, hoping to see Tasha's name on the caller ID. Instead, the phone identified the caller as TQ.

"What have you learned?" he asked without preamble. Luke had called the jinn after he'd parted from Sara, demanding satisfaction for Tariq's botched assignment that first night.

"Still Scotch, Luke?" Tariq asked, as Luke lifted his glass. "Still single malt?"

Luke hid his small smile behind the glass as his eyes searched the room. He should have expected the wily creature to be nearby.

He didn't find the jinn, but his blood pounded hot when he saw a lithe woman with cropped dark hair and feline eyes. *Caris.* He stood, upsetting the table in his haste, but a second later she was gone.

She'd either transformed into mist and left, or his eyes were playing tricks on him. He forced down a wave of discontent and concentrated on finding Tariq, ultimately locating him by the back door.

"Tell me what you know," Luke demanded.

"That depends. Will this do us square?"

"What does your conscience say, Tariq? It was you who wronged me. Does this balance the scales?"

"It does."

Luke stayed silent, remembering that cold night in Munich many centuries before.

"Dammit, Lucius, it does."

It did not, Luke thought. But that point could be raised at a later date. "Tell me."

"Then we're square?"

"I did not say that."

"Fucking-A. Fine. Got me under your goddamn thumb for the rest of my natural life."

"The countermeasures, my friend. Tell me what you know of the detention device and its countermeasures."

"They'll fry your ass if you get free of them," Tariq said.

"I don't recall saying that was my purpose. I'm a lover of knowledge, Tariq. Knowledge for knowledge's sake."

"Fuck," Tariq said. "It's your ass. Whatever. It's a fail-safe system."

"I expected as much."

"Security Section can release you from the device upon proper authorization from Bosch or Leviathin."

"And the judge?" Luke asked, thinking that perhaps Acquila had not yet outlived his usefulness.

"Nada. Once bail's granted, he's out of the loop."

"So Bosch and Leviathin are key?"

"That's the beauty," Tariq said. "The system's also tied in to the prosecutors and the lead investigator."

Luke tensed, the possibilities dancing in front of him. "Say that again."

"I know," Tariq said almost giddily, and then repeated himself. "Sweet, huh?"

"Together?" Luke asked, ignoring the jinn. "Doyle and the prosecutors must be together?"

"Any one can do it," he said. "Bosch, Doyle, Constantine. But they can't do it remotely. Gotta be in Division, in Security Section. Key in access to the primary system, then key in the abort code."

"Interesting," Luke said. He would take much pleasure in dragging Doyle's sorry ass back inside Division and making the para-daemon do that which would set Luke free.

But despite the pleasure he would undoubtedly derive

from such an adventure, he had to admit that the risks were legion, as were any attempts to use Bosch.

He frowned, not pleased by the possibilities. "Are there alternatives?" he asked Tariq. "Who installed the fail-safes?"

"Lucius," Tariq said. "Take the easy route."

"It's none of it easy," Luke answered. "We'll speak again." And then, before Tariq could protest, he terminated the call and thought of Sara.

At one time, he would have used her without hesitation, but that time was long gone.

He thought of Sara and her sense of rules, of justice. She would never agree to do this thing, and more than that, he knew that he could not ask her to.

There had to be another way, he thought, as he stood to leave, and somehow he would find it.

♦

Sara woke with a start, jerked awake by a sharp pounding at her door. Not that she minded too much—she'd been teetering on the verge of another nightmare—but at two in the morning, it was quite possible the visitor could be worse than the tormenting dreams.

"Coming," she shouted, sliding into a robe. She hurried to the door, checked the peephole, and found herself looking at Luke's sexy, scowling face. She keyed in the alarm code, opened the door, and soon discovered the reason for his scowl—her across-the-hall neighbor, Mrs. Fitzhugh, was standing in the doorway in curlers, her expression both shocked and disapproving.

And why not? With his long, dark coat, his warrior's

eyes, and the scar that cut across his cheek, Luke looked decidedly formidable. "It's okay, Mrs. Fitzhugh. He's a friend." Which wasn't the least bit accurate. Friends didn't make her melt from a single look. And it was only around Luke that she felt like her body was a fire that only he could extinquish.

And, she noticed as she ushered him inside, he'd brought her a flower.

She stroked her finger over the soft petals of the bird-of-paradise. "It's beautiful. Thank you." She frowned, looking more closely at the flower, and then at his slightly sheepish expression. "Where did you get it?"

"The garden in front of your building," he admitted. "There aren't many options at 2 A.M."

She bit back a laugh. "No, I guess not." She headed toward the kitchen to find water for the flower. "So why are you here? No news about Tasha," she added. "You would have told me already."

"I wanted to see you," he said, his voice somehow both strong and vulnerable. "I followed Stemmons's trail tonight. Tracking away from each of his original crime scenes as best I could. I found nothing."

"I'm so sorry."

"Afterward, I came here. You're in my head, Sara. I hear your voice. I smell your scent. I feel your touch." His shoulders lifted. "And I had to come."

Her heart tripped in her chest. "Oh." She swallowed, knowing she shouldn't say more, but unable to stay silent. "I'm glad you did."

"Are you?"

"We're probably breaking a lot of rules."

He moved toward her. "Oddly enough, I've never been good at following rules."

"Why do I believe that?"

"But the rules are important to you," he said. He caressed her cheek, making her want to break down and purr. "Do you want me to leave?"

She hesitated, knowing that for the sake of her sanity—and possibly her job—she should lie. Instead, she spoke the truth. "No." She looked at his face, the perfect, classic lines marred by the warrior's scar. A face that had seen death and a man who had surely wrought it a thousand times over. Yet right then he was looking at her with such tenderness it made her breath catch in her throat. "No," she repeated, her voice little more than a whisper. "I want you to stay."

"Good," he said, the simple word conveying a wealth of emotion. "Let me hold you."

She hesitated only a moment, then moved in and pressed her cheek against him.

Luke sighed, his chest rising and falling beneath her, steady and calm.

"Luke," she began, then stopped. She wouldn't tell him that she wished things were different. That they'd met under different circumstances. Instead, she told him the most basic of truths. "I— No matter how I feel about you, I will do my job."

"Do you think I don't know that?"

She tilted her head up to look at his face. "It doesn't seem to bother you overly much."

"You will do what you must," he said. "As will I."

She swallowed, knowing that as a prosecutor she should push, try to determine if he was intending to run, and if so, how. As a woman, though, she didn't want to know. Didn't even want to think about it. Because if he stayed, he would undoubtedly be executed for murder. And if he left, she would never see him again. Impossible.

"We met at the wrong time," she whispered.

"When would you have preferred?"

She laughed, considering the question. "I don't know. The thirties? Odds are good I wouldn't have been a lawyer back then."

"Except that you would not have been born," he said, his fingers lazily stroking her back. "And as inconvenient as it may be for us, I am fond of the woman you are."

"I am, too," she admitted. "Still, it would have been nice. To be with you, without all of this noise surrounding us." She thought back, enjoying the game, the fantasy. "Then again, maybe not the thirties. Maybe the 1800s, and I could have lived in the South and worn fabulous gowns."

"Ah, but then we would have to work so very hard to free you from the corset."

Her breath hitched as she imagined him undressing her. "If it was your fingers doing the unfastening," she admitted, "I'm not sure I would mind."

"Nor I."

It struck her suddenly that he surely had actual experience with actual corsets, and the realization was both fascinating and overwhelming. "Were you here during the Civil War? The American Revolution?"

His laugh seemed to rumble through her. "If I tell you that I was, will you run?"

"No," she whispered, trying to imagine all that he'd seen, that he'd experienced. It made her expected eighty or so years seem inadequate and puny. "My father would have loved you," she said, then immediately backtracked. "I mean, the history. He loved history, and you're like a walking archive. It's . . . it's overwhelming."

"Then we are even," he said, "because you overwhelm me as well."

His words seemed to trip over her skin, a skimming rock on a pool of water, sending little ripples of pleasure outward over her body. She wanted him—there was no point in denying it—and yet she knew damn well that taking this any further would be a bad, bad idea.

"Luke—"

"Hush." He brushed his lips over her hair, then tucked a finger under her chin and tilted her face up to his. She drew in a breath, knowing she should protest, even going so far as to form the words in her head. But they didn't come, and when his mouth brushed hers, she moaned with the pleasure of it.

The kiss was slow and gentle, a promise of future delights, and her body fired in anticipation, her breasts aching and her thighs gathering warmth between them. She clenched her hands, gathering his shirt in her fingers, and opened her mouth to his.

"Sara," he whispered, his lips brushing her ear in a wonderfully arousing manner. "I would have you in bed."

He didn't give her time to answer, simply slanted his mouth over hers even as he drew her close until their bodies pressed together, and she could feel every inch of him, including his growing arousal. She moaned, her lips parting with the sound, and he took full advantage, his mouth sliding greedily over hers. His mouth was both soft and firm, and he slid his tongue over her lips, between them, deepening the kiss as her body warmed under his ministrations.

Every inch of skin tingled, and her panties were damp with need. She shifted, wanting, and pressed harder against him. "Luke."

He stole his name from her lips with a kiss, hot and demanding. His hands were on her shoulders, and he pushed her back, hard, onto the couch, and the slow burn of passion transformed into something desperate and demanding.

She moved beneath him, wanting to feel him, to have more of him, and she heard herself moan, her body overwhelmed by the simple, exquisite touch of his lips upon hers.

When he added his hands to the mix—when he shifted to straddle her and his hands slipped inside her robe and beneath her T-shirt—her mind seemed to snap. There was no way—no possible way—that she could survive the onslaught, this bliss.

"I want to see you." Roughly, he shoved her shirt up. His mouth closed on her, teasing the erect nipple through the thin cotton. Sending delicious shocks through her body, loosening her. Readying her.

"Naked," she whispered. "Why aren't you naked?"

"I think I can remedy that oversight," he said, then eased back to work the buttons of his shirt.

"No," she said, her own nimble fingers taking over, enjoying the rush of touching him. Of being totally lost within him.

She pulled the shirt open and splayed her hands across his chest, the cool metal of the band he wore pressing against her palm. She closed her eyes, wishing it could simply disappear.

"It is not there," he said. "Tonight, there is nothing standing between us." He spoke with force, his hands reaching up to cup her breasts, teasing her and tormenting her as she arched against him until any thought of arguing melted from her brain.

"So beautiful."

Eyes closed, she smiled. She thought the same of him, and she fell greedily upon him, her mouth on his chest, his neck, his cheek and the scar upon it. "How—"

"An altercation with a sword before I was turned," he said with a wry grin. "The sword won."

As she laughed, he took her shoulders, rolled her over so that she was trapped beneath him, his busy hands and mouth sending all sorts of sensations rocketing through her. His mouth closed again over her nipple, the pleasure of the sensation so acute it was almost painful, certainly almost unbearable. She writhed against him, against her own roiling emotions, her back arching up toward him as she fought down a scream of pleasure. As she fought not to beg him for more, harder, faster.

He seemed to know what she wanted anyway, and his clever fingers dipped down, then ripped her panties off with a low growl. Then his hands were on her, cupping her, his fingers finding her wet and needy, and his moan of satisfaction almost enough to send her over the edge.

When he closed his mouth so intimately upon her, the edge did rise up, engulfing her, sending shocks reverberating through her body, so intense she had no choice but to cling to his shoulders for fear that if she did not, her body would explode with the intensity of it.

Wave after wave, his sensual assault continued, until she couldn't take it anymore and screamed for satisfaction, for his kiss.

He drew himself up, his lips still warm with the taste of her, finding her mouth, battering it, taking. *Claiming.*

She struggled to free him from his jeans, and once he was naked, he rose over her, a dark god, a fierce warrior, and she reached for him, wanting to be his spoils, his battleground, and knowing that he would fill her. Her body, her emotions, her deepest desires.

Her body trembled with anticipation, and she whispered one single word. "Now." That was all it took. His eyes darkened with desire, his fingers pushing her thighs apart, and then the sensual, erotic assault as he thrust himself into her.

She groaned, so wet and so ready, her body opening for him, taking him, drawing him in. The pleasure was exquisite, and she bucked against him, matching his thrusts, the need rising within her again as she cried for him to not stop, to never, ever stop.

His touch was a promise, his thrusts a caress, and as she traveled up, up, up, she knew that he was coming with her. "Now," he said. "By the gods, Sara, *now.*"

She exploded. Shattered. Her body—her mind—held together only by the force of her will and his firm hands upon her.

"Luke." The name was soft, like a tribute, and he pulled her close.

"Ah, Sara. My Sara."

And right then, with his arms tight around her and her body warm and sated, she could almost believe that she was his. Could almost believe that somehow, someway, they stood a chance.

CHAPTER 29

The security in Lucius's Malibu home rivaled Buckingham Palace, but that was hardly a deterrent to a man like Serge. He slipped through the defenses in mere moments, then stepped inside among the shadows that roamed within his friend's home.

The ocean, he told himself, eyeing the shadows with trepidation. *Not the manifestation of nightmares.*

The home perched on the beach, the west wall nothing but glass. And tonight, the moon reflected on stormy seas, the shadows cast inside the home both beautiful and frightening.

He exhaled loudly, scoffing at his own foolishness. A man like him jumping at shadows. A man who could kill with hands or fangs, who had done exactly that many times over. The very thought shamed him.

No more.

First, he had to find Tasha. That much, he owed to Lucius.

He lifted his nose and breathed deep, finding her subtle smell in the air. But how long she had been gone he did not know. Days, perhaps. Or possibly only hours.

A flutter of hope danced in his chest, and he followed the scent, searching for her room, hoping in vain that she had returned to this place.

He found what he was looking for on the second

floor. Not the girl herself, but the room that she had made. A child's room, a girl's room. White and pink, with porcelain-faced dolls on shelves that ran along the wall, a foot or so beneath the ceiling.

An innocent's dolls, but she wasn't innocent. Not anymore.

He could remember the look of her, the scent of her. And he had longed for the feel of her.

A low growl eased from his throat, and his cock, hard and ready, strained against the seam of his jeans. The daemon wanted to come out to play.

No.

Damn her.

And damn himself and the daemon within. He wouldn't succumb, couldn't destroy that innocence.

Except the innocence was gone, and he'd seen something new within her. But whether it had been there before, or whether Braddock corrupted her, he didn't know.

All he did know was that he wanted her.

Yes, he wanted to find her for his friend, to satisfy his obligation. To ensure that she was safe. And he told himself that was where his motivation ended.

That, however, was a lie. He wanted. Him. *Serge.* Daemon.

By the gods, how he wanted.

He could feel her, the scent of her enveloping him, caressing him. Soothing him.

He lay there, not moving, not even breathing. And then he reached for one of Tasha's porcelain-faced dolls and slowly and deliberately threw it against the wall.

◊

Luke left Sara's house well before dawn, and now the Mercedes's headlights cut a path through night as he maneuvered the curving Malibu canyons. He would have liked to have stayed—would have liked to have made love to her again and again—but he needed to be home during the daylight hours. He might not be able to hunt or prowl, but he could work the phone and the computer, and by the time night fell again, he would have a lead on Tasha. On Caris.

It was not over yet.

His phone rang, and he hit the button for the speaker, then listened as Slater's deep voice filled the car.

"Nothing yet," Slater said, "but I've got a bead on a few para-daemons the staff at the Slaughtered Goat says used to come in there about the time Caris first showed up. I'm going to track them down, see what they know."

"Get back to me as soon as you do."

"You got it. Something else, though, my friend. Some shit went down here the other day. Maybe you heard about it?" Slater asked, his tone making clear that he knew exactly who had killed Hasik.

"I've picked up some rumblings," Luke said. "What of it?"

"Apparently, there was a witness. Division's been called in."

Luke bit back a curse and thought of Sara. Of the disappointed way she would look at him when they met again. "Interesting."

"Thought you might think so. I'll keep you posted,"

Slater said, then clicked off as Luke considered this new inconvenience. *Alinda*. There was no other explanation. Nick's little elf had gone and ratted him out.

It was not, however, a problem that he could address now, so he put it out of his mind, focusing instead on sliding the car into the garage, and then stepping inside his beachfront home. Not as convenient as the home in Beverly Hills, but he longed for the sound of the ocean. More, he had no desire to spend his nights surrounded by the lingering scent of Ryan Doyle and his RAC team.

No lights burned in the house, yet the moment Luke opened the door, he knew that someone had been there. Not Tasha, though. *Sergius*.

Luke tensed, nostrils flared, shoulders rolling into a fighting stance as his temper reached the boiling point.

Back it up. Back it up and keep the daemon at bay.

This wasn't the time, he told himself. Not the time to lose control. Not when so much was riding on him remaining calm. On him thinking rather than acting.

"Serge!" he called. "Where the hell are you?"

No answer.

"Dammit, Serge. We do this now or we do it later. Choose."

Silence echoed in return. The house was empty.

The ocean.

The moment the thought entered his head, Luke knew that was where Sergius would be. Like himself, Serge had always had a fondness for the sea. For the sting of salt in the mist, the tug of the currents, and the mystery of black, unplumbed depths.

He stepped onto the back deck, then climbed down

the steps to the private beach, the sand glowing in the moonlight.

At first, he thought that he was mistaken, for he saw no sign of Serge. Then he looked closer and saw the faint outline of a body prone in the sand, the surf crashing over it. He stalked to the water, then stood over his friend, who lay sprawled in the surf.

"Get up," Luke said, extending his left hand to his friend to draw him up, the slow burn of rage and disgust growing within.

"Fuck you. Fuck me. We're all fucked anyway, aren't we?"

He pulled Serge to his feet. And when the other man had steadied himself, Luke reached back with his right arm and punched his friend and fellow *kyne* hard in the face, knocking him back down into the sand. He fell upon him then, his hand splayed wide over Serge's heart.

"Do you remember?" he whispered. "Do you remember what we did? In the village outside of Prague? How we took over the town? How we killed our competition?" His fingers tightened on Serge's breast, nails digging into skin. "There are only two ways to kill a vampire, friend. A stake through the heart or a blade to the head. But the heart doesn't have to be inside the body for the vampire to live. Do you remember, Sergius? Do you remember how we cut the hearts out? How we lined them up? And how we let our victims watch as one by one we staked them into oblivion?"

His eyes met Luke's, the pain evident behind the daemon-fire. "I would die rather than be that monster again."

"I would not give you the satisfaction," Lucius spat

as the daemon rose up in fury, preening and roaring and ready for a fight. "You lost her," he hissed, as his fists rained down on his friend, face, bone, and cartilage breaking under the assault. "I trusted you, and you lost her. You touched her. Did you fuck her, Serge? Did you fuck my ward?"

The answer was immaterial. It was only the wrath that mattered. As hot as molten steel, as sharp as any blade, and the daemon fed on it. Tasted it. Sucked it in. And, yes, grew strong.

With clawed fingers, he reached down, his hand over Sergius's heart as he clutched, hard, wanting to rip through flesh, wanting to dig through muscle. Deep within, a voice yelled for him to stop, to wait, but he was too far gone, and soon the man he had once called friend would be gone, too, the daemon having taken action, having gotten rid of traitors and fools.

Hot hands clutched his wrist, and Lucius met Sergius's eyes. Serge may have wanted to die, but the same could not be said of his daemon, and Lucius gave a roar of satisfaction as the beast met him, challenged him in combat. A pretty fight it would be, he thought, as Serge rose up, slamming his forehead into Luke's and knocking him backward.

Sergius did not waste the advantage, springing up and attacking, the daemon within not hesitating, not planning or considering.

They'd been changed on the same day, and both men and daemon were equally matched. This night, however, Serge held the advantage, as his daemon flowed wild. Lucius knew the cost, and held back, determined even within the throes of daemon-fire to cling to the shred of both humanity and sanity.

Serge's heel intersected with Luke's jaw, rattling his teeth, and Lucius considered that sanity was overrated. He rushed, sideswiping Serge's steadying leg before the kick came back to center. Serge lost balance and Luke pressed his advantage, falling hard upon his friend, his enemy, his brother.

He had no stake, but that seemed hardly important at the moment. He crushed his hands against the sides of Serge's skull. Beheading killed a vampire just as well, and right then, Lucius could rip the bastard's head off.

Deep within, Luke pressed back, trying for control. Trying to surface.

On the beach, Lucius held fast, eyes on Serge's face, relishing the moment when the fiend was ripped apart.

"I didn't," Serge said, his eyes flashing red, but his body going limp.

Lucius hesitated, the daemon wary, looking for some trick. "Speak," Lucius demanded.

"I did not touch her," Serge repeated, the fire fading from his eyes. "I swear."

Within Lucius, the part that was still human battled back, taking advantage of the daemon's surprise, finally beating it under. "Serge," he whispered, releasing his vise grip on his friend's head. "By the gods, Serge."

"We haven't fought like that in over five centuries," Serge said, drawing in deep chunks of air. "Now I re-member why." He rolled onto his side. "You always beat me."

"You are yourself?"

"For now," Serge said. "I don't know for how long. It comes," he said. "It stays."

"You're going to have to find the strength to fight," Luke said, fearful that strength was fading within him. It was far too easy for the daemon to come out this night. It needed release if it was to be crushed back, docile, within.

"My daemon is not the problem," Serge said. "Tasha is gone. Graylach was slaughtered. Your enemies, Lucius—"

"I know," he said. "Caris has taken her."

"Caris?" Serge asked, his confusion clear.

Luke kept his voice flat, unemotional, and told his friend all that had happened.

"What can I do?"

Luke unbuttoned his shirt. "Who designed this device?"

He watched as Serge's brow knit, as he reached out and touched the cold metal. "I've heard of these, but I have never seen one before." He looked up at Luke. "Someone of great power made this."

"Can you find him?"

"Perhaps. If not, I may have another solution. I'll leave word where and when to meet me tonight, and we'll see what can be done."

CHAPTER 30

"Nothing new on Stemmons's location," Sara said, hanging up the call from Porter and turning back to face her team. "So we switch gears for a moment and focus on the Dragos matter. We've got three weeks until trial."

Her attention moved to Doyle and Tucker as J'ared floated in and took a seat. "What more have you two got for me on the rape?"

"We've run down five victims now," Doyle said. "The judge was a damn prick, and hell on wheels for keeping secrets. But once we tugged on the thread, it all started to unravel."

"And Tasha?"

"Not a word, not a whisper." Doyle narrowed his eyes as he looked at her. "You ever consider that Dragos is blowing smoke up your skirt?"

"What are you talking about?"

"That he knew Braddock was dirty, and he's tossing you this load of crap about his ward figuring you'll do exactly what you're doing."

"Not buying it." She'd seen the pain in Luke's eyes. No way was she going to believe he was bullshitting. "So I want you to keep looking. And I also want you to flag the interviews with the other rape victims. Have Martella make copies and send them to Dragos."

"Are you fucking kidding me?" Doyle said, as beside him, Tucker almost choked on his salt-and-vinegar chips.

She turned to J'ared. "That rule plays down here, too, yes? We come across evidence that might clear the defendant, we have to turn it over?"

"Check," J'ared said. "Pretty sure humans took that one from us. An earlier incarnation of the PEC established that rule in, oh, about 600 B.C." He frowned. "Maybe 1600 B.C. Anyway, before that, it was pretty much anything goes."

"Reading that rule awfully broad, aren't you?" Doyle said, blood rushing to his cheeks, and his eyes flashing red to match. "Dammit, Constantine, do you want the guy to get off?"

"What I want is justice." She pressed her palms flat on the conference table and leaned over into his face. "And that means, Agent, that we don't try to stake innocent men. So if you find anything that suggests Dragos didn't murder Braddock—or if you find anything that suggests mitigating circumstances—then you flag it, you copy it, and you send it to the defendant. Are we clear, Agent?"

"I get you," Doyle said. "But we're not going to find anything. Dragos is a son of a bitch. And for once—finally—he's going to get what he deserves."

His phone buzzed and he answered it with a growl, then looked up at Sara with the kind of bright smile that made her very nervous. "Well, well. Look what we got here," he said. "A double murder in Van Nuys, and an eyewitness who swears it was Dragos."

♦

"That's him," the girl named Alinda said, pointing a bony finger at an image of Luke.

Sara felt her mouth go dry. "You're certain."

"Totally." She turned toward Doyle. "Just like what I said when I called it in. I was in the alley, and I saw him break in."

"Hasik and Tinsley died late Friday. Why are you coming forward now?"

She licked her lips. "I was talking with people. Checking Web pages, for the news, you know. Our news, I mean. And I saw his picture. He's the one who killed that judge, right?"

"Lucius Dragos is the defendant in the Braddock matter," Sara said. "Had you seen him before?"

"His kind don't much come into a place like this."

"His kind?"

"Vampire," Doyle said. "This is a were-den. Mostly, anyway. Get a few hellhounds, a few daemons. Vamps mostly avoid it. The breeds don't really get along."

"But he didn't come in, right?" Sara said. "Didn't you say he went in through the alley?"

Alinda nodded. "There's a keypad. He used it."

"Did he know the code?"

"Sure," the girl said. "He got in, right?"

Sara didn't bother answering.

"Let's go in," Doyle said. "Don't know what we're going to find. Can't catch an aura without a body."

"Guess we'll have to rely on old-fashioned detective work," Tucker said, then cringed under Doyle's dark look.

"Hardly a challenge," Doyle said. "We got an eyewitness. This thing is wrapped."

The owner, a burly man named Viggo, escorted them to a small office off the back hallway. There was nothing remarkable about the crime scene. The victim's office looked as Sara imagined it always had, slightly unkempt, very lived in. It wasn't until Doyle passed her his PDA with the crime scene photos that the full impact of what had happened here—of what Luke had done—hit her.

Two bodies seemed to cover the floor. One, a heavyset man with his neck broken, his head lolling at an obscene angle. The other, a wiry creature that lay in a pool of its own blood originating from the long gash across its neck.

She closed her eyes as bile rose in her throat, the acid taste lingering in her mouth. She'd seen thousands of crime scene photos and dozens of actual crime scenes, many much more brutal and bloody than this.

But she'd never before seen one rendered by Luke's hand.

Around her, Doyle and Tucker inspected the room. "Got security cameras?" Doyle asked.

Viggo shrugged. "Tinsley had cameras. Whether he bothered to turn them on—"

"Pull them."

"Don't bother." They all turned toward the doorway and saw Nostramo Bosch stepping into the room. The victory evaporated from Doyle's expression, replaced with cold wariness.

Bosch turned to Viggo. "Leave us."

"What the fuck are you talking about?" Tucker said, the moment Viggo closed the door.

"Prosecutorial discretion," Bosch said. "We'll not be pressing charges against Dragos. Not for this."

"Fuck that!" Tucker said, even more loudly than Doyle.

Even Sara, who had no desire to see Luke charged, couldn't comprehend the insanity of Bosch's statement. Yes, she'd reviewed the file. And yes, she'd read the list of terrible things that both Hasik and Tinsley had done. But that didn't mean they should be cut down in cold blood. So why the hell would Division decide not to press charges when they had two dead bodies and an eyewitness?

Bosch, however, wasn't saying.

Doyle took a step forward. "This is bullshit. God-damn vigilante Alliance bullshit." He shoved a finger in Bosch's face. "It's not right," he said, and with that, Sara had to completely agree.

◊

The moon hung heavy and bright in the sky, silently watching as Luke moved through the thick clusters of trees. He moved with purpose, despite the lack of a path, his steps never hesitating, his way certain.

And when he reached the clearing, he stood in the shadow of a tree and waited.

Serge had said to meet him there, and now Luke could only wait and hope that Serge's efforts to help him remove the detention device had paid off.

Around them, the forest was quiet, though not silent. The baleful hoot of an owl cut through the night, as if echoing Luke's concerns. Minutes passed, and Serge didn't show.

Restless, Luke paced, irritation building, then shifting into cold, hard dread as minutes shifted into hours.

Serge wasn't coming. Of that, Luke was certain.

He was, however, equally sure that his friend would never betray him. Would never make a promise he did not intend to keep.

And that could mean only one thing: The daemon within Sergius had won the battle, and his friend had disappeared into the dark.

He was on the verge of turning around when he heard footsteps in the brush. He peered into the trees, and watched as Nicholas stepped toward him.

"You fired me," his friend said without preamble.

"I had no choice." Luke turned, pointedly looking around the clearing. "You came all this way to complain about our advocate-client relationship?"

"I came to deliver a message," Nick said, his voice clipped with emotion.

"What?" Luke said, worried now. "Serge?"

"The fool approached Tiberius."

Fuck. "In the state he was in? With the daemon so close to the surface? Why the hell would he do that?"

But even as he asked the question, Luke knew the answer. Serge had wanted to make amends for failing in his promise to protect Tasha. Unable to find any other way to free Luke from the detention device, he'd foolishly approached Tiberius, hoping the vampire leader would use his influence and pull the necessary strings. "The goddamn fool."

"Damned is right," Nick said. "Tiberius tried to put him down." A small smile touched Nick's lips. "It didn't go well."

"He's gone rogue."

Nick nodded. "His daemon's out, Luke."

"I understand," Luke said. But at least his friend was free. Had Tiberius captured him, Sergius would be no more.

"Tiberius has assigned me to search for him."

Luke's brow lifted. "What will you do?"

Nick lifted a shoulder. "I'll search. Doesn't necessarily mean I'll find."

Luke nodded. For the time being at least, Serge was safe from Tiberius. From himself, though...that was a different matter.

"I'm also here with a message. Tiberius sends his regrets about Alinda's betrayal."

Luke almost smiled. "I'm sure he does."

"He said to tell you that he's arranged to make the problem go away. It won't come back to bite you in the ass, Luke. All things considered, that's better than nothing."

CHAPTER 31

Luke's sprawling Malibu house had been built into the side of a hill and took up at least half a city block. Formidable, and yet alluring. Much like the owner himself. She almost hadn't come. Had, in fact, been driving aimlessly in the night for more than an hour, trying to wrap her head around what she'd learned at the Slaughtered Goat.

The truth was that she didn't know what she was going to say. All she knew was that she had to see him. Had to see the Luke who was in her head, and erase the image of the Luke who had sliced that creature's throat. The Luke who had broken Ural Hasik's neck.

The Luke who had lived up to every horrible thing described in his file. Crimes for which he would never be prosecuted, and for which the dead would never have satisfaction.

A set of wooden steps surrounded by lush greenery led down to a solid steel door beside which she found an intercom panel. She pushed it, then heard a faint click. She tried the knob, found it unlocked, and stepped inside.

"Luke?" she called, tentatively at first, and then with more power. "Luke, are you here?"

There was no answer, so she moved all the way inside, shutting the door behind her.

The house was less ornate than she would have expected for such a ritzy address. Instead, she found it homey, lived in, as if Luke had long ago abandoned pretense for comfort and had been concerned with pleasing only himself. It pleased her, too. The bright colors. The overstuffed pillows. Luke undoubtedly never saw the room in the light of day, but it was bright and cheery nonetheless, with a long glass wall at the back that opened onto a wooden deck and a stunning view of the Pacific.

She imagined standing there with him and watching the sunset, then felt a pang of regret that they would never in fact see the sun together. A foolish notion, especially considering her purpose in coming here tonight.

Except, of course, that she wasn't certain what her purpose was, other than to see him. Was she expecting him to deny his actions? Or to promise he would never do it again? She wasn't naive enough to believe the first, but she couldn't quell the fear that he would absolutely refuse the second. Fear, because unless he did step away from the blood and death that papered his file, she knew that they would never find a common ground. And a common ground was something she so desperately wanted with him.

"You are a fool," she whispered. At the end of the day, what did it matter if they solved one set of problems? There was another looming—the trial.

After a few minutes of standing alone in his living room she called his name one more time, then debated leaving. She couldn't bring herself to do that, though, and instead moved through the house, determined to see him.

She found him upstairs, in the first room off the hallway. A room filled with pink and white, the walls lined with dolls that stared down at them, their faces full of bland disapproval.

Beneath the porcelain-faced audience, Luke stood at the window, looking out at the white-tipped waves. He knew she was there, of course. Even were her image not reflected in the glass, he would have known simply from the scent of her.

"I came in here to think of her," he said. "To remember the way she would sit on the bed and play with her dolls. To picture her running on the beach in the moonlight, her face lit with a smile. Innocence," he said. "And that bitch and her human cohort have sullied her."

"I'm so sorry. But I still believe you'll get her back."

She watched as his shoulders sagged. "I know."

The silence loomed between them, and still he didn't turn around. He had to know why she'd come, but he didn't say a word about it. This was her issue, her battle. And she was going to have to strike the first blow.

"I've just come from the Slaughtered Goat," she said.

"Are you here to arrest me, Counselor?"

"No. There won't be any arrests in that matter. Prosecutorial discretion. No charges being pressed."

She thought she saw the slightest relieved sag in his shoulders before he lifted his head so that she could see his face in the glass. He was looking straight at her with unmistakable heat, and she felt desire stir inside her, her body responding to nothing more than the intensity of his gaze. She drew in a breath and stood still, determined not to show it—at the same time certain that those damn vampiric senses could hear the increased tempo of her heart and find the scent of her desire.

"Then why are you here, Sara?" he asked, his tone both an invitation and a challenge.

"Because of you. Because of me. Because there can't be a you and me if you do that."

"Do what?" he asked. "You're a prosecutor, Sara. Aren't you trained to be precise? The word you're looking for is *kill*."

"Yes, dammit, it is. And you can't just go out and decide who lives and who dies."

He turned away from the window to face her. "Do you condemn the man who killed Jacob Crouch?"

She blinked with sudden understanding. "You? You killed Jacob Crouch?"

"This is who I am, Sara. It's what I do. And you will either accept me or you won't. But I will know that you understand it. All of it."

"No." She shook her head. "No. I don't want to know this. I don't know what you expect me to do with what you're telling me."

"I only want you to admit to what you already know. That justice is not necessarily found in the courtroom."

"Just because I wanted it—just because I praised you without even knowing you—that doesn't make it right."

"How is it wrong, Sara? He was a murderer, a beast. How was it right to let him continue to inflict pain on others?"

"What do you want me to say? Do you want me to say that it was right that you killed Crouch? Fine, I'll say it. But that doesn't mean you can leap from that one event to a general rule. It comes down to something so basic it's a cliché—the ends don't justify the means, dammit."

"Sometimes," Luke said, "they do." He took a step toward her. "Meet me there, Sara. Come at least that far with me."

"I don't know if I can." She couldn't hide the pain in her voice.

"The world isn't black-and-white. Especially not this world. Did your father's stories of history teach you nothing? The world is painted in shades of gray, an infinite number all blending together to make a pattern."

"I don't see it that way."

"Then you don't see me," he said. "I do what I do to calm my daemon."

"Surely there's another way," she said.

"Perhaps. But I'm not going to seek it out. There are some rules in this world of ours, and one is to move through it with the daemon harnessed. There are those who don't subscribe to that rule. Who kill humans with glee and torment their own kind. Those who haven't tried to subdue the evil within. I hunt them down, Sara. I hunt them, and I kill them. Which is no more than they would do to me."

"I get that, Luke. I do. But it still doesn't make it right."

"And that's the fundamental difference between us. You see right and wrong while I see an evil that must be stopped." He took a step toward her, his body tense, his expression dark. "I was once the very thing I now hunt. And make no mistake, the daemon lives in me still, and one day I may not always be strong enough to contain it."

"You are," she said, her voice weak, her mouth dry. "You will be."

He caught her wrist and pulled her close, then bent down to whisper in her ear. "Are you certain?"

There was danger in his voice, along with a warning. She didn't heed it. Instead, she embraced it, her pulse quickening, her skin suddenly so very sensitive. "I am," she whispered.

His hand went around her back, and he pushed her toward him until their bodies ground together. "You play with fire, Sara, and yet when I'm around you, the daemon purrs. You soothe me. But right now I don't want to be soothed."

His mouth crushed hers like an invader, vanquishing whatever remnants of hesitation remained within her. His tongue plundered her mouth, and she met him stroke for stroke savoring the taste of him. Scotch and heat and pungent desire.

His hands gripped her rear, drawing her closer, fitting her tight against the erection that strained beneath his jeans. She whimpered, her hands clutching the material of his shirt, holding tight against the rising sensations that filled her, claiming her and begging for more.

She broke the kiss, tilting her head back to look into eyes that reflected the depths of her own desire. "Luke." It was a plea, a prayer, and an invitation, and he accepted, scooping her into his arms and carrying her into the hall as if she weighed no more than a feather.

"My room," he growled. "My bed."

A huge bed dominated the room, lit from above by moonlight from the glass ceiling. She still had enough of her sanity left to look for the shutters, and found the metal blinds tucked in at the sides, ready to close as dawn threatened the sky.

"I've missed the feel of you," he said, laying her gently on the bed, his large hands struggling with the tiny buttons of her blouse. "Screw it," he said, then grabbed the material and tugged, sending buttons flying and making her laugh as the cool air brushed over her naked skin.

His finger caressed the lace of her bra, tracing the swell of her breast against it. "So beautiful."

"Touch me," she begged, longing to feel his hands on her breasts and the weight of him pressing down upon her. "Touch me now."

He wasted no time fulfilling her command. His hands grazed down her belly, finding the button on her linen slacks. He tugged them off, taking her underwear at the same time, until she found herself naked from the waist down, clad only in her bra and her open blouse.

"Beautiful," he whispered, his hands caressing her thighs, stroking the soft skin and sending ribbons of white-hot heat curling throughout her body. "Clothes," she said. "Off."

He took care of that quickly, stripping naked as she watched, his body as magnificent as she imagined any god's could ever be. "Better?" he asked, sliding once more to brush his fingers up her legs.

She couldn't answer. Could only moan, the ache growing between her legs forcing her silence. She craved his touch, the velvet stroke of his fingertips, his breath against her clit, his cock filling her. She wanted everything—all of him—and she was absolutely certain that she would die of frustration if she didn't have it all right then, right there.

"Here," she said, taking his hand from her thigh and pressing his palm against her sex. "Now, please, now."

A low growl rose from his throat as his finger slid inside her. "You're wet for me, Sara. Tell me how wet you are for me. How much you want me."

"I am," she said, spreading her legs for him, giving herself to him. "I do."

He moved up her body, exploring her with his mouth as he went. With deft fingers he unfastened the front clasp of her bra and released her breasts. His mouth closed over her nipple, laving it with such intensity she thought she might come right then.

He pulled away, leaving her mourning the distance, then twined his fingers in her hair. "Kiss me," he murmured even as he descended hungrily upon her. She matched him, their mouths meeting, warring, *claiming*.

Between her legs, his erection twitched, hard and ready. She reached down, lifting her hips, her hand finding him. He was velvet steel beneath her fingers, and she guided him to her core, straining up, silently urging him to take her. To fill her.

He didn't disappoint. With a low groan of pleasure, he pushed slowly inside, giving her body time to adjust, to take him. But when she was ready, when she'd clasped her legs tight around him, all pretense of easiness evaporated as he thrust inside, their hips pistoning in perfect time as the deep, carnal pleasure crescendoed.

He took her right to the edge, then slowed—the torment enough to have her crying out—biting her shoulder through the shirt she still wore. He wasn't finished with her, though, and as he entered her in long, measured thrusts, his hand slipped between them, the pad of his thumb stroking her until it was pleasure—and not frustration—that had her pressing her lips tight together to try to keep from screaming as she came, the world bursting into a million particles of light.

Her fingers clawed at his back as he thrust harder and faster, finding his own release even as the last starbursts of her orgasm fizzled and popped around her. "Oh, wow," she said, as he collapsed beside her, pulling her tight against him, their bodies as connected now as they'd been during sex.

"I think that sums it up nicely," he murmured, the grin on his face reflected in his voice. He shifted, propping himself up on his elbow, his massive body shadowing hers. He traced his finger lazily over her stomach and up near her breast, the effect anything but relaxing.

"Your body is like a treasure," he whispered. "More beautiful than the statues carved by the masters themselves."

"You're very sweet. Insane," she added with a laugh, "but sweet."

"Insane, am I? How can you doubt a man who watched the masters themselves? Who knew the models personally?" There was a tease in his voice, and she fought not to laugh. "I assure you that I know what I'm talking about."

"That must have been amazing."

"At the time," he said, "it was only my life. Looking back now—seeing the way the world has changed—yes, it is amazing." He sat up, pulling her into his lap and tucking her close to his chest. "I would love to show you my past. To walk you through Rome, through Britain. To tell you the stories of what I saw on the streets and the people I once knew."

A deep longing filled her. "I'd like that. I'd like to hear your stories." She eased close, head tucked against his chest, suddenly melancholy.

"Sara? What is it?"

"Foolishness," she said. "It's just that for you, I'm not much more than a blip on the calendar."

"Never," he said, with conviction so warm and strong that she was sure nothing would ever shake it. "I will walk through history with you, and we will make these years our own."

She laughed, forcing herself not to think of the looming trial, the very real possibility of his demise. "Even if we did, it would be a short history. I'm longevity challenged, after all."

He stroked her hair. "To me, a single moment with you is more precious than a century with someone else."

The sentiment delighted and flattered her, and she snuggled closer, then lifted her face for a kiss. "I don't want this to end," she said.

"Then let's make sure it doesn't," he said, and caught her mouth in a kiss. He made love to her again, slow and sweet, then held her until she drifted to sleep in his embrace.

She awakened to the bold strains of Beethoven's *Ode to Joy*—and thought that the ringtone for her alarm was absolutely perfect.

She didn't want to leave his arms. There were no

nightmares here, no gaping voids between them. All her doubts were swept away.

But she couldn't stay. She sat up and swung her legs off the bed, then smiled when Luke's hand reached out to stroke her back. "I have to go," she said. "I have a meeting this morning."

"You'll come back?"

She wanted desperately to say yes. Instead, she twisted around to look at him. "Will you kill again?"

"Sara—"

She held up a hand. "You wanted us to be clear, Luke. For me to understand it all." She watched him stiffen. "I know the way the world works, Luke. I know you have powerful Alliance connections, and I can put the pieces together. So tell me now. If you're asked to step in—if you're asked to kill—will you go? Will you answer that call?"

She saw the change in him instantly, the hardening of his features, the slight downturn at his mouth. "Of course," he said. And she knew then that in the cold light of day, nothing between them had changed.

CHAPTER 32

She'd spent the day at the office dealing with the mundane, which, after viewing the dead so often, had been a welcome change.

The mundane, however, hadn't kept the nightmares at bay, and she'd had to fight the urge to go to Luke's when the long day had ended. Instead, she'd gone out for a drink with Emily, and listened to her friend rattle on about the new attorney in the office and how he was apparently both single and cute.

She'd called Luke afterward, telling herself she was only gathering information, trying to discover what he'd learned of Caris or Tasha. The answer had been nothing, and the frustration in his voice made her heart ache. All in all, it had seemed like a perfect day to stay home and catch up on all the things she hadn't had time for since she'd taken this job. Like laundry. And tossing out the spoiled milk.

After three loads, she'd settled in bed with a book and hoped that the nightmares wouldn't come.

Of course, they had.

Little girls, sharp fangs. Crouch. Stemmons. And the blood. So much blood.

And so she'd lain in bed, clutching the covers, wishing for Luke. Knowing that if he were beside her she could sleep, the nightmares tamed. *Safe.*

Giving up on sleep, she slid out of bed, then went into the bathroom to splash water on her face, hoping the chill would bring her back to her senses. It didn't. She still wanted him. More than that, she needed him.

Ironic, she thought, that a man who killed so easily could be the one person in all the world who made her feel protected. Safe. *Loved.*

Dammit. One little word, and it was completely messing with her head. She didn't want to go there. Didn't want to think about loving Lucius Dragos.

She feared, though, that she did. She loved him, and yet she didn't know how to be with him, this man who'd twisted Ural Hasik's neck until it had broken. It didn't matter that Hasik had been among the worst of the worst. Why stand up in court and argue for justice if men like Luke would go out to render it on a whim?

And why, despite all of that, did she so desperately want him beside her right then? Why did she long for him to stroke her hair and tell her that they would catch Stemmons? That they would stop him before he hurt the next young girl?

And why, God help her, could she imagine with sweet, visceral pleasure pressing her gun to Stemmons's temple and pulling the damn trigger?

"But you wouldn't do it," she told her reflection.

The trouble was, she didn't quite believe herself.

In the living room, she turned on the news, then watched as a grave-faced reporter described Stemmons's two victims and thickly announced that the police had no solid lead on the escaped killer's location. She grabbed a cup of coffee, knowing that the caffeine would be no balm against lack of sleep, then headed to the door to get the newspaper.

She keyed in the alarm code to disable the system, then opened the door. The paper was there on the mat, just as she'd expected, but she paid it no attention.

Instead, she stared at the porcelain-faced doll with the red lips and pink dress. A small sheet of paper was pinned to the doll's apron, one word scribbled across it: *next*.

With her blood pounding in her ears, she grabbed a pencil from the table beside the door, then used the eraser end to carefully turn the doll over. Still using the pencil, she lifted up the back of the dress to reveal the doll's cotton body—and the name written in black marker along the seam. *Tasha*.

◆

Sara cringed as Luke hurled what had to be a thousand-year-old piece of pottery against the perfectly painted wall of his Malibu living room, then watched as it shattered into a million pieces. He reached for the companion piece, and she jumped forward. "Luke! No."

"Goddammit," he raged. "He will not hurt her . . . He will not touch her . . ."

"They're doing everything they can. Voight's scouring my front hall right now hoping to pick up a trail."

"I need to go there."

"It's morning, Luke. You can't."

He stalked across the room, hands fisted, his entire body tense with rage and grief. She watched him, her heart aching. "You have nothing else on Caris's location?"

"Nothing," he said.

"Can I do anything? Can I be your eyes and ears during the day?"

He turned, and the raw emotion she saw on his face made her tremble. "There is one thing," he said.

"Anything."

"I will not lose you, too."

She shook her head, not understanding.

"I want you to stay here," he said. "With me."

"In case you forgot, you're the defendant and I'm the prosecutor."

"I think we've already destroyed whatever walls are supposed to exist between our two roles."

She couldn't argue with that.

"Stemmons or Caris left that doll on your doorstep," he continued. "They know where you live. And I will not see you harmed."

She opened her mouth to protest, but closed it when she saw his face. His concern was real, as was his determination. And she knew damn well this was not a battle she would win, even if she wanted to. "All right," she said. "I'm not entirely sure how I'm going to make that fly at work, but I'll figure it out."

"Thank you," he said simply. "There is another thing." Though he spoke firmly, there was a catch in his voice. A hint of reservation that surprised her.

"Luke? What is it?"

"My blood. I want you to drink from me."

His words surprised her, but what surprised her even more was that his words didn't repulse her. Slowly, she tilted her head, looking at him from this new angle. "Why? Why would I do that?"

"With enough of my blood in you, I can find you. I can reach out in my mind and locate you through your thoughts and sensations." He brushed her cheek. "You would be safe, and I would rest easier when you were out of my sight."

She bit her bottom lip, unable to deny that what he proposed was appealing. Erotic, even. The promise of a forbidden intimacy and the excitement of dancing on the edge but not slipping over. What would it taste like? Feel like? And would such an intimate encounter change her?

"No," he said, his words sharp in answer to the question she voiced. "I would not change you even if you wished for me to. I would not risk that with you, Sara. Not ever."

"Risk? You mean the daemon?"

"That is part of it." He stood and moved to the wall of windows, now covered by metal shutters that barred what would otherwise be a stunning view of the Pacific. "I told you before I would have you know everything. That there would be no secrets and you would understand who and what I am."

"Yes," she said, a hint of worry rising within.

"Then it's time for you to hear the rest of it." He turned to face her. "I killed my Livia," he said, his voice deceptively impassive.

She sat on the couch, her knees suddenly weak.

"She was so young, and death was upon her, a weakness that she was born with and only got worse as the years went on. I was newly turned and arrogant. I thought I could save her. But the daemon in me had not yet been bound, and it was too powerful. It rose up, and I surrendered to it. Instead of saving her, I took life from her, and lost myself utterly to the daemon. It was centuries before I went through the Holding. Centuries during which I did unspeakable things."

"It wasn't you," she said, feeling cold. Feeling sad. "It was the daemon."

"It was me," he said firmly. "The daemon is within me, and though I have control now, that power and that fury—that potential—is within me always." He sighed, looking back toward the shuttered window.

She pressed her lips together, willing herself not to cry. "Bosch told me that vampires who haven't controlled their daemons are rogue. Are hunted." She winced, thinking of him like that. "He told me you weren't rogue."

"I'm not," he said. "But at one time, I was. And there were those who lost their lives trying to put me down. My daemon is powerful, Sara, and it was not until I met Tiberius that I was forced to succumb to the Holding. For six months, I endured the torment of that ritual, and when I emerged, I had control, and I had regret. Tiberius stood for me, arranged a pardon for my actions, and in the centuries that have passed since then, I have battled to keep my will dominant. To control and use the daemon rather than it using me. Most often I have won that battle. But not always, Sara. Not always."

He reached into his pocket and pulled out a small ring, a coiled snake, so tiny it seemed to disappear into his palm. A child's ring. "Livia's," he said. "I keep it as a reminder of what I did. Of what I am capable of."

"Luke—"

He held up a hand, cutting her off. "No." She watched as he collected himself, then focused again on her. "When you drink from me, you will not be *vampyre*—you will not be able to seek me out, to feel my emotions. It works only one way without the change. There will be some increased strength, your senses sharpened. But no ill effects."

"Sounds like a good deal," she said with a wry smile. "But I don't get it. Didn't Tasha have to drink your blood when she changed? Why can't you find her? The same way you'd be able to find me."

"With Tasha it is different. I cannot feel her, nor she me. I cannot close my eyes and find her in the world. I cannot look at her," he added, moving to her side, "and sense her fears or her joys."

"Why not?"

He considered his answer. "Her mind," he said. "It allowed the change, but resists the connection. It is one of the reasons for the prohibition against turning those who are addled."

She heard the sadness in his voice and took his hand. "We will find her."

His fingertips brushed her cheek with all the intimacy of a kiss. "Will you do this for me? Will you drink from me?"

Her heart skittered, and she knew that what he asked of her was even more intimate than sex. But she wanted it—despite everything that still loomed between them, she wanted him. And, yes, she wanted all of him. "All right."

"Thank you."

"Luke, about your blood—you said it strengthens me. Will I live longer, too?" she asked, teased by the allure of more time with him.

He shook his head. "No, Sara. I am sorry. If I could have you with me forever, I would."

"But you can," she said, her mouth dry, her words surprising her. Surprising her more because she only then realized how much the idea tempted her.

"No." The word came out so harsh she cringed. "Do you think I would wish that horror upon you? To see you succumb to the tumult of the daemon? Do you think I can bear to think about your body, bloodied and battered, as you fought? And if you died before you were even given the chance to fight?" He stood and paced between the couch and the wall of shuttered windows, his fears and memories driving him. "For you to survive the bloodletting, I must control my own daemon, and that I cannot promise."

He saw understanding in her eyes. Compassion. "You were young then. You have control now. You turned Tasha, right?"

He bit back a bitter laugh. "Control?" He recalled the way he'd been lost when Annie's blood had flowed. The daemon had burst free, reveling in the blood, dancing in the power. He'd almost lost control. Taken too much, and Annie had nearly died because of it.

And he'd done so because he had imagined that it was Sara in his arms.

"I did not know Tasha," he said, trying to make her understand. "I did not love her. Not as I loved Livia. Not as I love you." He saw her lips part in pleased surprise at the admission. "The daemon latches on. It wants what it desires, and it would take all. It is strong, and I cannot guarantee that I am stronger. Not then. Not with my mouth on your vein.

"No," he said, taking her hand. "The change is not for you. Never for you. But my blood. Sara, I would share my blood with you, and I will swear to protect you always."

She nodded, overwhelmed.

"Then drink," he said, and sank his fangs deep into his wrist. She hesitated only a moment, then she looked up at him, her eyes locking with his as she lifted his wrist to her mouth, pressed her lips down upon him, and drew in his blood.

The tug of pleasure through him was instantaneous, and he drew his head back, his body already hard, his need for her desperate. He reached for her, his hand clasping the back of her neck. He leaned back against the couch and held her tight as she drew him in, as he met and merged with her, and gave of his strength.

Mine.

Hunger rose in him, but not the vicious hunger of the beast. Not the daemon. On the contrary, she soothed the daemon, brought him under control even as he lost himself utterly in the sweet pleasure of Sara's lips upon his skin.

"Enough," he said, pulling away. Her skin glowed from the power of his blood, and he could feel her desire, her arousal, the connection between them vivid and sharp.

"I feel you," she whispered. "I need you."

"I cannot wait," he said as he pulled her shirt up,

desperate to feel her skin against his, to plunge inside her. To ravage.

"Don't wait," she said, the passion in those two words bringing him close to losing it.

He needed no further encouragement, and he made quick work of the rest of their clothes, then thrust inside her, his palms pressed on either side of her, his eyes on her face, watching as passion rose within her. Within Sara.

Mine.

Yes, he thought, as the world exploded around him, she was well and truly his.

And he was hers, as well.

◆

The creak of the automatic shades startled Luke, so intent had he been on the computer screen in front of him.

He and Sara had spent the day in front of the computer and on the telephone, searching for a lead, a clue, anything that would lead him to Caris, to Stemmons, to Tasha.

"This," he said, tapping the screen. "I think I may have something."

Sara came over, her hand casually on his shoulder as she leaned in to read the screen. "What is it?"

"Property records for the house that I thought was Caris's. I've been following a paper trail and found an interesting deed from the 1920s." He pulled up the image, then showed Sara the name on the deed—CV Enterprises.

"Caris Vampire?"

"Could be. She always had an interesting sense of humor."

"And you found other properties owned by the same company?"

"I did," he said, pushing back from the computer. "Two commercial buildings and one house. I'm going to investigate the house now."

He saw the worry on her face. "Be careful," she said.

"Always."

She grabbed her purse, which made him frown. "You're leaving? You promised to stay here."

Confusion brushed her features. "Well, yes. But not every second of every day. I still need to work. And I need to go to my apartment and get some things."

He nodded. She was right, of course. "With an escort, though. Call Division. Have them send someone from Security Section."

She looked at him, silently noting the irony, then nodded. "All right. I won't leave until someone arrives."

His shoulders dipped in relief. "I could not bear to lose you."

"I know. Me, too."

She held out her hand for him, and he pulled her to her feet and into his embrace. He kissed her forehead, felt his body firing, and stepped away. "Later," he said, brushing his fingers over her lips. "We shall continue this later."

"We certainly will," she said.

His phone buzzed, and he reluctantly stepped away from her to answer it, frowning at the unfamiliar number.

"Lucius?" Tasha's voice, and his heart tightened at the sound of it.

"Tasha? Where are you?" He held out his hand and found that Sara was already beside him, holding him tight, keeping him steady.

"They hurt me. Said I'm broken. But I'm not broken, am I, Lucius? I'm a good girl."

"You are," he said. "Of course you are."

"I did a bad thing, though," she whispered.

Fear rippled through him. "What did you do?"

"The thing inside me. I let it out. I let it out even though you told me never, ever to do that. But I couldn't help it. I needed to get away. They were going to hurt me, Lucius. They were going to cut off my head."

His body tensed, the daemon within him rising, ready to fight. Ready to kill. "Are you safe?" he asked, grinding the words out past clenched teeth.

"Yes. But I'm scared. Will you come?"

"I will," he said, clutching Sara's hand. "I'll come right now."

CHAPTER 33

His daemon was snapping at the edges of his control by the time he found his ward, curled up in the single-stall bathroom of the gas station on Santa Monica Boulevard. The attendant was pounding on the door, screaming that customers were complaining. Lucius grabbed him by the shoulders and tossed him the length of the building, where he crashed into a row of newspaper machines, knocking them over and spilling quarters out over the sidewalk.

He didn't bother with the door handle—he simply ripped it off its hinges. Inside, Tasha screamed, then scrabbled to him on all fours, her now-gray dress dragging in the filth and muck on the bathroom floor.

"I'm here, I'm here," he said, holding her close to his chest and soothing her. "Are you hurt? Do you know where the son of a bitch is?"

"He drank from me," she said after several false starts. "The human. From me and from all those little girls."

"Was he alone?"

She shook her head. "A female. A vampire. She promised to change him. Promised to bring him over if he killed me. Said I was wrong. That I shouldn't even exist. Scared me, Lucius. Wanted to hurt me. Wanted to kill me." She pressed her face against his shoulder, and he held her as shivers wracked her body. "I let it out. The monster inside. And I got away. But they wanted to hurt me, Lucius. They wanted me to be ash."

"Nobody will hurt you," he said, calling upon all of his strength to keep his voice calm. Soothing. "No one will ever hurt you again."

"You'll protect me," she said, lifting her head to look at him, the pain in her eyes almost enough to bring the daemon back to the surface. "You love me."

He breathed deep, willing the daemon back down. "You are mine," he said, holding her tight. "And I will protect you to the death."

♦

Since J'ared had called while Sara was in her car with the news that the medical examiner wanted to see her, Sara skipped her floor altogether and headed straight for the medical tech section of Division. She found Richard Erasmus Orion IV eating a peanut butter sandwich in the break room. He was leaning back in his chair, his eyes closed as classical music blared, his cowboy boots perched on the shiny clean Formica tables.

She cleared her throat and he jumped, then immediately shut the music off and held out a sticky hand for her to shake.

"Sorry! Sorry! Hard to find fifteen minutes around here. I was just taking five."

"What have you got for me?"

"DNA," he said, cocking his head and leading her across the hall and into one of the labs. His Einstein-white hair shot out in all directions, and he wore a long white lab coat that flowed when he moved, revealing a hint of the Hawaiian-print shirt he wore beneath. All in all, Richard Erasmus Orion IV gave every indication of being an eccentric genius.

"I've already read the report on the DNA evidence," she said. "Was there an error?" She had the absurd fantasy that he would tell her that Luke was no longer implicated.

"More of an oversight," he said as he poured coffee into a mug that said *The Dead Do It Stiffer*.

"An oversight," she repeated. "What kind of oversight?"

"The kind where we find more DNA."

She paused while reaching for her own mug. "Would you mind repeating that?"

"Happenstance, really," he said. "I was taking another look at the wound, and that's when I noticed that the bite radius was a little hinky."

"How?"

"I'll show you." He punched a few buttons on a computer terminal and the familiar image of Braddock's neck appeared on a wall screen. "Ripped up a bit," he said, "but you can see the initial contact points of the fangs here and here," he said, indicating with a laser pointer. "But this was what caught my attention. See this? Another fang impression, right? But at a slightly off angle." He tilted his head to demonstrate. "Like our perp wasn't happy with his initial grip on the victim's neck."

"All right," Sara said, wondering what this had to do with DNA. She knew better than to try to rush him, though. She'd learned long ago that when an ME had a point to make it was best to be patient; eventually they'd get there.

"So I thought I'd check the bite radius. Just make sure it was our perp. And there you go."

"It wasn't?" She couldn't keep the surprise from her voice. "There was another biter? A first biter?"

"A cookie for the little lady," he said, tapping the side of his nose.

"And DNA confirmed that?"

"Did indeed," Orion said. "Not enough markers to make a match, but enough to definitively conclude that there was another biter."

"I need your report," Sara said, her mind churning.

"Not a problem." He went to a terminal, tapped a few keys. When he turned back, he held a ceramic candy dish shaped like a human hand. "Tootsie Roll?"

"No thanks."

"So how much damage does this do to your case against Dragos?" he asked.

"A lot," she admitted, unable to keep the smile off her face as she considered all the possibilities. "It messes it up a lot."

With Orion gaping at her, she raced back toward her office, her phone plastered to her ear, and J'ared at the other end of the line.

"Question for you: What if Tasha attacked Braddock? Took him just to the point of death. Self-defense because he was raping her. Where does that put us legally? If the DNA proves my theory, then that would knock Dragos down from a capital crime to a lesser charge, right?"

"Well, yeah," he said. "But whoa, golly, you think that's the way it went down?"

"Just go with me on this. Okay, so Dragos gets charged with a lesser crime—gets to avoid execution. But what about Tasha? If that's really how it happened, then what happens to her special dispensation?"

"Hang on. Hang on." She heard him typing. "Nope. No leeway. It's clear. She takes steps—she lets the daemon take control—she's terminated."

Sara leaned back, incredulous. "Even with evidence of rape?"

"Regular vampire wouldn't have such a raw deal, but, hey, she wasn't supposed to be allowed to live in the first place."

"Shit. Okay. Thanks." She clicked off the call and tried to sort through her thoughts, because she was positive she knew what had happened. Braddock raped Tasha. And Tasha, terrified, lashed out against him, her own daemon probably coming out for revenge. She went after Braddock, wanting to end the torment, and somehow Luke realized what she was doing.

He followed, found Braddock on the brink of death, and realized what would happen to Tasha if the PEC tied her to the murder. So he did what Sara had come to expect of Luke: He protected the girl. He put himself out there as a target to draw the fire away from Tasha. He staged the scene, leaving his ring, leaving his DNA. All of it, every bit, designed to lead the PEC to him.

He'd intended to run; of that she was certain. Draw them in, make sure he said enough to be determined guilty in absentia, and then escape. That had been the point of the nerve gas in his tomb that very first night.

Something had gone wrong, though, and he'd been incarcerated. And unless she introduced the evidence about Tasha, he would most likely die for a crime he didn't commit. Implicate Tasha, though, and she'd be staked.

There had to be a way to protect Luke without putting Tasha's head on the block.

And as she passed through the reception area and under the *Judicare Maleficum* archway, she realized that she knew whom to go to for the answer.

◊

"You're asking me to consider dropping a capital murder charge down to manslaughter?" Nostramo Bosch peered at Sara from behind his desk, the hint of gray in his temples glinting in the overhead light. She stood her ground, back straight, shoulders square.

"Yes, sir. I think the evidence will show that Dragos was protecting his ward. She was being subjected to repeated abuse by the defendant."

"You have proof of the abuse?"

"Working on it."

He stood up, began pacing behind his desk. "When you were first assigned this case, you told me your relationship with the defendant would not affect your judgment."

She bristled. "And it hasn't."

"Hasn't it?"

"Sir, I'm only asking you to consider this if it's supported by the evidence. Whatever my feelings may or may not be, they can't change the facts."

He stared at her, the scent of cinnamon filling the air. "What exactly are you looking for here, Constantine?"

"Reduced charges and house arrest. He wears the detention device until time served."

"This is a high-profile matter, and you're suggesting that we should forego incarceration?"

"Sir, he was protecting a woman who couldn't protect herself. What purpose would be served in locking him up?"

Bosch exhaled loudly, then drummed his fingers on the desk. After a moment, he nodded. "You prove the rape, I'll authorize the deal, subject to Leviathin's approval."

She swallowed, willing herself not to be too optimistic. Not yet. "Sir, I haven't worked here that long, and to be honest, I'm not sure if that's a good—"

"Nikko tends to accept my recommendations," he said, but he was smiling. "And Constantine? Stop calling me sir."

In the hall, she tried to walk without an added little hop in her step, but didn't quite manage it, and when she caught sight of Doyle and Tucker in the hall near her office, she hurried to meet both of them.

"What have you got? I need solid evidence that Braddock raped Tasha."

"We've got shit on the girl. Rape, yeah. Tasha, not a thing. We can't even prove he knew her."

They followed her into her office, then flopped into the two guest chairs as Sara paced. "Would there be physical evidence left?" she asked. In a human, she knew the answer would be no. For a vampire, though... She just didn't know.

"Hit or miss," Doyle said. "But if we can get her to agree to a session with a Truth Teller, that's pretty weighty shit. I thought she was missing, though."

"Apparently she's back."

"So we'll bring her in," Doyle said, pushing out of the chair.

"No," she said. "I'll arrange it."

He glanced at her, eyes narrowed, nostrils flaring. "You have his blood in you."

"The hell I do," she said, not willing to discuss her personal affairs with the likes of Ryan Doyle.

"That's a crime, Constantine. Directive 27. Ring any bells?"

"I told you," she said firmly. "You're wrong."

"Hope so," he said, his nostrils flaring. "Because I like you, Constantine. Not entirely sure why I like you, but I do. And I'll be damned if I'll stand by and watch that bastard hurt you."

"Then you don't have a thing to worry about."

CHAPTER 34

Lucius sat on the edge of Tasha's bed and held her hands in his. She was showered and changed, now in pink pajamas and a flowing pink robe. "You are centered now? The daemon well under?"

"I am." She licked her lips, her eyes wide and scared. "I was so afraid I wouldn't see you again. They wished to keep me away. Far away. And then they wished to kill."

He stroked her hair, then pressed his hands against her shoulders, willing her to understand. "You are here. You are safe. And they will never threaten you again." *Never.* As soon as she was steady Luke was going after Caris. He'd kill her. He'd kill Stemmons. And he'd do it in the most painful way he could devise.

On the bed, Tasha pulled a rag doll to her and hugged it tight. She tilted her head back, her nostrils flaring. "Girl," she said. "The scent of a girl fills my room." She lowered her head and stared at him with wide, guileless eyes. "Why, Lucius?"

"You have caught the scent of a friend of mine."

"I saw," she said, making him wonder. "Pretty girl. The way she touched you in that bar."

"What bar?"

"Before," she said. "Before you killed for me." She tilted her face up to him. "That's what he did to me. The judge. He did to me what you did to the pretty girl."

"It's different," Luke said, his blood chilled, and an unwelcome fear rising in him. A worry that there were things happening here that he had not seen. "You watched me, Tasha? You spied on me that night?"

"Spied on you. You spied on me." She rocked on the bed, and he knew that he was losing her again.

"Tasha, focus. The woman is important to me. And she will be staying with me for a while. Can you understand that? Can you be nice to her?"

Her eyes widened. "I'm always nice," she said, then her forehead creased. "Except when I'm not. I wasn't nice to them tonight, Lucius. The ones who kept me. The ones who wanted to hurt me."

"And to them you never need to be," he said, taking her hand and cursing his earlier fears, cursing himself for seeing cunning and contrivance even in innocence.

"Have to be nice to the girl, though. Your woman. Your Sara."

"Sara," he repeated. "You heard her name?"

"You love her."

His heart twisted. "Tasha, you know that no one will ever replace you."

"You do things with her," she said. "Naughty things. You've never done naughty things with me."

"And I never will." He leaned forward and pressed a chaste kiss to her forehead. "Rest," he said. "I must go take care of something. I'll be back soon."

She said nothing, and he left the room, his thoughts turning to Caris and the thousand ways he would hurt her.

The phone buzzed and he snatched it up, expecting Slater or Voight. "What have you got?"

"Your balls in a sling, you son of a bitch." Ryan Doyle's gruff voice filtered through the phone. "What kind of games are you playing with her?"

The fury that had been aimed at Caris took a sharp turn, as the image of Luke's fist intersecting with Doyle's face filled his mind in a most satisfying way. "I don't know what parasite is infecting your brain, Doyle, but if you have something to say to me, you can damn well say it to my face. Or are you too much of a coward?"

"You couldn't keep me away."

Luke clenched his fists at his side, forcing calm. "After so many insults between us, what the hell has happened now sufficient to have you darken my doorstep?"

"Sara," he said, making Luke's heart twist.

"What's happened to her?" Luke demanded, his voice tight with fear.

"You did, you shit. She drank your goddamn blood."

"She did," Luke admitted, "though it's no business of yours."

"It's my business when you mess with the prosecutor's head. When you seduce her into committing a crime."

"There's been no crime," Luke said. "The exceptions are clear. I offer her protection."

Doyle barked out a laugh. "The fuck you say. Whatever game you're playing, Dragos, it isn't going to work. You're not sliding out from this murder charge, and you're sure as hell not hurting that girl. I won't see you destroy her the way you destroyed my life, my woman," he said, his words bringing to the forefront the events so many centuries ago that had shredded the bonds between them. Luke clenched his fists. Now was not the time.

"I should have killed you then," Doyle continued.

"We all have to learn to live with regret."

"I'm warning you," Doyle spat.

"And yet your words mean nothing. You want to finish this, then get your ass here and we will. But don't come unless you mean it, because if you land the first blow, I will kill you. With no thought to our past friendship or the debt that I may owe you. I will kill you. And so if it's death you seek, then bring it on now."

"I'll be there in an hour," Doyle said, and before Luke could respond, he clicked off and the phone went dead.

◆

Sara had nicknamed the guard who'd been assigned to her Guido. Not only because he looked the part, but also because she couldn't for the life of her pronounce his real name.

"I'm not going to be long," she said, opening the door.

"You stay," Guido said, grabbing her by the shoulders and lifting her over the threshold. He plunked her down by the door, closed it, then pointed a warning finger. "No move." And then he disappeared for a rundown of the entire apartment. With only one bedroom and one bath, that didn't take long, and he was back with an efficient nod before her arms had even stopped aching from his clutch.

"Right," she said as he stationed himself in front of her door, as immobile as a Buckingham Palace guard.

She hurried to her bedroom and shoved some yoga pants and a few T-shirts into a duffel bag. She added a few work outfits, an extra pair of shoes, and her father's book. She paused for a moment at the bedside, then reached for the gun. After a second's hesitation, she chambered a round, then put it into her purse. If she was worried enough to have Guido following her around, then she was worried enough to be armed.

Out of habit, she hooked the portable panic button onto her waistband, then ran into the bathroom for essentials. Once she had everything she needed, she headed back into the living room to meet up with Guido, still standing perfectly still at her door.

She checked her watch and smiled—ten minutes past midnight. She'd managed to pack for an overnight stay with a man in less than fifteen minutes. That had to be a female record. "Ready," she said.

He nodded and stepped aside, allowing her to punch the exit code into the control box. As Roland had taught her, she held the portable panic button in one hand and entered the code with the other. "Gotta protect you in those few seconds when you don't know what's outside the door," he'd said.

The system disengaged, she peered through the peephole, and since nothing was there, moved to open the door. Guido got there first, edging in front of her with a stern wag of his finger. He opened the door and took one step forward—just far enough for the sword that slashed downward to lop off his head.

Sara screamed, her finger fumbling for the panic

button even as her mind registered the attacker—a teenage girl with auburn hair and an expression of grim satisfaction. And right by her side was Xavier Stemmons.

Sara pressed the button hard as she stumbled backward, tripping over the bag she'd dropped. Even as the gray mist of the security force filled her apartment, she grappled in her purse, her fingers closing around the butt of the gun. She yanked it out, and as Stemmons leaped upon her, she fired.

His body jerked from the impact, but he held tight, the woman holding on to him as well so that the three of them were locked in an unwelcome embrace.

And as Stemmons's blood spilled out upon her, Sara succumbed to the odd sensation of her body disintegrating.

The last thing she saw before her mind turned to mist was the dark form of the Shade materializing in her living room.

And the last thing she heard was the girl's singsong voice whispering, "Lucius is mine. Mine, mine, mine."

◆

Luke didn't wait for Doyle. If the para-daemon had a death wish, he could damn well wait at Luke's house for him to return home.

Luke had a more pressing engagement: Caris.

He raced down the Coast Highway, then maneuvered the busy streets until he careened to a stop in front of the private drive that led to the house his research had revealed was owned by CV Enterprises.

He hoped to hell she lived there. If not, he was all out of leads.

He killed the engine on his car, then sat in the dark, weighing his options. He ruled out approaching by car, as that would eliminate the element of surprise. As for climbing the fence and approaching on foot, the security cameras that dotted the landscape would similarly alert her to his presence, something he would rather not do. He wanted her weak. He wanted her vulnerable. And that meant that he needed the advantage of surprise.

His wants, however, weren't aligning with the physical reality of her home. As he was cursing that fact, he heard the low, strong purr of a motor. A Jaguar, unless his ears deceived him.

He smiled and stepped out of the car. The element of surprise had just been tossed back into the mix.

He eased back, out of sight, but still close to where her car would emerge. He stood still in the dark, waiting and watching, listening as the hum of the engine drew his quarry closer and closer. The first hint of headlights cut through the dark, and he tensed, his body ready to pounce. And then, as the gate opened and the car eased through, that's exactly what he did.

Caris turned as he leaped, slamming the car into park even as she began the slide toward the opposite door. It did her no good. He'd yanked the driver's door open before she was even half out of the car.

He lunged, snarling, his hand grabbing her shoulders as they both slid through the car and out the passenger door to land, hard, on the rough asphalt. Whatever surprise she'd felt, she'd recovered, and now she kicked back, trying to free herself from him.

"Nowhere to go, Caris. Nowhere to run."

She spat in his face, then froze, her expression one he knew well. *Transformation.* He clung tight to her, the hematite bands at his wrists and ankles seeming less of a burden now that their proximity was screwing with her abilities.

Confusion flashed in her eyes, and he closed one hand around her neck. With the other, he pressed a stake to her heart. "The truth," he said, "or you will die. Are you prepared for that, Caris?"

"What do you want, Dragos?"

"Tasha," he said. "I want revenge."

There was a pause, then her brow furrowed. "What the hell are you talking about?"

He reached down and ripped open the white linen shirt she wore, then pressed down on the stake, hard enough to draw blood, the daemon itching to press harder. To kill. "Do not fuck with me. I should end you this instant for the things you've done, but first I need you to tell me where Stemmons is." He leaned in close and lowered his voice. "Go ahead and resist. Trust me when I say I'll enjoy getting the information from you."

Not a hint of fear rolled off her. "Stemmons? That human worm? Like I'd associate with that kind of garbage. And you know damn well I'm not inviting little Tasha over for tea." Her eyes flashed. "So tell me what the hell you're talking about, or stake me. The asphalt's cutting into my ass, and I want to get up."

"Don't tempt me," he said, increasing the pressure on the stake. "And do not even think about lying to me. I caught your scent, Caris. At the Slaughtered Goat, and then at the scene of Stemmons's last victim."

"Well, color you clever," she said. "I had my reasons for being there."

"Share," he said, twisting the stake like a drill.

"Dammit, Lucius, I—"

"Tell."

"I had a project," she said. "A special project that you put the brakes on, thank you very much." She flashed him a harsh glare. "And then I learn about some human doing murder and making it look like a vamp—and, hey, that's my territory. So, yeah, I went. Wanted to see who was stepping on my toes, maybe planning on blaming me for things I haven't yet done. But there's no crime in that, Dragos. And I sure as hell don't have your precious fruitcake of a ward."

He opened his mouth to retort, but the words never came. Instead, his head seemed to explode, bursting apart from the force of Sara's scream all the way on the other side of the city. A scream and then the sharp snap of an image forced into his mind—the bastard Stemmons, and beside him, Tasha.

CHAPTER 35

Luke backed away from Caris, the image still sharp in his mind as the truth hit him with the intensity of a punch to the face. Tasha had played him. A game of revenge to punish him for wanting another woman, and to punish Sara for being the woman he desired.

He ran. He left Caris battered on the driveway, her face a mask of confusion, and he ran from the house, his blood pounding, terror raging through him. She was trapped. She was scared.

Snatches of her hand. Her gun.

And then the connection popped.

Gone. Nothing.

The lock he'd had upon her thoughts had snapped like a rubber band. They'd taken her, and in him, the daemon raged, screaming to kill, *to find*.

Calm, he told himself as he sucked in air, trying to find a center, a place where he could think and plan. Sara needed that. Needed him sharp. *Stay calm, and you can find her.*

He lifted his head, nostrils flaring, as if he could catch the scent of her on the wind. There was nothing, of course, but the motion, the effort, seemed to sharpen his mind. Allowed him to home in, bring him closer.

To see what she saw and feel what she felt.

Except there was nothing but the faintest hint of her

essence. Panic rose within him, and he fought it back. They'd taken her. Transformed her into mist. *That* was why he couldn't find her with his mind.

He needed help. And right then, he could think of only one person who could offer the help he needed.

He pulled out his phone and called Doyle. "They've taken her," he said without preamble. "Goddammit Doyle, Stemmons has Sara."

He heard the sharp intake of breath, then Doyle's gruff and steady response. "Where was she?"

He released a breath. "Her apartment. They took her. Transfigured and got her the hell out of there."

"Materialized yet?"

"No." He said the word forcefully, because he had to believe that the connection between him and Sara would remain strong. Once she was solid again, he'd find her in his mind.

Once she was solid again, he would save her.

"Tucker's on the phone beside me contacting Security Section. We'll meet Roland at her apartment. See if we can learn anything."

"I'm in my car," Luke said. "Call me the moment you know anything." He had to keep moving. Had to keep *doing*. If he didn't, he was certain he would go mad. God*damn* the detention device. It kept him solid. Kept him *there*. Kept him from moving fast and striking hard.

Dammit, dammit, dammit.

With no other way to unleash his fury, he took it out on the streets, flooring the Mercedes and careening around curves as he drove. Ignoring Tasha's betrayal. Ignoring his own blindness against the daemon that had been preening and playing all these years.

Ignoring everything except the singular task of getting to the woman he loved, and getting there as fast as he could despite the shackles on his body.

He moved through traffic like a wildman, running lights, cutting off the late-night, bar-hopping crowd crawling along the road at a fucking snail's pace. He was exiting I-10 for Wilshire Boulevard when Sara ripped into his head once again, her terror and pain enough to stab a thousand holes in his heart, the pain counterbalanced only by his relief in finding her once again.

He punched the redial button on his cell phone to connect with Doyle and focused on locating her, on pulling thoughts from her head. Thoughts that would give him help. A clue. Anything.

Fear.

Fear, and death.

Death all around her.

But no scent of it. Only the trappings.

Stone.

Bars.

And something familiar. Not to her—her thoughts were confused, ragged. But to him. He knew this place. The small flashes in her mind adding up to a picture of—

Luke!

I'm coming, he said uselessly. She wasn't *vampyre.* She couldn't hear him. Even so, he had to call out to her. Had to let her know. *I'm coming,* he repeated. *I swear that I am coming.*

"Where?" Doyle demanded, his voice sounding hard and fast over the speaker.

"Beverly Hills," Luke said. "My crypt. He took her to my own fucking crypt."

"Steady," Doyle said, his gruff voice surprisingly gentle. "We'll get her back. I promise you. We're going to get her back."

♦

"Please, no." Sara knew it wouldn't matter. Knew he couldn't be reasoned with, yet she begged anyway. Begged for the life he was about to steal from her. A life she now so desperately wanted to share with Luke. "Please. Don't do this."

"But I have to," he said, looking at her with glassy eyes. "You were very naughty."

"I was. Absolutely." Her head pounded, and she wanted to reach up and clutch her skull in her hands, but her wrists were bound. She was naked, her pants and shirt in tatters on the ground.

As if in a dream, she realized where she was. A crypt, cold and dank. And she herself strapped down to the lid of a hard stone coffin.

"The blood is the light," he said. "And my Dark Angel feeds on the light."

In her mind, she screamed for Luke and prayed that he would hear. But there was nothing there. Nothing but the pounding in her head and the shivers that wouldn't stop. Bone-deep trembling that shook her so much her teeth were chattering.

"You'll be warm soon," Stemmons said. "The dead don't feel the cold."

"I don't want to die."

"You won't at first," he said, and then he actually smiled at her. "First you have to give the light. To me and to my Angel. The light nurtures. The light heals. I have drunk my Angel's light, and it has healed. Soon, it will make me divine."

He'd fed off Tasha, Sara realized, and the gunshot wound now looked like nothing more than a scratch. All her fantasies about blowing him away only to learn that it wasn't a gun she needed. Not to kill a monster. Not in this world, anyway.

He stepped closer, and for the first time she saw the knife in his hand, glinting in the hint of moonlight that crept in through the bars of the crypt.

"I would say that this will only hurt a little, but I'm afraid that would be a lie." He smiled wide. "And I don't lie. That's very, very naughty."

She wanted to cry, wanted to scream, but no sound came out.

No sound that is until he dragged the tip of the knife across her belly.

Until he rent flesh and muscle.

When he did that, the scream burst from her, a desperate cry. A piercing plea for Luke to come, to please come, to save her.

And as the world started to turn gray around her—as Stemmons sliced his knife into her breast, her thigh, her neck—she imagined that she saw him there, her dark warrior, her life, her love.

He would come.

He would come for her and end this nightmare.

But as the world slipped away from her, she knew the nightmare was real, and this time, she wouldn't wake up.

◆

Blood.

Sara's blood.

He could smell it, could practically taste it, and the scent of it drove the daemon wild.

Lucius let it. He needed the beast now. The daemon's speed, the daemon's rage.

Needed to use the daemon to destroy the bastard who had dared to hurt his Sara. And as for Tasha...

His heart twisted with the pain of it even as he raced forward, feet pounding over the soft earth, Sara's scent drawing him, her thoughts—incoherent, terrified, pain-filled, but *alive,* still alive—calling to him.

She was close. So very close.

Luke...

The tiniest of echoes, but the beast within him unfurled, head snapping up, rage boiling.

He'd traveled by land, the route swifter than the tunnels beneath his home. And now he raced toward the familiar structure. Moving swiftly. Moving silently.

And then felt the shock of seeing her like a punch in the gut when he peered through the bars at the horror that lay within.

Stemmons was there, and he stood over Sara with a blade tipped in blood. Lucius tilted his head back and drew in the scent. *Tasha.* But not present. Not there.

Instead, her blood was within the human.

She'd not turned him, but she'd made him strong.

Deep within Lucius, the daemon growled. *Not strong enough. Not fucking strong enough.*

Sara was naked, her breath coming in stops and starts, and he could hear the shallow, weak beat of her heart. He could smell the blood that had been spilled on the stone. The life that was draining out of her.

No time, the daemon cried. *No time.*

With a guttural roar, Lucius ripped the door off the crypt, then tossed it aside. Stemmons turned, his eyes so wide it was almost comical, and found the beast barreling down on him.

"Die," Lucius said, and took the blade the human wielded. Then swiftly, purposefully, Lucius drew it across the man's own throat.

Blood gushed like a faucet, but its scent did not entice. The human was putrid. Rotten.

And only Sara mattered.

He rushed to her side, the daemon still raging, screaming out in denial and fear as he felt the life draining from her.

Back, Lucius thought, trying to gather himself. He had to think. Had to *think,* and could not do so with the primal beast raging in pain and fury within.

He felt the beast withdraw, as if understanding that the life of the woman depended on its departure.

"Sara." He stroked her forehead. "Sara, my love."

Her eyelids fluttered, and when he again caught the scent of her pain, a new swell of fury rose within him.

"I knew you'd come. Had to say good-bye."

"No." He stroked her face, held her hand. "No, you cannot leave me."

"No . . . choice." Her voice was so weak, but still she smiled at him, even as a vise tightened around his heart.

"I'll heal you. I can make you well." With grim determination, he bit his wrist, then pressed it to her lips. "Drink."

She did, but her eyes did not spark. The life did not return. She was too far gone, and he was losing her, his blood barely prolonging the inevitable.

He pulled his wrist away and brushed her hair off her face. Lost, so terribly, terribly lost.

Footsteps behind him, then Doyle's voice. "Oh, God. Oh, damn. That son of a bitch. That goddamn fuck-wad."

"Your coat," Tucker said. "Doyle, put your coat over her."

"Getting darker," Sara said as Doyle draped her. "No time." Her lips twitched, as if she was trying to smile. She looked straight at Lucius. "I love you."

His heart twisted, and he felt his eyes well with tears. He had not, he thought vaguely, cried in centuries. Now it felt as though if he started he would never stop. "You cannot go."

"I don't want to." Another flash of pain crossed her face, and her fingers twitched as she tried to grip his fingers.

"Do something," Doyle said.

"My blood is not healing her. She is too far gone."

"Dammit, Lucius, she's not there yet. You can save her. You can change her. Don't let her go. Not like this."

"I cannot." He thought of Livia. Of the daemon within. Sara was too weak, and he felt too much. He would go too far. He would fail.

And even if he succeeded, it was not what he wanted for her. The daemon. The horror. The never-ending battle within.

And yet...

He drew in a breath, felt a tear trickle down his cheek.

And yet he could not see her gone.

"What the fuck?" Doyle spat. "Cannot? The hell you can't. You're a goddamn bloodsucker."

"I cannot," Lucius said again, this time standing up and pressing a hand to his chest. "Countermeasures. One taste of human blood and the stake is triggered, and I must feed to turn her. The curse *vampyre* demands the exchange of blood."

Doyle sagged. "Ah, hell."

"There is a way," Lucius said, turning back to Sara and holding her hand. Her eyes were glassy, her grip weak. But her fingers moved beneath his. "Hold on," he said. "Hold on, my love."

"What way?" Doyle asked, and Lucius told him about the fail-safe, the mechanism by which the detention device could be released by either the prosecutor or Doyle inputting their authorization code back at Division. "You will go?"

A beat, then Doyle nodded. "I'll go."

He headed for the door.

"Ryan," Lucius said. "There is no time to drive."

He saw Doyle hesitate, and he saw the sharp jab of fear. Then Doyle glanced at Sara. He swallowed, then nodded. "Right," he said. "No time."

He turned then and faced the wall, his hands thrust out in concentration. The bones in his face seemed to shift, rolling beneath his skin, even as his eyes grew beady and red. His skin turned a pale orange, the color seeming to gather at his fingertips. He drew in a breath, then another, then whipped his arm in a circle, as if drawing upon the air.

In the wake of his hands, a hole opened, dark and black. He stepped inside, and the air mended itself, the hole disappearing.

"How long?" Lucius asked Tucker, who was staring slack-jawed at the place where his partner had disappeared.

"I've got no idea."

Lucius bit back a curse and knelt again at Sara's side.

"I trust you."

He clenched his teeth together, determined that she would not see the tears threatening his eyes. "You are not afraid?" He himself was terribly afraid, the memory of Livia close to the surface, his failure with her as fresh as if it were yesterday. And even if he did not fail again, he could not protect Sara from her daemon. That, she had to battle on her own.

"Safe," she said. "With you. I'm safe."

Her trust humbled him, and he thrust one hand into his pocket and pulled out Livia's ring. The reminder of how he'd lost control. The talisman that had soothed him before he'd found Sara. It would, he hoped, protect them both now. He slipped it onto her little finger, then clasped his hand over it as Sara struggled to breathe.

"Not long now," he said. "Not long, and you will be healed."

"Dark, Luke. Don't let me go. The nightmares."

Fear stabbed at him. Where the fuck was Doyle? "Hold on, Sara. Don't leave me."

Behind him, Tucker paced, his phone plastered to his

ear. "Where the hell are you?" Tucker shouted. He turned to Luke. "Now. He's doing it now."

Even as Tucker spoke, the band around Lucius's heart popped open. And as it dropped to the ground, Lucius leaned forward and sank his fangs deep into Sara's throat.

CHAPTER 36

She was his.

Sara. Her blood filled him. Primed him. Gave him life and strength even as he drew the same from her. He had to take her to the edge—right to the edge, and no further. Too far, and she would slip away, unable to be turned. But pull back too quickly, and she would never recover, alive but damaged from the loss of blood, the loss of this sweet, tangy life that he now drew from her veins.

This was the connection he'd craved. That the daemon within had begged for, yearned for. The sharing. The connection. The blood. The daemon within rose as he fed, crowing with joy and need.

It wanted to consume her, to feel her life within him, to draw her to the surreal point of death and take and take and take some more.

"Luke," Tucker yelled. *"That's enough. Luke! Pull back!"*

Something tight and firm closed on his shoulder, but he ignored it, instead clutching Sara against him, her body trembling next to his, his mouth curved to her neck, the sweet smell of her skin filling him, arousing him. And the blood. By the gods, the taste of it, such sweet nectar that he would lose himself forever in the sweet, decadent delight.

"Luke! Stop!"

He could hear her heart beat, its steady rhythm now spotty. Somewhere within, he realized he needed to stop, to pull back, and though he knew that, he couldn't do it. Couldn't push past the daemon. The lure of the blood was too intense, the cry of the daemon too strong. And then it was Sara inside his head, telling him to drink. To drink it all. To consume and live and glory in the allure of the blood.

Pater!

Pater, stop!

He froze. That voice—that cry of *father*—it belonged to Livia. His Livia. And the moment he realized that, his senses rushed back.

Sara.

By the gods, Sara. What had he done?

She was curled up in his arms, the beat of her heart almost indiscernible even to his ears. Her eyes glassy, her skin deathly pale. He'd almost taken her too far, but there was no time for self-recrimination. He bit down hard on his wrist, opening a vein, and pressed the wound to her mouth.

"Drink," he ordered. "Drink, Sara."

And despite his worst fears and premonitions, her lips closed over his flesh and she drank, her thirst strong and deep as life flooded back into her. As his blood warmed and changed her.

He held her tight as she suckled and said a silent thank-you to the gods and to the sweet voice of the child he'd once failed.

This time, he'd beaten the daemon—and Sara still lived.

◊

She woke to pain and light dappled across a velvet darkness. Her body, sore and weak, was covered with beads of blood rising off long, slim cuts.

Concrete walls surrounded her. Above her, a ceiling with drilled holes.

And in the distance, she heard the low, harsh growl of a monster.

A sharp blade of fear cut through her as she realized that she remembered nothing. And the fear grew steadily stronger as slowly, ever so slowly, memory returned.

Stemmons.

Tasha.

Blood.

And Luke. Always Luke.

She shivered, remembering suddenly the way he'd thrust his fangs into her neck. The way her body had arched in response, the pull of blood strangely enticing, all the more so when she took from him, drinking and drinking until she'd collapsed beside him. Until she writhed in the agony of death, then stretched with the strength of rebirth.

She'd wanted this. Despite the fear, despite the unknown, she'd wanted it because it meant that she would be with Luke. That they would be together, forever.

Now, though, the fear was rising. She was trapped. Alone with a beast. *Her* beast. Her daemon.

Dear God, what had she done?

Time to feed, Sara. Time to come out and play, play, play.

All around her, the room seemed to whisper. A soft female voice urging her to feed, to kill. *Her* whisper. *Her* voice. And as it spoke, the hunger rose within her.

She explored her mouth with her tongue, felt the tips of her fangs—and reveled in the burst of power that seemed to explode within her.

It's what you are now. It's who you are.

Nosferatu!

Vampyre!

Monster!

Kill! Feed! Live!

Each word struck as a blow, knocking her back, pummeling her flesh. "No!" She screamed the word, slammed her hands over her ears to shut out the voices and thrust her head between her knees to ward off the blows. But they were in her head—the words, the blows—and nothing she did would stop them.

That's the way. Hide, Sara. Hide and let me take over. Let me live. Release, release, release me and you will be free.

She tried to stand, dizzy from the voices battering her, her mind still fuzzy.

But she understood now. Understood that she couldn't close the voices away because they were within her. They were her daemon, and she was deep inside the Holding.

Deep in the ritual, and she didn't know the way out. She didn't want to succumb. Didn't want to stay hidden down here. Didn't want the daemon to feed while she cowered below.

But she didn't know how to stop it.

He hadn't told her how to fight.

"Luke!" she cried. "Luke, help me!"

This is all his fault. Stay away. Stay here. Stay down here and punish him for what he did to you. Easier, so much easier, to stay.

"No," she said, and then with more force. *"No."*

Coward.

Bitch.

Liar.

The words came at her like blows, knocking her off her feet. She fell, confused, then found a hand reaching down to help her up. "Luke?" She was safe. He was there. "Is it really you?"

He smiled at her. "I'm here to help you."

The Numen. It had to be. She nodded, and let him draw her up. "Your daemon is blood and fear," he said. "Do not give that to her."

"But I am afraid. And my body bleeds."

"Come," he said, and she melted into his arms. "Do not think about the pain." He laid her gently on the ground. From his fingertip, he drew blood, then traced it over her wounds. The skin knitted in his wake, leaving her tingling, her body suddenly awake and alive.

She realized with a start that she was naked.

"Pleasure," the Luke-*Numen* said, as his hand slipped down to cup her between her thighs. "Take pleasure from me. Take strength from me. And we will fight the daemon together."

His fingers had found her core, his mouth her breast, and she gasped, focusing only on Luke as the whispers around her grew louder, bolder. "Are you real?"

"I am as real as you need me to be." He flicked his tongue over her nipple, and a hot thread of desire shot through her, finding the finger that teased her clit.

"Please," she said, her hips bucking shamelessly. "Please take me."

"You need to go over," he said. "Do you see the walls?"

She turned her head, saw the walls of the room and realized that the ceiling had disappeared, replaced by a black sky, twinkling with stars. "Just get over the wall, and you'll be fine."

"How?" The walls were steep and slick and seemed to stretch up forever.

"I'll take you there," he said, and as he did, he thrust inside her, filling her.

She moaned, her hips rising up to meet him, wanting to take more and more of him in. Searching for that place, that way, that path up to the top.

"That's it. Yes, yes, that's it."

She looked at him above her, the love in his eyes urging her on.

"Please," she said. "More. Harder."

"Dear gods, yes," he said, and took her, slamming into her, battering them both. She arched against him, eyes squeezed shut, desperate, so desperate to climb, to take all of him. To consume him, to be with him, wholly and completely.

She was climbing. So close. So close to the top.

And then over, over, over, over.

It came upon her fast, her body's surrender, and when she opened her eyes, she was warm and soft and curled up within his arms.

His arms. Not a dream.

Luke.

It was over.

And then she wept, his soft murmurs caressing her as the tears spilled out.

"How long?" she asked when she could speak again. "How long was I in that place?"

"A week," he said, wiping her tears. "But you're free now. And you're in control."

She closed her eyes and looked within, where the daemon was bound up deep. "Yes," she said. "I won."

She smiled up at this man she loved, and who loved her. "I knew you'd be there. I knew you'd help me through it."

"I was so scared," he admitted. "Terrified that I'd lost you. That I'd failed you."

"Never," she said, pressing a hand to his cheek. "You saved me."

♦

"You're spoiling me," Sara said, setting aside the biography of Augustus Caesar that Luke had brought her the previous afternoon.

"And I will continue to spoil you," Luke said, stepping into the room with a breakfast tray. "So I suggest you get used to it." He settled the tray over her lap. An English muffin, sausage, coffee, and a thermal mug filled with warm blood. Looking at it, she realized how hungry she was, even for the blood, which she'd discovered was surprisingly tasty. Or, perhaps, her taste buds had simply changed. So far, she'd sucked down liters of the stuff, with Luke assuring her that the thirst would wane as time passed, and she would not feel the need to feed at such regular intervals.

She took a sip, then turned her attention to the muffin as he sat on the edge of the bed beside her. "I'm not an invalid, you know."

His mouth twitched. "Have I been treating you as such?"

She recalled the vigorous sex they'd had the previous night, and had to concede that he hadn't. "It's been more than two days, though. Bosch is going to think I skipped out on him."

"Two weeks off," Luke said. "And if my memory is correct, he instructed you to take it, or else."

That much was true. After the ordeal at the crypt, Ryan Doyle had apparently gone to Bosch and explained what had happened. Following a brief review of Sara's notes and a short interview with Luke, the charges in *Division v. Dragos* were dropped. In support of the dismissal, the PEC entered a stipulation formally outlining the facts as known. That Dragos's ward had not in fact prevailed during her Holding. That her daemon had broken free and was, as Ryan Doyle had once commented, clever enough to wait, silently watching the workings of their world even as the daemon became more and more entwined with the girl who'd become obsessed with having Luke all to herself.

She'd concocted a plan to force Luke to go on the run with her, and although no one knew for sure if Braddock had actually raped the girl, everyone was certain that Tasha had taken advantage of Braddock's past history. She'd gone to Luke hysterical, swearing she would kill

the judge for what he'd done to her. As she'd anticipated, Luke would not allow Tasha to risk punishment,
and had stepped in to protect her, going so far as to
drain the last drops of blood from the already critically
injured victim in order to frame himself.

"A decadent plot," the judge had said. "Maybe
someday we'll know all the pieces to the puzzle." And
Sara, who heard about the judge's words after the fact,
had to agree.

The judge had signed the dismissal of the charges
against Luke at the same time that he'd issued the war-
rant for Tasha's arrest. It was not a case Sara looked forward to prosecuting, because every day that Tasha was
on trial would be another twist of the knife in Luke's
heart. Another reminder of the depths of her betrayal.

"Has there been any word?" she asked.

"None," he said.

"There may never be any," she said gently. "She
could be on another continent by now. And you can't
keep me hidden in here forever."

His smile was small and sad. "You see too much
now."

"I see you," she said. The bond between them had
grown stronger since the change, but even without the
new connection, she would have known what he was
thinking. What he feared.

"We cannot close our eyes to the possibility that she'll
try to harm you again," Luke said.

"Well, for now the price isn't too bad," she said, trying to lighten the moment. "I get to sit here in this
incredible Beverly Hills mansion and read books and
be totally pampered. I've never really taken a vacation

before," she said. "I honestly don't know what to do with myself."

She was gratified by his quick smile. "You're not vacationing," he said, stroking his fingers lightly up her arm. "You're recovering. And if you're at a loss for ideas, I'm sure I can think of one or two things to keep you entertained."

"Yeah? You want to show me?"

"Very much," he said. "But I'm afraid we'll have to wait. Right now you have a visitor."

"Really?" She wanted to ask who it was, but he'd already crossed the room and stepped out through the door. A moment later, he returned with Ryan Doyle in tow.

"Well, look at you," Doyle said. "You look a damn sight better than you did the last time I saw you. You doing okay?"

"I'm great," she said, happy to see the investigator. "Thanks for coming. And thanks for taking care of the case. Working things out with Bosch."

He shrugged. "Least I could do, what with you almost dying." She noticed that he didn't look at Luke. Whatever trouble had brewed between them was still there. Perhaps, though, it had faded a little.

He inclined his head, then shuffled his feet, as if she'd embarrassed him, which considering the para-daemon's usually gruff demeanor she thought was particularly amusing, and chalked it up to the fact that she was in bed and wearing a nightgown. He was turning as if to go when Luke's phone rang. He opened it, pressing the handset to his ear, but with her newly sharpened hearing, Sara could easily hear both sides of the conversation.

"Pain, Lucius," Tasha said, her voice thick with tears. "And blood, so much blood! The daemon came out. It came out, Lucius, and I tried to fight it. Tried to do what you told me. Tried to be good, but it wouldn't let me." She sobbed. "It kept me under for so long. It kept me buried. It made me lie and hurt people. Hurt children! And it wouldn't let me find you."

"Tasha," he said, and Sara bristled at his low, calming tone. "Hush. Hush. It's okay. Everything's going to be okay. Where are you?"

"South. La Jolla. You'll come get me? You're not mad at me? I did bad things, Lucius. Naughty things. But it wasn't me. I wouldn't. I didn't, and I'm so scared now. Scared of me, and what's inside. We need to push it back again, Lucius. Together. We need to push the daemon back under."

"I'll get you," he said in that low, toneless voice. "I'll help you. You know that I will."

"Because Lucius Dragos takes care of what's his. I'm yours, Lucius. I'm yours, yours, yours."

"That's right, Tasha," he said, with a hard look toward Sara. "Lucius Dragos takes care of his own."

The moment he hung up, Doyle rounded on him. "What the *fuck* are you doing?" he asked, voicing Sara's exact thoughts.

"Exactly what I have to," Luke said, his face hard and his eyes sad. "I'm doing exactly what I have to."

◊

Tasha stood on the roof of the house across the street from Luke's mansion on Bellagio Way, miles away from the Los Angeles subway tunnels where she'd been hiding in grime and filth. A dark place, not right for someone like her. Someone precious. Someone extraordinary.

She tossed her arms out at her sides and let the breeze blow over her, causing the white gown to billow around her ankles. So soft. So pretty.

He should have wanted her. Should have taken her. And yet he'd never touched her. Never bit her lip and drew blood, sweet blood. Never thrust himself hard inside her.

She'd played, though. She'd played with other boys' toys, and there'd been blood and teeth and glorious pain and their thick bodies shoving inside, filling her up, making her spread her legs and draw them in and it was good and nice and she wanted it more and more and more.

But Lucius never saw it. Never saw her. He saw only the shell, not what was inside. What she kept hidden. What she let loose when she played with the other boys.

She had to show him. Had to make him see.

Needed him to prove he loved her. Prove he'd be with her always. *With her.* Inside her. And that he'd take care of her.

And he did love her. Did, did, did.

Wasn't that why he killed that pasty-faced Braddock? Hadn't she planned everything just so?

Except she hadn't planned for the bitch. And the bitch had swooped in.

And now the bitch had her Lucius.

And he was *hers.* Not the bitch prosecutor's.

Tasha had tried to get rid of her. Learned about the murderous human the bitch had trapped in a cell. Formed her plan. Played the rescuing angel for the human, the one who was almost worthy. And she'd been lucky that the vampire Caris had swooped into town, drawing Luke's attention away from the truth.

But still her plan hadn't worked. The worthy human was dead, and the bitch was in Lucius's house. In Lucius's bed.

Not for much longer.

From where she stood, she couldn't see into Lucius's bedroom. But she could see the garage, and she felt a trill of satisfaction when the door swung open and Lucius's Mercedes purred down the driveway, cleared the gate, and took off down the street. La Jolla was nearly two hours away. Plenty of time for a little talk with the bitch. Just girl to girl.

Getting in wasn't a problem. Lucius had changed the access code, of course, but she'd known his override code for a decade. Never bothered to mention that to him. Some secrets a girl had to keep.

The code operated both the gate and the front door, and Tasha was soon inside, the marble floor cool against her bare feet.

The bitch would be in the master bedroom. She'd be thinking that was where she belonged. There, in the bed, with Lucius.

She was wrong. Tasha would have to explain that to her. And as she climbed the stairs, she let the anger rise in her, the power that it gave calming her, making her strong, making her confident.

The bitch had changed, Tasha knew that, but a new

vampire was weak after the Holding. Weak, that is, unless it emerged in harmony with the daemon. Then there was strength and power. So sweet. So strong. So very, very clever. Had to be clever. Let the daemon show, and bad things happened. Stakes. Blades. Had to hide inside. Had to be smart.

She climbed the stairs slowly, quietly, then padded down the hall to the doorway that stood open to Lucius's room. The bitch was there, sitting pretty in the bed, and she looked up, eyes wide with surprise at Tasha's presence.

"Tasha? I—are you okay? Luke just went—I thought he went to get you in La Jolla."

"Changed my mind. Allowed to do that, aren't I? Change my mind?"

"Sure." She shifted on the bed, one hand holding a book, the other under the sheet. "Ah, um, do you want to call him? Tell him you're here?"

"No, no, no." She took a step toward the bitch. Easy. Was going to be so easy.

"You know I'm prosecuting the Braddock murder, right?" The bitch's tone was chatty, and Tasha wanted to giggle. Death was in the room, and she didn't even know it. "I was wondering if I could ask you something. The detectives have some questions and—"

"Ask me no questions and I'll tell you no lies."

"Will you tell me the truth?"

"Maybe, maybe, if I like the question."

"What did Braddock do to you?"

"Bad man. Naughty man. Said things to me. Mean things."

"What did he say?"

"He insulted us."

"Us?"

"Me and I. I and me. We are we."

She almost laughed as the bitch frowned, trying to figure that out.

"Insulted the daemon? Is that what you mean?"

She touched the side of her nose. "Clever, clever girl. But no prize for you. Clever girl's been bad. Took what didn't belong to her."

"Did Braddock touch you?" the bitch persisted.

"Wouldn't. Not at first. Told him to. Lucius wouldn't, so I told the judge to. He wouldn't, either. Said he was being good now, and no touching allowed." She smiled, thin and cold. "But I changed his mind. Told him what I wanted. All the naughty things in my mind. Told him, and touched him, and then he did them. Naughty and nice, and all for me. Do you want me to tell you, too?"

"No." The bitch frowned, as if she didn't like the story. "Luke went after him to protect you."

"Sweet, sweet Lucius," she said. "I got there first."

"Because you knew that Lucius would cover for you. Knew that he'd put himself at risk for you."

"He loves me. Had to show me. I had to know." She took a step toward the bed. "So you see, he can't be yours. He'll always be mine. Mine, mine."

Tasha smiled, and drew a stake from the folds of her gown. "I think it's time to say good-bye now."

"I don't," the bitch said, and suddenly she didn't seem so small and vulnerable. Suddenly, she was up in the bed, a stake in her hand, too, and she had it aimed right at Tasha.

Tasha laughed. "You think you're a match for me? For us? Newly made against so, so strong?"

"No," the bitch said. "I don't."

"But I am."

Luke spoke from behind Tasha, having moved to her with lightning speed, the edge of his sword now pressed hard against her neck. She turned slowly, eyes wide. "Lucius...Where—"

"Closet," he said, flicking his head only slightly to the closet in which he'd waited and watched and listened.

"But you went away. You drove off to get me. I saw you. I saw you leave."

Luke thought of the Mercedes with its tinted windows, and Ryan Doyle in the driver's seat. "Psych," he said.

She closed her eyes in concentration—then opened them again, surprised.

"Hematite sword," he said. "You're not transforming, Tasha. You're staying right here."

Fear filled her eyes, and he steeled himself. Remembering what she was. What she'd done. To Sara. To those murdered young girls.

"Lucius, no. Please. It's me. It's Tasha. You love me. You protect me. You watch over me. I'm yours, yours, yours."

"You are," he said, remembering the snowy night when he'd succumbed to the horror of what he was— a night when he'd tried to find redemption for the death of his daughter in the immortality of this addled young woman. His hubris had been dwarfed only by his pain, and he'd made a foolish choice, then compounded it by arguing so vigorously for special dispensation.

He'd looked at Tasha and seen Livia. He'd looked at her and seen life and love and the promise of a future without the pain of his errors hanging over his head.

He'd been a fool, and now they were both paying the price. And though it tortured him, he knew that now it was time to step up and do what he had not had the strength to do so many centuries before.

"You are mine," he repeated. "My child. My ward. My responsibility." And with preternatural speed, he swung the sword out and around, the razor-sharp blade slicing through the skin and tendon and bone of her neck. "You are," he repeated as the body collapsed to the ground. "And I do now what I must."

He closed his eyes, steadying himself, letting go of regret and loss and sadness. And then he looked at Sara through tear-filled eyes. "There will be no trial," he said. "No court. This is your justice, right here, rendered by my hand." He looked at her, saw the anguish in her face, and knew they'd reached a line across which Sara might not follow. "Can you stand for that?"

She looked from him to the lifeless body of Tasha, the child who'd been his surrogate daughter. The daemon who had betrayed him.

Then she moved across the room and pressed her hand into his. "I stand with you," she said, and relief poured through him. "And I always will."

◊

Moonlight cascaded through the leaves, casting long shadows across the graveyard as Tasha's casket stood closed, ready to be moved into Luke's crypt, the first body ever to be placed there. Sara stood by Luke's side as he looked down at the simple steel box, her fingers twined with his, so overwhelmed with love it took her breath away. She wished she could make this night easier for him, and at the same time, she knew that he had to do this. Had to say good-bye to the young woman he'd once thought to save, the young woman he'd once loved and protected.

"Not all of her was vile," he said, looking not at her, but at their reflection on the cool metal lid. "There were moments when it was truly Tasha under my protection." He shifted, then met her eyes. "I have to believe that."

"And you should." She thought of the girl he'd once described to her who'd danced on the beach and played with her dolls, and in her heart she knew that he was right. The real Tasha, that poor addled child, was hidden somewhere beneath the daemon. "You freed her, Luke," she said, then blinked back tears. "No matter what else happened in that room, the Tasha you once loved is free now."

He pressed a hand to the casket, closed his eyes, then nodded. "I'm ready," he said after a moment, then stepped back from the casket.

She nodded to the men standing near the crypt door, and they came slowly—Nick, Doyle, and Tucker.

The four men lifted the casket, then carried it into the crypt, settling it into one of the previously unused stone sarcophagi. Nick stepped back, then pressed his hand to Luke's shoulder. "Shall we slide the stone into place?"

"Not yet," Luke said.

Sara started to follow the men out, but Luke held her back with a hand to the arm. "Don't leave."

"Never," she promised.

He reached over and lifted the lid on the coffin, and when he looked in on the girl, she could see the pain on his face, and tightened her hand in his.

"Luke?"

As she watched, he pulled Livia's ring from his pocket, then gently placed it on Tasha's finger.

He turned to her, and she forced herself to speak through a throat clogged with tears. "You're certain?" He'd carried it with him for so long that she feared he would miss not having it in his pocket.

"I am," he said. "It's time."

Gently, she lifted her hand and placed a palm to his face, a warrior's face, strong and scarred, yet soft with love.

He had buried two children tonight—Tasha and Livia—and the pain he felt burned through her. Yet he stood tall and strong beside her. He would heal, she knew. They both would.

"Come," he said, taking her hand. And together they left the crypt and stepped back into the night.

EPILOGUE

"Are you nervous?"

Luke's soft words from behind made Sara jump, and she twisted around to smack his hand away with her pen. "No. Of course not." *Hell, yes, she was nervous.* "Now go sit down. You're supposed to be in the gallery, not at the bar."

"I believe, Counselor, that court is not currently in session."

No, it most definitely wasn't. She knew because she'd been stalking the halls of Division for the past six hours, waiting for the jury on her first trial to come back. A daemon who'd set up shop on the Internet, luring in aspiring actresses for screen tests, then using a specially manufactured camera to suck the life out of the human females as they read their lines. She'd been prepping the case for more than a month now. The facts and the law were solid.

Now all that was left was for the jury to do its job.

According to Martella, the jury had finished, and the parties had been asked to return to the courtroom for the verdict.

Sara had been the first to arrive.

"There is very little more nerve-racking than waiting in a courtroom for a jury's verdict," Luke said.

She lifted a brow. "And how would you know?

You've avoided the courtroom in at least as many cases as I've tried."

He pressed a hand over his heart, his overly innocent expression making her laugh. "Counselor, I'm shocked. I don't know what you're talking about."

"I only wish that were so." But she was teasing as well. Over the past several weeks they'd reached a tentative sort of truce. Luke stayed out of her courtroom—well, out of the defendant's chair, at least—and she wouldn't question what he did for the Alliance. What he did, she knew, to keep his own daemon at bay.

Nostramo Bosch pushed through the gate with a curt nod toward Luke. Sara shooed him away, then watched, exasperated, as he took his time moving out into the gallery to sit directly behind her.

Slowly, the courtroom filled, and when all the parties had returned, the bailiff—a skinny gremlin—announced the judge with a shrill, "All rise!"

The judge, a wizened old vampire who sipped blood during testimony from a plastic travel mug, polled the jury, then asked the defendant to stand as the foreman read the verdict.

Sara held her breath, certain she could feel Luke's support wafting from behind her.

"Guilty."

Sara sagged with relief. Beside her, Bosch offered a hand in congratulations, along with a hearty, "Good work, Constantine."

At the opposite table, the defendant snarled as the bailiff came forth with the shackles.

In the gallery, the applause was deafening, as all the

prosecutors and staff from Sara's section celebrated her first trial, and victory, within Division.

She saw both Martella and J'ared, each of whom smiled and waved. She returned the gesture, but the man she was really looking for had already pushed through the crowd and was standing beside her at the table.

"You did good, Counselor," Luke said, laughing after she drew back from the kiss that she swore she wouldn't give him, not while she was at work. "Perhaps we should go home and celebrate?"

"I can't think of a better idea," she said, hooking her hand in his and tugging him toward the door, following the path Bosch had taken.

In the hallway, she paused as a reporter from one of the Shadow news organizations fired questions at her. "The defendant was a true monster," she said, "and there's no doubt that justice was served."

She clung tight to Luke's hand as they walked toward the elevator, ignoring the additional questions shouted behind them. *Justice.* She'd thought a lot about what was just and right since she'd joined Division. Since she'd met Luke. She thought of Jacob Crouch. Of Tasha. Of Luke himself.

"You're right, you know," she said, stopping in front of the elevator.

"About what?"

"Sometimes, things *are* gray. Especially in this world." She pressed her finger on the button, focusing on it instead of on him. "I can't condone what you do, but maybe I understand it. A little." She shifted, nailing him with a hard glare. "But don't ever let me see you in the defendant's chair again."

His mouth curved up, his smile reaching his eyes even as his arms pulled her in. "Ah, Sara," he said, then brushed his lips softly over hers. "I promise, I'll never let them catch me. You, though," he added, his tone tugging at her heart. "You, darling Sara, have captured me completely."

Can't get enough of
J. K. Beck's sexy Shadow Keepers?

Get ready to sink your teeth into *When Pleasure Rules,*
the next book in J. K. Beck's hot new trilogy.

WHEN PLEASURE RULES
Coming from Bantam October 2010

Seven innocents have been brutally murdered on the
streets of Los Angeles, yet the Shadow Alliance has no
suspects and no leads. And as more bodies are discovered, the age-old feud between the vampires and werewolves threatens to explode and turn the city into a
living nightmare.

With her back to the wall, Lissa Monroe—a strong-
willed, ravishingly beautiful succubus who entices men
to surrender their souls—agrees to go undercover for the
Alliance. Her mission: infiltrate the mind of werewolf
leader Vincent Rand, a ferociously alluring enemy who
has a powerful hold over her. Lissa has never lost control of her deepest desires, but Rand is an impenetrable
paradox, a principled soldier who fears nothing—except
perhaps the darkness of his own past. As the City of Angels teeters on the brink of apocalypse, these two adver-
saries must join together to have even the slimmest
chance of surviving a more lethal enemy hidden in plain
sight.

Turn the page to take a peek inside....

The moon hung heavy in the Parisian sky, its silvery light choking out the feeble glow of distant stars.

Ninety-two percent waxing gibbous.

A dozen years ago, he wouldn't have had a clue what that meant. Now the phases of the moon pulsed through his blood.

Any other day, ninety-two would be too much, the animal within struggling to break free.

Not tonight. Tonight, he wanted the full meal deal, one hundred percent. *No.* Not full. Better a ninety-nine percenter. When the moon was full, the wolf took over, focusing on nothing but the hunt. The kill. But at ninety-nine, Rand kept a hint of control, a little bit of awareness.

Tonight, he wanted to be aware. Very aware.

Tonight, he wanted the kill.

He made no noise as he moved over the cobblestone surface of the Avenue des Peupliers toward the Avenue Neigre in the Cimetière du Père-Lachaise. On either side of him, the houses of the dead rose in the moonlight, their smooth stone surfaces gleaming.

It ends tonight.

He eased into the shadows and closed his eyes, letting the sounds of the night surround him, the scents find him. He'd been a soldier before the change, a hunter who used his training and skill to track down enemies of the state, men selected for quiet elimination by an unseen force.

He remained a hunter now. A man searching for an enemy. A wolf hunting its prey.

There.

He opened his eyes, his nostrils flaring as he twisted his head, catching the para-daemon's scent. He followed it, the fevered excitement of the hunt burning in his gut as he moved in silence down the rough cobbled street and then onto the narrow gravel lane that was the Champs Bertolie.

The bastard was here. Nearby.

Hidden.

Tree branches shivered in a light breeze, and Rand searched the shadows for his quarry. The change that had intensified his senses and augmented his strength became more pronounced as the moon grew full, and now he could see into the deepest shadows, could hear the softest whisper. The brush of wind over wood. The scurrying of insects. But what he hunted didn't breathe, and as long as Zor remained still, Rand couldn't find him.

He couldn't remain still forever.

Tonight, Rand had the advantage of surprise. Not to mention the raw rage that flared when he thought about what Zor had done.

The para-daemon would die tonight, even that ultimate price insufficient payment for the females' lives he'd taken.

Rand froze, then slowly lifted his chin. *Movement.* Only a hint, but enough for Rand to know he'd found what he'd come for. He made no unnecessary moves.

Did nothing to telegraph his presence to his quarry. But within, he tensed, coiling his muscles to prepare for the strike.

With the moon at only ninety-two percent, his canines hadn't erupted and his claws hadn't extended. He was human, or appeared to be so. But the beast was close, straining and yowling, half-crazed by the thought of the kill, and Rand would call on the animal tonight. More than that, though, he'd rely on the weapons he'd brought with him. The knife sheathed at his thigh. The switchblade in his hand. The length of wire he habitually kept in his pocket.

He'd dressed in black, his clothing and dark skin nothing more than a shadow in the graveyard, his shaved scalp covered by black knit so as not to reflect the snatches of errant moonlight through the thin blanket of clouds. He shifted his gaze left, then right, trying to pinpoint the movement. As he searched, a faint metallic click sounded in the dark.

Rand cocked his head, calling on both skill and instinct to isolate that one small noise now heard only in his memory. *Left.* He veered in that direction, moving swiftly but silently between two marble tombs, the cold stone gleaming in the moonlight.

He paused, realizing that the sound had been the sharp snap of a grate creaking open. His quarry had entered one of the tombs, and Rand lifted his chin, nostrils flaring as he tried to determine which tomb had been breached, tried to catch the stale, earthen scent of the para-daemon he'd been chasing. Like rotting acorns.

He couldn't find it. What he smelled instead was fear. *Fear?*

A hint of foreboding twisted in his gut. Because there was no way he had scented Zor's fear. Even if the para-daemon knew he was being tracked, he wasn't smart enough to fear Rand. Yet the scent was unmistakable, and as he reflected on the oddity, he realized with sickening surety the source of the fear.

A female.

The goddamn bastard had abducted another female.

Even though he'd received no word that any more Parisian were-women had gone missing, there could be no other explanation. Zor had taken another, and even now the female was trapped and terrified and quite possibly dying.

White-hot fury pummeled through him, so intense that it threatened to overcome reason. He pushed it back, calling up his training to use the rage rather than be used by it. And when he was certain that control was once again within his grasp, he followed the scent, easing toward the north and curving around the monument until he stood, back pressed to the stone, near a wrought-iron gate that acted as a door to where the dead lay within.

Another step, along with a slight tilt of his head, and he could see inside, his superior vision finding the woman kenneled in the corner, eyes rimmed in red, her lips pressed tight together as if she refused to give her captor the satisfaction of seeing her cry.

Alicia.

He shook his head, pushing away the memories and forcing himself to concentrate on the moment. On Zor. And on this terrified woman now cowering in a cage.

The female was naked, and even from a distance, Rand could see the long red welts on her back. Not from a beating, but from the methodical removal of the skin. Zor would strip every inch of skin off the woman, feeding on her pain. Taking his own pleasure from her suffering and forcing her to endure the unbearable. And only then, when his appetite had been fulfilled, would the para-daemon free the captive. Not from her cage, but from her suffering.

Seven females. Eight including this poor woman. And all of them compelled to endure horrific brutality, all for the purpose of feeding a para-daemon's perverted appetite.

No more.

He checked his perimeter, finding no sign of Zor himself, then approached the cage.

"*Non.*" The woman scrambled backward, eyes as wide as coins, but the word was dull, without conviction, as if she understood that protesting would do no good but had to go through the motions anyway.

"I will not hurt you," Rand said in the woman's language. He studied her face, recognizing her as a female from the fifteenth arrondissement, though he did not know her name. "*Je suis un ami.*"

The words were hollow, though, and she remained in the corner, as far away as possible.

He crouched down and inspected the cage into which she'd been shoved, and the anger he'd boxed up flared again when he saw the dog dish filled with kibble next to a bowl of stale water. One lone water bug moved across the surface, disturbing a thin layer of grime.

After a moment of searching, he found the hidden

hinges as well as the lock that kept the cage sealed. He tugged at the door, but it didn't give.

Apparently he would have been better served bringing acid and C-4 and leaving the knives behind. He peered at the woman. *"La clef?"*

A hint of hope fluttered across her shell-shocked features. *"Je ne sais pas."*

Rand had expected as much; most likely Zor kept the key on his person. Still, he stood and moved purposefully through the small room, unwilling to abandon the hope that Zor kept the key in the tomb, hidden, but convenient for accessing his prisoner.

Nothing.

Two ancient sabers hung mounted on the wall, forming a cross above an interred soldier. As Rand considered the swords' usefulness for freeing the woman, a new sound caught his attention. The rough scrape of stone against stone.

The woman's cry of *"Monsieur!"* filled the chamber as Rand spun toward his attacker, the switchblade extended and tight in his hand, as comfortable as an extension of his own body.

He sliced through the para-daemon's shirt and knocked the bastard backward, but not before the para-daemon grabbed the hilt of the knife sheathed at Rand's thigh, taking the weapon with him as he tumbled away. Zor's reflexes were sharp, honed from his recent feeding, and the monster sprang back to action almost immediately, greasy strands of pure white hair covering his face as he crouched near the opening to the tunnel through which he'd entered, the stone still shoved aside to reveal a dark maw that smelled of dirt and decay.

"Running, Zor? Go ahead. You won't last long."

"Against you? I'll barely have to flex my muscles."

"I wouldn't bet the ranch." The para-daemon might have the advantages of age and a preternatural strength that exceeded Rand's weren gifts, but in this fight, Rand knew he wouldn't lose. He had fury on his side. He had his memories, and most of all he had the wolf snapping inside him, demanding release.

Zor would die tonight, and it would be Rand's hand that delivered the killing blow.

The para-daemon seemed to hesitate, as if he could see the certainty shimmering around Rand and was wary of it. For the briefest moment, Rand thought that the creature really would dive into the tunnel and run. But Zor wasn't so easily intimidated, and instead of bolting, he attacked, Rand's own knife tight in Zor's hand as he lunged at Rand with all the focus of a daemon determined not only to survive but to destroy his enemy.

Rand dove to the side as the beast lunged, the blade slicing through the back of Rand's shirt and the flesh of his shoulder blade. The wound was hot and deep and stung like a bastard, but Rand ignored it. *Not the time; not the problem.* Instead, he rolled over, taking his weight on the wound as he kicked up and out, his heel intersecting Zor's wrist, forcing the beast to drop the blade, which skittered across the stone floor until it was consumed by shadows.

His own blood stained the blade now, and Rand could smell it—covering the steel, seeping into the floor, soaking the shirt on his back.

He breathed in deep, the scent and the pain rousing

him, thrusting him into the familiar black where nothing mattered but the hunt.

He sprang up, fueled by an overwhelming need to end the para-daemon right then. *Not possible.* Even as strong as the weren infection had rendered him, he was still no match for Zor, whose heritage lay in the bowels of hell. Thoughts of a quick kill might fuel his imagination, but the soldier in Rand knew that he needed to seize whatever advantage he could. Take, and kill.

And so the battle became a defensive game, with Rand holding his own as he looked for opportunity, the para-daemon's exceptional life span and equally impressive arrogance working against him. They both knew that the beast had defeated elder werewolves with dozens of years on Rand. Hundreds even.

In Zor's mind, a werewolf barely twelve years into the curse—and not even fully affected by the lunar pull that night—posed little threat.

And that, thought Rand, would be the beast's downfall.

Sure enough, the creature leaped forward, wiry muscles propelling him high into the air. He lashed out on descent, his kick soundly intersecting Rand's chin, and although the blow sent Rand's neck snapping back, he didn't falter, managing to snag the beast around the ankle and sending the creature to the ground.

Rand didn't squander the advantage. He lunged forward and slammed his knife through the para-daemon's gut, releasing a gush of snot-yellow liquid through which ran thin strands of crimson blood, together but separated, like oil and water.

The scent rose, and the wolf within him snapped and

growled, begging for release, and for the first time since he'd been made weren, Rand didn't fight it. He'd never felt the tug so strong at only ninety-two percent, but damned if he didn't want it now. Damned if he didn't need it. Because although he had the upper hand at the moment, this fight wasn't over until Zor's body lay limp and lifeless on the cold stone floor.

He crouched over Zor, snarling, teeth bared, feeling the strength surge through him. Not fully a wolf, and yet not still a man. *Cursed.* But right then, with Zor pinned beneath him, the curse felt like more of a boon.

He leaned in close, hot breath on the beast's ear. "If I could destroy you eight times over, I would." He gripped Zor tightly around the neck as he straddled him, his knees crushing into the beast's sides as he kept him pinned to the ground. "Eight painful deaths for each of the females you tortured. Eight descents into hell. Eight times you would look into my eyes and know that I brought about your demise."

"Destroying the mortal shell will not destroy me, you foolish animal." Zor's eyes filled with loathing. "You, however, will stay dead."

His body seemed to erupt from within, the force of the internal assault tossing Rand backward and knocking the knife from his hand. Zor leaped to his feet, larger now, all sinew and muscle and taut, tight skin. Even the wound through his stomach had healed, with no indication that there had ever been an injury. His eyes glowed a savage orange, and when he spat at Rand, the spittle ate a hole in Rand's shirt. *Acid.*

"Playtime is over, wolf cub. Time to die."

He charged, and Rand didn't even have time to wonder

how he'd so quickly lost the advantage. He could only react. Could only trust his training and his strength and the wily cunning inherent in his animal nature. He spun out of the way, slamming himself against the side of the tomb and using the momentum to propel himself at an angle to the opposing wall. He came to a halt under the crossed sabers, and he reached up, grabbing them down even as Zor leaped behind him.

Rand couldn't see the beast behind him, but he could smell him, could feel the shift in the air, and without thinking, he extended the sabers at his sides, then whipped around, scissoring his arms as he did so. It worked. The steel made contact with the daemon's middle, the blades sinking into the daemon's flesh, too dull to cut all the way through, but it didn't matter. Rand had him now, and he used the force of the blow to knock the beast backward.

Zor fell, his expression one of utter disbelief, and he had time only to haul back and spit before Rand pressed his foot on the creature's forehead, held him still, and used the saber as an ax to chop off the creature's head.

Only after the head rolled to the side, eyes staring blankly, did he realize that a bit of the spittle's spray had landed on his face. He reached up and wiped it away, ignoring the acrid scent of burning flesh as he bent to pick up his switchblade. Then he turned to the woman, whose wide eyes contemplated Rand with an expression usually reserved for quarterbacks and MVPs. The only hint of her fear, in fact, was the pure white of her knuckles as she held tight to the bars of her prison.

"We'll get you out," Rand said, and when a pat down

of the daemon failed to turn up a key, he lifted the head, jammed the blade of his knife into the back of the beast's throat, and then used the acid that spilled from the ripped salivary gland to eat through the lock.

The door swung open, and he took off his shirt and tossed it gently at her feet. She bent slowly, then put it on, the hem hanging down almost to her knees. She stood in the doorway of the cage, looking at him as if waiting for a signal.

Rand rolled the head across the tomb, out of sight. Then he retracted the blade. *"Il est fini."* He turned toward the door, then back to her when he realized she hadn't moved. *"Allons-y. Vous êtes sûre."*

Slowly, very slowly, she walked toward him, pausing a few feet away. *"Mon mari?"*

"We'll find your husband," Rand promised. "We'll go right now."

Her eyes flickered, as if trying to smile, and she reached for him, wanting comfort, but he wasn't the one to give it. He'd given her life; that would have to be enough.

Slowly, she lowered her hand.

"Let's go," he said, then saw her eyes widen with fear. In one motion he turned and put his back in front of her, blocking her petite frame as he flipped open his blade. He let it fly toward the tomb's doorway, a rectangular void highlighting the form of a man who lashed out, slamming his hand against the knife and shifting its trajectory.

"Have I been that poor a leader that you would seek to take me out by a blade to the heart?" Gunnolf asked.

He reached down to pick up the knife, then slid his fingers along the blade's edge, drawing a thin line of blood. "A steel blade will render no permanent harm to a werewolf, lad. You know that, aye?"

"That was a warning," Rand said, inclining his head both in respect to his leader and to hide his amused grin. "But next time maybe you shouldn't sneak up after a fight."

"Och, aye. You have me there." He crossed the room in three long strides, his wild mane of fiery red hair more suited to a Viking than a political leader. Not that the Shadow Alliance was a typical political entity. Nothing within the Shadow world was typical.

It had been Gunnolf who'd found him, confused and angry and changed. Gunnolf who'd tended him and sheltered him. Gunnolf who'd taught him what he now was, and who took no shit when Rand railed against the reality that had been thrust so rudely upon him.

Gunnolf glanced down at the woman, who now stood behind Rand, clinging to his shoulders. "Do you know who I am, lass?" Gunnolf asked, compassion softening his sharp features.

The woman nodded, stepping close, finding the comfort with Gunnolf she hadn't found with Rand. *"Oui."*

"She needs to find her mate," Rand said. "And she needs medical attention."

"It will be done." He pressed a hand to the woman's shoulder, then glanced down at Zor's body. He shot Rand an ironic smile. "You found the bastard, then?"

"I did."

The Alpha turned slowly, disgust filling his features as he took in the tomb, the cage in the corner, the rank smell of death and decay, and Zor lying dead across the floor. "You took a hand to the matter yourself, I see," Gunnolf said, his meaning clear. Rand had gone after Zor without official sanction. Without involving the Preternatural Enforcement Coalition, the organization with jurisdiction over all the Shadow creatures.

"Sir, you wanted the problem solved, and I solved it. He killed our women."

"Aye," Gunnolf said slowly. "You did right." He paused, stroking his chin. "There is another matter. A delicate one."

Rand stood at attention, waiting.

"There are not many I can put on this task," he said, shooting the woman a quick glance. Rand understood his Alpha's shorthand. He was referring to the *kyne*, a secret group of warriors assigned to each of the Alliance representatives. "Of those I can ask, you are the one I want."

"There is very little I would deny you." Gunnolf said nothing, and the heavy weight of dread settled on Rand's shoulders. He shook his head. "No. Do not ask me."

"I haven't."

But he had. Even in silence, Gunnolf was asking him to do the impossible. "The answer is no."

Gunnolf looked pointedly at the female. "Let us return the woman to her pack, and then we can discuss this."

"Now."

Gunnolf's shoulders dropped, and for a moment Rand thought he'd pushed too far. Then Gunnolf lifted his chin, and though Rand saw compassion in his Alpha's eyes, what he saw most was determination. This wasn't a request; it was an order.

"I need you to go home, Rand. I need you to return to Los Angelés."